GW01045637

THE

PROVIDENTIAL ORIGINS

OF

MAXIMILIANO RUBÍN

A NOVEL BY

LAWRENCE BATTERSBY

Tre
Cappelli
Editions

First Published in Great Britain in January 2020

by

Tre Cappelli Editions

Paperback ISBN 978 1 913 33200 6

A CIP catalogue record for this book is available from the British Library.

Printed and bound in Great Britain by Clays Ltd, Elcograf S.p.A.

Cover picture by permission of Casa-Museo Pérez Galdós. Cabildo de Gran Canaria. www.casamuseoperezgaldos.com

Cover design by *Anythink*, Paris. abeauhaire@anythink.fr

Tre Cappelli Editions

14 Derry Avenue, Plymouth, PL4 LBH United Kingdom.

www.trecappelli.com

For Roberta

NOTICE

The Providential Origins of Maximiliano Rubín is a novel of historical fiction. Whilst it includes many real names, and real places and takes inspiration from several real incidents, the portrayal of these characters, places and incidents, as well as the addition of fictional characters, places, and incidents is entirely a work of imagination.

BOOK ONE

Man is neither good nor bad; he is born with instincts and abilities.

Honoré de Balzac
(*La Comédie Humaine* - Foreword)

PART I

GLORIOUSLY YE FELL

Friday, 25 September 1868

I came home because of the storm three nights ago. It seemed portentous to me. You can imagine the effect it had on our mother. The sky blackened and the rain blew in from the eastern sierras behind Vélez. All night the wind wailed, fell and rose. It pummelled the panes and slammed the shutters. Luckily, we had prepared. Everything here was tied down — except for our brother Gabriel.

In the morning the silence made mutes of us all. It was as if the livestock and even the wild birds were holding their breath. That is when we discovered Gabriel's bed was cold. He had gone missing, again. However, we rarely worry about him because he is often somewhere else and can be relied on to show up when it is time to eat. Instead, we concentrated upon clearing the yard and counting the damage.

It was around seven o'clock in the morning when our mother spotted a group heading from the town in our direction. After the excitement of the past few days we wondered if this was the town's dignitaries come to complain about my parent's running naked a few days ago, or General Caballero de Rodas' men on their way to prevent royalist soldiers from landing on Vélez' beaches. The General would have been welcome here. Since we could not be sure who this crowd were, my father felt it necessary to be toting his ancient rifle. As they got closer, we could hear the sound of lamentation and saw these were not Caballero de Rodas' men. Gabriel was at the front leading them right to our place. Behind him were three black horses with uniformed riders and a crowd of lamenters from the town. They were two hundred metres from the house before we recognised Captain José García from Daniel's army unit and understood that the flat-cart they were pulling was a hearse.

As I write this entry, my eldest brother, Daniel's body is laid out downstairs in an open coffin placed on the dining table. Mother could not bring herself to do it and so my sisters have prepared him. They have coloured his face, neck, and hands. They did their best but he still looks like a grotesque army doll. Of course, he is not lying there alone: Cayetano has obtained compassionate leave from the seminary. He has climbed on top of the table and has lain down beside his adored brother.

There are, or rather there were, three years between Daniel and Cayetano. They looked so alike and shared so many things — clothes, books, even a secret language: one-third Castilian, one-third Latin, and one-third an odd guttural code known only to them — people just assume they are, or rather, they were, twins. Mother is worried what Cayetano may do to himself. Although he has seen the three bloody bullet holes in Daniel's body he refuses to believe his eyes. He curses and pulls lumps of hair from his own head and repeats *Dei Gratia Revenio* over and over but even God cannot answer this incantation: no one can bring Daniel back.

Cayetano says he understands we have to bury Daniel in the morning, yet he places his hands on Daniel's chest and says he can feel Daniel's heart beating and puts his cheek close to Daniel's lips and says he can feel a warm breath. We shall have to find a way to tranquillise Cayetano, and perhaps also our father because he seems to half-believe that a prayer from Cayetano will return us to yesterday — when he had four sons.

6

BENITO

TALL, THIN AND unwashed, forty-three year old Benito Pérez Galdós rams the misaligned door-bolt into place. He returns to the ladder-back chair he has placed under the bathroom window. He sits arms crossed and stares again at the rifled medicine cabinet. He rolls his haggard moustache ends, then decides he shall do what Maximiliano Rubín would do.

He kills the candlewick. A mild glow of light dies as he steps onto the last rung of the chair. He reaches and unlatches the window then pushes against its stiff shutters. Rusted hinges rasp in the dark and sylphs of clammy air stream in as he clambers out. Behind him, the chair tips over.

His angular body is not well adapted to this adventure. Nevertheless he continues his manoeuvre along the wide, third floor windowsill. Should a neighbour glance from their window and see him — a stick-like figure seated on the ledge — might they take him for a thief? Or perhaps a man-sized version of that sinister children's puppet everyone is talking of? *Mistaken for a pilfering Pinocchio*, he suppresses a titter at the absurdity.

Although he moves unsteadily — from all he drank after the Devil had left last night's talking-shop —

curiously, out here, his mind feels sharper than it has in months. In a way, the *tertulia* has been the tipping point Concha wanted. It could only have been worse if she had trotted in with Luis Simarro in tow. One thought looms larger than any other, whichever direction he takes to traverse his personal rubicon there can be no turning back.

He sits on the ledge, looks at his dangling legs and shoeless feet. His mind races back a quarter of a century and he imagines Sisita's face and voice and wonders what she might say if she could see him there: *Never leave the house without shining your shoes*, comes to mind.

That girl could always find the humour when their situation needed it. Her mimicry of his mother was beyond sublime. She could give those frequent maternal exhortations in the same raw squawk of his mother, Mama Dolores. Sisita would secretly tilt her head to the side; roll her eyes; wag a long finger and hiss: *Look at me, Benito, I'm the shrieking balloon losing air.* And they would laugh until tears rolled down their cheeks or Mama Dolores appeared on the horizon.

It surprises him how frequently he has been having these visits from the waif-spectre, who remains forever eighteen. He wonders what a grown-up Sisita would look like. What else might she say if she could see him perched out here? Especially since this is the nearest he has been in months to leaving the apartment. Perhaps she would say it was an unconventional exit. After all, this is what they say about him. That, and his being non-conformist.

Sadly, Sisita is not here to say anything. Neither is

the owner of the apartment he occupies — his sister-in-law has gone away with who knows whom for a long weekend — and the housekeeper is in her top-floor cubby hole, probably dreaming of Prince Charming. Only his sister, Concha, is here tonight. *Spare a thought for Concha*, he thinks. If he loses balance it will be Concha who shall have to scoop up the scraps of his wrecked limbs, his wracked brains, and be baffled by their pecuniary puzzle. The latter would be a mystery for them all to solve.

Where has all the money gone? The truth is he cannot tell them. Not because he wishes to hide anything. Simply because he does not know. And this, not knowing, lets them whisper another reproach: *feckless in finance, reckless in romance.* Even Concha says it. It is as well that Sisita is not alive to know what has become of him.

The night is starless. He shifts his weight on his wrinkled, skinny buttocks and feels the folded-up tax-demand in one back pocket and in the other pocket a folded-up career-killing critique of his last novel, *Lo Prohibido*.

He wants to touch the farthest end. So, he moves along the ledge. The only sounds are the clicks of his quickly cooling bones as he continues his slow, sideways, slither in the bitter cold. Halfway across, he opens his eyes wider and leans gently forward. From here, he can see into the bleak abyss below.

Human eyes have never seen their courtyard from this angle before. In the dark, his pupils adjust until they discern odd shapes ninety-feet below his wiggling toes. Outlines of huddled handlebar shoulders and basket-faces stare up at him, as though concerned he may disturb their peace.

'Bastard bicycles,' he mutters to himself.

His train of thought circles back to Concha. *She's probably fallen asleep, anyway.*

No matter the occasion, Concha can be relied upon to drift into the kind of deep, dumb sleep that has eluded him these past few months. He has been jealous of her ability to do that since this all began.

The bicycles would have me and she'd sleep right through it, he concludes.

The night air starts to clarify his thinking. He begins to compose the letter he has long procrastinated over. For the moment, he still does not know to whom he would address it. So he settles for *to whom it may concern*. He delights in the pompous *faux* gravity of that salutation.

One thing he is certain of, it should contain three parts. Part one, an epistle to the past. A love letter to the long-interred Sisita. Those who really understood him would expect that. Part two, a plea to the present. Present debtors that is, asking that they forgive his debts and leave his sister unfettered. Part three, for his ex-mistress, that irrational Hispano-Francophile literary critic, whose heart-felt critique crumples in his trouser pocket. To her he would say, *I'm also moving on.* And he might add *en-passant* that he has more than just a notion of what is required to transform his next '*personnage principal*' — Maximiliano Rubín — into a realist masterpiece. As a postscript he imagines he might also say *and to hell with you.*

His face and hands begin to chill. His teeth chatter. He gazes once more into the lacuna. The bicycles are surely goading him, bloody well daring him. He knows he cannot sit out here for ever. He closes his eyes, breathes in deeply, and re-summons Sisita. This is his most revered, beautiful, sweet image of her. It is the last time he ever saw her; standing beside his mother, waving goodbye, and mouthing their secret. It is a memory that evokes measures of love and hate, tenderness and violence, in equal measure.

On the other side of the bathroom door, Concha is contemplating a rescue. She is fifty-eight years old, short and rotund. Although dressed in her nightgown and dressing robe, she has not been sleeping either. With a deathly cold draught around her ankles how is it possible to sleep? Her face projects the weariness that comes from taking care of Benito – their gentle *espiritu turbado* — their timid genius who fears his writing career is over.

'So, what if it is?' she told him last night after the *tertulia* ended.

It was clear he did not appreciate her frankness. Too bad! Diplomacy is not what she is noted for, and anyway he needed to be told. She accepts she can be *like that*: brutally direct. Even Benito, who is so rarely provoked, has chided her.

'That's why you'll never find a man. You're too much of a modern Mama Dolores,' he said.

'Who says I'm looking? And anyway, who the hell are you to talk?' she replied.

Of the ten of them, only the eldest two are married. Thus, Concha, Benito and six of the others are in the same position: spinsters and bachelors. She comforts herself in the knowledge she really could get a man, if she wanted. After all, she is not unpresentable. Even Benito has said so. She keeps herself tidy, is always elegantly turned out and she is perpetually prepared for the unexpected. Even now, well past midnight, her hair is still dressed for a chance rendezvous: crimped at the front and ribboned at the top, a black, silk ribbon around a greying bun.

You never know who might show up here in Plaza Colón, is how she explains her readiness to herself.

Close to her spinster chest and steadied in a tin cup she holds a half candle from which a flicker of feeble light laps around her neck. She avoids the mirror in the corridor. Circumvents witnessing the rings of sleep deprivation that surely must be around her baleful eyes.

She turns the handle of the bathroom door and unwittingly transfers the ink from her reading of the evening editions to the door handle. The door does not open. She grips the handle again, a little tighter this time, and turns it once more, with a little extra violence. Still it does not give. She begins to push at the door with both hands, and then pull again at the handle, and finally starts shaking it in a light frenzy.

'I know you're in there,' she says, her voice raised.

But there is no answer.

She cocks an ear, puts it to the door. A draught darts past her ankles. She puts her eye to the keyhole. She sees a chair on the floor and no sign of her brother. Her response is more frantic. She braces and shunts the door with her broad shoulder. The door flinches in its frame. She steps back, readies for another effort when a muffled sound emerges, as though coming from somewhere beyond the bathroom.

'Don't worry.' A surreal whisper from afar.

'As if I'd worry,' Concha answers. Her tone reeks of fake insouciance.

She puts her ear to the door again. She hears scuffling, reminiscent of a rodent racing to escape his pursuer. 'What are you doing in there?'

'What do you think I'm doing?' His voice sounds closer.

'I suppose it must be the call of your realist muse.'

'Sarcasm is not permitted on a Sunday,' Benito says.

'It's already Monday,' she answers.

This brother of hers is always ready with a quip. But there are signs he cannot hide. Already naturally nervous and thin, he has lost weight. His furtive looks in the mirror, trying to cover up missing patches of his hair, do not go unseen. His skin has sprouted dry red patches. He has exiled himself indoors and rarely sleeps without his sleeping draught. But cohabiters catch on. How can they, especially how can she, not worry?

On the window ledge, Benito reflects on his sister's interference. It has waxed and waned but however hard he has tried he cannot get it to wither and die. She is always so well-intentioned in her determination to get him to move on. Take Saturday night. She considered: if he will no longer go and listen to the debates in the Ateneo then she will bring the Ateneo to him. They would have their own little talking-shop *tertulias* right here in the apartment in Plaza Colón. She told him how she coaxed his best friend, José Ferreras. Between them they rounded up more than a handful of the Ateneo's talking windbags and brought them home to see Benito.

'Cheer you up, bring you out of yourself,' was how they justified it.

In Madrid the lure of free food and drinks is a powerful charm. Thus, caught cold, he had no choice but to play along. He supposed the visitors could still be duped by his coherent, quippy, self-awareness: 'What can I say, except my well-known passivity is currently in its dominant phase,' he told them.

Most of the visitors laughed at that one. Most seemed taken in. Except for the Devil, Rafael Salillas.

Unbelievably, Salillas had managed to inveigle himself an indirect invite, and as the others left Salillas stayed behind for a 'pep talk.' Or so he told Concha. 'So, he's taking it all in his stride?' Salillas had asked.

'It's just a little writer's block. He'll be back out prowling the streets for stories soon enough,' José answered.

'I'm probably one of the few who's actually read *Lo Prohibido*. It shows uncanny insights,' Salillas said.

And that is when Benito stepped back into the conversation going on between Salillas, José, and Concha.

'Uncanny insights?' Benito asked.

'Only an alienist or, dare I say, perhaps someone suffering the symptoms could have written it so well,' Salillas said.

'The critics don't seem to agree,' Benito said.

'They don't know what they're talking about,' Salillas said.

'I suppose their criticism is more about the overall literary effect,' José Ferreras said.

'Overall literary what's-it? Who cares about that? I'm talking about the medical conditions. I couldn't have done better myself,' Salillas said.

Whilst Salillas was talking, José Ferreras stood behind him, silently laughing and drawing circles in the air with his finger. Benito's pleading eyes and pallid face eventually signalled to his circling sister: *Get him out.*

It was whilst leaving that Salillas asked his hideous question: 'We were wondering if there are other depressives in your family?'

Benito's skin still crawls at the humiliation. He finally understands there is only one way to put an end to this. He smiles and regrets he is not wearing shiny shoes.

LUIS

LUIS SIMARRO IS homesick, again. His despond would disappear if only he could ditch his sense of obligation for these nights. Swanky soirées with French entrepreneurs looking down their long noses, speaking at him in stuttering Castilian. Them; always full of allusions to the 'good old days' when Napoleon's brother ruled Spain. Him; feigning surprise with 'Oh, really?' when they claim they have distant tribal relations in Toledo.

'Why do we have to go there and make small talk with these people?'

Four times a year he asks Mercedes that same question. Tells her he hates these evenings at the consulate because they are always so stultifying. Brimming with barely lucid braggarts, most of them retired and wrinkled.

'Do stop your maudlin moping. There's bound to be plenty of Spaniards too,' she says in her sweetest tone.

'A pack of mongrels from La Mancha?' Luis says, 'hardly Spanish at all.'

If he seems on the edge of another argument it is because he knows, as well as she does, they are compelled. Four times a year they wear their best faces, dress in Spanish elegance and clap hands when the little orchestra starts. Deep down, Luis suspects Mercedes finds some pleasure in these evenings of chamber-music, socialising, and champagne.

'It could be worse,' she says.

'What's worse than listening to a gaggle of inter-bred ex-dignitaries, babbling on about their "Hispano-Gallic" genealogies?' Luis asks, punctuating with his fingers.

'Where else in Paris can you make the same connections?'

Luis thinks about answering. He knows of several good asylums in the vicinity with an abundance of well-connected aristocrats. But each time he tells her that, she laughs a little less.

Unlike Luis, Mercedes has read tonight's guest list. She has informed him of tonight's guests-of-honour: Adaro and Aranguern, a duo of Spanish architects. Eduardo Adaro is the younger of the two, probably Luis' age. His partner, Tomás Aranguern, known to be tall, taciturn, rumoured privileged, and may be a distant relative of Mercedes. Perhaps she is right about tonight. This could be one of the better evenings.

'Are you sure they beat the French?' Luis asks.

'Twice!' Mercedes says.

Luis loves the idea the consulate mansion will be packed tonight with French architects come to fawn at the feet of these guests. Yes, this evening promises something a little different.

'Tonight we'll be treated to their phoney Gallic amiability,' Luis says.

'You've become so ungracious.'

'Better that, than their habitual Gallic arrogance,' Luis says.

Mercedes ties his cravat over-tight in feigned strangulation. Luis loosens the knot and begins laughing. His maudlin mask is gone. The maverick alienist is back, ready and willing to be enraptured.

'Something to enjoy then *n'est-ce pas?*' Mercedes asks, and turns her back for him to button-up her dress.

It is her favourite; silk, light-blue like the winter sky in Valencia. A scooped U-cut neck, puffy, short sleeves and white lace around the neckline and cuffs. This is the robe she reserves for consulate events. However, she habitually accompanies it with different flowers in her hair or pinned upon an epaulette. And a different necklace or pendant always adorns it. Tonight she wears large pearls as white as the lace above her breast. No earrings, hair pulled back tightly and face well-scrubbed. A natural rouge.

Luis takes his time buttoning her dress. He gets half way done before he stretches his arms around her. She wears flat shoes and tonight he stands an inch or two taller than her. He leans into her, breathes in her perfume —peach — rubs his face and wiry speckled grey beard against the nape of her neck.

'Time to leave,' says Mercedes.

A carriage is waiting for them outside their apartment.

'Makes a pleasant change,' Luis whispers, when he sees the situation in the consulate.

'What does?' Mercedes asks.

'Spaniards coming up here and causing the French to feel inferior.'

It turns out that Mercedes and Aranguern do have distant family relatives in common, so she does not complain when Luis leaves her with Aranguern and a field full of fogeys who mill around him.

He goes to corner Adaro. The young architect yappily expresses his delight in attending another celebration of their last competition win, especially as this had not been just any old competition: This was the most important architectural competition since the contest to design a new central bank. A contest, which incidentally, they also won! Luis wants to hear about everything. But it is the gossip of the next big design project that most piques his interest.

'First the central bank, then model prisons, and now I'm hearing rumours,' Luis says.

'Are you?' Adaro slurs, 'I suppose I can let you in on the secret.'

They are speaking in Castilian, but Luis has learnt to be wary of the many near Hispanics in Paris that make it their business to overhear.

'Shhhh,' Luis says, and he places their empty champagne glasses on top of a covered piano. He takes two brimming glasses, puts a finger to his lips, and leads the way.

'Follow me,' he says.

Over the past five years, Luis has become a minor celebrity amongst Spanish expatriates in Paris. He has become intimate with the reception rooms of the Spanish Consulate. He knows where to herd Adaro. They move out of the main reception room away from the crowd. Pass through a grand, wide, corridor with shiny parquet where open doors lead to six anterooms especially commandeered for tonight's event.

Luis angles Adaro towards the furthest anteroom. They are about to enter it when Luis spots, on the far side of the room, a group of loud, impeccably dressed French architects. Luis had noticed them earlier, filling up their glasses, and talking of art and architecture. The group is arguing aloud about a painting hanging there. It is, Luis thinks, appropriately named *Los Borrachos*; *The Drunks*.

They seem spellbound.

'What secret?' Luis whispers to Adaro, stopping him on the threshold.

'Are you sure I can tell you?' Adaro grins.

'Of course.'

'We stole the best ideas for this project.'

Perhaps it is the alcohol, but at first Luis can hardly follow Adaro's confession. Then it occurs to him, he is thinking of the gossip concerning the next big architectural project, whilst Adaro is thinking of some secret related to the last two projects.

'Stole? From whom?' Luis asks.

'Borrowed. I meant to say we borrowed them,' Adaro recovers his slip.

'Where from?' Luis asks.

'Well, from the other one of course,' Adaro says and puts a finger to his own lips.

'You mean your designs for the model prisons were based on your designs for the central bank?' Luis asks.

'Yes,' Adaro slurs.

'Well, I suppose that makes sense. Both being

places where you lock something up. You borrowed your own designs. So what?' Luis says.

'Ah... but we borrowed them at the suggestion of one of the judges,' Adaro whispers and taps his nose again.

'Oh, I see,' says Luis, 'an insider.'

Adaro leans in closer, and surreptitiously slurping over his champagne flute looks across at the art-loving French architects.

'Plenty foxy foreigners tried to win it too, you know,' Adaro says, then slyly swivels his eyes towards the art lovers.

Luis turns to watch the still-enthusiastic, half-drunken group in the corner as they continue to stare and comment loudly on *Los Borrachos*. He thinks about revealing to them they are looking at a copy. Would they know, or even care, that the original Velazquezian masterpiece had been stolen years ago? By their compatriots as it happens.

'People are appropriating ideas all the time,' Luis says.

'I suppose you're right.'

'In histology, we'd never make a single advance without building upon the ideas of others. Why do you think I came to Paris?' Luis asks.

'Oh, everyone knows why you came here,' Adaro says, 'but no one knows why you stay.'

The remark needles. Luis attributes Adaro's insight to Cardenas Espejo, the Spanish ambassador. Espejo is always telling visitors he is wasting his time here: Tonight, it was: 'Let me introduce you to Spain's best alienist.' Guests suitably impressed until he adds, 'He's served more time here than any of us.'

Espejo liked to make Luis' time in Paris sound like a prison sentence.

'Relax, Adaro. You had a friend tip you off and you re-used your own ideas. I wouldn't become over-anxious,' Luis says.

'But we appropriated those ideas from the French.'

Luis tries to parse this privileged information. They borrowed their own prize-winning ideas and used them to win another prize. But, those first prize-winning ideas had been appropriated from the French. Is that it? Luis can hardly follow the trail, but he is curious.

'No need to beat yourself with a measuring stick,' he says.

He has still not got Adaro talking about the next big architectural competition. The one which the alienists are all interested in. But at least the tipsy architect is talking.

'Appropriated from them?' Luis asks, and lets his eyes point across the room to the drunken French draughtsmen.

The inebriated architects have congregated around a second painting: *The Death of Pedro Velarde*. It shows the defence of the Monteleon Barracks during the Spanish War of Independence against the French occupation. The Ambassador borrowed it from a good friend of Luis', the young artist Joaquín Sorolla. Joaquín had tried to be diplomatic: 'Won't it be a provocation to hang it right where your French visitors will see it?' he asked. 'Yes, it will,' Espejo replied and grinned.

Adaro does not respond to Luis' question. Instead, he stares at the architects who argue over how much

'French influence' they can identify in Sorolla's painting.

Luis feels the presence of someone. He turns to find Tomás Aranguern has arrived to lead Adaro back towards the ballroom. Aranguern leans over and sniffs the air in the direction of the French architects.

'They can't complain,' Aranguern whispers to Luis. 'They're the pre-eminent pilferers of ideas.'

'Are they?' Luis says.

'Of course. You know where *they* got the idea in the first place?' Adaro asks.

'I hear you architects get many of your ideas from nature these days,' Luis answers.

'Don't make me laugh. They got it from Havilland,' Aranguern intervenes.

'Who?' Luis says and raises an eyebrow.

'The Brit! Those Brits,' Aranguern says, 'have incarcerated so many of their population that they're way ahead of everyone. Happy to share their ideas, too. Any decent library has the lot in minute detail.'

'Havilland? That name sounds French to me. Anyway, if he gave his ideas freely...' Luis says and extends his palms up, as though offering a gift.

'Quite! French got them for free,' Aranguern says. 'So why not us? No shame in taking inspiration from wherever you find it.'

'I suppose not,' Luis agrees.

'Be sure of it. Ideas are a pile high for a peseta. You want to know what makes the difference?'

'Tell me.'

'Pragmatic application. That's what makes all the difference.' Aranguern takes Adaro in arm. The partners wander away, leaving Luis to reflect.

The rot already set in last year, but if anyone in the future was to ask Luis, he will likely put his finger on this precise moment when his pining for Madrid takes a more serious turn. When he knows he will soon do the thing he has been putting off for so long. Of course, his decision is simpler now that Freud has arrived for training. Since that young Austrian has shown up, Professor Charcot has lost his edge. And even Ranvier seems seduced by the sophistry. Freud's continued presence at Hôpital Salpêtrière is all the proof Luis needs; to know that he himself no longer belongs in Paris.

Luis watches Adaro and Aranguern stagger back to the source of the chamber music and he waves to Mercedes, who makes her way past them in his direction.

'What were you talking about?' she asks.

'Pragmatic application.'

'You do talk such gibberish,' Mercedes answers.

'I feel it's time to go home,' Luis says.

It will be another day before he explains to her which 'home' he means.

CAYETANO
61 CALLE MAYOR, MADRID
SUNDAY, 18 APRIL 1886

CAYETANO SITS SLUMPED at the small table. His crooked arm supports his tired head. A weak dawn light rouses him as the grey hue of Sunday enters and sets about dislocating the night.

He stands, stretches his arms, picks up his brothers' notebooks of adolescent-to-mature musings. Although he promised Alonso he would not do it any more, he finds he has once again made some margin notes — 'sometimes the present can only be understood in the light of the past.' At least they are in pencil this time.

He opens flimsy louvred doors and steps through on to the bland narrow balcony. This past few months it has become a ritual for him to stand here in this tight space, his face to the breeze, his senses awakening. From here he sees the positive in his situation: rent-free lodgings, and this spectral view across the roofs of Madrid.

The early skies are grey, mixed with reds and blues. Buildings in the distance appear as though placed behind a translucent curtain. Some sleepy windows are black, and others are orange. Impressions of hazy homes in a theatre set. Cayetano leans over and takes in the view below. Calle Mayor courses three-floors beneath, like a wide river. He sees pale silhouettes of flower sellers already flitting across Madrid, pushing their wheelbarrows full of palm leaves, living their maxim: *carpe diem quam minimum credula postero* — seize the moment, trust little in the future.

Last night, in those hours between confusion and elation, he decided he would do likewise. He swiftly returns from the balcony, crosses the room, opens the top-drawer of the commode and remove a bitten ebony holy cross on a silver chain, and a leather-bound bible.

Both of these are bequests from his blessed brother, Daniel. It has been seventeen years, six months and three weeks since Daniel was taken, and these have been with Cayetano every day since.

He slips open the drawer beneath and places Alonso's journals back in their usual home. After a moment, he kisses the little cross and places it with the journals.

His hand hesitates a moment before he removes the Euskaro from the same drawer. Another bequest from Daniel, but not bequeathed to Cayetano this time. Daniel left this particular gift for Alonso. It is more than a legacy. It is a means of defence. These are trying times in Madrid. Still, he has never felt the need before today.

He slips the Euskaro into its custom sewn pocket. Deep and double lined, tucked away on the inside of his tile-black soutane. The pocket is his own handiwork. It is his personal 'Bellingham billet'. He named it that since he knows English history almost as well as he knows Spanish history.

He continues to move around Tránsito's apartment in slow-motion, as though he were a burglar, not a lodger. His limbs are bent and his breath is bated. He tiptoes over the thinly carpeted corridor. Gathers up his shoes, opens the door and exits. The door creaks. It always creaks. Even he can hear it. His thirty-three year old landlady, Tránsito, does not stir. He departs his temporary haven and mouths a silent farewell to her.

Actually, Tránsito is more than a landlady. She is also his cousin, once-removed. Formerly a nun, she is currently an angel. In the past they had been assigned to the same church. But that all changed. She understood his situation and he understood hers. He does not wake her now. Even celestial bodies need to sleep on a Sunday morning.

In his stockinged feet he descends three gloomy flights of stairs. At the street door he slips his clacky shoes on, goes outside, and waits for the lock-tongue of 61 Calle Mayor to click into place.

The flower-sellers have vanished. Calle Mayor is now an empty artery. A gust of dirty wind whistles up like a reproachful sirocco cast out from the Creator. It stings, causing his eyes to water. He pushes away another intrusive thought. On a different day he might have considered that a presage.

It is a short walk before he reaches Calle de Ciudad Rodrigo. Once there, he picks up his pace. He is almost running, nearly laughing, when he enters the Plaza de la Constitución by its western arcade. It is there that the Euskaro swings and batters his left shin.

'Christ Almighty,' he says, and bends to rub his

freshly welted tibia.

He looks up, sees two women walking across the plaza in the direction of La Casa de la Panadería. In unison the women clear their throats, like a well-practiced duet. 'Good morning, Padre,' they mouth across the plaza.

He is not giving them his better ear, but they are not so far away that he cannot read their lips or guess what they have said. He smiles at them, abstractedly. He does not know them. He raises an arm, a halting wave.

He crosses in the direction of Café Hernández. He is nearly there when from the corner of an eye he sees black diamond shapes hurtle towards him. They are almost upon him when suddenly they swerve away, shooting back into the sky. He watches as other swirling house-martins join them. He stops to enjoy the show. Some people in this city consider them to be vermin. However, this scene always reminds him of home.

He had once shared this fact with Tránsito and quickly regretted doing so: 'I don't understand why you even think of Vélez as home?' she said.

'Where else can I consider home to be?' he replied.

'You haven't lived there in nearly twenty years.'

But she already knew the reason he could never return to live there. He told her often enough: Daniel's aura haunts the place. It is a troubled presence and Cayetano always feels it. Be that as it will. The house-martins of a spring day in Madrid will always have him nostalgic for Vélez.

The birds continue to make circles in the sky

above the rooftops, and then like arrows they swoop once more. They descend right into the plaza coming close to his feet. This time he kneels and sees what they see: freshly thrown crumbs. He is a statue watching their fearless jerky motions as they collect this morning's offerings inches from his toes.

Suddenly they scatter. Their bird-loving benefactor, a crumb throwing waiter, has created too much clamour and crashing as he begins to set out several rows of small tables. The waiter leaves, then returns with chairs and copies of several of last night's editions of Madrid's press.

Cayetano takes a seat in the row nearest the cafe. He picks up a copy of *El Dia*.

'Good morning, Padre,' the waiter says.

Cayetano tilts his head to give the waiter his good ear.

'Right. So it is. One to crown all mornings.'

The waiter nods in agreement, because in Madrid one hears all kinds of riddles every day.

'You're up early, Padre.'

'So I am,' Cayetano answers.

'Coffee?'

'No. I'll have a hot chocolate and something sweet.'

His order given, he turns to gaze back over the way he came. From here he can see the hands on the clock-towers of Casa de la Panadería. According to the clock on the left, it is seven in the morning; according to its brother, it is ten minutes past.

Cayetano takes out his own watch. It shows five minutes past. It does not matter which is correct, because in his determination not to be late, Cayetano is far too early, by any measure.

Where better to let the time pass. He will enjoy the warmth of the rising sun. Its rays are weak for the present, but soon, barring a cloud sent to mask the moment, the sun will show and caress his shoulders.

He scans *El Dia* but, once again, another newspaper has not published what he hoped to see. He takes a cursory look at the front page — a report from England, about how Prime Minister Gladstone has told the House of Commons there will be fifty-million pounds over the next three years to buy land in Ireland; a report from France, of how the French Government will arbitrate between a coal mining firm in Decazeville and its employees; and a report from Italy, where there has been a decree to dissolve government ahead of new elections.

A slight movement in one of the toad-eyed garret room windows draws his attention back towards the other side of the plaza. In the garret-room a curtain twitches. A face materialises at the window. A hand rubs away condensation. The face disappears. The curtain falls back. He throws the newspaper on to the table adjacent and watches the house martins come and go.

The waiter arrives with his drink and a complement of churros.

'Sorry it took so long.'

Cayetano sips his hot chocolate. Bites into a churro. Feels the sun rays on his neck. He is savouring the moment when he hears a voice at his back.

'Well, if it isn't our noble Cayetano.'

Cayetano is startled. He recognises this voice,

although he hardly expected to hear it again.

'Ferrándiz?'

'Don't you look a sight,' Ferrándiz says.

Cayetano closes his eyes, inhales deeply, and clears his throat. He wonders if Tránsito might be right. Has he become unkempt? 'I can hardly believe it's you. What are you doing here?' he asks.

Ferrándiz takes a seat facing Cayetano and with a similar jerky motion to the house-martins he reaches over the table and helps himself to a long, sugary churro.

'I'm back.' Ferrándiz points to the garrets: 'New digs, new life, new habits.' He smirks at his own wit.

'Have another churro,' Cayetano says.

'All change for me now. I'm up with the birds and everything.'

Cayetano watches as Ferrándiz throws sugar and crumbs at the house-martins. Perhaps it is the surprise of coming across Ferrándiz after all these months, but Cayetano is unsure of what to say. Unsure of how much Ferrándiz could know. He waits for his old friend to talk.

'I'm making my fortune,' Ferrándiz says, 'but what are you doing here?'

'I heard that you'd left Madrid,' Cayetano says.

'Well, I'm back now. And I'm fine, thank you!'

'Sorry, I should have asked. Are you really fine?'

'Better than that,' Ferrándiz says.

'You look different.'

'I am different. That whole disinvestment thing was a blessing.'

'Disinvestment?' Cayetano says, unable to prevent incredulity in his voice.

'Don't you prefer that? I mean, defrocking sounds so vulgar.'

'If you say so,' Cayetano says, wondering whether Ferrándiz will ever be serious about anything.

'I'm teaching Latin now.'

'You? Teaching it?' Cayetano almost spits out his hot chocolate.

'I wish Bishop Narciso had come up here and disinvested me years ago.'

'Well, you were never a serious priest.'

'You can all have a good laugh, but it won't be at my expense. This pays twice as much as the old stipend. And I get the garret-room.' Ferrándiz points over his shoulder again. 'I can't complain.'

'That'd make a change.'

'You should think about it too, Cayetano,' Ferrándiz says, in a conspiratorial whisper, 'It's an easy living. Everyone seems to want to learn Latin these days.' And then, since he apparently sees some joke that Cayetano does not, Ferrándiz starts laughing, a whimsical, near hysterical laughter, like the old times.

'Calm yourself, Ferrándiz. This wouldn't be the moment to choke on a churro.'

GABINO

IT OCCURS TO Padre Gabino Sánchez that whilst he is not as tall as he used to be, at seventy-six years old neither is he as short as he could be. Since his 'loss' —as they are calling it — several of his old acquaintances have come here to stay and grieve with him. There are plenty of beds here in the palace, therefore they can stay as long as they wish. He is thankful they have remained with him until it is almost all over.

Although almost twenty years have passed, they say he looks the same as when they last saw him. He knows it cannot be true because he has become whey-faced and beneath his robe is a frame more stringy than sinewy. However, he does still have need of the augustinian pudding bowl for an occasional hair-cut whereas they do not.

It is possibly his eyes; still alive and full of his customary curiosity that provokes their compliments. In all of this he finds it amusing they have not mentioned he has become taller than them. They used to be one or two centimetres taller than he and now he discovers they have shrunk faster!

There is no secret of how he has been able to delay the inevitable shrinking that is nature's joke: he is, or rather, until six months ago he was the most mobile priest in Madrid. Within the city and sometimes beyond it too he rarely takes a carriage, no matter how far he must walk.

He has been walking or marching like this for more than sixty years. He has carried arms and fought in two civil wars and would have done the same in the last one too but being nearly sixty when it started they thought he could better serve the Carlist cause by training the youngsters.

Now he hardly walks anywhere. He is virtually blocked in here because for six months the Tormentor has been pursuing him. The man will not leave Gabino Sánchez in peace. He hardly dare venture out for his walks without finding the Tormentor lurking around a corner. He has made inquiries of who the fellow is. He knows everything of the man now. Apparently, some people call him the 'Liberal Crusader.' Perhaps they think of him as a contemporary Saint Jude. But Gabino Sánchez senses nothing liberating in the man's intentions. From his point of view the fellow feels oppressive like storm-cloud shackled to his zucchetto.

In the palace they have other names for him: the Tormenting Crusader, the Bane and the Thorn amongst them. Alas, the man is their burden to bear. Even now on the eve of the sentencing he continues to come around and pester them; as though this will change anything. Finally, for the sake of serenity, Gabino Sánchez instructs them on what to do: 'If the Tormentor shows up, banging on our door, clanging at our bells, bring him to me.'

Gabino Sánchez has been thinking about the

power of cathartic cleansing of the spirit. His doctor has encouraged it, saying it is an especially potent remedy in cases such as this where one suffers a 'deep and irrational feeling of culpability.' *There's nothing irrational about this!* Gabino Sánchez thinks.

Yet, perhaps it would be therapeutic just to talk about it. And Gabino Sánchez already understands, by now knows it to be inevitable, he shall talk, and he will embellish the story. He will take poetic licence here and there. No one could deny him the right, especially not The Tormentor. And anyway, a little gilding of the story would not change a thing, just as the Tormenting Crusader's insistence on a meeting changes nothing.

When they finally open the door, and let the Liberal Crusader in. Gabino Sánchez first spies him in his library, enthralled by what he is seeing there. Gabino Sánchez gets to talk about it all in the elegiac way he has foreseen. He sees the Tormentor is an attentive listener, and notetaker, and, as far as he can see, will be an efficient re-interpreter of facts.

Probably this story, if it ever gets told, will be a mixture of their recollections; Gabino Sánchez' decorated discourse, blended with the Thorn's barbed rehashing.

He tells his tormentor, first you have to know what happened. It was like this: the bishop's carriage entered Plaza de la Cebada and triggered thunder. Ancestral roars erupted and ricocheted around the plaza. Echoes rattled windows in those low-roofed buildings and there was a spontaneous clapping of hands and whooping.

'It's noisier here than at a bullfight,' Bishop Narciso shouted above the chaos to his three fellow passengers.

They all seemed to agree. But only Gabino Sánchez and the bishop himself shared that precise picture of that particular Corrida.

'We should pause here,' the bishop suggested.

None of them argued. And the bishop was correct. A neutral observer would say it was as though they had entered the Grand Plaza de Toros in Aranjuez instead of this secondary plaza in Madrid. This was a place to take the pulse.

Gabino Sánchez watched as his protégé bounded out of the carriage and quickly slammed the door behind himself. The bishop went among his public. He shook hands with the men, embraced the women, and tousled the hair of the children.

Inside the carriage, Gabino Sánchez and two other men: Rector Nicolás Vizcaíno, and the bishop's cousin, the cherubic Doctor Juan Creus y Manso, waited patiently. Up above, the coachman and the driver peered from their perches. Occasionally one of them leaned over to calm the horses, ready to crack a whip. They could easily retrieve the bishop, should there be a need. But there was no need. There was only joy in all of that jostling.

They all understood this gesture of communion between the bishop and his flock; Madrid's true faithful. Thus, the trio inside sat shuffling their feet and waited. Each of them grinned at the other, each of them fiddled with their timepieces.

Eventually, it was the younger of them who took a deep breath and stuck his head out of the carriage window: 'Your Excellency,' Rector Vizcaíno pleaded, 'we risk being late!'

It worked, but part of the crowd accompanied the bishop back towards the carriage and surrounded it. The horses became nervous again.

Rector Vizcaíno sat back down inside the carriage, muttering, and patted his leather purse, into which he had placed a pre-loaded pistol earlier that morning. He was, of course, oblivious of Gabino Sánchez' knowledge of the pistol's presence.

'We'll be late,' Rector Vizcaíno repeated to no one in particular, and stared again at his watch.

Bishop Narciso finally entered the carriage and sat adjacent to his personal confessor and dearest friend, seventy year old Padre Gabino Sánchez. As the carriage moved forward and squeezed slowly out of the Plaza de la Cebada, the bishop continued waving. Finally, when they were beyond the plaza, he looked over at Gabino Sánchez and said, 'I felt for a moment as though I were El Espertero.'

'You pranced more like the bull than the toreador,' Gabino Sánchez said, as only he would be able to.

The bishop turned to take in the perspiring young Rector Vizcaíno.

'Try to relax, Nicolás,' the bishop said.

'I am relaxed,' Rector Vizcaíno, who was never late for anything, answered.

'It's natural they're excited now that Madrid has its own bishopric,' Gabino Sánchez said.

Rector Vizcaíno said nothing more. After all, what could he say? It was his idea to take this longer route and 'give the flock more chance to witness the splendour of the moment.'

Gabino Sánchez regarded the two men facing him.

The young rector was quiet, studying his own finger-
nails, which were already bitten to the quick. Adjacent sat the ample-cheeked Doctor Juan Creus, who
was grinning broadly and patting the small black
leather bag which sat on his lap. Gabino Sánchez
turned away and half leant across the bishop, towards
the still open window.

'You hear that, Your Excellency?' Gabino Sánchez
asked.

The bishop carried on waving and smiling in bene-
volence.

'They're saying you're just what Madrid needs,'
Gabino Sánchez added.

'They'd say that about anyone who took this job
on,' the bishop answered.

But Gabino Sánchez had known Narciso too many
years to accept this. He had a point he wanted to
make: 'Well, I'm proud of you, Narciso. You've
worked hard. You've taken risks. You've given Madrid
the lustre of magnificence it merits. Enjoy this moment with a little good grace.'

The carriage clipped on up Calle Toledo in the
direction of the Pro-Cathedral, San Isidro. The bishop continued to look out the window, acknowledging
the crowd. He thanked them, blessed them, and
bowed his head to them.

Gabino Sánchez turned again to stare at the bag
sitting on Doctor Juan Creus' lap. He raised his
eyebrows at Juan Creus, for he believed he knew
what the contents were likely to be — brandy, and
probably not much else. Juan Creus had been semi-
retired for years, and for all those years the closest
he had been to any medical situation had been to

blether on about how the 'old ways' of doing things were better.

As they approached San Isidro, they could hear music, bells and mayhem. They drew level and lurched to a stop. After a few moments the coachman clambered down and opened the kerbside door.

'Time to be regal,' Gabino Sánchez said. Then he surveyed the many thousands present. San Isidro had never seen such a crowd. Gabino Sánchez smiled at Narciso and reflected upon how much they had given to reach this point in their lives.

'This is worth everything,' the bishop said.

And that is exactly the way it was. At least that is the way Padre Gabino Sánchez remembers it.

SUNDAY BEST

CAYETANO SLAPS FERRÁNDIZ on the back. If Ferrándiz were choking to death on a churro is there any doubt Cayetano would be the first to try to save his old friend? He has not forgotten his debt. How, when he first arrived in Madrid from Vélez, it was only Ferrándiz who did not treat him like a throwback to Cervantes.

At the time, Ferrándiz seemed as bemused as the others that this bearded cleric clung to ideas better suited to another century, but he never judged nor made fun. Instead, he took him under his wing. He showed Cayetano where to go to have his shoes properly mended at a fair price. He introduced him to those few trustworthy city butchers who sold fresh meat on credit terms that did not cost your entire stipend. And when he did not have a peseta in his pocket it was Ferrándiz who showed him where to turn.

In exchange, he taught Latin to Ferrándiz, and never joined the others in saying Ferrándiz was a 'fraud' or a 'libertine'. Nor did he take any delight at Ferrándiz' defrocking when Bishop Narciso showed up on his mission to 'cleanse' the new bishopric.

He knew Ferrándiz would evolve and survive.

Ferrándiz was one of his best ever pupils of Latin. The fellow did everything with zeal. But Cayetano understood where Ferrándiz' real passions lay. Though who was he to judge anyone? Judgement is the domain of a higher authority. Ferrándiz disappeared after he was, as prefers to say now, 'disinvested.' And though friendship is hard to come by in Madrid, Cayetano never went searching for him. But he rarely stopped wondering.

'Anyway, now I don't have to listen to all of you fundamentalist Jesuit naysayers telling me that I'm going to hell for my sins,' Ferrándiz says.

Cayetano closes his eyes. In his imagination he crosses himself and asks forgiveness for Ferrándiz. 'I don't remember ever saying you'd go to hell,' he reminds him, 'I simply suggested you'd be happier in another vocation.'

As Cayetano takes another sip of his hot chocolate, he inspects his former colleague. It is true, Ferrándiz looks more content than before. He is clean-shaven, his clothes are well pressed, his shoes pristinely polished. He is certainly passable as a Latin master. Whereas, he seldom seemed so as a priest.

'How long's it been? Eight, nine months? I expect you'll have a wife or a mistress now, or both if I know you,' he teases Ferrándiz, and despite himself he feels a kink of disapprobation in his face.

'There's no need to put on your pious imposture, Cayetano. Do you think you're fooling anyone?' Ferrándiz reacts, in a fizz.

'*Quin taces.*'

'Hold your own tongue,' Ferrándiz answers.

Cayetano leans across the table. He stops with his

nose almost touching Ferrándiz' nose, and his black eyes are locked in a rare atavistic animosity straight into Ferrándiz' eyes.

Ferrándiz summons the gall to stare back. Yet there is no denying a fear in his eyes. He probably knows he has gone too far. He runs his tongue over his lips, as though readying to speak. 'It's not me that's saying it,' Ferrándiz says.

'Not you?' Cayetano answers and pulls away.

'You know how it is around here,' Ferrándiz says, quietly, 'blah blah, blah, there goes Cayetano pretending to be holier than the rest of us.'

'Is that what they say?'

'Oh, they say more than that,' Ferrándiz says. 'Got his own "chick-in-the-nest" and have us believe he's not been plucking her feathers.'

Under the table, Cayetano aims a kick at Ferrándiz' legs.

'That hurt,' Ferrándiz says.

'Just crossing my legs,' Cayetano says. 'Who was that supposed to sound like?'

Ferrándiz loses his chirpy look. Then recovers to grin and even wink at Cayetano.

'Take your pick.'

'I'm not surprised you were defrocked,' Cayetano says and smiles.

'I was "disinvested", if you don't mind.'

'If you say so,' Cayetano says.

'Look, I apologise. I shouldn't have spoken that way about your cousin. But they don't know you like I do.'

Though Ferrándiz seems half sincere, he lingers perhaps too long on the second syllable of the word cousin. Cayetano chooses to ignore the provocation. This is not the best moment to deal with Ferrándiz. Better to have him gone.

'Apology accepted,' Cayetano says, and he extends his hand across the table.

'Thank you,' Ferrándiz says. 'And, so here you are, back in the fold.'

'I suppose,' Cayetano says.

'Now you'll stop writing those letters?' Ferrándiz says.

'You heard about those?' Cayetano says.

'Some were published. They made you seem like the crazy one.'

'If you say so,' Cayetano answers.

'Come on. Do you honestly think they care? Do you imagine that the archbishop, the pope, or the prime minister are that interested?'

'They should be.'

'And the bloody Queen of Spain too! What were you thinking?'

'It was not fair.'

'Anyway now you're back in the fold,' Ferrándiz asks, 'what's it like over there?'

'Over where?'

'Everybody knows Gabino Sánchez rescinded your disinvestment,' Ferrándiz says: 'Offered you the mass over in Chamberí.'

'Then everybody should know the terms weren't right.'

'The terms not right? Are you telling me you haven't accepted the position?'

'Would you?'

'Of course! Don't tell me you're waiting for them

to apologise! It'll never happen.'

'Who knows?' Cayetano answers.

'Pride is a sin too, remember?'

'It's complicated,' Cayetano says quietly.

'It'd be easier if you could tell a little white lie. Just now and again! Mister marvellous noble man. Can't you do that?' Ferrándiz hisses, and with his thumb and index finger he measures out a little-white-lie; small and ephemeral.

Cayetano smiles, as he always has in the past when Ferrándiz hissed and called him mister marvellous noble man. 'You think lying would be easier?'

Ferrándiz snaps back, 'You wouldn't be the first. You could've said you came from a family of Carlistas. Covert of course but Carlistas all the same.'

'They know where I'm from.'

The effort to remain calm causes Ferrándiz' veins to pulsate in his neck and his cheeks to redden. 'Not every single bloody citizen in the whole of Vélez-Málaga is a republican!' he says, his mouth twisting as he spits each word.

'Vélez-Málaga is not so big, you know,' Cayetano says.

'Now you think it's funny? There were a dozen other things you could've said. But, you're so stubborn. Never willing to compromise.'

'Lying is not a compromise, it's a debasement of the soul.'

'You could've said you supplied guns for the Carlistas while you were away all that time in Puerto Rico.'

'But I didn't,' Cayetano answers.

'What would they know about that?' Ferrándiz argues.

Until last night's visit to the Bishop's Palace, Cayetano might have dismissed Ferrándiz ramblings. But the wounds of the revelations he learnt there are cutting deep into his conscience. He will never tell Ferrándiz this. Ferrándiz cannot know he was right all the time. 'I've told you, the Church is above politics,' he says.

'It's not, though. Is it?' Ferrándiz says.

Cayetano leans forward and lowers his voice.

'If this was only about politics, how would you explain your own situation? Why were you defrocked? Which particular body politic had your attention?'

'Empathy is just wasted on you,' Ferrándiz says, then mutters under his breath as he looks pensively back towards his garret.

Cayetano takes the opportunity to pick up the penultimate churro. He slips it into his mouth, then rubs away the sugar from his fingertips. The old friends fall into silence.

It is Ferrándiz who eventually breaks it.

'Anyway, where *are* you going all dressed up?' Ferrándiz asks, then seeing the last of the churros on Cayetano's plate, he quickly reaches over.

Cayetano smiles darkly as though he could break Ferrándiz' arm.

'Have you forgotten what day it is?'

'Still rather early, and Palm Sunday hasn't quite the same appeal for me,' Ferrándiz says.

'Right. Of course. You're in a different line of business now.'

Ferrándiz takes out his watch, 'I've a rendezvous,' he says as he feeds the final churro into his face. Then he stands up, abruptly, and shakes Cayetano's hands. He places two pesetas on the table, says, 'The waiter can keep what's left.'

'I'll pass on your regards to anyone that remembers you,' Cayetano says.

Ferrándiz turns and looks once more towards the toad-eyed attics. 'Mine's the top garret on the left, if you're ever looking.'

Ferrándiz then strides through the arches, towards Calle Toledo.

Cayetano licks the sugar off his own lips. He watches his old friend walk away. He already knows this friendship is lost.

INSOLVENT

2 Plaza Colón, Madrid
19 April 1886

BENITO'S SILHOUETTE IS framed in the bathroom window. His legs dangle and his unshod feet touch the cold wall as he listens to Concha shake the bathroom door with increasing violence. Her alacrity almost tips him backwards. He imagines windows beginning to open behind him in the surrounding apartments, with gawpers hoping for a little domestic drama to pepper their dull existence.

'Benito! Are you all right?' Concha sounds desperate.

He has the momentum now and so tips himself forward over the ledge. He lands with a thump on the bathroom floor.

'Of course,' Benito answers. 'Why don't you go back to bed?'

He stands up, unlocks the medicine cabinet, and for the second time tonight stares sock-eyed at the solitary circle of dust. A murky ring bears testament to the absence of the chubby brown bottle of chloral hydrate. Concha refuses to obtain further supplies. Benito shrugs his shoulders. Defeated. He opens the door and steps into the corridor where Concha, the confiscating sibling, awaits with her arms folded.

'I thought having visitors might cheer you up,' she says.

'Look, we already had this out,' he says.

'José agreed with me! Everyone's worrying, about you, didn't you hear what they were saying?'

'What's their gossip now?'

He need not have asked her that, because he already over-heard them.

'They say you look odd and inert. I heard someone say you look suicidal.'

'Pfff. They're all artists. You know how they love a melo-drama.'

In the gloom of the corridor Concha stares at him. Shakes her head.

'Your worry-sticks look like rat tails, again. And you smell. What were you doing out there anyway?' She raises an eye-brow.

He holds back his laughter at her reference to his mous-tache as 'Worry sticks.' She has guessed exactly where he was but that should not be a surprise. He has been out there before — perched between places. Concha knows this, al-though she prefers not to recall.

He could tell her that tonight, or this morning or whenev-er this is, that his imagination — or the alcohol — has him wondering: Imagine opening a window, crouching on a ledge and then pushing away to oblivion, just slipping out to some kind of freedom.

He could say it is an option he is considering for Maximili-ano Rubín. He could say he was living the moment, and she would know the truth of it. But he dare not tell her everything that flashed through his mind whilst on the ledge, like — *don't look down, do that and you'll be distracted. What if there is no instant nescient oblivion? Only the shame of a broken body, a traumatic, deferred death, and in the meantime, your survivors will have to seek the services of a lawyer to dig into your affairs*. It exhausts one just to imagine it.

'It's exhilarating,' he says.

'It's stupid,' she answers.

'It's infinitely better than sitting at a desk all day, waiting for a trickle of words that you'll only kill before the night's through.'

The candle-flame flickers, and Concha moves a chubby hand to keep the light from dying. 'I'll take your word,' she says, then forces a smile. However, her face betrays that inside she is not laughing. 'And Salillas didn't seem that bad,' she adds: 'After all, he did say *Lo Prohibido* was a good novel.'

'Do you think Salillas actually understands *Lo Prohibido* is intended to be ironic?' he asks her.

Benito realises the question is an unfair one. Concha is the first to read his manuscripts, but how is she supposed to know that Salillas is yet another devotee of determinism? Before he can apologise to her, she already spits out her fractious riposte.

'Did *anybody* understand it was irony?'

'Touché!'

'But those who know me understand I'd never seriously write an homage to hereditary.'

He grins, places an arm around her shoulders and then remembers one more thing he loves about his sister, before he gave her cause to transform into a harpy. He watches her bite her lower lip. She seems to be thinking of something else to say to him. She never runs dry of ideas to get him 'restarted.'

'I bumped into Doctor Tolosa Latour yesterday,' she says.

Benito smiles. It amuses him that after twenty years she still calls him 'Doctor Tolosa Latour.'

'It's almost two o'clock in the morning and you get up to tell me you met Manolo?'

'It's almost two o'clock in the morning and you get up to be brilliant on the bathroom window ledge?'

'What does Manolo say?'

'He says you should stop feeling sorry for yourself.'

'Manolo said that?'

She steps forward, looks at his shoeless feet. This is her in her defiant, unafraid, straight-talking posture, which even at two o'clock in the morning is fully functional.

'And... write a better book.'

He supposes Manolo has told her to say that, told her to 'shock' him. Probably told her this would help him 'relativise' the whole thing. Manolo says that a lot.

'I thought at least you understood. There was nothing wrong with the last one.'

'You said no one is buying it,' she reminds him.

'That's true.'

'And that all the literary critics hated it,' she adds.

'That's also undeniable.'

'Can't you just forget this thesis novel stuff for a while? Write something more like the others. Write something that'll sell thousands of copies. And if that doesn't shut them up at least it'll solve your money problems.'

'Who says I have money problems?' Benito snaps back.

Concha winces. 'You think we don't know?'

He has tried to hide the extent of his financial problems. Told them his pocket-watch was in for repair. But they can guess plenty. They probably know which pawn broker has it. He is frequently borrowing from everyone. His business partner, Miguel, expects to be 'tapped-up,' even seems to enjoy the concomitant re-ordering of relationships.

That would be tolerable, except nowadays Benito is borrowing from his sister and sister-in-law. They never refuse. They would empty their neighbours' purses if they thought he needed it.

In return, what has he been to them? Certainly not the most gallant of distracted bohemian middle-aged artists. How often has he said he would not be living here, in Madrina's home with the two of them, if he could afford his own place? How distant that dream has become these past few years. In his lowest moments, he has begun to believe he will die owing money. The knowledge he is inexorably plodding towards insolvency, like some dumb acquiescent cow clopping to its last meal in an abattoir, distresses him.

He would sell his only possessions: the summer-home in Santander, perhaps even the Losada, but they say the mortgage-debt would not be covered by the sale proceeds, and anyway the Losada is not entirely his to sell, at the moment. He has confided all this to José. Now, he must suppose José has in turn confided it all to Concha.

'Do you really think that just because Madrid's malevolent community of literary hack-critics have mangled me I might have jumped?'

Concha does not answer.

'You imagine for a minute I'd have given Salillas that pleasure?'

She hauls the hem of her nightdress above her slippered feet. She sniffs. She holds out her stubby inky fingers and looks at them closer.

'I didn't say that,' she says and sniffs again. 'We were just thinking, you know, if you could get back to work that might resolve your… situation.'

'We?' Benito steps forward, takes Concha's chin and tilts her face, looks at her directly in the eyes. 'We?' he repeats.

'You know, Madrina, and I. And José.'

'Just the three of you?' Benito asks.

'And Doctor Tolosa Latour,' she adds.

'And how about the neighbours?'

A nervous giggle, a shake of her head. There is no one else. At least no one else she will admit to right now.

'It's just that, apart from their criticism, I can't seem to get this character — Maximiliano Rubín — properly into his own skin.'

'We all know why. Do you think we don't see how it's affected you; all of this drinking and smoking and barely eating? You're going to be forty-three in a few weeks and look at you. You'd pass for sixty-three years old!'

'I suppose my good fortune has to end sometime.'

'Look who's being dramatic now,' Concha says and heads towards the kitchen.

Benito follows in his sister's tracks.

'I'll make us a coffee, and we'll chat,' Concha announces.

Benito has experienced these kitchen-coffee-chats of hers before. Her voice already drips with the same broody portents.

It is clear, she wants to tell him some 'harsh truths.' He watches her move ahead; her jaws firmly clamped.

He wonders: is this the moment to reveal to her the depth of his financial debts and the shallowness of his creative palette? Is it now he should share his own 'harsh truths' for once?

CAYETANO'S PRAYER
SAN ISIDRO, CALLE TOLEDO, MADRID
18 APRIL 1886

THE SUN HAS begun a sly pirouette. It hides amongst clouds and then reappears. The plaza is inhabited by strangers. He leaves. He crosses Calle Tinteros, enters Calle Toledo. He pauses to stare at San Isidro. Seen from the North, even against a limpid daylight the Pro-Cathedral San Isidro seems magical, taller and grander this morning.

In moments he arrives, alone on the street in front of San Isidro. A place of peace, his own sanctuary. He walks up the steps, kneels in front of the vast locked gates, and prepares to offer a silent prayer.

He is kneeling on the last step leading up to San Isidro when a dandy wearing a dark three-piece suit and sporting a light-coloured handkerchief in his top pocket materialises behind him. Cayetano stands up, looks around, and concludes the man must have appeared from the seminary next door.

The suited stranger walks up the steps, past Cayetano, and unlocks the gates. He passes through, arrives at the main doors to the cathedral. Humming to himself, he opens the cathedral's main doors, enters, and lets the doors slam behind him.

Cayetano closes his eyes, kneels on the penultimate step and prays:

Dear God in heaven,

Today is a beautiful spring day and the start of Holy Week. I should be readying myself in church, blessing the palms and celebrating your arrival in Jerusalem. Instead I am here on the steps of San Isidro.

Without knowing so, I have waited a long time for today. You, of course, always knew. And even though I have lived a good life in your name these past forty-seven years, my soul will not rise up.

And though I have suffered a great deal, I have never complained, because I always knew in my heart that it was your will, and one day everything would make sense. Finally, it makes sense, and since you see more than me, and hear more than me, you know why I am here. And since only you know the truth only you can judge me. I do not ask for forgiveness nor absolution.

In the name of the Father, the Son and the Holy Ghost. Your faithful servant, Padre Cayetano Galeote Cotilla, Amen.

Cayetano is crossing himself when the dandy re-appears. The man has a broom in his possession and is smiling as he comes back down the stairs.

'Dean Almaraz would be pleased if you wished to wait in the cathedral.'

'Have we met?' Cayetano responds.

'I'm Don Manuel López-Oliva from the City Council.'

They exchange handshakes. López-Oliva starts sweeping the steps before adding, 'I presume you're part of Dean Almaraz' welcome group?'

Cayetano fumbles in his pocket, then stares up and

down Calle Toledo. It makes perfect sense that the dean would be there to welcome them too. He could join that party. Perhaps he should. But instead he looks away and mutters, 'I'm with the others.'

'Pity you,' López-Oliva says.

López-Oliva starts sweeping Cayetano's step. He throws back his shoulders and puffs up his chest. Cayetano descends one step. Even from there, when he raises himself to his full height of five feet and ten inches, he can look López-Oliva directly in the eyes.

'The dean's got it all planned. He'll throw open the doors just at the moment the Bishop's foot alights on these steps.'

'How dramatic!'

'It will be,' López-Oliva answers. 'Anyway, I can't stand here all day talking to you. Maybe you'd like to come inside and watch the rehearsal?'

'It's a better view here. I'll wait here.'

But Cayetano does not wait there. Instead he re-traces his steps back up to the crossroads of Calle Tinteros and Calle Toledo. To slow his thoughts, he counts, aloud, the number of red-painted tavern doors he passes. There are many.

From a distance, he waits and watches as Dean Almaraz and his welcome committee arrive and tuck themselves up inside the cathedral.

It is only just after nine o'clock in the morning, but the flock are beginning to congregate. Cayetano hurtles back from his vantage point. Disciples are flooding into Calle Toledo. They arrive from every direction: Calle Tinteros, Calle Grafal, Calle Concepción Jerónima and Calle Collegiata. Everyone is gathering and talking in front of the cathedral. He has to spin around to make out what they are all saying. He wishes they would shut up. Determined, he moves amongst them, irrationally intent on getting back his own place.

'Excuse me, excuse me,' he says.

He elbows his way through to a spot that exists now only in his mind. He pushes closer to the kerb. But the crowd keeps arriving from that direction too, forcing everyone back towards the steps. With his better ear he can distinguish occasional, urgent, anonymous imperatives:

'C'mon, move back there. There's plenty of space at the back. C'mon, give it up. Leave a space for the others.'

The chattering in the street transforms itself to a hum, and the sounds of his own thoughts barely reach him anymore.

To hell with them, he thinks.

He looks around and takes them all in, their smiles and their chatter and dressed so fine. Still Cayetano is forced further and further back. Minutes pass and he finds himself situated on the first step leading up to the cathedral doors.

This is too far away.

He decides he will not be budged. Now, when people back into him he pushes them to the side.

'Watch what you're doing,' a short, bulky, brown-suited man says to him.

The man is on the verge of pushing backwards once more with his enormous rear-end, but perhaps he has an intuition, or some survival instinct. He turns to face Cayetano. He observes the tall priest who has wild black eyes, who seems a crusading Christian from another century.

'Sorry, Padre,' the man says and bulks his way in elsewhere.

The steps behind Cayetano continue to fill up with even more of the faithful. But now Cayetano manages to hold his ground on the centre of the first step. There are thousands of people surrounding him. The faithful are everywhere: in the vestibule, on the steps, on the pavement, even hanging out of windows across the street, and next door too.

He can barely move, and he no longer even sees the kerb of Calle Toledo directly in front him. This was not the spot he wanted. But he has no choice, they will arrive in five minutes. He tries to remain calm. Concentrate on his own welcome. Except now his thoughts start to feel hemmed in too; they race faster and faster. His breathing retreats, becoming shallower and shallower.

Then blankness. He has forgotten everything. What was it he wanted to say? He cannot remember. All of his thoughts are being pushed and jostled. They lurch this way and that way. There is a throbbing sound. Loud, discordant music screeches from every corner: there are guitar players, organ-grinders, and singers, everywhere.

Ten chimes from the cathedral bells. The last bell peals and a new cacophony of discordance rises up, falls back, then crashes into a momentary silence.

The carriage is sighted coming up Calle Toledo. The babble stops and a children's choir situated somewhere to the left begins singing.

Cayetano strains to hear but cannot quite distinguish their words. All at once, parts of the crowd in front of him shift like snakes, slithering aside to create a narrow path through their midst.

He sees blinkered horses stride into view: a pair of Andalucían Greys. The Greys vent their vapours and Cayetano wills them to halt. *Stop*! He hears in his head.

And they do. Spume sprays from trumpeting horses' nostrils as they draw up. The carriage sits at the kerb for several seconds. There is an odd silence followed by cheers.

He sees right inside the carriage. Old Gabino Sánchez is there, and Rector Vizcaíno too, and the bishop himself. There is another figure in the carriage, someone Cayetano does not recognise.

Seconds pass.

A footman arrives from the opposite side and opens the carriage door. The bishop steps down. The crowd flows towards the carriage. Feet rumble behind Cayetano. Suddenly, the cathedral doors are prematurely being opened, with a flourish.

Cayetano's pulse quickens as the path to the bishop's carriage closes up and then reopens. The crowd is sucked away to allow the bishop sight of the steps leading up to San Isidro. The bishop strides forward. His entourage is lost somewhere, lagging in his path.

Cayetano feels himself being pulled by strangers' hands. They tug at him, but he remains clamped, quite steadfast. Other pathways through the crowd open and close as onlookers jostle. The crowd clap hands and some stamp their feet.

'Over here! This way, Your Grace,' a voice says.

Cayetano leans forward, looks along a clearing in

the crowd. The bishop appears. He seems to be heading right towards Cayetano. Cayetano looks beyond the bishop, searching for Gabino Sánchez. Eventually he spots the old confessor trailing far behind the bishop, and further behind him is the rector. The crowd pushes again. The pathway narrows and then closes. Suddenly, all three are gone from view.

GOODBYE PARIS

HÔPITAL LA SALPÊTRIÈRE, PARIS.
10 JANUARY 1886

LUIS SIMARRO IS with his namesake and mentor Louis-Antoine Ranvier in their shared laboratory. It is clean and bright and has the perfect temperature. This is Paris; modern and magnificent. And this is the man Simarro most admires of all those geniuses he has worked with since he arrived here.

Some of the other histologists have mistaken them for cousins. Both stocky, both black haired — although despite being fifteen years younger, Luis' hairline recedes more than his mentor's. Ranvier's massive untidy sideburns and beard are already more flecked with grey.

Luis' sideburns and beard are tidy and trim and match his waistcoat. But one day he will take the grey and the girth of Ranvier — he is already on the way — and they will seem even more like cousins. Ranvier is also from the South. Not Valencia, like Luis is, but from Lyon. And so, not only is Ranvier's accent also different from the others up here but his entire way of being has the same exuberance of his eyes, mouth and big colourful words. Just like Luis.

They are taking pleasure in dissecting a brain. Luis is summoning the courage to be pragmatic. He thinks of all the things he loves of Spain and they come to mind, sharp and packed with odours and sounds and laughter. There are some darker images that cling to the fringes of these happy souvenirs. They are dim, archaic and dusty. Whereas, from his

60

recent conversations with the architects he has confidence that these memories are scabs of another epoch. The world has moved on. The scabs are being scraped from the modern Spain.

'I've been thinking of going back,' Luis says.

'Back where?' Ranvier asks.

'Madrid.'

Ranvier lays a scalpel on the bench they share.

'Why would you want go there?' Ranvier says, unable to hide his surprise.

'I hear things are moving there.'

'I thought you hated the place.'

He knows even better than Ranvier and the others that Spain is fifty years behind France, and it sticks in his throat when they say it is a 'backwater.' However, the champagne of the prior evening has left Luis light-headed. He has become a bubbled-up risk-taker, ripe for the argument. After five years away, Luis misses the sun, misses speaking Spanish and misses the food.

'I'm serious. I think I'll need to have a chat with Professor Charcot,' Luis says to Ranvier.

'*Comme tu veux, mon ami. C'est votre funèbre.*'

When Luis finally has the opportunity to talk directly with Jean-Martin Charcot, the astute Charcot has other ideas. Charcot is not in the mood to lose one of his best researchers. And he knows where to probe for doubt:

'Things are changing in Spain, are they, Luis?' Charcot asks.

'Yes, they are, absolutely.'

'Remind me again, who's running the country's asylums these days?'

'Well, the Church is, still, but there are already a few

private asylums too. Then there's talk of this whole new programme.'

'Talk! I've not seen much research being published from there. Have you?'

'It will take time, sir. There are important reforms already underway, you know. They've already built a new model prison in Madrid.'

'You're thinking of entering that profession?'

'Prison alienist does not yet exist in Spain. But it'll be model asylums next.'

'They're just buildings, Luis,' Professor Charcot reminds him.

Of course, the French already have their system of model asylums, their model prisons, their model everything. Even Charcot's state-funded university chair in histology is now a chronicled artefact, not a 'model' anything.

Privately, Luis is worried. He wonders if Spain is serious about catching up with France. Yet, the young architect, Adaro, seems more than enthused. He said there was cash, derring-do, and political will. It is all materialising now.

That is how they could produce their modern pentagonal design for the prison blocks: five floors, a purpose-built chapel, a hospital in the grounds, humanely configured solitary confinement cellblocks and even an avant-garde on-site mortuary, according to Adaro. Luis wonders if Charcot could name one city in France where you can find a prison like that. 'The argument is being fought now, sir. It's time for me to go home.'

Luis remembers, too, what else Adaro said about the philosophical changes and political reforms — 'Spain's no longer impervious.'

And neither is Luis, he has decided.

Charcot is magnanimous. He can afford to be, since there

is a queue to take Luis' place. 'If that's how you feel, you're probably right to go back.'

'My fiancée misses Spain too,' Luis answers. He is glad she is not here to contradict him.

'Naturally, she does. Anyway, as you well know, we're looking in different directions now, you and me.'

'I thought you believed this non-science was simply a fashion,' Luis says.

'Perhaps it is, but this is where the funding is now. People are fascinated by the *unconscious*. And what would a fellow like you do with an idea like that?'

'Absolutely nothing, sir!'

'I tell you, even Ranvier's coming around to it, now.'

'Is he? Maybe he is sir, but as I've said many times and you used to say yourself, the unconscious doesn't lend itself to scrutiny, nor dissection.'

'True! We can't lay the unconscious on the slab, not yet.' Charcot says.

'My point, precisely,' Luis presses. 'If we cannot see it, nor isolate it, how can we ever know anything about it?'

'There's a growing enthusiasm for it, you know.'

'Not from me,' Luis says.

'You don't think this young Austrian is on to something?'

'No, I don't.'

'I trust you will have no regrets,' Charcot answers.

'I trust you'll have none either,' Luis says and wonders whether either of them would ever admit to a single regret.

STILLNESS IN THE HIATUS
SAN ISIDRO, CALLE TOLEDO, MADRID
18 APRIL 1886

CAYETANO CONTINUES SEARCHING. He weaves this way and that way. He feels the Euskaro hit against his bones. There are so many faces, they all meld together. Nothing distinguishes one from the other, until amidst the hats and heads he catches sight of the bishop's white and gold coloured mitre.

He stares at the mitre and tracks its starts, stops, twists and turns. Occasionally, it disappears from view but reappears like a flag heading ever towards him. He searches too for Gabino Sánchez but there is no sign of the old confessor, nor of the others that arrived in the carriage.

The noise around him increases, and suddenly, the bishop is only yards from him, almost upon him. Getting closer to San Isidro's wide steps. The crowd resume their insistent calling, they all want to touch the bishop.

'Over here!' A woman's voice is loudest.

'This way, Your Grace,' a young boy calls out.

They try to get the bishop to come in their direction. He has a confused air about him. He looks towards Cayetano but takes a pace away in the other direction towards the young boy. Just then, Dean Almaraz steps out from behind the main door of San

64

Isidro, starts clapping his hands and insisting the crowd clear a path.

For a moment, no one moves.

It is for Cayetano to help the bishop. He pushes his neighbours aside and raises his voice, 'Your Excellency, this way,' he calls.

The bishop pauses and stares again at Cayetano. A slight breeze gambols up Calle Toledo. In that moment, Cayetano spots the small cluster of bright, pink flowers, pinned to the bishop's cassock. They flutter in the limpid air — *cercis siliquastrum* — the flower of the Judas tree. Of course, it could not be any other.

Even though people begin calling again, just as insistently as before, Cayetano continues to take the initiative, 'Señor Secretary,' he calls louder than before. 'This is the way, Señor Secretary.'

The bishop screws up his eyes as though trying to get a better look. He shakes his head. Perhaps he wonders how it is that this priest might have known to address him as *Señor Secretary*. But all the time he continues moving towards the main doors, towards Cayetano. When he reaches Cayetano he pauses for a moment to ask: 'Do I know you, padre?'

Cayetano kneels. The irony of the bishop's question is not lost on him: '*Felix qui potuit rerm cognoscere causas*,' Cayetano whispers.

'What's that you're saying?' The bishop asks, leans over slightly.

'Fortunate is he who learns the causes of things,' Cayetano has perfectly recalled what it was he intended to declare.

But the bishop seems not yet to have understood

the significance of Cayetano's words. He carries on, tries to side-step Cayetano. He tries to proceed past the bearded priest and up on to the second step, towards San Isidro's great doors. But Cayetano takes hold of the bishop's hand. He kneels and kisses the episcopal ring.

The bishop halts, he leaves his ring hand in Cayetano's, and with the other he waves to the crowd. All the time he continues to smile for the faithful. He is still smiling when two thousand witnesses hear the delayed explosion of the first shot.

Instinctively the crowd throw themselves down.

As they make themselves small and cover their ears, a bullet tears through the bishop's cassock. It splinters his spinal cord and lodges in the left side of his body. He collapses forward, a wrecked deckchair on a breezy morning.

Cayetano, still kneeling, fires again. A second bullet rips through the bishop's shoulder and out the other side. It flies far into the sky over San Isidro. The violent voice of this second detonation merges with the unfaded fury of the first.

Amongst the two thousand prostrated members of the flock, only Gabino Sánchez, dares rise and show himself.

Cayetano pulls the trigger a third time. This time, no bullet discharges. Calmly, he pulls the trigger again. The third bullet discharges and thuds into the thighbone of the prone and bleeding Bishop Narciso. The wrath of gunshot howls, merges and dies in the distance. An unnatural stillness descends.

A single, plaintive voice is heard; the sound of Cayetano, loud and furious. He looks skywards, shakes his fist and cries out the words he came here to say: '*Mea est vindicata, mea est vindicata.*' Then he starts laughing. Some may say he appears hysterical. In the hiatus Cayetano points Daniel's bequest towards the only man standing. It would be impossible to miss the old confessor — *but there is no dignity in that*, Cayetano reasons.

Gabino Sánchez, seeing the revolver pointed directly at himself does not sink to the ground, instead he closes his eyes and waits for release. Thus, he does not see Cayetano turn the revolver to his own temple and squeeze the trigger one last time.

PART II

TAKING CARE OF TRÁNSITO
61 Calle Mayor, Madrid
18 April 1886

Alonso races up the stairs as fast as he can. At forty-one years of age he is no longer able to rely on the agility he once had, thus when he arrives, the police have already posed their questions, purloined interesting papers, and seized random souvenirs. A photographer has even set up his tripod and taken the 'necessary' ambrotypes of the apartment. Worse, he is about to take pictures of her.

Alonso takes command. His experience in the Civil Guard means that certain gestures still come to him automatically. He knows the law and especially how to be an obstacle to it. 'I'm sorry I wasn't here when they arrived,' he whispers to Tránsito Durdal. Then looks around at the signs of the police visit. Books and papers are piled on the wrong shelves, drawers are half-closed, carpets turned at the corners. In the bedroom her clothes lie heaped in a corner.

'It's not your fault,' she tells Alonso.

'If I'd got here sooner, maybe you'd not have this mess,' he says.

'Lucky for me you're here now,' she says.

Indeed, it is fortunate for her that Alonso arrives when he does. He soon puts an end to the photographer's preparations.

'She is not a suspect in anything. Is she?' Alonso directs his question to the police captain.

The captain nervously pinches at an imaginary speck on

the arm of his own tunic.

'However, she's a witness,' the captain says.

'So am I for that matter.' Alonso is curt. 'You've no right to take an image of her.'

The captain shrugs his shoulders. The photographer gets the message and puts away his equipment. Alonso stands in the middle of the small salon and keeps them all in view. He thinks of what she had said about luck. She thought she was lucky? In fact, once again, it is his brother Cayetano who has all the luck.

Of the four boys, it was always Cayetano who sailed calm waters. Always Cayetano who seemed impervious to life's doubts, pressures, and temptations. True, that was due to the grace of his temperament. They all knew that. Not only that, there were the serene Málagan Jesuits who had taught Cayetano equanimity for whatever winds serendipity served him. That had prepared him well for dealing with whatever life threw at him, but not for dealing with the death of a loved one.

When Daniel was killed, Cayetano's grief was deeper than everyone else's. They all understood that too, because no brothers ever loved each other more than Daniel and Cayetano had. Daniel was barely in the dirt when Cayetano rushed off to negotiate every priest's suicide posting — Fernando Pô. No one in Vélez, nor Málaga, nor even all of Andalucía could remember a single priest who had taken that posting and returned.

Alonso could barely believe it when his mother told them: 'Fernando Pô? You're certain?' he asked their mother.

'Yes.'

'He has a death wish,' Alonso said.

'He's too sad here,' their mother had replied. 'He can go

out there and help people.'

He could always stay here and help us out, Alonso thought.

'Your father feels it will keep his thoughts from turning inward,' she added.

So that had been that. Cayetano had left. They all waited with a certain dread to hear of his demise. But Cayetano remained lucky. He did not die in Fernando Pô. But he did not return to Vélez either. It seemed he was determined to deplete his reserves of good luck by taking on other suicidal posts.

Meanwhile, at home in Vélez they learnt to do without his presence and contribution. They considered Cayetano had gone, for good. From time to time they heard how he kept taking on and surviving new suicide postings, until none remained. Eventually, after twelve years of crying in the colonies, Cayetano came back to Spain.

He swept into Vélez as though he were Don Quixote and gave away all of his savings — twelve years unspent pay, doled out like chicken feed — to his family, and family of family also. He kept enough money to live for three months and then left them again, this time for Madrid. They still all feel their debt to Cayetano.

Thanks to Alonso, there will be no picture of Tránsito in any of Madrid's newspapers. Perhaps a debt is being repaid here today. But the police are greedy. They cannot have their ambrotypes, so they want something else. Alonso watches the captain secure two journals under his left arm and hold the other journal open.

'These aren't evidence,' Alonso says. 'They belong to me.'

'You'll have to prove it,' the captain says. And does not let go. His clear irritation compounded having conceded over the photographer.

Alonso estimates his irritation is about to worsen: 'You see that name, here, embossed in silver?'

'I suppose that's you?' the police captain says. He exhales loudly and his lips vibrate like a stallion after a gallop. He appears not to be in the mood for argument. But he would be a fool to ignore Alonso's experience or rank. The captain's face hardens as he hands the journals over.

Alonso wraps his writings back in their cloth, ties them, and returns them to the commode where Cayetano has habitually hosted them.

The captain points to Tránsito: 'She says he was reading them, obsessively.'

'And so what if he was?' Alonso says. 'He's been reading the *Bible* constantly and *El Liberal*, *El Correo* and a dozen other newspapers.' Alonso gathers up those items as he names them. 'Do want to show up at headquarters with all of those?'

The captain hesitates but evidently has no intention of reading all of the cited material: 'Nothing moves from this apartment,' he warns Alonso. 'I could come back with a court order.' He signals to the others and they all head for the door.

They leave Alonso and Tránsito in peace. They did not ask where the priest got the gun. Alonso wonders if she would have told. He decides she would not have said anything because she could have volunteered the information anytime she wanted. *Let them work that one out for themselves*, he thinks. Then tips an ear, as he listens to the police tramping down the stairs.

There must have been something in the air last night. Once again, he dreamt of Cayetano. But this incubus was different. This was not the same vision he has been having for years. There was still that ancient, scruffy albatross yoked to his shoulders. But in last night's dream the albatross slipped free: it rose, then flapped, and laboured for a second or two, but suddenly it broke clear. It flew away into the clouds.

Tránsito clears her throat, 'Were you there when it happened?'

He had been in San Isidro. No one in there had understood anything. They heard the percussion of gunfire. He had not even got out in time to see his brother trying to shoot himself, nor witness him laughing, saying he had been avenged. He had not seen any of that, but all around him they described it and how the shooter had been taken away in the bishop's own carriage. For hours, no one was allowed to leave the scene. As soon as he could, he had tried to go to the police station but was not permitted to see Cayetano.

'It's not your fault,' Tránsito tells him. 'You've been a great brother, to him.'

What does it mean to be a 'great' brother? Alonso is not sure if can claim this. Yet, since Cayetano's troubles all started; seven months, he has been coming up here to Madrid every month. And they *have* become so much closer. He wonders if he could have foreseen this? Was this written somewhere in their past? When did he first felt the burden of the weight of his eccentric older brothers? Was it when Daniel got killed? After Daniel was gone, looking out for their family should naturally have fallen to the second son, to Gabriel. But in their family this was impossible. They had learnt that Gabriel's frequent convulsions have a label — epilepsy — and were not God's 'punishment.' But Gabriel needed taking care of. It could not be him taking care of them.

If the first son is dead, and the second is himself occasionally incapacitated, naturally it would falls to the third; to Cayetano. However, he was gone. His contribution to the family farm and business had always been tenuous. On the other hand he made no demands and seemed to have no expectations. Therefore, whilst Cayetano's absence forced a rearrangement of routines and responsibilities in their extended family junta, it also rendered some aspects of the future clearer. That was, until he returned, hale and hearty, believing he was Don Quixote. But he bestowed his fortune and was quickly gone. He took a train to the North for an unspecified period. Alonso supposes this time Cayetano's absence from Vélez will be permanent.

'Maybe if you hadn't brought up that valise this would not have happened,' Tránsito says, bringing Alonso out of his reverie.

'There was nothing in it he could not find somewhere else,' Alonso says. 'Except for the journals and he asked for those.'

Tránsito begins pacing again. She tugs at her hair. Alonso opens his arms wide. He waits to comfort her. She returns, and this time she accepts his embrace. She lets her head rest on his chest. 'I don't know what to do,' she whispers.

Alonso pulls her a little closer.

Tránsito pulls away, she walks towards the balcony. He sees tears strain at the edges of her eyes and her chest move in quiet spasms. She tugs back a corner of the curtain and looks through the window into the distance. 'Cayetano will go to hell because of me,' she says.

'Don't let their allusions colour your spirit,' Alonso says. His earnestness has an eager edge to it. As though he wants to convince himself more than her. 'I have an idea,' he says. 'Let's do something naughty.' He goes to the commode, takes out the three journals, undoes the old bootlaces from around the muslin and unwraps the cloth. He stands in front of the small fireplace. 'Let's burn them!'

'Won't you get into trouble with the police?' Her eyes

sparkle, but there is hesitation in her tone.

'They're mine. I can do what I like.' But Alonso does not immediately light a fire. He strides away, reaches up and pulls open the curtain. With the journals still in his other hand he opens the balcony door and steps outside. 'Or we could tear them up, page-by-page, and throw them to the wind.'

Tránsito crosses to the commode, takes out a slim, rolled-up mattress. 'Or you could come here.' She throws the mattress on the floor, 'and we might see what was so interesting to your brother.'

EPICUREAN SWERVE
Vélez

16 AUGUST 1858

Their parents think no one can hear them when they are quarrelling in their bedroom. Yet, except for Cayetano who does not hear so well, over the years all of the children, in their turn, simply went outside and sat under the open bedroom window and listened to their parents' terse whispers.

Only in winter, when the window is often closed, are the children uninformed. Otherwise, they hear almost everything. This is how Alonso and his younger sister, Remedios, confirm what they already suspect: their family is poor and Alonso is brainy, for a boy!

It is Remedios who sees their parents signalling time for a jaw-jaw, and so she signals Alonso and they loiter under the window-ledge.

'I think he should go back this autumn, their mother says.'

'We've discussed this a hundred times. I need him here,' their father answers.

'But you said yourself he's even smarter than Daniel and Cayetano were at that age.' Their mother's voice is already raised.

'Exactly! So, he's already learnt as much as the Jesuits can teach him. And we can save a wage here. I'm getting more and more veterinary work and that pays well.' Their father's voice is calm, for now.

'That's another reason he could stay on at school. At least until he's fourteen. We can afford it,' she says.

'You think so?' their father answers.

'Even if we can't, Brother Ricardo says he's happy to wait for payment.'

That is when their father raises his voice, 'I knew Brother Ricardo was behind this.'

Sitting under the window, Alonso and Remedios hear their father's footsteps, as though he is circling the bedroom.

'He's only saying we should think it over.' Their mother sounds calmer now.

'He never said that when it was Gabriel's turn to leave school, did he?'

'Meaning what?'

Mother's hackles always rise at any insinuation Gabriel may be 'different.'

Father knows when to retreat. 'All I'm saying is they already have Cayetano for God's Army. And, heaven knows, they nearly had Daniel before him.'

'So?'

'If we send Alonso back in September, they'll have him a noviciate before November,' their father reasons.

'Would that be so bad?'

'Surely one from four is enough? They should be paying us.'

'All you think about is money,' their mother says in her loud shaky voice — the voice father says makes her sound just like Grandmother Cotilla.

'Are you saying you'd be happy with two sons as priests?'

'It's not really fair, though, is it?'

'What's not fair about Alonso working here with me?'

'He'd be like a slave, chained here working on improving the farm, paying his grandfather's debts, but he'll never own anything, will he?'

'But he'll always have somewhere to live, and food for his table.'

'But only Daniel can take over the lease or buy this place; if he ever has the money!'

'I don't make the laws of the country.'

'All meat for the progenitor and all gristle for the others!'

'They'll be all right,' Father says.

'Daniel will! With his army pension and his farm lease. And the Church will take care of Cayetano, once he's or-dained. But what about the others?' Their mother's voice trails away.

'Shh, yourself woman. Aren't we putting something aside for the others?'

'You shh, yourself, man! And anyone would think you'd have more sense than put a peseta in a bank, after what happened with your own dumb father.' As usual, their mother probably imagines she has the last word, and surely their father cannot argue with her because he is the one always going on about how the banks ruined Grandfather Galeote.

But their father has other ideas: 'Your family would have had money in the very same bank, if they'd had any. But they were so poor they made Saint Francis seem prosperous!'

They hear their mother, laughing and then the window slams shut.

For weeks afterwards, Remedios loiters near their parents' window, cocking an ear when she can, and later filling Alonso's head with gossip.

'I'm telling you they are starting to feel bad. Maybe they'll change their minds. Give you another term or two back at school.'

'Probably they won't,' Alonso says.

'But if they did, you'd like that, wouldn't you?' she says.

23 August 1858

With exaggerated ceremony, his mother hands him a small rectangular object. He sighs. The shape is unmistakable. It is what he knew it would be. The book is doubled-wrapped in thick black paper, and a thin red cord neatly holds in place a white card containing his brother's unmistakable scripture: *Happy thirteenth Birthday to Vélez' own Nebrija.*

Today is Alonso's thirteenth birthday, and at the kitchen table his parents and sisters wait for him. But he is not in a hurry to unwrap this parcel. He already knows what it will contain, because there is no mystery in their household, there is only tradition. Alonso is number ten in the series of Galeotes and so it can only be one thing.

Since it is his birthday, he has the privilege of occupying his mother's place at one end of the long kitchen-table whilst she sits tearful to his left. His father, the culpable parent who accorded him the nickname 'little Don Nebrija' sits in the shadows at the other end of the table.

It's been five years since Alonso spontaneously started writing down any new words he hears his family say or has learnt at school. None of his three elder brothers has ever done that, and he has no idea why he wanted to do this. He simply wanted to. But, according to his father, he was 'compiling a dictionary'. And for years they have been calling him 'our little Don Nebrija'.

That is apparently in honour of Antonio de Nebrija, another of his father's iconic literary phantoms, even older than Cervantes!

Alonso is proud of his dictionary, but it has been ages since he came across any interesting new words. Now that he will not be returning to school, he has told his father this is a good moment to stop keeping the dictionary. Alonso wishes there were some literary figures of this century his father could have chosen to worship. He looks up and feels his father's eyes burning into his own, as though his thoughts have just been read.

'Go on. Open it!' his mother urges Alonso and she smiles knowingly at the object.

'Couldn't I just open it later?'

Alonso places the parcel on the table.

He looks beyond his mother to solicit the sympathy of his sister, Carolina; she is eighth in the series of Galeotes. On her thirteenth birthday, she received *The Illustrious Kitchen Maid*. Carolina is grinning at him, as though to say, 'Open it.'

He turns to Soledad for a crumb of compassion. She is number nine in the series of Galeotes. Last year, she received *The Two Damsels*. Alonso grits his teeth when he sees that Soledad too is almost bursting to laugh. They all know who is in line for number ten in the *Series of Exemplary Tales*.

All these years his father has never deviated, not once. And here's the thing: no one in Spain actually knows the order of composition of Cervantes' *Exemplary Tales*. No one except, of course, their father. Even though some Vélezians swivel their eyes in their sockets and refer to their father as 'The dubious Cervantes savant,' none of them can actually show he is wrong because no one in Vélez has even half his obsession.

Years before Alonso was born, his father has marked *Lady Cornelia* as number ten in the compositional order, and so it is that which Alonso is in line to receive.

Father stirs in his seat and clears his throat. Alonso does not look up at him, but he feels certain of what is coming.

'Come on, Alonso, hurry up.'

But Alonso is surprised when his father adds: 'By the way, I have something else for you.'

Something else? What else?

Perhaps Remedios is correct after all. Perhaps they feel

guilty. Is there a post scriptum? Another term at school? A rifle of his own?

Alonso removes the small white card written in Cayetano's handwriting and slips it into his trouser pocket. He pulls away the red cord and pockets that too, then picks up a clean knife and slits the double-wrapping along two sides. He begins to reveal the book. Even before he has seen it, his siblings are clapping, cheering and laughing.

In Alonso's hand is *Volume I* of *The History of Don Quixote*. Alonso begins laughing too. He realises just how much he has dreaded receiving an *Exemplary Tale*. Not because he thinks he will enjoy the *Don Quixote* tale any better, simply he has less explaining to do when he meets his friends.

Alonso turns his mind to the 'something else' his father has promised. And he wonders who has managed to persuade his father to break the Galeote family tradition. Is it someone present at the table? Or perhaps Daniel or Cayetano, neither of whom could be here today? Alonso looks down the table in the direction of his father. They exchange half-smiles and his father raises a glass, brimming with red wine.

'Happy Birthday, son,' his father says.

'Thank you, Father,' Alonso says.

'Here's that other thing I mentioned,' his father says and passes a small parcel down the table.

It is quickly in Alonso's hands. Alonso slips the knife in and removes the contents. He holds up another book, this one with silver lettering: *Alonso Galeote y Cotilla, Journal August 1858*. Remedios starts to smirk until their mother stares at her.

'A journal?' Alonso asks.

'Since you've stopped keeping a dictionary, I thought you'd appreciate it.'

'Thank you, Father,' Alonso answers politely.

'Remember, that's how Cervantes got started, as I might have mentioned before.'

Alonso supposes his father will likely quiz him on *Volume I* of *The History of Don Quixote*. Better that than be quizzed by friends on *Lady Cornelia*.

'You're not going to ask to see it. Are you?' Alonso has the courage to ask.

'Certainly not!'

'I'm not even sure how to start.'

'That's easy,' his father says, 'imagine you're writing a letter to one of your cousins in Puerto Rico.'

'Which one?'

'Facundo would be around your age.'

'Facundo's at least four years older,' his mother says.

'Is he? Well, anyway, you can imagine him whatever age you like,' his father says. 'They all like to hear about the old country.'

'But not everyone's life in the "old country" is as interesting as Cervantes' life,' Alonso answers.

'Of course it is,' his father answers. 'Everyone's life is full of drama. Packed with events. The sun rises, the sun sets, the stars appear. A stranger visits. A baby arrives, a brother leaves home. One book pleases, another book disappoints. A train arrives at the platform, a boat sails from the quay…'

'I think he gets the point,' his mother interrupts.

Worried about appearing ungrateful, Alonso vows he will think of something to write. For now, he places his journal on the kitchen table, picks up *Volume I* of *The History of Don Quixote* and begins to read the dedications.

Remedios has taken nearly a half page for herself. She has sketched a drawing of three figures. This is typical of her. If there is a space, she must sketch in it. The smallest figure of the trio is seated at a desk, a pen in hand. The other two stand next to him, one with a rifle on his back, a holy cross hanging from his left hand. The other has no rifle, only a holy cross around his neck. Alonso understands that the little figure at the desk is supposed to be him.

'I don't see Gabriel in this drawing. Where is he?' Alonso asks.

'Probably outside stealing oranges,' Remedios says. Her laughter has the others laughing too, until Mother tells them to hush.

Alonso remembers the white card and takes it from his pocket. He turns it over to read the message from Cayetano, their noviciate priest, currently studying something he says is metaphysics. It is enigmatic, as usual — *Dear little brother, you'll have had a pleasant surprise today. You see, not everything our father does is* pre-ordained. *A barely perceptible Epicurean swerve is all it takes to escape* Lady Cornelia. *Enjoy!*

Alonso has no idea what Cayetano means, except it must be related to his last visit home. Father and Cayetano stayed up late to play *Democritis and Epicure*, a game of chance where the loser has to do something out of character chosen in advance by the winner. He supposes Cayetano must have won.

MORE HARSH TRUTHS
2 Plaza Colón, Madrid
19 April 1886.

In the kitchen, Concha seems to be bristling for this opportunity. She frees her jaws from their clamped silence. Talks fast and firm.

'It's time you heard some harsh truths, brother.'

'Is it?'

'You're not the first writer to receive bad reviews,' she says.

'This is different.'

'Nor the first to have been dumped by their mistress.'

Her remark catches him by surprise. Is there nothing that can be hidden from her? Anytime she announced that the 'countess' was at the door he always insisted their liaisons were of a literary nature. But no matter how intimate a thing is, it is never safely hidden from her. She is uncanny in knowing where to scratch. Once she even asked him if he could ever imagine killing their mother.

'Bad reviews are only words,' she says, bringing Benito back to the moment.

'Shall I remind you of what they wrote?'

'I wouldn't bother,' Concha says and wrings her hands.

'I'll tell you anyway: *Galdós has lost his touch. The reading public should look elsewhere for their entertainment.* Shall I go on?'

'That was only Casanovas,' she says. 'What do you expect from "The President for the Preservation of Happy Endings,"

Plaudits?' She stabs a finger in the air.

She has got the measure of Casanovas because she has often heard Benito, José and the others talk of him. They say he is too dumb to absorb the function of realist writing.

But Luis Alfonso Casanovas is not the only critic. There are the others: serious critics, people whom Benito respects — or, in the case of the countess, maybe more than respected. 'Don't forget Ortega y Munilla,' Benito says.

'What about him?'

'Even he wrote *Lo Prohibido* was, *Too Depressing an analysis of heredity* to expect anyone to read it *for entertainment.*'

She pulls her dressing robe tighter around her shoulders. Her knuckles whiten.

'Then what about Clarín?' she counters.

'What about him?'

'He said it was authentic, and candid, and rooted in the real world.'

'He's a friend.'

'But at least he liked it.'

'Even Clarín hopes I don't get back onto the subject of heredity in my next novel,' Benito reminds her.

'Perhaps he has a point,' Concha says quietly.

Benito places his coffee cup on the kitchen table. Leans forward. Takes both ends of his greying moustache between his fingers and thumbs and rolls them like cigarettes.

'I've told you: heredity is the only story that can make any sense after *Lo Prohibido.*'

'So what! You can't finish it,' she says.

Benito falls silent. Slumps into his seat.

'Anyway,' she presses him, 'do people really care about *your* view of this heredity argument?'

He stiffens. Sits back up again, as though pulled by invisible strings. 'You may not have noticed, Concha, but how this ends can affect us all.' Benito looks away, towards the kitchen window, as though it were a dark portal to another Madrid.

Instinctively, her gaze follows his, then she shakes her head as though realising her own absurdity.

'And Salillas and his coterie are the ones who seem to be winning,' Benito adds.

'Who says so?' Concha's disbelief is clear.

'Well, of course they are. Every day it's those dinosaurs who get heard on the matter.'

'Perhaps the public are interested in what they have to say on the subject,' she says.

'But it's pseudo-science,' Benito answers. 'And it's not just the alienists laying this on. They have archbishops, police chiefs, politicians, and even bartenders spouting the same nonsense.'

In her seat, she mirrors her brother's languid posture. It is as though they have both been battered into submission by Benito's assessment of where public opinion is being led.

'Don't you believe the alienists know something about the causes of madness. Understand whether free will exists?'

'I've read everything Salillas and his cronies have read. There's no proof of anything.'

'But isn't it their job to say how mental asylums should be run?' she argues.

'Why wouldn't it be a writer's job too?'

'You keep saying that, Benito, but you're not actually writing anything.'

He purses his lips. Leans over and blows into his already cold coffee. He tries to avoid her stare. 'And you know why that is,' he reminds her.

'Because the loose lady said Bueno de Guzmán was two-dimensional?' As his first-reader, Concha knows all about the straw man of *Lo Prohibido*. She could probably even tell which real person had inspired the character. Not that it matters now. All that matters is which critic has said loudest the character was a parody.

'She's a bitch!' Concha blurts.

'Her name's Emilia,' he responds and raises his eyebrows.

'This is all her fault!'

Her vehemence has Benito wondering whether his sister has a point. Is this why he cannot write anymore? Has she so battered his self-belief? Perhaps she has. She was never just an ordinary, uninformed, literary hack.

'What the hell does she know?' Concha asks.

Her question makes him smile. He considers answering: *Quite a lot, actually.* They had talked incessantly — on the reform of asylums and prisons — whilst he worked on *Lo Prohibido*. All this talk of modernising institutions was a wonderful and necessary distraction for them, as much as it was for everyone else. He cannot remember, but it might even have been Emilia who suggested it was the novelist's job to write a 'thesis novel' about the 'burning issue' of the day. Well, where has listening taken him? To the fringes of bankruptcy, and wearisome ridicule from hacks who tire at three hundred words!

'Harlot!' Concha says and grins.

'I feel they were quite right: Guzmán *was* rather two-dimensional,' Benito says.

'What's Guzmán got to do with anything?' Concha seems a little unsure. 'You're not planning to resurrect him in your new novel, this "coda" as you call it. Are you?'

'Of course not. I've got Maximiliano Rubín. He'll have all the same so-called degenerative antecedents.'

'So you're saying Maximiliano Rubín will be just like Guzmán?'

'Everything that Salillas and his cronies expect — all they

claim makes a person predestined to be deranged — Maximiliano will have. I'll even have him being suckled by a goat.'
Benito laughs.

Concha laughs too. It's been a while since they laughed together like this.

'So, why don't you just get on with writing it? Wouldn't that be a wonderful way to spite the countess?'

'Something's not quite as it should be. It was Emilia who put me on to it. I need to look from *both* sides.'

'Pretentious rich hussy!'

'With Guzmán I was concentrated on looking from the outside-in.'

Concha appears uncertain of whether Benito does know how to remedy this problem. But at least he has begun to laugh again and has that old gleam in his eyes. Perhaps a little push would do it. 'Maybe if you went down to Leganés?' she suggests.

'There's nothing there for me.'

'But you went in the past when you needed authenticity for your "troubled" characters.'

When he and Luis Simarro were on talking terms, this idea might have been sound. Anyway, Simarro's gone from the Santa Isabel asylum at Leganés and since then things have not been so favourable for writers, nor inmates come to that. The chaplain, the rector and the sisters of charity are running Santa Isabel again. Benito's last visit there did not go well. A fact he has not yet shared with Concha. Telling her is overdue: 'Forget it. The chaplain has forbidden me access for as long as he has "air in his lungs". And sadly they're still full.'

'Why?' She sounds offended on Benito's behalf.

'Because my writing is a "heinous crime" against the Church.'

'He actually read *Lo Prohibido*?'

'He was talking about *Doña Perfecta*.'

'It's been ten years since that was published.'

'True. And he admitted he'd not actually read it. But apparently it was "anti-clerical filth". According to his sources.'

'He said that?' Concha slaps her thighs in apparent rage.

'He said worse.'

'How can he say it's anti-clerical, if he's not even read it?' Her voice is raised.

'Faith?' Benito smirks at his sister who still holds on to her own faith.

'You're not funny.' Concha sits down.

Santa Isabel asylum has gone back to its old methods. All traces of a person's individuality are progressively wiped away. It is done through drugs, reward, and punishment. The moment an inmate arrives they are dispossessed of any personal property, whether tangible (clothes, books or jewellery), or intangible (ideas, beliefs and rituals). Any anchors to personal identity, any hinge holding the person to their past, is untethered.

Benito hears that quinine, opium, morphine and belladonna are much favoured again in Leganés. No, you do not go there looking for authenticity. You may find a husk if you search long enough amongst the four hundred inmates but that is all.

'You know the funniest thing?' Benito asks.

'There's something funny about this?'

'Chaplain del Mazo is the name of the new director!'

'Mister Mallet?' Concha starts to giggle and her shoulders shake. 'You're making that up.'

'I'm not,' Benito insists. 'It's Señor del Mazo running the show.'

She laughs uncontrollably. Benito too is caught in the moment. As this memory of an argument with Mr Mallet takes hold and renders him deliriously happy, Benito knows he has not laughed like this in months, not since Emilia left.

Concha leans across the table and hugs her brother. She fumbles in the pocket of her dressing gown. 'You really must read this.' She slips an envelope into his hands.

'What is it?'

'You're never going to imagine what happened whilst you were comatose on chloral hydrate.'

He had only slept ten hours. She had slept too. How much she exaggerates! He takes the envelope and puts it in his pocket without a glance.

'I'll read it later. Where were we?'

'I insist Benito, you must read that straight away.' Concha readies to leave the kitchen.

'I'm going to bed.'

Concha's eyes roll at Benito's stubbornness. 'You'll never believe that front page. You should read it, then go and visit José.'

'How do you know I'm ready to leave the apartment?'

'You returned from your bathroom bravado didn't you?'

'I'll visit José.'

'And while you're there ask him about Luis Simarro!' she shouts as she hurries away from the kitchen.

THE LAST STALK

THE TORMENTOR LISTENED, a glass of port in his hand, as Padre Gabino Sánchez told of what happened next. There was a white flash, an ugly crack in the sky, and a boom sounding at its tail. The unmistakeable portent of a pistol shot. The faithful flung themselves forward. They flopped to the ground like stalks scythed with a single sweep.

An unearthly silence. Two further gunshots.

Padre Gabino Sánchez dared tilt his head upwards. There was no sign of Nicolás Vizcaíno. There was one stalk — the bishop — which took longer to fall than the rest.

Padre Gabino Sánchez stood up; watched. He was unable to utter a sound as his beloved Narciso collapsed to his knees. For a moment, the bishop's back remained upright, rigid as a pole. Then his head flopped sideways like a mishandled marionette before he tipped forward and fell on his face. Gabino Sánchez stared in shock. Mouth agape, he watched as the gunman rose up and looked around. He heard the assassin rant in Latin. The man was dressed in priest vestments and he turned to stare directly at Padre Gabino Sánchez.

They recognised each other. It could not be anyone else. Padre Gabino Sánchez was transfixed, but he did not move. He simply closed his eyes and waited as Padre Cayetano pointed the pistol in his direction.

The gun, an Euskaro, misfired. Gabino Sánchez opened

his eyes to see the priest had not been aiming in his direction. He had turned the pistol against his own temple and was still ranting when he pulled the trigger a second time: another misfire.

Hot tears trickled down Gabino Sánchez' face. He remembered the Euskaro holds five bullets.

How many shots have already been discharged? He asked himself.

He continued to watch Cayetano, who had the pistol pointed at his own temple. He knew it was not a Christian response but he prayed to hear a click of detonation. He willed a bullet to slip out of the gun-chamber, blast through the barrel and blow Cayetano's head to smithereens.

He watched Cayetano frantically pull on the trigger and rave in Latin.

It was then, with Narciso lying in his own blood and the glassy-eyed Cayetano making empty, catatonic trigger motions that two policemen appeared. They disarmed Cayetano without a struggle.

Still there was no sign of the whereabouts of Vizcaíno, but Gabino Sánchez heard a voice howl above all the others.

'Don't let him be dead! Don't let him be dead!' Juan Creus howled and scurried towards the bishop.

Coming in the opposite direction, more policemen appeared. They commandeered the bishop's carriage and carted Cayetano away. Gabino Sánchez heard them order the coachman to drive to Calle Juanelo.

The crowd rose up in little groups and took in the scene. Despite his bulk, it was Doctor Juan Creus who first reached Narciso's bleeding body and begged for assistance. Help arrived in the form of anonymous, pale-faced parishioners who had risen up from the ground and begun to surround the body of the bishop. On Juan Creus' instructions, they lifted him up by his arms and legs and carried him the few yards into the cathedral gatehouse.

In the melee, another man ran behind them calling out to Creus: 'Let me through, I'm a doctor.'

More police appeared, one of whom remained outside the gatehouse door. Gabino Sánchez pushed through the crowd. When he arrived, Narciso was already laid out on a marble-bench situated under a dirty, opaque window. Juan Creus was being assisted by the other man, whose medical bag was already open. Shiny surgical instruments protruded from black, rolled-up leather sheaths.

'This is Doctor Moreno y Pozo,' Juan Creus said.

'We've already extracted a bullet.' Doctor Moreno sounded pleased.

Padre Gabino Sánchez wondered at their efficiency. How had it been possible to extract a bullet in the few minutes it took him to reach the gatehouse? He stood watching blood trickle down the front of the marble-bench, forming a shapeless scarlet stain on the floor under Juan Creus's feet. There were bloody footprints everywhere. In the dim light, Juan Creus and Doctor Moreno bent over Narciso, searching frantically but unable to locate other bullets.

Gabino Sánchez heard a low moaning sound. At first, he was unsure if it came from Narciso or one of the others. Juan Creus stood up and moved away from the bench. Gabino Sánchez stared long into Juan Creus's eyes, and saw they were full of fear. Juan Creus reached into his medical bag, took out a small, thin-necked bottle of water and started to sprinkle the contents over Narciso.

Gabino Sánchez recognised the bottle; Narciso had gifted it to Juan after visiting Lourdes.

Will there be a miracle today? Padre Gabino Sánchez wondered.

A commotion from just beyond the door of the gatehouse disturbed them all.

Rector Vizcaíno's raised, angry voice: 'Let me through!'

Vizcaíno entered the gatehouse and took in the scene. He must have recognised the bottle in Juan Creus' hand. Vizcaíno's fury was etched in black lines upon his face. Creus thrust the bottle back into his bag.

'I wondered where you were,' Gabino Sánchez said.

Rector Vizcaíno ignored him and began to take control. He gave out orders, spoke loudly to the others: 'We're taking him home,' Vizcaíno said.

'He can't be moved,' Doctor Moreno replied.

'Well, he's not staying here, laying on a slab,' Vizcaíno argued loudly, and under his breath added, 'with some old fool splashing water on him.'

BACK ON THE STREET
MADRID
19 APRIL 1886

AFTER MONTHS COOPED up, Benito is outdoors. It is not yet
five o'clock in the morning. He is in Plaza Colón. He is on his
way to see José Ferreras. Concha will claim the credit for
shooing him out of the apartment, but the time was right,
anyway.

The city seems preternaturally still. Its fragrances and
sounds more acute than he remembers. He sits on a park
bench. He reads the front page. He still cannot fathom the
news. He puts the newspaper down, picks it up and re-reads it
over and over. Then repeats the same motions. The headline
screams: *BISHOP ASSASSINATED BY PRIEST*

The drama happened here in Madrid, less than twenty-
four hours ago. Everything about it galvanises his sensibilities.
A tragedy! A waste of a life! A new flashpoint for the country?
But there is something about these characters — a bishop,
and a priest — something Shakespearian, something Cervantian. What harm must a bishop have done to invoke such
wrath in a colleague of the cloth? In its tragedy and complex-
ity this story is calling him. He intends to eviscerate this one
too, but not from the outside in, this time.

It frustrates him too that he was at home tucked up in a
sleeping-draught-assisted, self-absorbed exile whilst just a few
kilometres away the Bishop of Madrid was being murdered.

Manolo was right, this self-pity of his had gone on too

long. Nothing will keep him from writing any longer.

He wonders why no one came to tell them. Then again, would they have known if his assistant has been banging on their door? Their natural and assisted state of dormancy had lasted the entire day and night of Sunday.

He slept whilst the grief stricken were likely running in the streets a few kilometres away from where he is sitting now. He wonders: *Where are they now? At home searching their closets for weapons and planning their revenge?* But then, who could they take their revenge on? Because, when a priest kills a bishop, one cannot blame the republicans, or the monarchists, or even God.

So, who is to blame?

He rises and strides away from Plaza Colón towards Plaza de Cibeles. He could take a carriage but prefers to walk. He continues on his way, ruminating, already understanding that this story has a larger importance for him.

His senses stutter back to life. The street odours are fresh, and sharp. Some are acute. Unattenuated by habit, they flood in. The scent of coffee from a street-corner café, from another open door a touch of aniseed, and something else. Almonds, perhaps?

He sidles on, pausing at the bakers and patisserie-makers now also opening their doors to temptation with their *pestiños*, *churros* and *buñuelos*, and early Easter *torrijas*.

He evades their enticement. Walks past. His head is light, his feet are heavy and his thoughts are loud. There is a joy to being out here, but also a deep sadness. A murder of this magnitude will fan the flames that have flickered for this past year over the country's burning question. But what price must they pay?

Everyone will have something to say. Commentators with clap-trap theories will be just as loud as ever; louder probably, than any rational well-reasoned Kraussists. He already sees what he must do.

He picks up his speed. The city dwellers are tentative in emerging from the shock; thus no one impedes him. He need not skip around a street-seller here, or make a sleight to avoid a beggar there, or stop in the trail of some pedestrian who has pulled their internal deadman handbrake. He can slow-walk or fast-march as he wishes. This novelty of being outside renders him more alive than ever, even in the shadow of an awful death.

What will José make of it? Benito is sure that when he arrives, his friend will take everything with his habitual composure and detachment in the face of a news story. In the immediate moment, José will place everything in perspective. José will see the outline of the entire play, not just this act.

As these thoughts coalesce in Benito's mind, there is something else there, some dull and nagging irritation, like a flat stone in his shoe. This is when he remembers Concha's words about asking after Luis Simarro. He already has a sinking sense of knowing why she may have said this.

INTERESTING HIPPOCAMPUS
41 Arco de Santa María, Madrid
20 April 1886

Seven scientists squeeze into Luis' makeshift dissecting sanctum. Luis wears the white laboratory coat he brought with him from Paris. It has a pocket at the level of his heart, under which is emblazoned *Hôpital Salpêtrière*.

Luis sits in one of his two adapted bosun chairs. His friend, Santiago Ramón y Cajal, sits in the adjacent chair. The others crowd around. They stare over the shoulder of Luis and Cajal as Luis bends forward across his recently installed mahogany workbench.

Previously, a white-marble kitchen sink had occupied the space. The sink was ancient and beautiful. It came from the same quarries as *Michelangelo's David*, but it was an encumbrance. Therefore, it had to go to make room for the elegant cutting slab. As far as Luis knows, the sink has been ferreted off to the farm owned by some cousin of Mercedes.

In exchange, Luis has the buck brains needed for today's advancement in histology. Today they might answer the question: do aggressive male rabbits have different brains from shy brothers?

Standing behind Cajal is Juan Madinaveitia. Juan is a colleague of Luis', so he is allowed to handle Luis' precious Leitz microtome. The others — the 'youngsters' as Madinaveitia calls them — are scattered around, behind these three wise men.

It might seem to the inexpert eye that chaos reigns on the workbench. Bottles and jars of assorted sizes and shapes are scattered. These vessels containing fluids of oddly vivid colours — shades of red-orange, black-browns, and some green-looking liquids — may seem randomly situated. But look closer and see the scientist's scheme of order. See the labels scripted in Luis' handwriting. There are a variety of solutions: dichromate, chromic acid, formaldehyde and osmic acid, as well as alcohols of various concentrations. Several paraffins too, but each safely in its right place, relative to the other.

Yet danger does lurk; half a metre away a cylindrical gas-lamp sits on the workbench. It is not yet dusk, but the lamp is already lit. A slight moment of complacency, an instance of inattention and we will have an explosion that will deprive the country of its finest cadre of histologists.

Part-way up the lamp's body, a skirt sticks out like a ballerina's, silvered on the interior, black on the exterior. Luis brought that lamp from Paris too.

Further to Luis' left, just beyond his reach, are some rag-stopped bottles and jars: potassium bichromate, ammonia and silver nitrate. Next to those, placed directly in front of Cajal, is a book open at *Section IX, Metodi di Indagine, page 183*. Cajal does not read Italian but occasionally he steals a peek at the book anyway.

'This is the research protocol section,' Luis tells them as he holds the book open.

Luis was four years old when he left Rome and, although he no longer loves that place where his father died, he has never lost his love for the music of the language. By necessity of circumstance, Luis has become a polyglot. He also speaks flawless French. His linguistic aptitude came in useful whilst working in Paris when Professor Ranvier brought in some of Camillo Golgi's researchers from Pavia. It was Luis who organised their lodgings. Some even lodged with him. And Luis acted as interpreter, ensuring Golgi's methods were clear to Charcot's students, and Charcot's teaching was understood by the Italians. His new Italian friends made sure that Golgi's latest publications always came his way first.

Luis tenses. Pushes his elbows firmly against the armrests of his chair. Obtains the stability he wants. His long-fingered hands hover above a rectangular metal dish. The others stare at his fingers as though he is Paganini.

Luis and Cajal had already completed the fixation, embedding, and sectioning phases, before the others arrived. It is this next step they have all come to see. Luis pauses for dramatic effect. He arches closer, expertly manipulates a pair of toothed forceps then places the last of four freshly sliced sections of brain tissue into the metal staining dish.

'Number one: treat each section with potassium bichromate, or ammonia if you don't have the former, and silver nitrate. Number two: treat with a mixture of osmium bichromate and silver nitrate. Number three: treat the tissue section with potassium bichromate and chloric mercury.'

Today, the tissue sections are of rabbit. Even here in Madrid, it could take weeks for Luis to get his hands on a human brain. For their purposes, the hippocampus of a rabbit will be sufficient. They kill time, wait for the results, but experience tells them Luis will have been able to replicate Golgi's methods.

When they see the results they are in awe of the clarity: ganglions, fibres, and those elements the French call neurones are all visible, all ready for tracing. They applaud. Luis bows.

Despite his showmanship, they know Luis intends to put aside his cutting instruments and advance on another front. They know he has come back home to blow another trumpet in another battle.

Luis says when they win this struggle, never again will an alienist, or psychiatrist as the younger ones have taken to calling themselves, have to take instructions from an unqualified cleric. Nor will patients be called inmates.

As he pulls his chair away from the workbench, Luis looks into the eyes of the one man amongst them who has the dexterity and the patience to devote himself to perfecting Golgi's staining technique.

'It's over to you now, Cajal,' Luis tells his friend.

'Let's hear what Cajal has to say about the unconscious thoughts of the shy buck rabbit mind,' Madinaveitia says.

'On the subject of rabbit minds, you'll never guess who wants to meet with Luis,' Cajal says.

Cajal's question is directed into the air, asked of no one in particular. But most of them can guess who Cajal is talking about; Luis' lost literary friend.

The others collectively shrug their shoulders. Eventually, one of the trainees, Miguel Gayarre Espinal, speaks for them all: 'Benito?'

They know of the rumours of Benito Pérez Galdós and Luis' fan-letter writing fiancée, Mercedes, but a collegiate vacant mist covers all their eyes, as though there are a dozen men of that name.

'Maybe he wants to donate his brain to replace the rabbit's!' Espinal quips.

Only Luis and Cajal do not snigger. Luis understands what association Cajal probably had in mind when thinking of Benito Pérez Galdós — the introverted rabbit, not the promiscuous buck.

Espinal does not go so far as to draw a line between the notoriety of the sex lives of rabbits and the subject of their discussion, but the air is thick with the allusion.

'Can anyone think of another creature who knows better how to back out of the limelight?' Luis asks.

They laugh, because everyone is reminded of Galdós' shyness in company.

'What does he want?' Cajal asks.

'I imagine he's interested in the bishop's assassination.' Luis says. 'He's probably already getting in touch with the killer's family.'

They all know instantly what this means. Some of them have read *Lo Prohibido*. All of them know Galdós' alienist friend, Escuder. Galdós has revealed to Escuder and Escuder has told them: *Lo Prohibido* is a red herring: dripping in irony. A set-up, just seeming to support determinism. But, in his coda, Galdós plans to subvert the entire premise of degeneracy. He could do it. He is capable — none of them could name another novelist in Spain, or in Europe, better read in their medical texts than Galdós is.

'Who'd want to read another of his boring thesis novels anyway?' Espinal says.

Amongst the others there are a great deal of 'humphs' and chin stroking.

'I imagine he'll try to exploit this situation to sell his next book,' Cajal says.

'Especially since no one bought the last one,' Espinal says and the youngsters laugh.

'The way Escuder tells it, Galdós is serious,' Cajal responds. 'He actually believes degeneration theories are overstated.'

'He should just stay out of this,' Luis says. 'He'll likely end up getting the bloody priest garrotted.'

'Why would the priest even bother to talk with Galdós?' Cajal wonders aloud.

'If Galdós tells the priest he can keep his neck out of the

garrotte what does he have to lose?' Luis says.

Espinal says the unsayable. 'If not, at least you'll get your hands on a fresh degenerate brain specimen.'

The others groan.

'That could be an interesting hippocampus for perfecting this new tinting method,' Cajal says.

'There'll be plenty of time for that,' Luis says. 'It'll serve us much better if the degenerate priest's actions reminds the public of the risks and solutions.'

'Solutions?' the naive Espinal asks. 'What solutions?'

'The obvious one, you fool. Model asylums, run by professionals,' Cajal says, before Luis can.

GABINO'S WORD
BISHOP'S PALACE, CALLE SAN JUSTO, MADRID
5 OCTOBER 1886

WHEN POMP IS no longer your objective, you take the direct route from the Cathedral San Isidro back to the Bishop's Palace. The distance is short and the time needed to travel it would ordinarily be brief: a stroll of under ten minutes for an elderly gentlemen of Gabino Sánchez' epoch.

However, during the time the bishop lay bleeding in the San Isidro gatehouse, witnesses to his shooting had risen from the ground, but gone nowhere. Asked to leave the vicinity they seemed not to comprehend. And those that did leave Calle Toledo simply gravitated up the street and around the corner, taking their grief and candles with them to the palace in Calle San Justo.

Thus, when the police returned to the cathedral with the bishop's carriage, and Rector Vizcaíno organised for the bishop to be carried from the gatehouse back to it, thousands of grievers and some gawpers were already gathered all the way along the five hundred metres separating San Isidro from the palace.

Though the distance is short, for Padre Gabino Sánchez, it felt like the longest, bleakest journey he had ever made. He held Narciso's hand and watched from the carriage window as the congregation carried lit candles in the middle of the morning. The collective, supposed to be celebrating one man's triumphal entry into yonder were, instead, yawling like some macabre cortège at another man's certain exit.

As the carriage approached the doors of the palace, Vizcaíno leapt from it. He was quickly followed by two policemen. They cleared a path and carried Narciso into his palace. They laid the unconscious bishop on the couch. A small group gathered around him. Moments passed before Doctor Moreno arrived and asked Vizcaíno to clear the room of everyone that was 'non-essential'.

As strangers slouched away with the reluctance of unpaid scene fillers in a shoddy Teatro Español performance, only Juan Creus retreated with any grace. He slipped quietly to the back of the room and remained motionless, next to the closed windows overlooking the garden.

Rector Vizcaíno and Padre Gabino Sánchez stood next to Doctor Moreno as he administered more morphine. 'He's putting up a fight,' Moreno said. 'Come and see, for yourself, Doctor Creus.'

Juan Creus smiled and re-emerged into the centre of the room. 'I feel we must find the other bullets.'

'I think I've changed my opinion on that,' Doctor Moreno answered quietly.

'Then maybe it would've been better not to have extracted a bullet back there in the gatehouse,' Vizcaíno said.

Padre Gabino Sánchez had held that same thought on the edge of his mind for the past hour. He stared at Moreno, but still not saying what was on his mind.

Moreno sighed, shrugged his shoulders, then turned to Juan Creus. 'Our main focus should be on pain relief.'

All through the day, Doctor Moreno attended the bishop and Juan Creus assisted. With the help of Rector Vizcaíno, they stripped, cleaned, and bandaged the bishop.

Eventually Moreno located a second bullet which, with Creus' agreement, he extracted. They continued searching. It was late in the afternoon before they understood the third bullet had traversed the bishop's body — in one way and right out the other.

Occasionally the bishop regained consciousness and when he did, he was sometimes lucid, sometimes delirious. It was early evening when he suddenly seemed stronger. It was not clear to anyone if this was the start of a recovery or the start of the end.

It was then the bishop asked to be left alone with Padre Gabino Sánchez.

'It was him, wasn't it?' Narciso said.

'It was a stranger,' Gabino Sánchez replied.

'No, it wasn't a stranger. I forgive him.'

'Don't talk any more,' Gabino Sánchez urged. 'Rest. Keep your strength up.'

'If you say so,' Bishop Narciso whispered.

The outside light faded and Gabino Sánchez searched for more candles. He remained alone with his ebbing protégé.

The morphine doing its work, Narciso slept and woke in lengthening cycles. Just before dawn he awoke again but seemed a phantom. 'I'm going to die,' he said. 'I'm ready. Let them all come to see me.' He laughed in pain. 'Send for the queen.'

When Gabino Sánchez told Vizcaíno of the bishop's request, they argued violently. Padre Gabino Sánchez had to explain it to the bishop.

'Vizcaíno feels there should be no visitors, and especially not her.'

'Nicolás is young,' Narciso insisted. 'Reconciliation is what we need, particularly with her.'

Doctor Moreno was sent for. He administered further morphine. The word was passed out, visitors could come. They all started showing up. The first to arrive was the Papal

Nuncio, then Cardinal Zeferino González Díaz Tuñón. All through the day, there was a queue of the good and the great, apparently in degrees of distress.

The widowed queen could not come, but she sent her handsome representative who said that she was in tears when he left her.

'Had she not been afraid of giving birth at any moment she would have come personally,' the queen's representative said.

'And most welcome she would have been,' responded Rector Vizcaíno, without the least hint of irony.

All the while, Gabino Sánchez remained impressed at Vizcaíno's performance that still fooled the others.

Narciso was not awake when Prime Minister Sagasta arrived but Sagasta stayed for a long time and chatted with Gabino Sánchez and the Cardinal and the queen's representative.

'Why must it take a tragedy to bring us three together?' Sagasta said as he was leaving.

'I think those were precisely the bishop's words,' Padre Gabino Sánchez replied.

As the dregs of life drained from him, Narciso awoke and although his pained muttering became fainter and fainter he occasionally could enunciate words or phrases that Gabino Sánchez could understand: 'You see how far we've come?' he managed to say to Gabino Sánchez.

'I do.'

'Don't waste this opportunity!'

As the bishop lay dying in front of his eyes, Padre Gabino Sánchez gave his word.

INHERITANCE
61 CALLE MAYOR, MADRID
19 APRIL 1886

ON THE BALCONY he watches everything happening three floors below him in Calle Mayor. However, he is not fully concentrating on the crowd outside. Instead, he closes his eyes and reflects on her offer. There is no need to rush anything here. She is still Cayetano's landlady, still their cousin-once-removed.

He hears drawers open as she returns to the commode, presumably to find the cushions that belong with the mattress. He re-enters the salon, closes the doors behind him and opens the curtains. He has never been here before in the absence of Cayetano. The place has a heartless emptiness.

An uncomfortable reality inhabits his mind. The farm business in Vélez-Málaga is part-hocked; it can hardly be considered an enviable inheritance to covet, and he already knows being last in line was never worth fretting over, but he should probably make plans. He, Alonso, the smallest, as well as the youngest, of the four brothers will be the one inheriting.

For years, he has been permanently drenched in a mist of hand-me-down hopes. His shoulders ought to droop with the weight he has had to carry all this time. But they have not, because they are resolute, toughened by life. As he has been too.

The salon is humid. It still holds the sweat and odours of

Cayetano. Tránsito stands in the centre of it, holding two cushions. The reddened rawness and circles of sadness around her wide, beautiful, dark eyes are visible to him, even across a light-deprived room.

For a moment, he permits himself a longer glance in her direction. Tránsito Durdal y Cortés, to give her her full name, has barely changed. That little chrysalis, that adolescent, who might have become closer than a once-removed cousin, has metamorphosed into a thirty-three year old woman with the same artless sensuality she always had.

She holds his look and smiles.

Is it any wonder Cayetano never said anything? he thinks.

'How long will they stay out there?' she asks.

'Probably until they need a drink,' Alonso answers.

'I don't think I can stand it anymore.'

He remembers marks carved in a tree, long before he grew up, married, and had children. That was another moment, another Tránsito.

'I'll stay here as long as you like,' he suggests to her.

She tries to smile but this time her smile seems broken; it doesn't work.

'Or maybe you should leave here,' he says looking around. 'Think about taking a room in the hotel.'

She does not answer. Instead she twirls her hair around a finger.

Suddenly, there's a thwack against the wooden window-shutters.

Tránsito leaps in fright. 'Christ! What was that?' she asks.

He hears a stone drop. It lands, then rolls across the thin terneplate lining the floor of the balcony.

'Probably a hack with somewhere else to be,' he says.

'Why don't the police stop them?'

'It might even be the police who threw it,' he laughs.

'What do they want?'

'A story. Perhaps they'll even offer you money for it.'

If Alonso talks quietly, calmly and dispassionately, this is not due to a paucity of pity on his part. In truth, empathy has never been scarce in him. It is just he has learnt to bury it deep. He is trained to be this way. Harness your perceptions, perfect your poise, then move to action — those are the core elements of instruction in the Civil Guard. They can save your life, or perhaps someone else's.

Alonso has learnt how to act in the face of real danger. Honed his perception of all his senses and perfected the ability to respond with just the requisite violence. And in the face of danger, he has known how to kill. As has his brother, Daniel, before him. Now, as unpredictable as it is undeniable, the gentlest of the four Galeote Cotilla brothers — Cayetano, their noble throw-back — has learnt it too.

A FRIEND IN THE KNOW
14 CALLE PIZARRO, MADRID
19 APRIL 1886

THE DOORMAN IS discretion-in-a-uniform. His eyes flicker recognition. He does not need to ask anything because he knows everyone: why they come here or why they stop coming. He nods to Benito and watches him take the door on the left: the tradesman's entrance, which slinks along a corridor directly to José's office.

Benito knocks, but does not wait to enter.

José Ferreras is already at his desk, which is as wide as a caravel. He is a spider surrounded by a web of files. He appears startled to see Benito. He places a file on top of a flat wooden cigar case — a gift from Benito given pride of place on his desk — and clears his throat before he bounds around the desk.

'Benitín, you never said you were coming!'

'It was unplanned.'

'Why are you here? Do I owe you money?'

Although they last saw each other only two nights ago, they hug warmly. They both know Benito has beaten his melancholy — after months of self-exile he has crossed the threshold.

They have not always been this close. Twenty years ago, José the serious, savvy writer (a salaried journalist for *La Nación*) and the gangly Benito (who spent too much of his time in the

113

offices at *La Nación* working for free) did not always see eye to eye. José never hid his contempt for any of the students who spent time at *La Nación* pretending to be reporters, whilst their parents continued working and paying for university lessons their prodigals rarely attended.

'They inevitably find out,' José had said. 'Parents will always sniff out a slacker in the family.'

Benito never hid his disinterest in being judged by José. Yet the threat of his mother, Mama Dolores, showing up in Madrid worried him. He hated to be reminded.

Something in the air must have travelled the sea to Mama Dolores, warning her that her youngest child — far from her censorious coddling — was serving another kind of apprenticeship. Occasionally Mama Dolores would contact a cousin in the capital and get them to track Benito down. Said cousin would come by the office of *La Nación* carrying a letter from Mama Dolores who wished to be reassured: *How are Benito's legal studies going?*

'Why are you so afraid of her?' José had asked.

'I'm not,' he lied.

'Then, tell her the truth. Say you're doing what you want to do, not what she wants.' José made it sound simple.

But Mama Dolores had her own dreams and surely she was entitled to them? Even if Benito considered he had a compelling case to despise her, he did not enjoy his lie. He tried to rationalise it away.

'Even Balzac had to disappoint his mother,' Benito said.

'But Balzac had talent.'

Mama Dolores eventually discovered the reality. By then Benito had stopped showing up for classes, even those classes he seemed to enjoy. All of this because writing for *La Nación* had become an addiction. He felt he had a *purpose*.

It was reporting on the St Daniel's Eve riots in '65 that

caused his relationship with José to change. With all that was happening during the riots, they soon got split up. But José saw Benito just as he was confronting the police. José told the entire editorial office what he saw.

'Are you sure it was him?' they asked. 'He wouldn't confront a goose!'

'It was definitely him,' José insisted.

And when Benito arrived back in the office, bloodied and bruised, any doubt was removed.

'Why'd I do it? No choice,' he told them.

'There's always a choice,' José said. 'Try using those long legs nature gave you.'

It had not crossed Benito's mind to ask José why *he* had not stayed behind.

'But didn't you see what they were doing? Some of those being dragged away were friends of mine.'

'And you got yourself a thick lip! Do you think that helped them?' José asked.

'It was an impulse,' Benito answered.

'Impulse? Or the liberal crusader's rage?'

The police had given Benito a light beating for his troubles. The next day José wrote his article: *You know things are bad when even the most placid of students are moved to protest against this corrupted puppet government.*

Everyone at *La Nación* knew whom José was talking about; was there any reporter more placid than Benito?

The next line removed any doubt: *Assaulted! Our very own cub-reporter with his penetrating little piggy eyes, large ears, high forehead and dandy, high flat-brimmed hat. Yes, he, with his cravat and Prince–Albert coat, his mother-of-pearl coloured trousers, high-heeled shoes; this whole ensemble topped off with our classic Spanish cape, was battered whilst reporting from the barricades.*

The entire office laughed as it was read back to them.

'Why did you have to write it like that?' Benito asked.

'The public should know someone harmless was unfairly assaulted,' José said.

'Isn't it obvious it was unfair?'

'They'll say you were a "threat to security". Who's to say otherwise?' José said.

'But you made me seem ridiculous.'

'They use coercion: we use comedy!'

'What questions do you think you're asking here?' Benito asked.

He had heard José use that expression every day: 'Our job is to give the public stories that ask questions.' It was possibly that, and Benito's earnestness and bloody nose, which led José to continue the conversation, sympathetically.

'I'm asking what threat you possibly posed,' he said. 'What was your crime? Was it the impertinence of owning a modern, liberal point of view?'

'Couldn't you have done it without describing me in that way?'

'But did I write one word that's not true?'

Eighteen years on, they still look like themselves: José's jowls hang further and his neck is thicker than it used to be, and maybe he looks wiser. He carries the weight of growing gravitas with a certain aplomb. And what of the undernourished Benito? He is no longer the dandy but he still has the same troubled, if slightly more emaciated-looking, face. Now, however, he has a body in need of running repairs. His mother might say Benitín looks sickly.

'If you owed me money, I'd have sent Paco. And stop calling me Benitín.'

The friends share the joke; since they both know that Benito's assistant, Paco, is the least likely person in Madrid to come looking for money. Paco is, perhaps, the only person in Madrid more timid than Benito.

'I suppose you're here to reproach me for Salillas?' José says.

Benito waves a hand, a gesture which says he knows the game José is playing.

José clears a space on the desk. Benito joins him in the task. The friends work in unison. They both know why Benito is here, but they say nothing of yesterday's tragedy. They simply return the web of spine-marked files to their drawers, before José restarts his game of distraction.

'Then, I suppose you're still in a quandary on what to do about that character, what-do-you-call-him, Marco Ruffiano?' José says.

'Actually, it's Maximiliano Rubín. And no, I'm not in a "quandary" as you call it.'

'So, you're stuck with the other one then: Madame Malchance? She's such an awful tart.'

'She's called Fortunata. As you well know.'

For years José pretends not to remember the names of Benito's characters. Benito has learnt to ignore the provocation, move on to something else. He removes the folded-up pages from his pocket and passes it to his teasing friend. 'This is why I'm here.'

With enormous hands, José unfolds and flattens the newspaper on his desk. The front and second pages are taken up with the story.

'I knew this would get you out of the house,' José says. 'Three times, we sent someone round to your apartment. No answer! I was starting to worry.'

'We were sleeping.'

'Sleeping? At eleven? At three? And at eight?'

'Never mind. I've got to meet with this priest,' Benito says.

'So, you'll be back to your old habits.' José says.

'Meaning?'

'You know, keeping odd hours, engaging in a little recreational breaking and entering, following people around Madrid past midnight, that kind of thing.'

'Don't forget who trained me,' Benito answers.

'But times change my friend,' José warns. 'You know what happens now to people who do that and get caught, don't you?'

'It's necessary research,' Benito says. 'Realistic characters make for realistic stories.'

'That argument might have passed muster for your buddy, Mister Balzac, but this is Madrid.'

'So what?' Benito says.

'If you're caught creeping around a whorehouse,' José says, 'you're not considered a researcher on a quest for facts. You're a whorehouse creeper on a search for fornication. See what I mean?'

'No, not exactly.'

'In the light of the night, all cats are grey.'

José often disinters some old phrase like that when he wants to warn Benito. And Benito is usually in too much of a hurry to defend himself, at least with the eloquence he wishes. Usually he will conceive a witty answer two days later. For now, he points to the page on José's desk: 'I want to know all there is to know about the priest.'

'Then you've come to the right place. I sent one of my best around yesterday. He managed to talk with the priest's, what will we call her, landlady?'

'Landlady?' Benito asks.

'Young and attractive and it's her name on the rent-book. Not forthcoming though.'

'You always seem to find people.'

José shakes his head, slowly, from side to side, and rolls his eyes. 'Where do you suppose they took him?' he asks. Then, as is habit in these particular moments, he answers his own question: 'The nearest police station! Which would be where?'

'Not sure,' Benito answers.

'In Calle Juanelo! You've become rusty, Mister Realist-Writer. My shadows find everything.'

Benito would not be surprised to discover that police officers are numbered within José's far-extended 'family' of part-time shadows.

José takes a folded note from his trouser pocket and, ensuring they are not observed, slides it across the desk.

'Why so nervous?' Benito asks, and opens the note. He reads the address: *Third floor, 61 Calle Mayor.* He knows of this address. It has some buried familiarity. He cannot exhume the significance, right at this moment but is confident it shall arrive in due course.

ARMS & LETTERS

Thursday, 26 August 1858

Dear Facundo, it was my thirteenth birthday three days ago. I do not expect you to know that since we have never met and I am not sure of your age, nor can I say with certainty when your birthday is!

It is partly thanks to you that I'm keeping this journal. Having you in mind when I sit down to write makes it easier. That was Father's idea. He knows I have always wanted to become a writer and so he bought this journal and told me to 'Practice, practice, practice' like his favourite writer, Cervantes. I shall try to write longer entries in the future, but that all depends on how much work I have to do.

Monday, 30 August 1858

Dear Facundo, last night we all went over to the 'Palace' to celebrate my birthday. Before you become too excited about our social connections, I should tell you that I am not talking about the queen's palace. I am talking about my eldest sister, Teresa's place. We, I mean myself, Carolina, Soledad, and Remedios have a nickname for our older brothers and sisters. We call them the *Seven Elder Berries*, because they are old, stiff, fruits. It is just as well no one will read any of this! That makes us the *Four Young Fruits!* We quite like that idea. Anyway, Teresa is the Queen of the Elder Berries and Daniel is the King. I suppose Gabriel and Cayetano must be princes.

Teresa has been living in her palace in Plaza de las Carmelitas since she got married, four years ago. The previous tenants died during the last cholera epidemic and so the rent is cheaper than anyone thinks. You should see how non-proletarian Teresa has become!

Father says it is a good thing that Teresa got married and moved out. Having her and our mother in the house at the same time was a stress. Teresa also loves music, and dancing. And when she is not working she always has people over at her place. She moans a lot too! She cooks well and like Mother rarely refuses a drink when offered. By the end of my party, Teresa and Mother were singing those anti-monarchy songs that cause Father to be anxious.

'We'll get a visit,' Father said, 'you never know who's listening.'

'This is Vélez,' Mother said. 'It doesn't matter who's listening.'

Luckily Antonia was able to get Teresa and Mother to sing other songs too. Asides from Antonia and Teresa, we also had Laurencia and Gabriel present from the Seven Elder Berries. Ana-María could not come up from Málaga because she and her husband Big Bernardo were too tired.

No one is certain where Daniel is but according to Father his unit took a train up to Córdoba for military manoeuvres. And Cayetano was in his seminary in Málaga. He is not allowed leave for something as banal as a brother's birthday party. Anyway, I am not sure I would have wanted him to come, wearing his trainee-priest clothes and being miserable just because Daniel was not present. They are outrageously good fun when together but on their own they seem lost. So, without Daniel and Cayetano, I would say it was a little quieter this year at my celebration than last year at Soledad's.

Ana María and Big Bernardo are always 'too tired'. They spend their lives chopping up animals and selling them in their shop. Mind you, they sent masses of meat up to Teresa's place for the party, same as they did last year. And like last year, we ended up taking some of the leftovers around to Teresa's neighbours again before going back home.

Father got tipsy and went off to find someone to tell his Cervantian Four Genealogies tale to — this time to the old mute Martínez of the Taberna Majanillo in Vélez. That was funny! Nearly as funny as last year when Daniel and Cayetano invented a new family genealogy type and tried convincing father.

'There's a fifth type of genealogy,' Daniel said.

'Is there, now? What would that be?'

'It'd be us, the Galeotes!' Daniel said. 'We're the type that start out with nothing and end up with less than nothing.'

Father pretended to kick Daniel on the backside, telling him: 'We might never recover our little patch of wealth but we'll always have our dignity.'

On our way to Teresa's, my father had us walk by the *barrio* Arrabal de San Sebastián, where Grandfather Javier was born. He was getting ready to start on his Cervantes Four Genealogies spiel with us but Soledad saved us. She sped off, muttering, 'Not that again!' And the rest of us Young Fruits ran after her, pretending to try and catch her.

Thursday, 2 September 1858

Dear Facundo, I hope you don't mind if in future I stop pretending I'm writing to you and I just write to no one in particular. Tonight, Father said he wanted to 'talk later.' I wracked my brain wondering what he had found out. Then I thought maybe he had changed his mind and was going to send me back to school. I got a headache for nothing. All he wanted to talk about was the Four Genealogies!

We went for a walk, and so I was stuck with just him. In the end it turned out quite pleasant, only us two, walking and talking like that. He asked if I understood why he was always harping on about the four genealogies story. We were getting along so well I told him the truth. I said no.

'I've been thinking about these four genealogies. I may have made a mistake,' Father said.

I never heard him say he made a mistake, before. Especially when it comes to Cervantes.

'I've not actually got to that part of *Don Quixote*,' I answered.

He said all this time he has been talking too much about one genealogy; the type that start with nothing and end up with wealth. When really the way to embellish the Galeote family name is through virtue not money, and certainly not some mad pursuit to buy back grandfather's old house in Vélez.

'What do you mean?' I asked.

'You'll understand when you get to that part of *Don Quixote*,' Father said. 'You'll learn that virtue through "Arms" or "Letters" is much more attainable for people like us than trying to accrue wealth.'

Obviously, I have had to skip forward in the book: *Arms* means becoming a hero and bringing honour on the family through valour, like Daniel is doing. *Letters* means bringing honour on the family by being erudite. I suppose for us that means the priesthood — where else could a half-deaf boy like Cayetano hope to learn about philosophy, Latin, scripture, and theology?

School starts next week, and I'll not be joining. I imagine it'll be 'Arms' for me.

GOD'S POLICEMAN
14 CALLE PIZARRO, MADRID
19 APRIL 1886

JOSÉ FERRERAS RECLINES on his seat. He removes two Habanas from his cigar box, pushes an ashtray to the middle of his desk. 'There are people who should never learn of that address,' he says.

'Who do you have in mind?' Benito asks.

'People who burn houses.'

'I think you're letting your imagination run too far. And talking of burning, isn't it early to be smoking?'

'Now you've left your lair,' José says, 'we have something to celebrate.'

José knows too many of Benito's pleasures. He knows it is not just opera but Rossini, not just cigars but Habanas and not just women but, well, he knows too much. Benito watches his friend cut both cigars and push one across the desk in his direction. He picks up the cigar, appreciates its colour, weight and odour.

José strikes a match, lights Benito's and then his own cigar. He puffs slowly, inhales deeply. The tip crackles like a miniature furnace. He sighs and blows the smoke in Benito's direction. 'Since you're so interested in this priest's story, I've got some material to get you started,'

'Such as?'

'The rantings of a madman; an honest pleading for justice; a warning?' José says. 'I can't quite decide which it is. I'll leave it for you to work out and tell me.'

'Are the newspapers going to lead with the usual "madman" headline?'

'That seems to be the consensus.'

'And claiming he's a degenerate too, no doubt?'

'That chestnut,' José says, and takes his turn to flick ash.

'What about the defence?' Benito asks, certain that José will already be just as informed.

'Tricky! Because the priest himself claims to be as sane as any man,' José says.

'Doesn't surprise me. I have the feeling there'll be more to this situation than we're seeing.'

'*He* might be adamant he's sane,' José says, 'but as far as others are concerned that's a sure sign he's not.'

'Who's talking about madness then?' Benito asks. 'His defence lawyer, the Church, or the alienists?'

'The alienists for certain,' José says.

'Obviously, since they need a sacrifice for their altar of social experimentation,' Benito says.

'If he is actually mad, does it matter where they say his madness originates?'

'You know it does.' Benito splutters on his cigar. 'Being mad is one thing. Being labelled mad on account of your bloodline is another.' Benito knows José is as sceptical as he is himself by the lack of scientific proof behind popular degeneracy theories. 'I'd like to meet this priest.'

'I can see that you might because you need a new Guzmán for mental evisceration. But does this priest need you and your thesis novel?' José's voice carries something in its texture. Perhaps it is not sarcasm, but there is admonishment, or might it simply be concern?

'I've told you before,' Benito says, 'this novel I'm working on won't feel like a thesis novel. It'll read like a straightforward realist novel. Written to entertain, not to inform.'

'What about your character, Rubín? Won't it be obvious to everyone he's intended as the antithesis of Guzmán?'

'Remember, the novel is called *Fortunata and Jacinta*, not *The Coda: Maximiliano Rubín defies the determinists!*' Benito flattens down an upturned lapel of his own jacket.

José pushes back in his seat, blows circles of smoke. 'How about the bishop? Aren't you interested in him?'

'Of course I am.'

'Good, because you seem to have forgotten I met him.' José stubs out his cigar.

'Slipped my mind,' Benito says.

'That's because he was the type of socially engaged politico-cleric you hate so much,' José says.

'I wish you'd stop saying I hate clerics. I just can't stand anyone preying on the superstitions of feeble minds.'

'Someone has to guide the flock,' José says and grins.

'But it's not their role to try to be everywhere, interfering in our lives. They should decide what they want to be — priests, politicians or philosophers.'

'Should they really? What about you, Benitín? When will you decide if you want to be a writer or a politician?'

This reproach from José is hard to take. He was the first to tell Benito he would be mad not to accept Prime Minister Sagasta's cronyism — *cunerismo* they call it here in Madrid. If José had not encouraged Benito to accept the offer of a place in the Congress of Deputies, he may have turned Sagasta down. He ignores José's mischievous provocation: 'It's not the same thing,' he says and slaps the desk.

'All right, relax,' Jose says. 'You're a writer with a conscience.' He leans down and pulls out a grey file from a low drawer. The file has a neatly hand-written title in black ink: *Bishop Narciso Martínez-Vallejo Izquierdo*. A sub-title pencilled below, reads: *God's Policeman.*

'Pithy, don't you think?'

'I suppose it is,' Benito answers.

José flips open the file. 'These are my notes from the interview he gave us when he was assigned here last August.'

'Only eight months since the bishopric was created? Seems longer.'

'I don't suppose there will be so many queuing up to take the job,' José answers.

'They'll find someone,' Benito says. 'Martyrdom is an accepted occupational hazard in that career.'

'Accepted? I doubt that,' José says. From the file he extracts an envelope, from which he teases out an ambrotype, and places it on the desk. 'That's your man right there.'

Benito leans across and stares at the bishop's face. 'Can I borrow this?'

'Certainly! We have another. Take this too,' José says. He grins and slides the envelope across the desk.

Benito slips the ambrotype back into its envelope. 'I don't suppose you have one of the priest?'

José shakes his head. 'No, I don't. But I can tell you plenty about the bishop. It's all here.' He begins to read aloud the contents of the file: 'Narciso Martínez-Vallejo Izquierdo, born in Rueda, Molina de Aragón on 29 October 1831.'

'Fifty-four when he was shot,' Benito says.

Like a grand actor, José clears his throat and reads louder: 'Graduated from the seminary of Sigüenza, before coming here to study for his doctorate in theology.'

'Well, well, he studied in Madrid too. We have something in common then,' Benito says.

'He probably never had to lie to his mother though.'

'He didn't have Mama Dolores for materfamilias,' Benito answers.

José laughs. 'It's good to see that you're back amongst us, Benito. Where was I? Ordained a priest in Sigüenza in 1857.'

'And then what?'

'Six years later became a Canon, then appointed as Secretary to the Archbishop of Granada,' José says.

'What about his family? Wealthy?'

'He liked to say he was from modest stock. Told me his parents were humble labourers.'

'Humble? I doubt that,' Benito says.

'The bishop was a member of the clerical Carlista party,' José says. 'Got himself elected as Deputy for Molina de Aragón in 1871'

'Sound like the son of a labourer to you?' Benito asks.

'I don't know. He was forthright with me. Happily admitted being a Carlista during the sixties.'

'Bishop, politician, and soldier. You wonder when he found the time to say Mass,' Benito says, and shakes his head.

'Come down from your own pulpit, Benito. You know their history of toting rifles was borne of necessity, just like your Jesuit uncle Domingo.'

'My uncle was fighting the French,' Benito says, 'and that's not the same thing at all.'

'Well, anyway, after the revolution of '68, our dear Narciso calmed down, became Bishop of Salamanca. Did wonderfully well. Moved here in August '85 to repeat the feat. And you know the rest.'

'He volunteered all of that?'

'We do our own research too, you remember?'

'Who could forget?'

'You want these?' José slides his notes across the desk.

Benito starts to read them for himself. He sees that Salamanca is where José's sources picked up many of their echoes concerning the bishop, including, perhaps, a child. 'Seems he was loved by many and loathed by a few.'

'If he considered you worthy, he was ready to do anything for you,' José says. 'However, unworthy atheists would not be given a drop of water in the desert.'

'Mama Dolores would have adored him,' Benito says.

'He was a good talker too, as I remember,' José says.

Benito continues reading. José's notes reveal the bishop had sharpened his oratorial skills in the Congress of Deputies. By the time he left, he was considered amongst the most powerful and passionate orators, especially if some Liberal Deputy was proposing a new civic freedom.

'Not a fan of civil marriage then, it says here,' Benito grins widely.

'Well, be fair, which bishop could tolerate a marriage outside the Church?'

'Did you tell him that you had written an opinion piece in favour of civil marriage?'

'We were getting along just fine. It would have been rude to ruin it.'

Benito is near the end of the file when he reads José's note that the bishop was *under no illusions* about what awaited him in the new Bishopric of Madrid-Alcalá. 'What did he mean?' Benito asks. 'You think he knew what he was in for?'

'Well, this is Madrid, everyone knows the risks,' José answers. 'And don't forget, he had someone who knew Madrid.'

'Who?'

'His personal confessor, Padre Gabino Sánchez.'

Benito reads José's post-script: *Organise a meeting on the Bishop's first anniversary.*

'He never made it. Who'd have predicted that?' Benito says.

'I can think of someone,' José answers.

BOOK TWO

Those who have had direct contact with offenders know that they are different from other people, with weak or diseased minds that can rarely be healed. Alienists in many cases find it impossible to neatly distinguish between madness and crime. And yet legislators, believing exceptions to free will to be rare, ignore the advice of alienists and prison officials. They do not understand that most criminals really do lack free will.

Cesare Lombroso (A founding figure of Criminology)
L'Uomo Delinquente (1876)

PART I

THE BETTER SIDE
2 Plaza Colón, Madrid
19 April 1886

BENITO HOLDS THE ambrotype at arm's length. Daylight streams through the long, doubled-paned windows of his
study. He tilts the ambrotype. No matter which declination
he tries, the portrait seems waxy. Bishop Narciso's expression
is phlegmatic. Benito notices how he has turned his face at a
slight angle, the pose suggestive that the bishop was present-
ing his preferred profile, his better side.

Benito is as enthralled as any other Madrilian by this ongoing fascination for taking pictures. There must be sixty
studios in Madrid now. He remembers when there were less
than ten. He does not closely study the arguments concerning
which could be the better development process, but these
precisions about the impact of capturing light, the quality of
the paper or the chemical processes do not elude his comprehension. He finds the European and American competition
for supremacy in this sphere as fascinating as it is in others.
But it is the diversity of subjects' faces and poses he sees in the
portrait galleries that most ignites his own creativity.

He lays the ambrotype face-up on his writing table, adjacent to his manuscript. He picks up his magnifying glass and
moves in closer. His method of interpretation of ambrotypes
has never changed. He knows the sitter's pose is largely a
negotiation between the sitter and studio, who both search for
a *look*; the telling of some personal story. Firstly, he explores

for a hint of movement in the posture. Then for some implied relationship between the arranged objects.

No trope appears in the ambrotype by accident. And every talisman has an association to transmit. Each studio has its favourites: in a situation such as this one, it could be a hand that clutches a cross or bible, or eyes which fix on some partially glimpsed enigmatic divinity.

It is the bishop's dead and shallow eyes which call to Benito. They seem familiar. Eyes in constant judgement. Eyes coated in a layer of something: a mix of knowledge, of supremacy, and of contentment? Benito remembers this same look from a long time ago. These are the eyes of Mama Dolores. Also he has seen lips like these before: lips of cold, dry devotion, perched above a hard and righteous chin.

He lets out a long sigh, puts the magnifying glass to one side, walks around his desk. After a moment he returns and stands over the ambrotype. His detachment has returned. He can look again at the image of the bishop with the necessary dispassion. He notes the oval-shaped *passe-partout* acting as though it were a grand halo. Within it the bishop's head, shoulders and chest are all visible. Arms and hands are obscured by his *mozzetta*. On the centre of his breast the bishop wears a holy cross, as long as a man's hand, held in position with a fine-looking chain.

Benito places the ambrotype face down. An indescribable darkness sweeps over him as he remembers this morning's detour to San Isidro Cathedral.

The still-discoloured steps, vivid brownish patches of blood already mixed with the dirt thrown on top and brushed away. He arrived early but was not the first. There were already others, equally bewildered, talking randomly amongst themselves.

'Did you see it happen?' one man asked another.

'No. I was inside.'

'What about you?' A woman asked Benito.

'I was ill. Couldn't leave the house,' Benito answered.

'I'd have thrown myself in the line of fire to save him,' she said.

'Me too,' others echoed.

Benito fell quiet amongst them. When he left, he saw they all had tears in their eyes.

He picks up the ambrotype once more and stares into the face of the dead bishop. Alone here in his studio he sheds private tears then continues writing in his notebook. This is his impression of the deceased figure staring out from the ambrotype:

> The bishop's mouth is closed, tight shut. The lips are thin and flat, but it is not a metaphorically cruel mouth. The nose sweeps down, nostrils are large and flared, but not exaggerated; the nose is not aquiline, not at all like a vulture. He has a mole, high above his left eye, which seems to emphasise his receded hairline. This makes him look intelligent, not barren. Some hairs protrude slightly under and outwards from his Zucchetto, they are sparse; nevertheless still virile. Taken all together there is something steely in the bishop's countenance. One of God's soldiers trying his best.

Benito feels a presence, puts down his pen and turns around to face the door. Catalina is there. She has probably knocked before entering but Benito has only become aware of her now when she is already standing in the middle of his study.

'You wanted to see me?' Catalina asks.

'Did I?'

'Concha said I had to see you before I go out.'

'You're quite right. Sorry, I was elsewhere. Where is Concha?'

'She has gone out. To the concert, sir. Have you forgotten?'

'Isn't it early for that?'

'She said something about collecting your Losada,' Catalina says and smiles from one edge of her mouth.

Benito groans.

'Shall I prepare the Santander set?' she asks.

This look of hers — starched white, immaculately clean, and trimmed on the pockets and cuffs with blue all topped by a blue bonnet — is exactly the same as her mother.

Catalina is twenty-two years old but for as long as Benito has known her, even when she was a baby, she has always looked older than whatever age she happened to be. Her uniform reinforces this impression of austerity. It is, in his opinion, over-formal and he has told her plenty of times she does not need to wear it here. But she insists upon it.

Every time he looks at her, he feels guilt and astonishment that she is still here and that takes Benito's mind somewhere else.

Until three years ago, Catalina's mother was employed by Mama Dolores. She had been in Benito's family even longer than Benito had. She had been nursemaid to his older brothers and sisters; then cook and housekeeper. But one day she had the temerity to excitedly interrupt Mama Dolores who was getting the family ready for church.

The reason for her excitement? She had gone to the harbour to buy fish and had been amongst the first people in Las Palmas to receive the newspapers from the mainland. On that particular day, they carried a story that talked of a banquet held in Benito's honour in Madrid. She rushed home to tell Mama Dolores the news.

Mama Dolores had visitors and told her, 'Keep quiet, there's nothing to get excited about.' But she continued excitedly talking and telling Mama Dolores she should be 'Proud'.

No one ever tells Mama Dolores she should be anything. So just like that, after forty years' service, Mama Dolores dismissed her.

Discretely, Benito's sisters and brothers — those who had not escaped from Las Palmas — took care of their old nurse maid and her daughter, Catalina, went along too. They paid full fare for them to travel to the mainland. According to Madrina a housekeeper was needed here anyway.

When she first arrived, Catalina had that modest, coquettish but discreet way about her that many island girls have. Taller than Madrina and stronger than Concha, it did not take long for Catalina to make an impression in Plaza Colón — and not just on the household tasks. When her mother returned to Las Palmas, there were certain of Benito's friends who seemed especially delighted that Catalina chose to remain.

According to Concha, Catalina has made friends here: close friends. Whatever the reason, Benito is glad she chose to stay. Especially since it is Catalina who endows a feminine aesthetic to Madrina's apartment here in Madrid and to Benito's place in Santander.

Certain things she surely learnt from her mother: there are always pristine, clean and pressed towels in the bathrooms, the curtains are changed with the seasons and the bed linen is changed every Wednesday. But there are other little touches she has added for herself. Such as the flowers in every room: a vibrant, colourful mixture of Spanish bluebells, red carnations, mixed lilies, and geraniums, according to the month. It seems odd to Benito that the creator of all these many vivid and animated colourful bouquets is herself so understated.

On the occasion she and her mother travelled with Benito to his sanctuary in Santander, it was her mother who had spiced the bargain in the Sunday flea-market. Since it was decorated in Catalina's favourite colours of blue and white, it was Catalina who got to give the name — *the Santander set.*

Of all his friends, the most pleased when Catalina chose to remain in Madrid was José Ferreras. Despite being married for almost a quarter of a century and having children around Catalina's age, José occasionally dared jest with Benito: 'Don't you think this beautiful young lady is just waiting for the right man-of-experience to chance along?'

Naturally, when Catalina's mother was present, José never dared to be even remotely suggestive. The old lady had worked things out. Before she began her journey back home to Las Palmas, the last thing she warned her daughter was: 'Watch out for Ferreras. I've seen the way he looks at you.'

But Catalina had little need of her mother's counsel. It amused Benito to see how easily she was able to deal with José. After a few drinks, José would go through the same histrionics to arrive at the same joke. He would say how beautiful Catalina was and how only a man of 'experience' could appreciate her, and she would giggle and push him away. Then he would make a big sad face and say, 'Catalina has repulsed me, but things would be so much simpler if she repulsed me.' He would laugh, enormous belly laughs, until Catalina herself was laughing too. Then he would ask if everyone got the joke.

Benito places his notebook on top of the ambrotype. Turns to face Catalina.

'I understand Señor Ferreras is coming tonight,' she says.

'Indeed he is. On his own,' Benito answers and watches her face for a reaction. 'There'll be no need for the Santander Set, Catalina. After all, do you know anyone, apart from myself, less likely to appreciate *Regal* crockery than him?'

Catalina smiles and fiddles with her hair, tucking it in to her bonnet.

'All right, sir. I'll prepare the Las Palmas set instead. I suppose I should check the wine and cigars too, sir?'

'Don't worry, Catalina. I'll take care of that. Just some food in warm plates in the kitchen will be all we need. Thank you.'

'Everything's already there.'

'Then enjoy your night off.'

'Are you sure, sir?'

'Of course, and if you do return before Señor Ferreras has left, best ignore us.'

He notices that again Catalina smiles at the mention of Ferreras' name. Even the mention of it provokes a response from her these days. No doubt Concha has got it right too about Catalina and José's boy.

MODEL PRISON
La Cárcel Modelo, Plaza de la Moncloa, Madrid
21 April 1886

LUIS SIMARRO SITS facing Governor Del Pino. They are in Del Pino's office on the top floor of the administrative block of Madrid's model prison. Del Pino's large desk is a border crossing between the two men.

Salutations have been exchanged, but at this moment neither man speaks as Del Pino reads the instruction from the State Prosecutor's Office which Simarro has handed him.

Luis Simarro looks across the frontier separating his country: the scientific study of the brain, of observable behaviours and predictive events; from Del Pino's country: the pastoral caring for criminals, killing with kindness and praying for miracles. He takes the moment to observe the short, stocky governor. A specimen in his late fifties, Del Pino seems unremarkable; speckled grey hair, dark eyes, a pair of gold-coloured, round-rimmed spectacles. His complexion is bronzer than the typical Madrileño, and as he frowns, his countenance turns two shades darker, but his eyes glint mischievously behind his glasses. He has the appearance of a southern headmaster more than the uncompromising governor the Madrid judiciary are so enthralled with.

Finally, with a certain formality and an accent that removes any lingering doubt of his sunshine roots, Governor Del Pino leans forward on his chair. 'I know all about you, Doctor Simarro. And your interest in establishing a system of model asylums. But no matter what authority you think you have been given, in here there's only one person who decides.' The governor stabs a stubby finger into his own chest.

Luis says nothing but thinks: *And I know all about you too, Governor Del Pino.*

Luis has been briefed on Del Pino's reputation for innovation blended with a benevolent attitude towards his criminals. It is far too early for anyone to say if Del Pino's methods are working here, but every other gaol he has led has seen levels of re-offending fall to amongst the lowest in the country.

'You understand, if I feel your presence here is contrary to the wellbeing of any inmates in my care, I must ask you to leave,' Del Pino says.

'There's no need to worry, Señor Del Pino,' Luis replies 'we're fighting the same battle.'

In their briefing the Madrid Judiciary said Del Pino had the collie dog's dedication to his inmates, but the bullmastiff's readiness to rip off your arm if you raise it at the wrong angle.

'Are we?' the governor replies. Then he holds up the letter and for a moment re-examines it. He stares at the signature of the Provincial Prosecutor as though wondering if it can possibly be genuine.

In his other hand the governor holds a second letter; an indemnity letter, signed: *Doctor Luis Simarro, Alienist.* Del Pino's eyes flit from one document to the other and he re-reads quietly whilst simultaneously nodding. Finally, he places the documents flat on his desk and fixes Luis with a disconcerting stare as though he is assessing the renowned alienist.

His curiosity apparently satiated, Del Pino removes his spectacles, places them in the breast pocket of his black linen jacket and leans back in his seat. 'You can go meet your subject now, Doctor Simarro.'

'Thank you.'

'I'm looking forward to being enlightened by your assessment. Although I fear I already know what you will conclude.'

There is a finality in the way Del Pino says this and also in the speed with which he pushes himself upwards, out of the reach of his grasping dark chair. As he stands, he grimaces, and his chair creaks under his stocky form.

Simarro reaches across the desk, accepts Del Pino's handshake. 'Thank you, Governor.'

'Goodbye, Doctor Simarro.'

On this signal, two waiting gaolers open Del Pino's office door. Luis picks up his satchel and jacket. The trio make their way down a corridor. They proceed down a steep, stone, internal stairway. Luis feels himself already smiling. Since he came home, things have got better each day. The model prison towers beyond the shadow of hubris. It is what he wanted it to be. And he has no regrets about coming home.

He looks closer at his two companions. They are identically dressed in dark blue serge suits, with polished brass buttons, gold-coloured braiding on their sleeves. Each with a cap on his head. Neither utters a word to Luis. They continue their descent — ground level, past a set of secure double doors. The administrative block is behind them. They re-enter the centre of the pentagon, where the older of the gaolers — who appears to be around forty years old — takes the lead.

'You can leave your jacket, here,' he says, 'and your satchel too.'

'I'll need my notebook and pencils.'

'Those you can bring.'

They pick up their pace, proceed towards secured wings radiating from the centre, and accessible only through guarded entrances. They no longer walk upon marble floors, as in the corridors of Del Pino's block. Instead they are walking on grey, featureless granite. This is a place where the aesthetic gives way to the functional. Luis appreciates functional. He smiles at both gaolers.

'A good ten minutes to get to where we're going, several more secure areas to pass through.'

'I know,' Luis says.

'I don't recall you being here before,' the gaoler says.

'I haven't. I met the architects. I know what you have here: modern but secure, like a star-shaped bank. Five wings, five floors, three sets of secured doors along every confinement wing,' Luis reels off.

'You'll not be planning an escape today then.' The gaoler laughs at his own humour.

Luis feels a human connection is being made. He is glad to hear the man being so convivial. They pass through the first set of secure doors on the ground level. The walls along this corridor are also pierced by dusty, barred windows which appear grandiosely tall. But, again, to Luis, it all seems highly functional.

Murky daylight punches into and along the corridors, pushes under doors. Despite the strange surfeit of dirty light, there is a deficit of clean air. Luis gulps behind his hand and reminds himself that on the other side of these thick granite walls, just beyond the heavy rumbling iron gates marking the entrance to the prison, there is the oxygen-filled, wide-open Plaza de la Moncloa.

'Is it my imagination?' Luis says and breathes in deeply.

'It's the sealed doors. Tell that to your architect friends,' the fellow says and laughs again. 'We'd open the windows if we could be sure the inmates wouldn't try to leap out of them.'

The mention of 'inmate' has Luis wondering about Padre Cayetano. What condition will he find him in? He is still considering this when a loud grating sound obliterates his thoughts and a second set of doors is opened. The trio step briskly through and the doors are locked rapidly behind them.

'Not long, Señor Simarro.'

A mild odour of urine vapours pass underneath black painted cell doors, and muffled menacing sounds penetrate the air. In this corridor the walls are a sedating, heavy, blue-black colour.

They approach the final set of doors. Waiting guards anticipate their arrival and hold them open. The younger, mute, gaoler remains here with the guards as his superior and Luis pass through.

'Next up: solitary confinement.'

'Looking forward to it,' Luis jokes.

'He's the only prisoner we've got in solitary at the moment.'

They enter. There are five cells. Numbered seven through to eleven. The space is morbidly quiet. Luis feels a chill coalesce that is unlike anything he felt in those other parts of the prison he walked through. It penetrates his clothes. Icy fingers trace a line down the back of his neck and shoulder-blades. He shivers. Notices the old gaoler in his thick uniform is not shivering.

'Colder here than I expected,' Luis says.

The gaoler enters an empty cell, returns with a grey woollen blanket. Hands it to Luis.

'Take this.'

'Who's out there?' a voice from cell eleven calls.

The gaoler slides open an eye-level viewing slot in the door and peers in.

'You can put your book down, you have some company, Padre.'

Metal clanks as the occupant moves within the cell. Taking

a ring of keys from his jacket pocket, the gaoler turns one lock, then another. He smiles reassuringly at Luis and pulls the cell door wide open.

'This is Doctor Simarro. He's come to visit you.'

'I didn't ask for a doctor,' Cayetano says from the rear of the cell.

'Not that kind of doctor,' the gaoler says.

Luis' eyes sweep the interior of the cold, cubed space. Cayetano is standing at the back of the cell under a small, barred window. Rays of daylight streak in, radiate down the wall and across the floor, illuminating Cayetano's shackles.

A folded bed is attached to a wall on Luis' right. It has incongruous black bed-knobs, perfectly rounded, the size of a small orange. And to his left, a small round table supports a wooden jug and two wooden drinking bowls. In front of the table sits a solitary wooden chair.

For a moment Luis and Cayetano stare at each other. Cayetano has the same hazel skin of Governor Del Pino. Unlike the governor, he has a beard. His hair is black and is longer than Luis would expect for a priest. But it is Cayetano's eyes, blacker than his soutane and ceaseless in their movement, that most draw Luis' attention. It is as though they are searching for something.

Cayetano fixes Luis with a stare. Then addresses the gaoler. 'I never asked for any kind of doctor.'

'Consider it a gift from the State,' the gaoler says.

The gaoler and priest seem to be on good terms. The gaoler is chuckling as he closes the door.

'Don't worry doctor, the cell door is unlocked, and I'll be sitting outside for as long as you're sitting inside,' he says.

'You won't need that,' Cayetano says, and points to the blanket. 'It warms up here very quickly.'

Cayetano moves away from the window towards the bottom of the bed. His shackles grate against the granite wall separating cell eleven from ten. He lifts a lever and the bed lowers on hinges. 'You only have to imagine this is your *chaise longue*, not a prison bed,' Cayetano says and smirks. 'And this,' he waves a hand around in a circling motion, 'your office, not my cell.'

Luis hangs his blanket over the seat and wonders how to begin this conversation.

COVERING THE ANGLES

Saturday, 15 October 1859

Daniel came home last night on one week home leave. He has a full beard now. He does not talk much, but he did say they have to report back to their barracks in Granada by next Friday. This morning, I was under the window and heard mother hissing at father.

'Have you ever seen him before with a face like that?'

'Yes.'

'Not me! He's never been that quiet. He can't hide it from me. He can't keep anything from his mother.'

But Daniel hides whatever he wants to. Mother always sides with him in the end. Like when he left the seminary and walked all the way to Granada. He came back three days later with a signed army attestation form in his pocket. But she blamed our father.

'It's your fault for going on and on about the Four Genealogies and bloody family honour,' she said.

'Look on the bright side, Mother,' Daniel replied, 'at least, our unit's not a Bourbon one.'

This situation with Morocco has her very worried. Father is himself: serene and trying to get her to be the same: 'Calm yourself, María. It'll probably come to nothing.'

Father told her that Sultan Mulay Mohamed may be young and cussed, but he is not stupid. Morocco will just pay the compensation O'Donnell is asking for and things will calm down again. Daniel will likely see no action there. He said all of that but he knows it is not true, because Daniel whispered to him last night that General Zavala has given all the officers a week's home leave because they will be in Morocco within the month.

Cayetano gave a small black crucifix to Daniel, saying, '*Ubi bene ibi patria*'. Then they began chattering in their secret code. The cross is supposed to protect him.

Saturday, 22 October 1859

O'Donnell declared war on Morocco today. Daniel's unit is probably already on its way. Nobody in our house wants to tell our mother, so my father sent me over to Loja to fetch my uncle Tonto. We call him 'Tonto' because he acts crazy. Father says my uncle is no worse than mother when she has a reason to be uptight. But at least Tonto knows how to calm her down. He is her favourite brother.

Uncle Tonto talks slowly and dresses with clothes that are too short or too baggy. He has been doing this for a few years now and many people cannot remember when he used to be sensible. He makes Mother laugh a lot and she says she can remember when he was not crazy, as does Father. Some of the younger folk around here say they are not fooled by Tonto — they say he is pretending. Personally, I cannot tell either way.

Friday, 16 March 1860

It has been six months, but Tonto says the war with Morocco is coming to an end. We listen to him because he usually knows what is going to happen before it happens. I think that is another reason why some people are leery of him.

Sometimes he will say that so-and-so is in for a bad end if they carry on treating us common folk as worse than animals, and then paff… no more so-and-so! If Tonto says the war will soon be over, we believe it. Maybe Daniel will be disappointed though, because in his latest letter he was on about his promotion for valour and meeting Prim. It seems he likes war, more and more.

Tonto says this is all great because our boys are getting good experience for the day of reckoning. Tonto is always on about that: 'Mark my words, you young 'uns, before I'm dust, we'll see t'end o' these bloody Bourbons.' Then he will turn to Father and say, 'Anyone here with dewy-eyed Carlistas for friends needn't think we'll be dumping one corrupt Bourbon dynasty in favour of the other!'

Last month Cayetano was here for the weekend. Remedios took the lot of us on a walk to Nerja. All the way there and back, Father kept up his fretting with Cayetano.

'Keep your wits about you, and your ears open.'

'Why?' Cayetano asked.

'Because they try to turn young priests into soldiers for the Carlista army.'

Gabriel thought it was funny, asking Cayetano to keep his ears open. Father told him to stop laughing and carried on haranguing Cayetano.

'You're there for honour through letters. Let the others occupy themselves with arms.'

'You do remember my seminary is in Málaga not Sigüenza?' Cayetano said.

'They'll try anywhere,' Father said.

In Nerja we all went fishing and then lazed on the beach for hours whilst Remedios was in the caves copying wall paintings. She came out and straight away sold everything she had copied, to a group of English tourists.

On the way back home, I had a chance to take Cayetano aside

and tell him what Father has been suggesting concerning me joining the Civil Guard.

'Father's turned into all angles covered pragmatist,' Cayetano said. 'He's married into a crazy, republican family. He has one son already a sergeant in a liberalist army division. Another son is training to become a priest, so why not suggest the Bourbon Civil Guard for you? That way every option is covered.'

Uncle Tonto says it's a brilliant stratagem. 'You've become more cunning than Basilius,' he said to my father.

Later I asked my father who Basilius was.

'Time for you to re-read Don Quixote,' he said.

Thursday, 5 July 1861

Yesterday, I was taking the feed up to the goat shed and had the fright of my life. I heard a noise under my feet and when I pulled open the doors, I saw Tonto in the cellar. He was hiding in there with his veterinary friend, Don Rafael Pérez del Álamo. They were wearing masks. For a moment I did not know who it was until my uncle Tonto spoke. He said the army has arrived in Loja. They killed a lot of the protestors who had installed themselves in the town hall and tore down their flag.

Pérez del Álamo said there must be a hundred dead and maybe four or five hundred being held prisoner. Apparently, it was General Narváez, personally, who chose the units sent down to Loja. The protestors were not sure if the army would go easy on them on account of Loja being Narváez' hometown. But their actions last week embarrassed him.

What happened last week was that a little band of protestors took over the Civil Guard barracks in Iznájar and started waving republican flags. That led to singing "down with the Queen" and "bring on the revolution." Narváez told his

Queen, they're only a bunch of rabble rousers. It'll all be over tomorrow when they sober up. But after a couple more days the protestors went on to Loja. That's when Queen Isabel must have got worried.

They're saying Narváez told the army to 'show no mercy because none would be shown to them.'

Uncle Tonto and Pérez del Álamo said they were going to stay hidden up there for a few days. They said I must not tell a soul. But I told Father, and he sent me back up with blankets, some *torta turron*, a bottle of *vino santo* and cigarettes. But when I arrived, there was no sign of Tonto or Pérez del Álamo. No one knows where they are, or if they are alive or dead.

SOOTHING THE ARTISTIC CONSCIENCE
2 Plaza Colón, Madrid
19 April 1886

A LARGE ENVELOPE under his arm, José steps inside the apartment and nimbly evades Benito's grasp. 'Don't be so impatient, Benito. Pleasure first,' he says.

'I've been waiting for this envelope the entire day.'

'There's time. Where's your suffragette sorority tonight?'

'It's not a sorority,' Benito says and makes another bid to get the envelope from José.

'Well, whatever you call it. Where are they?'

'It's just the two of us. Concha and Madrina have gone to a concert. Some tenor named Tamagno. He has the voice of a barking dog, but they say he's handsome.'

'Do they? And what about Catalina?' José asks.

'She's out, too,' Benito says. 'I gave her the night off, but she left an excellent meal for us.'

José acts crestfallen. 'Well, at least I'll have something to look forward to later.'

'She'll be back late.'

'A good argument is worth the wait,' José jokes.

The friends sit and eat. Over dinner, José seems as interested in the priest as Benito is: 'I've had a report back from Vélez,' José says. 'The priest has two brothers, one of whom suffers from epilepsy, and five sisters.'

'Epilepsy? Are you sure?' Benito asks because he knows what the alienists will make of it.

'I knew you wouldn't like that.'

'It's simply one more condition on their list. They have no real body of proof for their purported link between epilepsy and degeneracy,' Benito says.

'There was another brother. He died in 1868 and two other sisters who both died young.'

'Unlucky family! What happened?'

'The brother was in the army. The sisters died giving birth.'

'Giving birth? Not good! You know what the determinists will try to make of that,' Benito says.

'An epileptic brother, and couple of sisters that die young. A clear-cut case of degeneracy,' José says and grins widely.

'Don't you start too! What about the priest, himself? Any more about him?'

'People say he's solitary, old-fashioned and belligerent.'

'In what way, belligerent?' Benito asks.

'When he's riled. And he enjoys hopeless causes. A bit like you: belligerent and crusading.'

Benito does not rise to José's baiting. Instead he changes tack. He asks José about his own family. They are all doing fine, except for his eldest son, Juan, who still wants to be an engineer, a scientist, or an inventor. José wants his son to be a professional musician, which is what José would have become himself had he not needed to earn a living running a newspaper.

'It's good that he still wants to become an engineer,' Benito says. 'How many wealthy musicians have you ever met?'

'I don't expect you to appreciate my problem,' José answers.

'Blame yourself then, for not properly cultivating his artistic side.'

'I blame his mother,' José says. 'She's encouraging him to

march up and down Madrid demanding the vote for women.'

'That's a problem?'

'There are plenty of good men who don't have the right to vote yet, either,' José says.

'True, but it need not be one or the other. It can both.'

José removes a placard from his pocket and unfolds it. The card is thin and, fully unfolded, measures around twenty-four inches by ten-inches. Written on it is *What Are Men Afraid Of?* 'I found this in his jacket pocket.'

Benito recognises the slogan: coined by Emilia. Also the hand-writing is unmistakably Catalina's. He puts his fist to his mouth to suppress a laugh.

'You know I'm in favour too,' José says. 'Just as much as you and that sorority you have on the go.'

'Why do you insist on calling them that?'

'They're not shrinking violets are they?'

'But you said you agree with them.'

'I do. But Juan will be marked down as a trouble-maker. He needs to be cautious these days in Madrid.'

Benito is not keen on the conversation turning to the type of women he has "on the go" as José puts it. It will surely lead to some discussion of where things are with Emilia. 'Anything else about the belligerent priest?'

'You may be interested to know the state's expert witness has been appointed and has already been in to assess the priest's mental capacities, and antecedents.'

'It's Simarro, isn't it?'

'The person you'd least want?' José arches his back into his welcoming editor's seat.

'I'll have to meet with him,' Benito says.

'Will his fiancée be there?' José asks, grinning. 'That could be a frisky meeting.'

Benito knows he did nothing to encourage Simarro's

fiancée. However, he also knows he could have done more to be discouraging. Anyway, all of that misunderstanding is in the past. And who knows if they are still together? 'Not necessarily tense; we became a little better acquainted after that misunderstanding.'

'You mean when you went to see him at Leganés?' José says.

'For instance. Yes, he helped me out then.'

'So, you're friends?'

Benito considers his relationship with Luis as having four distinct phases: Firstly with himself as an *admiring spectator*, secondly himself as an *unwitting innocent cuckoo*, and thirdly — after Giner de los Rios reconciled them in the easy ambiance of the Masonic Lodge, where he learnt of Luis early disappointments (father died of tuberculosis in Rome when Luis was only two years old, mother who tried to kill herself and Luis in Rome but failed only to succeed in Valencia two years later) — as an *embryonic friend*. But now, after they have taken diametrically opposing views on the question of free will, he supposes they are in the fourth stage: *polite enmity*.

'Friends? I couldn't go that far.' Benito shakes his head.

'Pity,' José says, 'because if you want to align yourself with the priest who swears he's *not* mad, then you're going to be in a battle with Simarro.'

USED TO BE FOUR
61 Calle Mayor, Madrid
19 April 1886

SHE BRUSHES PAST but is so close to him he smells her lavender perfume. With boldness, she reopens the balconette door and picks up the stone freshly thrown there. She leans over, and for a moment he believes she is about to hurl it back where it came from.

'They already have enough,' he says. 'I doubt they need it returned.'

He holds up the three journals in his hand. She slips the stone into a pocket in her dress and draws her head back slightly.

'Maybe I'll just take them home to Vélez,' he says.

She tilts her head, screws up her eyes and they both listen to the street below.

'Degenerate, degenerate, degenerate,' she hears them chant and stamp their feet.

'They probably spotted you there,' he says. 'Better to come back in.'

He lowers himself on to the mattress. He sits upright, his spine erect, his back against the wall. He opens the first journal. But she does not join him.

'It sounds like there are more of them now,' she tells him.

'They don't even know the meaning of what they're saying. I should go out there and shoot them. Maybe that's what they are waiting for. Another degenerate Galeote to come out toting a gun.' His voice is relaxed, though his body is tense.

Tránsito finally comes to join him on the mattress. She places her own back against the wall. Her shoulder touches his. Alonso sees that she holds a small black wooden crucifix in her hand. And for the first time since the police left, her breathing has stopped racing.

'This belonged to Daniel too?' Tránsito asks as she turns the small crucifix over in her hand.

'Yes, Cayetano got that,' he says. 'He'd given it to Daniel in the first place.'

'What did he leave for you?'

'His medals. His horse. His gun. His albatross,' Alonso laughs.

'His albatross?'

'I'm joking. Let's talk about something else.'

'Why did you bring all of that up here?' she asks.

'I thought it would cheer up Cayetano.'

'Really?' She is still repeatedly flipping the cross, letting its wispy, silver chain lie against the dark skin of her wrist.

Alonso places an open palm on her wrist. She puts her free hand on top.

Alonso leans in, asks: 'Do you remember when we first met?'

'Of course. It was Málaga. No, wait! Was it Marbella? I remember when we last met, before Madrid. That was in the convent. I think. Actually, I'm sorry, I can't remember exactly.'

He leans out, removes his hand from her wrist.

'It was the year of Cayetano's ordination.'

'Málaga then!' Tránsito says.

'You really don't remember?' he asks.

'I thought it was later, in Marbella. I was only twelve at

Cayetano's ordination.'

'Can you remember any of it?'

'I seem to remember all the young priests lined up for their ordination, including Cayetano,' she says. 'Then someone pushing me forward, someone saying I should assist in the putting on of the vestments.'

'So, you remember helping Cayetano to put on his stole and chasuble?'

'Yes, of course, then we all went over to the seminary: San Sebastián y Santo Tomás de Aquino,' she says.

'And Cayetano introduced us to Bishop Cascalluna and to Canon Ruiz y Blasco,' Alonso smiles.

'Well, I don't actually remember them. There were so many of you all,' she says.

'Now do you recall? I was in my well-pressed cadet uniform,' he says.

'We were all dressed fancy, like we were going to a wedding,' she says.

'I was standing just behind you when we were singing the Litany of the Saints,' he says. 'I wasn't standing there by accident.'

Tránsito's expression ripples, her eyes examine the ceiling.

'You were behind me? I just remember there were so many cousins, and first cousins once-removed, and second cousins, and aunts, and uncles, and great-aunts, and great-uncles.'

Tránsito may not recall him, but he remembers her. *As pretty today as she was then*, he thinks: *all legs, and bones, curves, and awkwardness. That same face, too.* She has always been a beauty, this cousin of theirs.

But growing up in Vélez, it had seemed to Alonso that someone like her, from Marbella, would think their ways too provincial. And then there was her infatuation with becoming a nun. Someone like that was unattainable and dangerous, at

160

least for someone like him. Although once or twice there were moments of adolescent bravado when he considered he might take the journey and travel the one hundred kilometres from Vélez to Marbella. But endeavours like that were for adventurers, not dreamers.

It's all in the past, he thinks, and sighs for the lost opportunity.

At least she seems to have remembered when he went to Málaga to see her in the convent. But it was already too late then, for both of them.

Alonso rubs his hands together, licks a thumb and flicks open the first of his three journals to page one. It is dated 26 August 1858.

'Look at that hand-writing. I've always thought I should be in the Royal Academy wearing a sash, not in the Civil Guard wearing a tricorn hat.'

Tránsito puts a hand to her mouth and laughs.

He takes her free hand in both of his.

'Tell the truth, Tránsito. You did notice me all those years ago.'

'Maybe if you were the one being ordained, I would have noticed,' she answers, but leaves her hand in his a little longer than he expects.

'This was all my father's idea,' he says, pointing to the journals.

There is still a faint chanting in the street outside, but this distraction is working. She seems to be relaxing. Her shoulders are less rigid, her face less tense.

'Ten years is a long time. I'm impressed by how long you kept it going,' she says. 'Shows a lot of discipline.'

'It's easy if you approach it the way he suggested. All you have to do is imagine you're writing to a cousin in Puerto Rico. At least that's how he got me started.'

'Ah yes, more cousins! Puerto Rico branch!' She laughs. 'Who had he in mind?'

'Cousin Facundo,' he says, and shows her the first line of the first entry: *Dear Facundo, it was my thirteenth birthday three days ago.*

She laughs again, more easily this time.

'Of course, I couldn't expect Facundo to have known that. After all, I didn't know when his birthday was,' Alonso jokes.

He begins to flick through pages. In the warmth of the room, they loosen their clothes a little.

'I wonder if Facundo kept a journal too?' she asks.

'Who knows? But given the Galeote's obsession with Cervantes, I wouldn't be surprised if he did.'

'Is it true they call your father, Vélez' Cervantian Oracle?'

She shifts her position on the mattress. Alonso can feel the warmth of her breath on his neck as she turns towards him.

'Yes, it is. I'd never have kept the journal going so long except I knew it would disappoint him if I gave it up sooner.'

'Do you think it's a sign?'

'What?'

'The pistol misfiring like that,' she says.

'Cayetano's always been the lucky one,' he replies, 'but maybe the Euskaro not going off is his first stroke of bad luck.'

'I don't understand,' Tránsito answers, adjusting her position so their shoulders no longer touch.

'What I'm going to say will seem cruel to you, but it's better to die with a bullet to the head than a slow bolt through the neck.'

He brought it up because he could no longer hold it down. And for the first time since he arrived, Alonso's tears for his brother begin. This thought of Cayetano facing the garrotte now comes between them. Real tears roll down his face. He cannot stop them. Nor can he prevent his sobbing, and gasps of despair for this cursed, absent brother of his. He would prefer if she were not watching this.

Although he tries, he cannot get the picture out of his mind: there used to be four Galeote sons, then there were three, and soon there will be only two of them.

Tránsito puts her arms around Alonso and rocks back and forth with him.

'It's not fair,' he says.

'He was so stubborn,' she replies, and continues rocking him.

Alonso wipes his tears away.

'You cannot imagine. I see him on the garrotte. This slow, crushing, painful death that's going to be his. To think they're calling him a degenerate.'

'Shhhh.' Tránsito puts a finger to Alonso's lips. 'There's someone banging on the door.'

MISGUIDED MÁLAGUEÑOS

Sunday, 30 October 1862

Guess who came to visit? Here is a clue: her brazenness caused the townsfolk to almost forget their preparations for All Saints Day. Another clue: consider the person most unholy and most immoral you have heard of. A woman who would be well-advised to remain as far from Andalucía as she could. A woman who especially should never think of setting foot in Málaga.

You surely have her in mind now. The woman whom even the English, in their fake polite manner say has no redeeming features: Queen Isabel came to visit. Everyone showed up to see her. Even Tonto made a sortie from his new job as principal undertaker at St George's.

'She is rather repulsive in the flesh,' Mother said of her.

The queen came to Málaga to try and make peace. The Town Council were courteous. They kept her busy, and they managed to extract some money. What else could they do? She inaugurated the new railway. And now we are connected to Córdoba.

'The Army can travel from Madrid to Córdoba. And from Córdoba to Málaga in less than two hours, now,' the queen's spokesman said.

'She may come to regret that, because trains run in both directions,' Tonto whispered.

It has been one year since his disappearance. At first, we did not recognise Tonto. Remedios insisted on making a drawing of him. He is thinner and his hair and beard are a little longer, and you can more easily see the grey in them. He showed up with his grave-digger friend, Pérez del Álamo and some other republican disguised as a priest. Mother says neither Tonto nor Pérez del Álamo have seen a razor since they became phantoms. And, she does not trust the one disguised as a priest.

'What's his name?' she asked.

'Whose name?' Tonto replied.

'That one,' Mother said, pointing. 'He looks more convincing as a money-lender than a priest.'

'José Bailon.'

'He's as mean-looking a character as I've seen,' Mother said.

Whoever would have imagined Tonto working and hiding in an English cemetery? He said there were 'revolutionary guerrillas' hiding out in Málaga. Those we saw looked more like beaten, half-starved dogs. One wonders can they really be the feared militia that the royalist newspapers talked about so often this past year?

Tonto was wearing a pair of wire-rimmed spectacles he acquired from a St George's widow last year. Mother is convinced his eyesight will become faulty through wearing them. Tonto and Pérez del Álamo were in good spirits, the two of them joking about their camouflage and Tonto's grave-digging job.

'No one would ever think to look under their noses,' Pérez del Álamo told us all.

'I suppose not,' Mother answered, but you could sense she was angry that Tonto had not been in touch.

'The cemetery has more life in it than any other meeting place in the city. More messages are left and picked up behind

Robert Boyd's headstone than the busiest telegram office in Málaga,' Pérez del Álamo bragged.

'Boyd?' I asked. 'Did you say Boyd?'

I saw the life fizzle from Father's eyes. The name Boyd is whispered along with the revered saints in our house. The day Boyd was executed, Father was part of the small group of Vélezians who had known about the planned landing of Robert Boyd and the others whom General José María Torrijos y Uriarte had recruited.

The problem was that the Governor of Málaga, Don Morales Moreno, was in on it too, and he tricked them all. He had the Vélezians locked up, and by the time Father and his comrades were released from prison General Torrijos y Uriarte and his crew were already prostrated on St Andrew's beach. More than fifty corpses, their hands still tied behind their backs, and their brains shot out, Robert Boyd amongst them.

There was to be no 'proclamation' that day.

General Torrijos y Uriarte tempted Boyd and the others with the lure and lustre of tomorrow's silver. They all loved sailing and fighting. Some travelled from Londonderry to London, and then to Gibraltar. Some, like Boyd, said they were only there for the cause. Morales Moreno betrayed them all. It seems the backstabbing Governor later shot himself. But there were no witnesses, so who knows?

Father smiled at my uncle Tonto. 'Boyd would be delighted to know that thirty-one years later he can still help us achieve our republic. It's a pity I can't do the same.'

'Time to let the young un's take up that cudgel,' Tonto said.

Just before arriving in Andalucía, the queen declared a pardon for all those 'misguided souls' of Málaga, who had been 'tricked' into participating in the riots in the region last year.

'You are all forgiven,' she said.

So that is that. My uncle Tonto and Pérez del Álamo and the rest can stop hiding from the queen's men. All those captured, half-dead men laying in gaol, can get up, put on their own clothes, open their cell doors and go home. Even those men that have been dead a year are 'pardoned'.

It would have been difficult to follow the queen on her travels because she was too quick. She went everyplace: to the train station, to the cathedral and to the hospital San Julián where she left behind 4,000 reales.

The Malagueña Civil Guard accompanied the queen out of the city with her big entourage and tiny husband. Pérez Álamo says it's clear that the Bourbons have no idea of how risky that was because the Civil Guard here is changing. On the outside it looks the same as it always did but inside a different heart is beating.

'It's all part of the plan,' Tonto said, and then winked at me. 'They pay good money too, just ask around.'

FIVE DUROS FOR CALDERÓN
CALLE MAYOR, MADRID
19 APRIL 1886

OUT OF VIEW, tucked up in a bookshop doorway on the even-numbered side of the calle, Benito wears his battered, beige-coloured Montego sunhat and holds two books under his right arm. Occasionally, he peers into the dusty windows, as though scrutinising the sun-bleached books and manuscripts.

The shop will not open for another three hours. He expects one of the journalists will eventually cross to this side of the calle and saunter past, but he easily passes for another anonymous bibliophile with something to trade.

His concentration oscillates like his heartbeat. One moment he is home in Plaza Colón with Concha, who already knew. And the next he is in Calle Pizarro with José, who confirmed the worst: Luis is back and he is 'state expert'.

The school of degeneracy theorists has called on its brightest advocate. What future now for the priest and his family? What chance now for the character Maximiliano Rubín to ride the slipstream of this hobby horse?

Is there a way anyone might diminish Luis' dogmatic certainty? Is it hypothetically possible to force a little swerve to Luis' swagger? Could he ever be persuaded to acknowledge even a flicker of free will? Because, if Luis could, then others would. But what are the chances?

'Why so glum, mister? It might never happen,' a passing

journalist says.

The surprise of not having seen the journalist approach jolts Benito to the present. He almost drops the books he is carrying. He does not answer the passing stranger, nor emerge to look across the street. He backs further into the recess. Looks through the glass door and stands with his back to the street. He pretends to be searching his pockets for keys to the bookshop.

When the stranger's footsteps are no longer audible, Benito returns to watch the dirty reflections in the bookstore window. He strains to hear if the journalists opposite are already restless. He listens to the rabble and understands one of them has picked up and hurled a stone at the window of the third floor.

Now they are chanting, 'Degenerate, degenerate, degenerate.'

A couple of them drift away from the crowd, walk past his side of the street, oblivious to his presence. The time of day hastens parched throats and pangs of hunger. More of them meander off in search of a bar. He reasons the rest will soon follow, like sheep, afraid of losing their place in the pen. None of them seem anxious about losing their rank outside the 'degenerate's' door. Soon, with no hacks to hold in check, the policeman potters away too.

Finally, Benito emerges and turns to face the building in which his interest lies. Number sixty-one looks like an afterthought, it is squeezed into a too-narrow space between fifty-nine and sixty-three, as though it does not belong in this street. It is an oppressed-looking structure of four floors, its sadness accentuated by its fancier neighbours.

Number fifty-nine is an ornate, *neo-mudéjar* dwelling of five-storeys fronted with columns and tall windows and capped by the trees on its roof-terrace. Sixty-three is less opulent, yet still elegant. Both abodes look down with chagrin at their tatty, narrow neighbour.

It does not take long for the street door of number sixty-one to open. A boy steps into the street. He is small, scrawny, and wearing clothes that are brackish, shabby, and loose. He is trying to keep his feet from coming out of his shoes that are several sizes too large.

It is not easy to say how old he is. He has the body of a young child, perhaps of eight or nine years of age, but the face belongs to an older urchin. Benito guesses he might be around twelve years old.

The boy looks furtively up and down, but not across the street to where Benito lurks. Suddenly he moves, turns left, and heads west along Calle Mayor.

Benito leaves his books on the door step of the bookshop, crosses the street in pursuit. He has almost caught up when the boy enters a small grocery shop. He loiters outside waiting for his quarry to leave the shop.

'You live at number sixty-one?' Benito asks when the urchin reappears.

The lad is not simple, nor easily taken in by a nervous man in a Montego hat. 'What of it?' he says, rocking on his heels, looking either side of Benito.

'Pedro Calderón de la Barca lived there,' Benito says.

'Who?' The boy asks. 'You better not touch me, or I'll scream.'

'Calderón de la Barca! Surely you've heard of him?'

'No.'

'You must have talked about him in school,' Benito says.

'De la Bote?'

'De la Barca! Calderón! He lived there,' Benito says and he points to number sixty-one.

'There's never been any Calderón's lived here.'

'Just a quick look inside. I'd really appreciate it.'

'I'm not stupid. I know you're one of those reporters, wanting to gawp at the third floor.'

'No one needs to know you let me in.'

'Five duros,' the boy tells him.

There is no negotiation. Benito is ready to pay double if necessary.

The boy slips the money into his trouser pocket. 'Thanks mister,' he says, a restrained grin on his face.

They walk back quickly. Pass through the unguarded street-door entrance and emerge into a dark, narrow hallway. Benito follows the boy up the stairs, past the grubby, brown-painted door of the first-floor apartment. On the second-floor landing, in front of an equally charmless and scratched door, the boy stops.

'If you tell anyone, I'll say you threatened me.' He takes a key from his pocket. He is grinning wider, showing his dental deficiencies, visible despite the shallow light. He opens the door to the second-floor apartment and slips behind it without another word.

Benito hears a clack and clunk of lock-and-bolt. He carries on up. On the third-floor landing, he removes his hat before knocking loudly on the door.

LOMBROSIAN CHOICE
La Cárcel Modelo, Plaza de la Moncloa, Madrid
21 April 1886

THE ASSASSIN PRIEST wears ankle-irons linked together by a chain long enough to permit walking but not running. He also wears fashionable black leather shoes. Luis finds this juxtaposition of the medieval and modern rather odd.

For a moment they continue to gawp at each other. Possibly, one waits for the other to make an utterance. A waft of air passes in through the barred but open window. Unlike the other cells he passed, the air here is not malodorous. Not of urine or perspiration but something else, faint, and pleasant.

Luis takes the initiative: 'I suppose you'd like to know who I am, and why I'm here?'

'You're Doctor Simarro,' Cayetano says. 'Have you forgotten you were presented a minute ago?'

'I'm here to get to know you. Provide an independent assessment.'

'Aren't you here because you want to know why I did it?'

'Actually no, I'm not. Those would be specifics for your lawyer.'

'You just want to know if I'm crazy?'

'I wouldn't put it quite like that. My function is to better understand what drives a person to ... well, you know.'

'You wouldn't believe me if I told you,' Cayetano says.

'That depends on whether you tell me the truth.'

'And nothing but the truth, so help me God? What if I

said my employers plotted against me and dismissed me for no good reason?'

'Are you saying they persecuted you?'

'Yes.'

'What, all of them?'

'Yes, sir, they did.'

'Who are *they?*'

'The rector, the mother superior, the bishop's personal confessor, and the bishop too. In fact I'd say the bishop was the worst,' Cayetano says.

'They all conspired against you?'

'Aren't you following me? I already said yes.'

Luis takes notes of what he is hearing. Cayetano's eyes follow the flight of the pen.

'Every single one of those people schemed against you?'

'Would you prefer if I just said a voice in my head told me to kill him?'

'That depends? Did a voice tell you to do it?'

'Would you believe that if I said it?'

'I might.'

'And what if I were to say I did it because the bishop deserved to die?'

'I'd find that more difficult to believe.'

Each man pauses. Looks the other in the eye. Luis pretends to be making a note. Eventually, he asks: 'So, do you hear voices?'

'Do you?' Cayetano answers.

Cayetano moves slightly, as though he will come further forward, but his leg-irons limit his movement. Luis nods in the direction of the bed fastened to the wall.

'Shall we sit down, Padre?'

Cayetano shuffles towards the bed, sits slightly bowed on the edge. An expression halfway between a smile and a sneer crosses his face. Despite everything that has happened: the assassination, the attempted suicide, and his incarceration, Cayetano seems more cat than mouse. To Luis' mind, he has a somewhat hypnotic quality about him.

Luis remains standing. 'No, *I* don't hear voices,' he says.

'Well, that's a pity for you,' Cayetano says. 'I do, all the time. Sometimes I hear music too. I'm hearing *La Calunnia*, from Rossini, right now.'

For a moment, Luis wonders whether Cayetano is serious. He searches his face but there's not the trace of a grin. He has to let this scene play out and decide later.

'I'm afraid I don't know that one,' Luis says.

'I'll send you the words. It's about slander,' Cayetano says and smiles.

Luis interprets the smile as sinister.

'Sometimes I even hear voices and see things at the same time. My dead brother for instance,' Cayetano adds sadly.

'You imagine voices and visions? Or do they seem real? Or can't you tell the difference?'

'Does it matter?' Cayetano asks. 'Why hasn't Alonso come?'

Luis looks at his notes. 'That's your brother? Right?'

'Yes, where is he?'

'I don't know. Perhaps your lawyer can answer that.'

'Are you sure you're not a lawyer? You look like one.'

'I'm an alienist.'

'Sit down then, doctor, and we'll see who's mad,' Cayetano says, and he points towards the other end of the bed.

Luis hesitates but he knows confidence is crucial here. In these moments you have to be masterful, you must keep the initiative. He sits on the bed a metre from the priest. A book lies open between them. Luis glances at it: *Religion and Science* is the chapter heading. He thinks he recognises this, but it can't be. Can it?

'You're something of a liar, doctor,' Cayetano says calmly and with no hint of aggression. He reaches over and closes the book.

'A liar? How so?' Luis remembers it is best never to contradict a lunatic.

'Presumably you're being paid to be here?'

'Well, nothing is for free these days.'

'Exactly! So, how can you be independent?'

'I am being paid by the state. But any assessment will be my own personal view, independent of any external party.'

Luis recognises the faint scent in the cell — lavender. 'Would you mind if I ask you some questions?' he asks and sets his notebook in front of him.

'I'm not mad,' Cayetano says.

'Can I ask about your parents? Are they both alive?' Luis asks, without pausing.

'Are yours?' Cayetano responds.

Luis sighs the sigh of orphans.

Without intending to — for he could not possibly have known — Cayetano has hit a nerve. The pain in Luis' expression and his hollow internal howl have travelled across the cell.

'I'm sad for your loss,' Cayetano says.

'You're unusually perceptive,' Luis says.

'None of us fell here from the sky,' Cayetano says.

'Learned too, I see.' Luis points to the book on the bed. The title is visible: *Studies in Philosophy and Religion*.

'It's Giner de los Ríos,' Cayetano says.

'Brought it with you?' Luis asks, unable to contain his surprise.

'Borrowed from the prison library,' Cayetano says. 'The Governor has quite a list.'

'I didn't know they had a library here.' Luis scratches his own head literally and figuratively. He cannot remember the architects having mentioned a library.

'You act like you don't know any priests.'

'I've met a few.'

'Then you know. Theology, Greek, Latin, scripture, and metaphysics, those are the bare minimum of our studies.'

'Makes sense,' Luis says.

'You might be surprised to know the Church is not blind to learning on scientific ideas. Nor on considering your version of free will.'

'I didn't know the Church had a verifiable position on that,' Luis says. He is lying because he does not wish to discuss a prehistoric precept.

'You didn't know *we* got there first?' Cayetano asks, and his tone has a salty edge. 'Were you unaware that Saint Augustin answered that question fifteen hundred years ago?'

In other circumstances Luis might talk about his time as soul-meddling Director of Santa Isabel mental asylum down at Leganés and his battles there with a medieval Church administration who made it their business to regularly evoke Saint Augustin.

'You'll probably want to say I'm some kind of degenerate,' Cayetano says.

If you only knew how helpful that might be in your position, Luis thinks.

'That's why you're asking me about my parents. You'll want to see abnormalities everywhere: early deaths, unconventional ideas, and killers lurking on the branches and roots.'

'It's routine to ask these questions,' Luis replies.

'But leave my family out of this.'

'The public needs to understand why a good man like Bishop Narciso was murdered.'

'Like I said, they'd never believe it. Let's simply settle on the fact it was his turn to die.'

'His turn? If you acted with premeditation they'll have no option but to execute you.'

'You're just like that lawyer they sent me. He wants me to plead diminished responsibility. Now you arrive and you want to know if I hear voices.' Cayetano moves backwards on the bed, stares with empty eyes at the ceiling.

Luis waits. He does not force the discussion. But takes a glance at his watch, looks around the cell. Locates the source of lavender odour: the priest's clothes.

Suddenly, Cayetano stirs: 'There's no long line of lunatics in my family. It would be slanderous for you to suggest otherwise,' he says loudly.

The guard knocks on the door, asks: 'Everything all right in there?'

'We're fine,' Luis says.

Cayetano walks around the cell, mumbling as though counting his steps.

'Sorry for raising my voice but when it concerns allusions about my parents, or their parents, I am duty bound to protect the family.'

'I see.'

'I've read what those hare-brained alienists like Cesare Lombroso are saying,' Cayetano says.

Luis feels his cheeks burning. He is surprised at Cayetano's knowledge but dismisses it as likely superficial. Anyway, Luis would never invent a case of degeneracy if there was no objective sign of it. He leans slightly forward and looks closer at the priest. He already knows the organic antecedents. He begins to integrate the subject's physiognomy and extrapolate the related mental condition. There *are* definite signs of stigma here. Now it is time to record them. 'Many alienists feel Lombroso was on to something,' Luis says. Then he takes a measuring tape from his pocket. 'Perhaps we can stick to the observable.'

Cayetano nods his assent. 'All right you're the doctor.'

Luis begins taking measurements, talking whilst measuring: 'What is your most vivid memory, Padre?'

'My brother's body laid out on the kitchen table,' Cayetano says.

'Open wide,' Luis asks.

Cayetano opens his mouth and Luis counts teeth.

'What's your most important memory, doctor?' Cayetano asks impudently as soon as Luis has finished counting.

'Better if I ask the questions. Since it's me that has to write the case notes.'

'Remember when you write your "case-notes" to emphasise that your subject insists on a death with dignity.'

'Wouldn't you prefer to live?'

'A life of ignominy is not a life,' Cayetano says. 'Execution is infinitely preferable.'

'Let's talk about the choices, shall we?'

PART II

WEIGHING THE ODDS
61 CALLE MAYOR, MADRID
19 APRIL 1886

THE DOOR OPENS just enough to permit her head and harrowed face to emerge. Benito is unprepared for this visage of weary sadness and grief. He says nothing, simply stares.

'Yes?' she says. She looks ready to slam the door shut but hesitates.

'Doña Durdal?' Benito asks and smiles at her.

'And you'd be?'

'Benito Galdós Pérez.'

'The writer?'

'Yes.'

'What do you want?' She leans forward a little more, tilts her head beyond the slight opening of the door, scans the space behind him.

'There's no one else,' he says.

She leans back inside, turns and mutters to the wall.

'I think I can help your employer.'

'My employer?' Her irony is unmistakeable. Lines form on her forehead, her lips turn inwards. A quizzical smile appears. She opens the door, slightly further. 'Are you saying you can help Cayetano?'

'Yes.'

'He's not my employer.'

'Sorry.'

'He's beyond anyone's help,' she says.

'Are you so sure?'

She takes a deep intake of breath, as if readying herself to scream, or burst her lungs and slam the door in a simultaneous action. 'What help can you offer him? Pity? He has plenty of that. Money? He has no need where he's going,' she says.

Benito has his answer ready.

'A fair hearing,' he says.

'The court already appointed a lawyer.'

'And I'm sure an entirely competent one. I meant a different kind of help.'

'Pardon?'

'I've just become a member of the Congress of Deputies.'

This information, not yet public, seems to have some resonance. She pulls the door open slightly further and Benito catches sight of the rest of her. She is wearing a long, black linen dress, as though she is already in mourning. But she still does not completely open the door, nor invite him in. Instead, she turns her head away and Benito understands why. She is whispering to someone tucked behind the door, someone who has been present all of this time.

'Maybe he *can* help?' she mouths to her concealed accomplice.

A male voice replies. The unseen man's voice is deep and strong; a contrabass used to exerting authority: 'In that case, Tránsito, perhaps we should listen to what Señor Galdós has to say to us.'

Doña Tránsito Durdal pulls open the door of the apartment.

Her companion steps briskly forward. He is uniformed in the green of the Civil Guard. He looks robust, albeit shorter than his voice suggested. He is probably in his early forties. In his turn he also looks over the shoulder of Benito and scrutin-

182

ises the staircase. 'We're pleased to meet you.'

Benito offers his hand.

When it is clear that no one else lurks on the landing, the mystery contrabass turns to Benito and smiles. He shakes Benito's still outstretched hand. 'You understand how things are, Señor Galdós,' he says. 'Do come in.'

Tránsito Durdal opens the door fully, and her comrade takes Benito's hat and places it on a hook beside a tricorn hat that matches his own uniform. He leads Benito down a short hallway speaking as he goes: 'Excuse my manners, I'm Don Alonso Galeote Cotilla.'

'Pleased to meet you, Don Alonso.'

'Alonso will do.'

Benito turns to face Tránsito Durdal. She is closing and locking the front door. She seems less guarded than before. Alonso places his hand under Benito's elbow and guides him through a door into a small dark salon overlooking Calle Mayor.

'Take a seat,' he says to Benito, and points to a small, rectangular table pushed up against the wall.

A pile of newspaper cuttings lie on the table and around the table are three spindly, faded, wooden seats, of the type you may find in a bar. Adjacent, a thin mattress lies on the floor. There are two or three notebooks on top.

'Thank you,' Benito says, and sits down.

Alonso pulls the curtains wide then opens the window a few inches.

Benito's eyes blink as daylight surges into the room. He sees out beyond the rooftops.

Alonso sits down in the chair opposite. 'You believe you can help my brother?' he says.

In the suddenly light-filled salon, Benito observes Alonso's cheeks are streaked, the skin below his eyes is puffed and red.

Alonso starts to gather up most of the newspaper cuttings on the table, folds them with precision.

'It can't do him harm to have a friend in the Congress of Deputies.' Benito lets his words find their import, whilst he stares out through the window. He has never been good with small talk and he hopes his social awkwardness does not reveal itself too early as a false deficiency.

Alonso does not answer. He leaves the table, crosses the room to a recess where more newspaper cuttings are already stacked on a wall-mounted bookshelf. 'Hmm, some influence in the Congress. I don't suppose it will hurt,' he says.

'Splendid views from here,' Benito says. Then clears his throat and points to the window.

'Some consolation, given the space is small, and the street noisy,' Doña Durdal answers and runs her fingers through her hair.

Benito looks around. The room in which he finds himself is perhaps fifteen square-metres, and likely accounting for about a third of the space of the entire apartment. 'Cosy though, Señora Durdal,' he answers.

'Tránsito, if you intend to be a friend.'

'Then Tránsito it shall be,' Benito says.

'I'll prepare us all some coffee,' she says, then leaves them.

She has gone into what Benito presumes is the kitchen. As far as he can tell, in addition to the salon where he sits and the kitchen where she has gone, the apartment has only two other rooms. He had noticed two doors lead off from the hall: one will be a bedroom, the other a bathroom-cum-water-closet. He looks at the mattress on the floor and wonders about the sleeping arrangements here.

A current of air breezes in through the open window and flutters the remaining newspaper cuttings left on the table. They seem ready to blow away. Benito puts a hand on them.

As fast as the breeze, Alonso strides back. He collects the last newspaper cuttings from beneath Benito's fingers. 'What's your interest in my brother?' he asks.

Benito knew this question would inevitably come. He has given the matter some thought. 'Everyone has their motives, mine are mostly humanitarian,' he says.

'What does that mean?' Alonso asks, his tone more curious than aggressive.

'Does it matter, as long as I can help?'

Tránsito re-enters the salon and places coffee on the table: 'Of course it matters. If you were an alienist, or a judge and your interest was humanitarian, well that could help. But a writer, even one elected a Deputy, I don't know what help *you* can be.'

'For a start I can help show he's not a degenerate,' Benito says.

'So you heard what they're saying?' Tránsito says.

Alonso punches a fist into the palm of a hand.

'It's shocking for you, of course, that they're already saying your brother is a degenerate,' Benito says.

'My father is going to die of the shame,' Alonso says.

'They don't even know what it is they're saying,' Benito says.

'What do you know that the alienists don't?' Tránsito says.

'I'm as well-read in their science as most of them are. More so than a good few of them,' Benito says.

'But you're a writer, not a scientist.'

'A writer with an interest in this question and some influence in Congress.'

'But what can you do?' Tránsito asks.

'Ask the right questions. Let me start by asking you. Do you think it's possible you lived here with a degenerate madman and didn't know?'

'Of course he's not mad,' Tránsito says and seems unaware that she is continuously stirring her coffee.

'And you, Alonso? What are the odds that you hail from a long line of degenerate lunatics and were oblivious?'

Alonso sighs then stares out through the window across the roofs — as though he is weighing the chances of that possibility. 'I know the odds of our father lasting the year are not good, if they continue to insist Cayetano is a degenerate.'

ALONSO & CAYETANO

Monday, 2 March 1863

The Queen of our fair country has had enough of O'Donnell, and his Liberal Union, and his liberal ideas. O'Donnell is yesterday and now we have the Marqués de Miraflores as prime minister. I believe Miraflores might be on my uncle Tonto's list — perhaps the Marqués may also soon be history.

According to Tonto, O'Donnell's demise is all the fault of the Progressive Party. But, he says, both sides in the Liberal Union will be equally sorry because it is only O'Donnell who could manage them.

'One side digging in for privilege and the other side digging in for doctrine,' Tonto said.

'And only a matter of time before the country rises again,' Father answered.

We have all noticed that since last year, Father and Uncle Tonto tend to agree more openly on many things.

I went to see my friend, Moreno. Uncle Tonto was right about that too. The pay in the Civil Guard is surprisingly good. And Moreno got a 'bounty-bringer payment' when I signed up. Of course he gave half to my father, who gave it to my mother.

During my training I'll be barracked here in Málaga. But I can get home to Vélez at weekends. There are arrangements too if I'm needed back at home for any emergency during the week. This way, no one in Vélez can complain that I am not there to lend a hand. It is not like Daniel and the army. There's a good possibility I can remain here after the initial training too — if I want to.

Monday, 20 June 1864

Cayetano is now ordained a Priest. Father is content because our family is now endowed with 'Men-of-Arms' — he means me and Daniel — and now a 'Man-of-Letters' too. Except of course Cayetano writes nothing! He prefers to read.

Mother thought the whole ordination ritual was magnificent. 'Very spiritual,' she said.

The rest of us thought it was a touch solemn. Even my own Civil Guard attestation ceremony last year seemed more joyful. I have never been to an ordination before. I do not suppose I shall ever go to another. Yet again, my mother was excessive, as usual: She had us light twenty-five candles when we entered the cathedral. Thus there was a candle for every year of Cayetano's life.

'He needs our protection and I suppose the Church needs it too,' she said.

Other trainee priests were being ordained. Their families were not as numerous as our lot. You can imagine where the greatest noise in the cathedral came from. Mother and my sisters — all the Elder Berry girls and all the Young Fruits too. Even my cousin Tránsito was there. Mother had sent a missive to the Cotillas and to the Durdals, as far down as Marbella. Practically all of the Galeote clan was there too. I half-expected all of our cousins from Puerto Rico!

Father arranged for a photographer to visit our home on Saturday. He says he spent more money for Cayetano's ordination than for Teresa's wedding.

Daniel and I wore our uniforms. Personally, I would say I looked smarter in my Civil Guard colours than Daniel did in his Army colours. I know the Young Fruits would agree with me on that. For the ceremony we changed into our "civvies" and then back into uniform, once outside the cathedral.

Tonto found all of this very amusing. 'You could have done the same as the bishops and priests do,' he said.

'Which is what?' Daniel asked.

'Just keep your uniform on underneath. Everyone knows that under their vestments they all wear the Carlista uniform.'

The whole huddle of Galeotes laughed loudly in the street and Father made my uncle Tonto swear not to repeat this when Cayetano was around, nor anywhere near Bishop Cascalluna or Canon Ruiz y Blasco.

Some of the other noviciates had arranged for a younger trainee from the seminary to perform the *putting on of the vestments*. One had arranged for his own mother to do it. Another had his sister. Guess who Cayetano wanted? Daniel, who else? But Daniel asked our cousin Tránsito to do it. Well, she had sung loudest during the Litany of the Saints.

'Go on, you do it,' Daniel said and handed her the vestments. Then nudged her forward. 'You're the trainee nun. This will give you practice for your own big day.'

So, it was Tránsito who helped Cayetano put on his new stole and chasuble. But once the Mass was over, Cayetano and Daniel went off on their own, babbling away. Cayetano was chatting on about honour and dignity. Daniel was chittering on about family. The indivisible Letters and Arms duo were back.

SLANDER IS A ZEPYHR

PUBLIC PROSECUTOR'S OFFICE. SUPREME COURT, MADRID
23 APRIL 1886

EXCMO D. MANUEL Colmeiro y Penido, on behalf of the Royal Academy of Medicine (RAM) I thank you for your confidence in our work. I am pleased to submit this, my Case Note Summary, which I hasten to add is strictly for your own confidential use in the event that your intervention may be required at the right moment.

Kindly advise our offices when a trial date has been programmed and a prosecuting judge appointed, at which moment a fuller (suitably redacted) version of this case note summary, plus a transcription of my Field Notes can be produced.

<u>Summary Conclusion (your reference only)</u>

The first essential information for you to know concerning this subject is he is dangerously delusional and an ongoing threat to the public. The second is that — for reasons outlined in the following sections — it is his destiny to be so. Putting to one side the personal tragedy for the victim of the shooting of 18 April, I feel sure you will agree with me that this case therefore arrives at a providential moment because it brings into focus those wider implications for the country, which so many state institutions have been concerned with.

At RAM we realise state funding is not fungible and will go to the most worthwhile causes. We feel your Ministry may consider this a providential moment to stake a claim. Thank you.

Subject Biographic Data

Name — Cayetano Galeote Cotilla. Born - 15 January 1839 in Vélez-Málaga, the seventh live-born and third male child of Cayetano Galeote Torres and María Cotilla Acosta.

Education — Attended Jesuit Brothers school in Vélez-Málaga for seven years, then their college, then the seminary of San Sebastián y Santo Tomás de Aquino, Málaga. Studied Greek, Latin, Theology, Philosophy, and Astronomy.

Employment — Currently defrocked. Ordained a Catholic priest in 1852, first employed in that position in Vélez-Málaga before volunteering (September 1868) for a mission in Africa (Fernando Pô). Subsequently having surviving said mission he volunteered for other overseas assignments ending with Puerto Rico. Returned to the home territories in 1880. Subject had been assigned to various dioceses in Madrid until August 1885 - when he was dismissed on suspicion of immoral conduct.

Subject's Physiognomy

Physical Condition — He stands five feet, ten inches tall. Currently appears under-nourished. Partial deafness in the right ear due to double otitis in childhood, otherwise generally in rude health.

Teeth — An irregular mouth. He retains four wisdom teeth: Consistent stigmata.

Gait — I concede it is difficult to be graceful in gait when one is chained, but the subject's gait was abnormally shambling; consistent therefore with the scale of degeneracy stigmata.

Skull (cranial capacity) — Given the subject's size, his

cranial capacity is smaller than normal. The frontal bone appears under-developed and the posterior, although better developed, seems raised. The auditory passages are higher up than usual. Overall, these factors combine to reduce cranial capacity to that of an imbecile. My experience suggests a dissection would confirm a microcephalic brain.

Prognathism — I am ready to accept there is some controversy amongst alienists as to whether this is a valid stigmata. Nevertheless, the man does have a discernibly projecting chin, and taking this with everything else — teeth, gait, and cranial capacity — the evidence seems indisputable.

Subject's Mental Condition

Memory — The subject's memory is unnaturally prodigious. There were numerous, over-vivid, recovered distant memories; mostly involving family members, especially a deceased brother. He claimed to have visions and demonstrated paranoia as well as delusional persecution (see field notes).

Emotional State — Despite facing capital punishment, the subject was flippantly insouciant of his situation. He fell silent, stared at the ceiling, seemingly catatonic.

Reasoning — Subject was capable of understanding abstract constructs but has irrational ideas (not worth repeating here) wholly unsupported by objective, scientific proof.

Subject Antecedents

Alienist Doctrine — Notwithstanding, some alienists are accused of having shown an over-enthusiasm for the dogmas of degeneracy resulting in their positions being open to misunderstandings by non-experts, I must take a moment to mention progress in ideas concerning hereditary antecedents. Alienists across the world accept the doctrines and use them to inform clinical diagnoses. Pioneering work, to contain the threat posed by and restrict the spread of hereditary madness, is being undertaken in countries less developed than our own.

Subject's self-disclosure — He has a brother suffering from epilepsy, at least one sister has had several miscarriages, and another has died whilst giving birth. Another paints, and sells her paintings, apparently preferring to maintain herself, and so she lives without a man's support. Whilst he does not admit to ever having suffered syphilis himself, he has been overseas for many years on missions, including Fernando Pô. (Who does not know about the endemic syphilis there?)

Genealogical Antecedents — For this case, Doctor Escuder is working under my direction. He has communicated to me his early data obtained in Vélez-Málaga. He reveals the subject's family as branch and root degenerates. He has met with representatives of four generations of the family and it is his opinion that the immutable laws of inheritance are in evidence.

Escuder has considered the cases of one hundred and sixty-three relatives of the accused, of which ninety-seven are deceased and sixty-six remain alive. There is evidence of hysteria, epilepsy, odd manias, delusions and criminal types. Escuder's report remains to be verified.

Doctor Luis Simarro,
19 April 1886

P.S. — Subject sent me the words of *La Calunnia*. I refute slandering anyone.

TELL HIM EVERYTHING
61 Calle Mayor, Madrid
19 April 1886

FAMILY IS FAMILY, and surely a brother will walk barefoot on a bed of blades for the whisper of a chance to save the life of his own sibling? Especially if that chance comes and knocks on his door. Unless of course said brother has something to gain from an older sibling receding from the scene.

And who could bear being labelled degenerate? What would a person not do to elude that ignominy and escape the 'shame,' as Alonso himself named it? That injury to a family's reputation has such a potency it could provoke the death of a dear elderly and much loved father.

'The idea of your brother being a degenerate madman,' Benito says, 'just seems ludicrous to me.'

'You sound very sure of yourself,' Alonso responds.

'Let me ask you, do *you* feel as though you are not in charge of your actions?' Benito asks. 'Are *you* on the edge of insanity?'

'Of course not,' Alonso says.

'Do you see any of this in your parents, your sisters, or your brothers?'

Alonso sighs, straightens some newspaper cuttings.

'Does it make sense to you that your brother reaches almost fifty years of age and is suddenly revealed to the world as a degenerate madman?'

'He's right, it makes no sense at all,' Tránsito says.

'There's little scientific justification for these claims in general,' Benito says. 'And I see none at all in this specific case.'

'Perhaps not a degenerate, but simply gone mad?' Alonso answers.

'I'm afraid they must have it both ways,' Benito says.

Tránsito clears her throat. 'There's someone I'd happily shoot,' she says. 'Probably, even enjoy it.'

For a moment, the other two simply stare at her.

'Does that make me mad?' she asks, then walks away before Benito or Alonso can respond.

As Tránsito leaves the room, an enigmatic smile crosses her lips.

Benito picks up some newspaper cuttings: 'Don't you wonder why they aren't inquiring about his motivations? And why all this fascination with degeneracy?'

He then produces a copy of this week's *The Truth* from his trouser pocket and passes it to Alonso. 'This is their weekly mouthpiece journal. Their leading article? *All human conduct is pre-determined.* You see where things are now?'

'Why are they so fixated?' Alonso asks.

'They want to convince the public they have the solution,' Benito says.

'Who does?' Alonso asks.

'Alienists with an agenda,' Benito says. 'Some, like Salillas, are blunt instruments. But this new generation, the Simarro's of this world, they are sophisticated in the art of persuasion.'

'Simarro's been appointed state expert.'

'I know, and unless something is done, he'll convince even your brother that his actions were inevitable.'

'Mightn't that impression be in Cayetano's interest?'

'Perhaps... if it were true,' Benito says. 'Do you think your father is ready to agree?'

'I don't believe so.'

'He would be right not to, because if you permit the lie then we should all fear your "degenerate" Galeote family.'

'Yet, if the state expert wants to assert my brother is a degenerate, how can we resist?'

'What kind of life has he led until now?' Benito asks.

'I don't quite know what you mean.'

'Would you say you are shocked by this turn of events?' Benito asks. 'Is it too much to say his story, until now, has been exemplary?'

Alonso looks towards the kitchen. Benito does too. Tránsito does not emerge.

Alonso strokes his chin, begins to pace back and forth.

'His story is what your brother should be judged on,' Benito says. 'Not a hare-brained idea that he hails from a long line of half-wits!'

'Whatever his provocation, his lawyer will surely find it and present it,' Alonso says.

'Really?'

'Why wouldn't he?'

'This suggestion your brother is a degenerate madman has to be interesting for him. Unlike you and your family, he won't care where the madness is said to originate. If he can convince the courts that your brother is simply mad then his job is done and Cayetano has a chance to avoid the death sentence.'

'That's what we all want,' Alonso leaps in.

Benito rocks back in his seat, as though to displace his earlier thoughts about what result might suit Alonso.

'The state expert's going to claim degeneracy,' Benito says. 'He has to. See if I'm wrong,'

Alonso stops pacing. He stares at the floor, then at Benito, but his eyes are an uninhabited *barrio*, revealing nothing of his head or heart. In the silence, it seems to Benito, a pivotal moment has arrived in their discussion. But neither man has time to develop their thoughts.

The warm voice of Tránsito Durdal and the smell of freshly made coffee, once again, takes possession of the small room. 'I've been listening to everything,' she says. She places a tray on the table.

Alonso frowns as though he does not welcome her return into the conversation at this particular moment.

'Influence. Friends on his side is what your brother needs,' Benito says.

'Influence cannot solve every problem,' Alonso says.

'Let's consider England. Bellingham shoots and kills the prime minister,' Benito says. 'Within a week they've got him sentenced and strung up.'

'And they say we're hot-blooded,' Tránsito says and raises her eyebrows.

'Bellingham's problem? He had no friends with influence.'

'Who can say it would have made any difference if he had?' Tránsito asks.

'Let's consider that. Along comes McNaughton. He wants to shoot and kill a prime minister too,' Benito says. 'He shoots the Personal Secretary, mistaking him for the prime minister. Kills him stone dead.'

'A frightening and violent place, England,' Tránsito says.

'Unlike Bellingham, McNaughton *had* influential friends. What do you think happened to him?' Benito asks, turning to Alonso and Tránsito.

'Obviously not strung up in a week,' Tránsito says.

'He was acquitted. Declared "not guilty" and sent to an insane asylum,' Benito says. 'But, as we all know, their asylums are like artists' rest-homes.'

'But that is England,' Alonso says.

'One man strung up within days. The other sent to an asylum. Same defence, same criminal motivation, and yet remarkably different endings,' Benito says. 'Which brings me to ask: what *was* your brother's motivation?'

'There's no mystery, Señor Galdós: "I am avenged." You'll find those were his precise words,' Alonso says.

'Avenged? What for?' Benito says.

Tránsito shifts position, she seems ready to respond to Benito's question. However, before she can, Alonso speaks again.

'Does that matter?' Alonso says, and he hands Benito copies of *El Globo*, *El Resumen* and *El Correo*. 'I don't believe revenge is considered a strong defence.'

This not being the moment nor place for academic detachment or a review of murder cases he has studied in the past ten years Benito chooses to let Alonso's rhetorical question pass. He hands back the newspapers.

'Bellingham and McNaughton claimed they were persecuted. Both pleaded diminished responsibility,' Benito adds.

'What point are you making?' Tránsito asks.

'The point is that their crimes were similar, their defences too, and their histories considered. But one had influential friends,' Benito asserts.

'They can't possibly let him off. Can they?' Alonso says.

'Not entirely, maybe but he needn't be Spain's Bellingham. He could be our McNaughton,' Benito says.

'And our father would die of shame, and our family be forever known as degenerates,' Alonso says.

'You misunderstand me,' Benito says. 'McNaughton was never labelled a degenerate.'

'Asylum or gaol, either way Cayetano wouldn't really be free,' Alonso says.

'But he wouldn't be dead either,' Tránsito says.

'They defrocked him,' Benito says. 'Put yourself in his shoes. The shame must have been unbearable.'

'But his reaction was disproportionate,' Alonso says.

'Perhaps their reaction was too. Why was he defrocked?' Benito asks.

For a moment Tránsito looks at Alonso. Her eyes, luminously lachrymose. Alonso returns her look.

'If it wasn't for me, Cayetano wouldn't be in this situation.' Tránsito seems ready to burst out with her confession. If that is what it is. She looks again at Alonso, as though expecting him to stop her from talking. Her chest heaves, she sighs deeply.

Alonso clears his throat. 'None of this is your fault. Tell him everything,' he says, and like an actor hoping now to fade from the stage he steps away into the recess where he clips more cuttings.

EXTRA-CURRICULAR
SEMINARY SAN PELAGIO, CÓRDOBA
25 SEPTEMBER 1868

PADRE GABINO SÁNCHEZ has come to calm their fears. It is six forty in the morning and today's scripture reading before breakfast is cancelled. The young seminarians gather and stare at him.

'You'll all have heard by now. The revolt has begun,' he tells them.

This latest group of 'young lions' already know all about their tutor, Padre Gabino Sánchez. But they seldom find him here in their canteen. Their tutor eats extraordinarily sparsely, rises early and is rumoured to eschew alcohol, except in a crisis. In return for those virtues he radiates an uncommon vitality in a priest of his generation.

He is, at first, his usual self. Serene, calm, and composed. He is their Apollo; nevertheless some aspect within him communicates an edginess. His eyes, perhaps? They wait for their tutor, this giant personality in a modest frame. They expect, as usual, his words will be hypnotic and soothing — even if it seems the subject may be stark.

'General Prim's flotilla is well advanced up the coast from Cádiz. They're likely on their way to strengthen the hand of Marshall Serrano,' Gabino Sánchez says.

He sounds rather matter of fact, unblinking, as though he is chatting about today's chores.

A quiet voice from the back of the hall floats forwards over their heads and towards the front. 'What will this mean for us, Padre?'

'We must wait and see. Perhaps a republic will be re-established. Maybe this particular branch of the Bourbon monarchy will snap off, give way to new healthier buds, perhaps not.' He smiles.

Another voice from the back of the room, a little more raised, a touch nervier, pipes up: 'Does it make any difference to us? Aren't the republicans just as anti-clerical as the current back-stabbing branch of the monarchy?'

'You all know our position; overt neutrality,' Gabino Sánchez says. 'Let the opposing political and military forces settle this between them.'

Feet shuffle. About half of the seminarians mutter or nod in agreement. Then a different voice pipes up, this one younger, more urgent and located nearer the front: 'And later, when the country needs us?'

'We'll be ready. But for now, spiritual guidance is what we're offering, not political interference.'

Some seminarians snigger, as though they know something the others don't, as though they know this 'we'll wait and see' response is a sham. After all, the whole country is aware that the Carlistas, with the Church's support, are the third force, just biding their time, as always. Some present could cite the words of several impatient Bishops who remain openly political, happy to interfere. That is why *all* Bishops are being watched, even the avowed apolitical. However, no one dares be openly militant, because too many clerics have disappeared.

Gabino Sánchez purses his lips. He casts a look over the young men's heads and waits until the sniggering has subsided. He clears his throat. It has been three days since the declaration in Cádiz; he understands some seminarians are nervy. However, no seminarian will yet ask him the questions he knows are in all of their minds: will the Church, and their political masters the Carlistas, really sit back? Won't they have to take sides soon? Won't they have to dig up their munitions, bury their soutanes and, in the case of some seminarians itchy for the fight, finally unbridle their bravado?

The same voice that began the questions: 'Does anyone believe the Isabellinos are just going to wait in Madrid for the rebels to march up there?'

Gabino Sánchez smiles and holds his arms up as though pointing to Madrid: 'We already know the answer to that. She's sent her man. General Pavia's at the head of her loyalist army, heading south to meet the rebel army. As we spend our time chit-chatting here, they are on the march.'

That sets them off: ten, twenty, conversations start up. Pavia's name is heard, over and over. For now, no one needs to call for order, no one has to ring a bell. The sound level keeps on rising but it is all a collegiate babble, not yet a rabble.

They all know of this General. He was once a Jesuit like they are now. Worse, he was born here in Andalucía; this 'traitor' knows the emotional topography of the terrain.

The voice from the back again, 'Why send him?'

This question starts them all competing for their particular theory to be heard above the others.

Gabino Sánchez takes a metal cup, stands on a canteen bench and coughs, one time.

Some seminarians turn to look at their fifty-eight year-old tutor. Observe how his skin covers his frame with much the same firmness that a younger man's might: nothing spare. He cuts a figure up there. Still moves light on his feet. He can chop pine logs as fast as most of the young lions under his tutelage. And, although there are plenty of grey flecks amongst the chestnut, his hair has not yet gone on holiday.

His face is lined but look closer and you'll see those are mostly laughter lines. Yet, what has *he* had to laugh about? He has borne arms in two wars in support of the Carlist challenger for the throne, he has probably killed men too. Yet look at him. Who amongst them can name a priest more pious-looking than Gabino Sánchez? There is no man they would prefer to take religious instruction from. No one more credible could stand on that canteen bench in front of them and keep them rapt. Not even his protégé, the Secretary, holds that power.

Gabino Sánchez raps the metal receptacle repeatedly with a fork. In an instant, there is silence.

They all gaze. See the wizened warrior. See the ready martyr. See the concerned cleric. See the man whose own warrior father was amongst those who freed Spain from French occupation, and whose uncle, also a priest, died in the same fight to liberate Spain. All the seminarians here know his history. They know that — irony of all ironies — Padre Gabino Sánchez' own father and uncle helped put Queen Isabel's father, Ferdinand, on the throne.

But then, which patriotic Spaniard had a choice? The whole of Spain rallied to defeat the French occupation. The whole of Spain made that same error. None knew how 'Ferdinand the Desired' would rule the country. Or what treachery he would sow.

'Are there any more questions?' Gabino Sánchez asks them.

Some heads shake. Some cubs grumble. But there are no questions forthcoming. Gabino Sánchez beckons them all forward. He stretches out his arms, as though embracing his pride.

'Anyone here worried about General Pavia?' he says.

They shake their heads again. Nothing worries them.

'Well, carry on about your normal business: breakfast, devotions and lessons, including the extra-curricular applied training,' he emphasises.

He steps down from the canteen bench and leaves them. He has barely passed the door when the seminarians start to break off and form their usual cliques. Some of them — those specially selected for Padre Gabino Sánchez' extra-curricular political affairs classes — move to an ante-room and begin to talk amongst themselves, speculating about the content of tonight's lesson.

Gabino Sánchez' extra-curricular applied training is where the best instruction in guerrilla warfare, spying, and survival can be acquired. Naturally, he does not do all of this on his own. He has help. For instance, Secretary Narciso Martínez-Vallejo Izquierdo makes the journey once a month from Granada to Córdoba to deliver his own particular contributions.

This semester, Secretary Narciso's specialities are 'blending in,' 'being invisible,' and 'misleading the enemy'. Although he is not due in Córdoba for another two weeks, a rumour is circulating within the seminary that Secretary Narciso has been seen in the vicinity of Bishop Juan Alfonso's Palace. Perhaps this explains why Padre Gabino Sánchez has quickly left the seminary and is now sighted by one of his own students hurrying along the path in that direction.

MOTHER SUPERIOR
61 CALLE MAYOR, MADRID
19 APRIL 1886

BENITO WATCHES TRÁNSITO. Her hands tremble and her lips twitch. She looks past him toward Alonso who lurks in the recess as though engrossed in his ordering of newspaper cuttings.

'I'm not sure I understand, Tránsito says. Previously, you were telling me to say nothing. Now you say I should tell everything.'

'I was talking about the police, then,' Alonso answers.

'But if they knew everything too couldn't that help Cayetano?' she asks.

'Don't be so naive. They didn't come here turning over your apartment so they could help Cayetano.'

'If there are confidences that you'd rather keep to yourself, I understand,' Benito says. 'Judge for yourself what you feel might help the public learn who Cayetano really is.'

'Would it help to know why I left the Augustinians?'

'I don't know,' Benito says. He now looks over to Alonso who has ceased cutting and ordering and is intently watching Tránsito's face. 'Does it have any relevance to what happened?'

She nods in the affirmative, then speaks rapidly. 'I didn't leave the convent for the reasons some muckrakers might imagine.' Her anger explodes in her articulation of muckrakers.

'Why *did* you leave, then?' Alonso asks. His tone seems part curiosity of a cousin once-removed, part wonder of an unbelieving spouse.

Benito is somewhat startled by Alonso's apparent emotion. Instinctively, he flings a remark like a quilt over a dangerous flicker: 'There's plenty of time for introspection. I mean you can think about that and get it off your chest another time.'

Tránsito and Alonso both swivel to focus on Benito. Her anger seems already dissipated. His curiosity seems already curbed.

'It was a mistake to have gone there in the first place,' she says. She stares at the two men, in turn, as though daring either to contradict her. Neither of them do. They are poised like poker players — ready to raise an eyebrow, or let their eyes say what is on their minds.

Go on, tell us about your foolish mistake, Benito's expression is surely saying.

'As soon as I arrive at the convent, I made another blunder,' she says. 'I confessed to old Sánchez.'

Him again, Benito notes.

'He was due for retirement,' she says. 'And always seemed to be asleep in the confessional.'

'Where better to go for a confession?' Alonso remarks.

'I'd heard him snoring and grunting in the box,' she says. 'I really needed to talk. I probably said it thinking he was not listening.'

'Said what,' Alonso asks.

'That I had doubts about my faith.'

Benito is still thinking about muckrakers.

'Well, it turned out that old Sánchez was listening all the time. He answered me — "My child, supposing the most devout have experienced those exact same feelings?" — Imagine the shock of the old goat opening his eyes and saying that.'

'I once confessed to my local priest that I had doubts about my mother's choice of a career for me,' Benito confides.

'Really? What happened?' Alonso asks.

Before Benito can answer Alonso, Tránsito continues her own thread: 'But the Mother Superior gave their game away.'

'What game?' Alonso asks.

'They were in cahoots. He told her everything. She knew my whole story.'

'She told you that?' Benito asks.

'No, but it was obvious. Suddenly she began to be kind. She'd notice the work I was doing and say things like "Sister, I don't think I've ever seen that floor look cleaner!" It was crystal clear.'

'Giving a compliment on floor cleanliness, that's her way of being kind?' Alonso says.

Benito shifts in his seat. He wants to ask Transito when she will talk of Cayetano.

'Other occasions she'd tell me I could finish my chores half an hour earlier and take some time to contemplate.'

'There's rarely enough time in a life for contemplation,' Alonso says.

As Tránsito recounts these memories her persona transforms, she seems more pious: 'I confessed twice more. And on each occasion Madre Mariana asked me to go to her room. She said that she had noticed I'd become less enthusiastic in prayers and singing. And asked me if everything was all right.'

Alonso's curiosity brings him fully out of the recess. He places his, by now empty, coffee cup on its plate and the chinking sound momentarily breaks into Tránsito's monologue.

Transito pauses, then looks into Benito's mind. 'You must be wondering what any of this has to do with Cayetano,' She continues. 'But don't worry, you'll see how their cabal operates and you'll understand the implications.'

Benito writes in his notebook: *A cabal in the convent with implications for Cayetano*. 'Do carry on,' he tells her.

'I decided I should just tell her directly about my doubts. Every morning, I'd awake at five-thirty and prepare for Lauds and think I'll go and see her straight afterwards. But she'd be stood like a stone in her pulpit, and I'd get cold feet. Then I'd think, I'll go and see her after Eucharist.' Tránsito's words trail away. Her presence shrinks as though this memory has exhausted her. Some tears leak in the corners of her eyes. She stares at the empty coffee cups, picks them up and departs, leaving Alonso and Benito to their own thoughts.

'It seems obvious where she is leading us,' Benito says.

'Maybe for you, but not for me.'

'Really? There's nothing new under the sun. I suppose your brother was assigned to la Iglesia de la Encarnación. Presumably he replaced the retiring Padre Gabino Sánchez?'

'Oh, I see where you're going. Let her tell you in her words. She's getting there.'

'I'm ahead of her.' Benito says. 'Let's say some sentiments were rekindled. Her faith is challenged. It's an old story. Even priests and nuns have urges.'

A lop-sided smile hangs from Alonso's mouth. His eyes are smiling too. 'Don't be so impatient. I don't believe this situation is what you think it is,' he says.

'What else is there?'

'Cayetano has known her since she was a child. Our maternal grandmothers are sisters.'

Tránsito returns and places another tray containing a fresh pot of coffee, three empty cups and a large jug of water on the centre of table. She has washed her face. 'I think I need more coffee, even if neither of you do,' she says.

'Thank you,' Benito answers and sips his fresh coffee.

'You forget how small this place is,' she says. 'I could hear you whispering. I'm sure Señor Galdós is not interested in knowing about our grandparents.'

'He thinks he has it all worked out,' Alonso says.

'Oh, I know that. He's a writer,' she says. 'They can imagine romantic liaisons everywhere. Even between cousins. Isn't that what were you thinking, Señor Galdós?'

Benito considers a confession of his own. Telling them he understands, better than they could ever know, that love between cousins can be as powerful as any other. It can last for an eternity, even in the perpetual absence of the other. He considers disclosing this, but of course he will never say it. Except, perhaps one day in a letter — ready to be opened when he himself is ready to be closed.

'I'm wondering, does it matter about your personal relationship with Cayetano?' Benito says. 'Our prospects of saving him don't really depend on that.'

'But you said it would help if people knew the entire truth about him,' she says.

He did say that. He meant it too. And it is clear to him that she wants to go on talking. It is as though there is something therapeutic in this for her.

'The truth is always worth knowing,' Benito says.

'Even if it will change absolutely nothing for Cayetano,' Alonso intervenes.

The brusqueness of Alonso's interjection causes Tránsito to gasp.

Alonso continues, 'He shot the bishop: Three bullets. Hundreds of witnesses. Does it matter if he is gallant?'

'If you want your brother to escape the garrotte,' Benito says, 'there are many prosaic things which might matter.'

Alonso shakes his head, he seems unconvinced. On the

other hand, Tránsito appears part persuaded that the truth cannot hurt.

'Even if you could help him avoid the garrotte,' Alonso says, 'they'll lock him up for the rest of his life, like your fellow, McNaughton. What kind of existence would that be?'

'Then let's set our aim a little higher,' Benito says. 'Begin with the assumption that Cayetano is not a degenerate madman. Can we agree on that?' He sticks his hand out, which Tránsito, and then Alonso, shakes.

'Let's ensure the provocation is revealed and measured by everyone,' Benito says. 'Perhaps that will favour a shorter prison sentence.'

'What harm can it do to set our sights high?' Tránsito says, directing her question and gaze at Alonso.

But Alonso does not respond. His lips curl inwards. He shakes his head in the negative, as though to say *stop dreaming*.

Benito breaks the awkwardness that has slipped over them: 'I was assuming before that Cayetano was likely assigned to la Iglesia de la Encarnación, to replace Gabino Sánchez?'

'Yes, but that's likely the only assumption of yours that'll be correct,' Tránsito answers.

'Perhaps, you're right,' Benito replies.

'And if you assume our Mother Superior, Madre Mariana, was content to have Cayetano in la Encarnación then you're as much a fool as I was.'

'Tránsito is convinced that her Mother Superior is partly responsible for all of this,' Alonso says.

Benito adds another name to his list — another superior mother that disappoints.

SIC SEMPER TYRANNIS

Sunday, 24 July 1864

I should not be surprised at Cayetano's latest efforts on behalf of Remedios. But I am. On the surface, he is like the rest of the Elder Berries and has tried to discourage her from painting. Yet he pays for her supplies. Now he has gone further. He has travelled here twice this month to show her drawings and paintings to his friend Canon Pablo Ruiz y Blasco over at the cathedral.

Remedios is happy. Us Young Fruits are too. But not everyone in the family is content with what Cayetano is doing, especially not Teresa. She rarely agrees with anything her younger sisters do. She is even preoccupied in the futile chore of finding a husband for Remedios. But Remedios is obsessed with drawing and painting everything — animate or inanimate, clothed or nude. Even the female nude, which she initials with the letter *R*, usually placed to hide a delicate zone. She is scandalous!

'Which sane young woman, does that?' Teresa asked.

Remedios did not even bother to answer.

Apparently, Canon Pablo Ruiz also draws and paints, and he has a younger brother, José Ruiz, who studies at the Real Academia de Bellas Artes de San Telmo de Málaga. I do not know if it was Cayetano's idea, but it seems José Ruiz is willing to give Remedios private lessons. In exchange for housekeeping responsibilities. You can imagine what the Elder Berries and Father think about that! However, Cayetano has told them there is nothing to worry about because José Ruiz y Blasco already has a fiancée. One of those pretty Picasso girls over at Calle Medced.

'We'll see to it that Remedios is not compromised,' Cayetano promised our family.

Now it is up to me, her nearly eighteen year old brother, training down the road in the Civil Guard barracks, to keep an eye open.

I just had coffee with Cayetano, Remedios and the Ruiz brothers. We went to a little coffee house near the cathedral. Remedios' brought some more of drawings and paintings. I could see the Ruiz brothers were impressed.

'Excellent, quite excellent,' José Ruiz said. 'Where does this talent come from?'

'From my grandmother,' Remedios answered.

I never knew that. I wonder if it is even true. What is true is Remedios starts as housekeeper and clandestine art student next week. She will even be paid a token monthly salary. And I shall be keeping my eyes well open.

Monday, 17 April 1865

It was supposed to have been a happy family moment for us: a new niece or nephew for me, another grandchild for my parents. Alas, I must tell you that two days ago Laurencia died giving birth. Her baby is motherless.

Our local priest has said it was God's will. But Cayetano, God's representative in our family, is unable to explain to mother why God is so cruel. The Doctor arrived as soon as he could but Laurencia was already dead.

We understand that our American cousins lost their Mr. Lincoln on the very same day and many of them feel father-less. I am sure their nation, especially his own children, will be grieving. Yet, if you could see our mother you would feel their entire continent cannot surpass her grief. She believes herself culpable for being unable to prevent it. Especially since only a few days ago, Laurencia had another of her odd premonitions: 'Mama, I dreamt of a torrent of blood pouring out of me, and people crying and slipping away from me, and then darkness,' she told mother.

Mother told her not to be silly, that she was twenty-four years old, strong, and healthy as an ox. She said, she would be there during the birth and would not let anything happen. And true to her word she was present and ever vigilant but could only watch as blood haemorrhaged — as it has in the past in these situations. She cannot understand the tyranny of this curse.

We hear that President Lincoln also dreamt clearly of his own death too. Perhaps he imagined this fellow, Booth, leaping over the balcony, shouting '*Sic Semper Tyrannis*' after shooting him in the head.

We hear too that some Americans believe their Mr. Lincoln was a tyrant, perhaps they should meet Narváez? Or lose a sister or daughter to another type of tyranny?

THE ODOUR OF NOSTALGIA
61 CALLE MAYOR, MADRID
19 APRIL 1886

THE CONVENT CABAL mystery begins to take shape in Benito's mind but there are so many elements he does not yet have the answer to. The more he learns the less he seems to know. But he is now on the inside of something. The answers just need to be unpicked.

'Why do you say your Mother Superior had a part in what happened to Cayetano?' Benito asks.

'The way she spoke about him,' Tránsito says, 'even before he arrived she was telling us he was a mercenary.'

'Then why did they offer him the position in the first place?' Alonso asks.

'It was not her idea. Some friend of old Gabino Sánchez arranged it,' Tránsito replied.

'A mercenary! They should have given him a medal,' Alonso says. 'All those years he spent serving in the dominions: Puerto Rico, Fernando Pô.'

'That didn't matter to her,' Tránsito says. 'According to her, he didn't belong and she doubted he'd last. She said the best we could do, for a mercenary like him, is try to civilize him whilst he was amongst us.'

'Mothers are not always superior nor can you rely on them to be charitable,' Benito says.

'She had never even met him,' Tránsito says.

'Then why was she so contrary?' Benito asks.

'She was very close with old Sánchez and at first we thought it was just the idea of a change that bothered her.'

'What changes could there possibly have been?' Alonso asks. 'After all, she was the one in charge, not an itinerant priest responsible for saying the Masses.'

'Some of the younger nuns hoped Cayetano's arrival might modernise our practices. That probably worried her.'

'Modernise? What is there to modernise?' Alonso says.

'Plenty of routines are discretionary. It's up to the Mother Superior to stamp her personality on the place,' Tránsito says. 'So, we imagined a priest from Andalucía might lead her to think more about the joy of faith, than the misery.'

'I remind you, you were not in Andalucía,' Alonso says. 'You couldn't expect the same kind of convent.'

'That was at the root of my unhappiness,' she says. 'The further I got from Andalucía, the less enthusiasm I had for my faith.'

'When we're there we can't wait to leave the place behind,' Alonso says, 'but as soon as we're gone we miss the sun setting over Andalucía, and for an hour of its absence we suffer a month of melancholy.'

Benito has not been back to Las Palmas since his father's funeral. His home province holds a power, but somehow far less than Alonso's and Tránsito's.

'There's a magic in nostalgia,' Benito says. 'Especially when it concerns Andalucía.'

'You're right. Everyone has an Andalucían anecdote,' Tránsito says. 'What's yours?'

Benito has several Andalucían anecdotes he could tell. For instance, he could talk of his first-time passing through Andalucía. He was nineteen, on his way to begin university in Madrid. It took three days for the boat from Las Palmas to reach the colourful, noisy, odorous Port of Cádiz. They docked at midday on the third day. His body was tired but his mind oscillated between the fervour of his delight in having escaped Mama Dolores and sorrow at having left Sisita behind. However, they had a secret. Soon, she would also be on her way to Madrid.

Far from the claustrophobic surveillance of Mama Dolores, they would be reunited. He thought they had played it perfectly. He had the expected argument with Mama Dolores. He wanted to study art. She would only finance — only tolerate — the study of law. He considered defiance: stay there in Las Palmas and be with Sisita. But his mother forced the situation and unwittingly gave him the idea.

Mama Dolores had decided a split was crucial. She wanted her last child to follow the path of her blessed brother in going to Central University in Madrid, to study Law. He would be far from Las Palmas, and especially far from Sisita. He was supposed to become a lawyer, build a career and forget all about his cousin.

Mama Dolores had said, 'Yes son, I see she is pretty on the outside. I see that you mean a lot to each other. And they have money too. But money is not everything. You have to set your sights higher. Don't forget, although it breaks my heart to say so; she's a bastard and it would do you well to remember that.'

The night before he was to leave for Madrid, Mama Dolores went to church as she always did, so he and Sisita stole the opportunity to meet. They talked it all out. They would soon be able to live together in Madrid. They imagined they had thought of everything. He had agreed to study Law, just as Mama Dolores had insisted, except that he would find a job and send Sisita the fare to take the earliest ship to Cádiz.

They would soon be together in Madrid. 'Enjoy these last

few days of your bachelorhood, but don't tell me anything about what you do. I don't want to know.' Likely, if he had known these were Sisita's last words to him he would never have acted the way he did when he got to Cádiz.

On his first night, he went with one of the women who lined the street just around the corner from his hotel. He remembers how his hand shook when turning the doorknob to the hotel bedroom. How everything seemed so intimate; her hand in his hand, her breath on his face, everything was new. He thought of Sisita the entire time.

The world is smaller and stranger than one can possibly imagine. At breakfast the next morning, he met his former teacher of Rhetoric and Poetics: Padre Teófilo Martínez y Escobar. The young priest was staying in the same hotel, and he was not wearing his vestments. Teófilo, not much older than Benito, was already confident in himself. He sat at the table across from Benito and smiled when Benito recognised him.

'Did you have a nice evening last night?' Padre Teófilo asked and grinned as Benito's face reddened.

Padre Teófilo was on his way to Madrid too. They agreed to take the train together to Sevilla. That night Padre Teófilo introduced Benito to strong Andalucían alcohol and the company of some women and men who liked to dance. They stayed an extra night in Sevilla. The next day, they took another train, to Córdoba this time. More drinking and dancing and another beautiful Andalucían experience. The following day they shared a quiet stagecoach to Madrid. Nowadays, he justifies himself by remembering his innocence, and what Sisita said about enjoying 'eligibility' for just a few more days.

He was two days late for the opening of the university. And he did not know it then but Sisita had already been dispatched on a ship bound for Cuba. Mama Dolores and her lawyer brother already had a wealthy match for Sisita in Cuba. It had been agreed to by Sisita's own mother who accompanied Sisita on the cruise ship. They told Sisita she was going on a vacation.

Benito has no idea what story they had told Sisita next. But he is sure his letters were never delivered. She was married off before the end of his second term at university and died nine months later whilst giving birth. Apart from Benito, only his sister Concha can measure the contorted feelings he holds for his mother.

He could speak of this anecdote, but the pain is never so dull as to suffer bringing it back into the light. So, he tells Tránsito and Alonso nothing of it. Only says, 'It's been a while since I went to Andalucía. I have an ache when I think of it.'

'Me too! I'm not sure what I miss most,' Tránsito says.

'My ears would claim the music, my eyes would claim the colours, my mind would claim the beaches, or mountains,' Alonso says, then steals a glimpse into the eyes of Tránsito before continuing. 'My heart would acclaim the company of other Andalucíans. But my stomach would say the food.'

Outside, the returning journalists can be heard. Their low grumbles and chattering in the street begins to drift up to the trio on the third floor. It disturbs the ambiance.

Alonso re-closes the windows and curtains. The apartment turns grey, disagreeable, and shadowy.

As their dialogue dies a natural death, Benito has an idea: 'I know a place with an excellent Andalucían cook. Why not continue our discussion there?'

MAN OF LETTERS
2 PLAZA COLÓN, MADRID
20 APRIL 1886

BENITO AND CONCHA sink back in their preferred seats. They light their own cigars. Pour their own brandy. Neither of them speaks as each listens to the gentle rising and falling rhythm of their own breaths. Eventually, Benito rests his cigar on the Mudejar ashtray on the table. He pushes the ashtray to one side and empties the contents of a large envelope on to a low table that either of them could touch with their slippered feet. A bundle of smaller envelopes tied together with red twine slips out.

Concha rests her cigar next to Benito's and leans forward to take the first envelope.

'When does he want them back?' she asks.

'José already has what he needs. They'll probably start printing them in the late editions.'

'How many did you say there are?' Concha is already scanning the letter she has removed from its envelope.

'Twenty-four. Delivered personally by Padre Cayetano Galeote on the eve of the shooting.'

'There's nothing here about why he did it,' Concha says.

'I'll tell you now, you can read the entire two dozen and still not know why,' Benito answered.

Concha hands the letter back to Benito. It is addressed to Rector Nicolás Vizcaíno.

Most Honourable Padre Don Nicolás Vizcaíno, Rector of the chapel of el Cristo de la Salud.

My very dear colleague, my character and dignity no longer permit me to tolerate the bizarre and unjustified conduct that you have practiced against me. I am obliged to point out that I am, like you, a priest, and somewhat longer serving. As someone who has, until today, earnestly fulfilled all my duties in the chapel and always been appreciated for that, I believe that some minimum level of fraternal respect is due to me.

If I have involuntarily committed a fault, surely that merits no more than a fraternal admonition on your part. Or should you consider the situation to be more serious then surely that should be deferred to a higher level within the church. Where, as a minimum, I would be permitted to respond to the charges against me and that way a reciprocal comprehension and appropriate resolution could be achieved. Awaiting your further orders, with affection,

Q.B.S.M. Padre Cayetano Galeote Cotilla.

Just as he did with José, hours before, Benito theatrically raises the letter to his nose and sniffs, as though expecting to find an olfactory trace of its writer. It is dated 9 December 1885, the same day Cayetano was dismissed from his duties at el Cristo de la Salud. It is brief, only two paragraphs long, yet Benito seems entranced by it.

'Why are you so taken with this letter?' Concha asks.

'It's not easy to explain, but it's as though in my head all these months I've been faintly hearing a murmur coming from the back of a cave,' Benito says, 'and now I have found the entrance and penetrated that cave deeper and deeper, until I can finally perceive the source and meaning of the sound.'

Concha has been around her brother for the creation of all his 'important characters.' There has often been such a break-through eureka moment.

'And so, you're hearing Maximiliano Rubín in these?'

'I am hearing someone reasonable, dignified, naive and, in the face of cold injustice, quite defenceless,' Benito says. 'That's who I'm hearing.'

He holds the letter up towards the nearby lamp. The paper more clearly reveals itself; greyish with variegated shades of near white. A bleaching process not well performed. He runs his fingers along the surface.

'Rough to the touch, and inexpensive,' he says.

'You do make me laugh when you pretend to be Chevalier Auguste Dupin,' Concha says. 'What did you expect you'd find, gilt edges?'

'I haven't finished,' he says. Then sniffs the letter: 'Too much chloride of lime!'

The paper is common and cheap, but in Benito's opinion the sentiments are rare and rich. He finds Cayetano's choice of words to be charming, and he appreciates the archaic tone of chivalric formality and evident fiscal paucity, all of which is transmitted in the absence of self-pity or self-consciousness.

'Doesn't he seem dignified and noble to you? He can't even bring himself to say why he was defrocked. What is this "fault" he has involuntary committed?'

'He doesn't seem like a lunatic, degenerate or otherwise. At least, not so far,' Concha says.

'Exactly! If I was a modern Sancho Panza, I might say, here's a pleasant fool, here's a contemporary Quixote. But I'm not Panza and so I'll only say, here's *my* Maximiliano Rubín.'

Benito sits far back into his armchair and puffs on his cigar. He looks content with his summation.

In response, Concha puffs her own cigar with even greater vigour than her brother.

'I suppose you've read them all?' she says.

'Of course. As Soon as José left. I stayed awake and read all twenty-four. Easy when there's no sleeping draught in the house!'

Concha puffs and blows a thick blanketed cloud in the direction of Benito's face.

Benito reaches into the pile and picks up another letter. This one is dated 17 January 1886 and also addressed to Rector Vizcaíno. He reads it aloud.

> *Purely by chance, I have learnt today that you held an Extraordinary General Meeting of the Council of the Congregation and you have repeated the same unfounded and disgusting accusations against me, in an attempt to have the Council ratify your decision of last week.*
>
> *Being absent, I was unable to defend my honour and dignity. This decision to dismiss me, taken due to your inexperience and poor counsel, is a matter for ecclesiastical discipline and should be referred to the offices of the bishop. I hope that you will respect this tradition and also cease from spreading disgusting lies.*

'I'll admit to some sympathy for your priest. But who acts out their disappointments in the way he has?' Concha says.

Benito is quick to spring to Cayetano's defence. 'Imagine you are in his situation,' he says. 'This injustice of unimaginable proportions has been perpetrated upon you and no one is listening to you. What do you expect you would do?'

'I'd become angry.'

'Correct. Now suppose you make a complaint. And still, no one listens to you. So, you become angrier. You take your complaint to the top. To the person your instincts assure you can be trusted as much as your own mother.'

'Who'd that be?' Concha asks, sounding intrigued.

'The bishop, of course,' Benito says, and he reaches to pick another letter out of the pile.

Excmo O Ilustrísimo Señor Bishop of Madrid Alcalá

I am Padre Cayetano Galeote Cotilla, residing at 61 Calle Mayor, 3rd floor. I was, until recently, charged with delivering the eleven o'clock Mass in the chapel of el Cristo de la Salud.

I respectfully expose the following facts to Your Excellency. I was verbally dismissed by the rector of the said chapel on 9 December 1885 and until now I have never received any written explanation for this dismissal. The rector stated that he only required the agreement of the congregation and that his decision was not subject to ratification by the offices of the diocese.

I was summarily dismissed in this manner and with only two reales pay, my dues for a single Mass. You will understand, Your Excellency, that my honour and personal dignity cannot permit such a thing, especially when it does not have the sanction of the Holy Office of the Bishop, nor have I received, in writing, some indication of what I am accused of.

I entreat your Excellency and place my confidence in your personal conscience, rectitude and sense of justice; which I am sure will not permit such an abuse to take place without being aware yourself of the minute details to justify such an action. May the grace of God protect you and grant you long life.

'Curious that he claims not to know why he was defrocked,' Concha says.

'Well, sister, now you're turning into Mister Poe's solver of mysteries too,' Benito says and rummages for another letter.' But to answer your question, yes, I also find that a little queer.'

Concha slowly opens and closes her mouth like a pike and creates circles of smoke between her and Benito.

Benito picks up the bunch of envelopes, apart from one, and holds them out: 'You can read them all at your leisure,' he says. 'Apparently, no one ever answered him. And as time passed, it's obvious he became desperate.'

Concha accepts the bunch of envelopes and extends her arm for the last of them.

He clings on to it. 'This one is the most interesting of them all, perhaps the saddest too.'

'How so?'

'The priest's frustration is evident, there may even be threats. But madness? I wouldn't say so.'

Concha curls and uncurls her finger, still insisting she wants that letter too. 'Let me see it.'

Benito continues to hold back the letter.

She tries to snatch it. Eventually, his fun over, he agrees to read it for her: It is dated 13 April 1886, five days before Cayetano would kill its addressee.

Excmo O Ilustrísimo Señor Bishop of Madrid Alcalá,

*I am compelled by circumstances to bother you again,
one last time. I say to you that I swear by the glory of
my mother that I am deeply ashamed to have agreed to
a truce on a matter so crucial to my honour.*

*So, I return to my request of before and demand due
reparation within 24 hours to the degree that I have
already expressed: Namely a full apology and material
damages at least to the amount of 18 reales and 56
duros which can be paid to Rector Vizcaíno or
whomever you believe appropriate.*

*If this is not forthcoming then don't doubt your Excel-
lency that I shall finally take action myself that will
deliver me from any debts I owe to recover the loss of
my family's name and reputation.*

Benito finally hands the letter over to Concha. She holds it in
her free hand.

'Perhaps not madness,' Concha says, 'but don't you find it
sinister to see him talk about taking action when you know
what happens next?'

'I'll concede a trace of premeditation there,' Benito says,
and has a puff on his own cigar. 'But there's not a whiff of
insanity.'

'And this swearing on the glory of his mother, isn't that a
bit last century?' Concha says?

'Not every mother is made of stone,' Benito says.

'Why must you always find yourself back there?' Concha
asks.

'You need to ask?' Benito says.

'Talk about something else then. This truce that he
regrets.'

'Another odd twist, you'll read it in the letters,' Benito

answers. 'Half way through this drama it seems they had had enough of Padre Cayetano causing a fuss. A priest called Gabino Sánchez intervenes. They offer Cayetano a position saying Mass in Chamberí diocese.'

'In Chamberí? Very swanky!'

'He accepts it but then something changes his mind. In the last letter you can see how much he regrets having agreed to a truce. He wants a full apology and material damages.'

'Material damages…you think he'd be happy to get his job back.'

Benito inhales deeply on his cigar and looks around his den, perched three-floors-high overlooking Plaza Colón. His gaze takes in their own material comforts: two enormous black-leather armchairs angled partly to the fire and partly to each other; that bust of Rossini; that easel; those charcoals; even those shelves weighed down by books. Everything here is ephemeral and will all one day be tipped to the wind.

'Can't you see, Concha? He can't be happy with just getting a position in one of the most genteel dioceses in the city. And the why of it is in plain sight, written in the man's own words — his family name and personal reputation are crucial to his honour. It is *dignity* which is critical to his existence. It is that which must be restored. Without that life has no value.'

GETTING CLOSER

Tuesday, 25 April 1865

That must be a marching drum I can hear in the distance. I tell you a civil war is on the way! Something is stirring. Even Cayetano has come to town.

All because, two weeks ago a Professor Castelar wrote an article critical of the queen's sale of state assets. Narváez told Castelar's boss, Rector Montalbán, he must dismiss Castelar. He would not do it. So Narváez fired both of them. Students protested. Then they killed ten students and wounded one hundred. Now, neurotic Narváez has decreed that every university professor in the country must take an oath of allegiance to the Spanish Monarchy and to the Catholic Church.

The professors are to take their oath during special private Masses. Cayetano is here for the special Mass being held in Málaga. I can tell you, he seems different, walking around in circles on the edge of his feet. And, for once, he has barely mentioned our brother Daniel.

I'll be on duty for their special Mass of the Malagueños Professors. Cayetano has asked a favour of me.

'Can your lot ensure the oath-taking really is private?'

'Why?' I asked.

'Who's to say what oath the professors might actually take?'

'Won't your bishop be under instructions?'

'Perhaps the bishop takes his instructions from a higher

source than Narváez,' Cayetano said and made the sign of the cross.

'What'll they swear allegiance to, then?' I asked.

'Whatever their conscience decides,' he said. 'The Church and something else no doubt, perhaps not the current monarch.'

Can you believe that? My brother's turning into a revolutionary!

After the Mass I'm going to visit Remedios. I can hardly wait to tell her. Cayetano says he will be calling on someone too. I would not be surprised if he went to visit cousin Tránsito. You remember her? The nun? The one I told you about?

Sunday, 25 June 1865

It's still not blossomed but the flower of a Spanish Republic is getting palpably closer. Tonto says when you pick the peasants pockets the end move is near. At the moment we're still getting paid, albeit in arrears.

Narváez is out of favour with the queen, again. Not because of the fiasco in April but because he could not dissuade General Prim and that lot from secretly plotting and preparing their next insurrection. This, despite his being buddies with them and even allowing them to enter Madrid. Narváez has not lived up to the queen's expectations. Mind you, no one here is crying for him, even if he is from Andalucía.

She has brought back Leopoldo O'Donnell. So now it is his turn to try and get Prim and his Progressive Party to give up their policy of non-participation in a Liberal and Union coalition government. Uncle Tonto says there is no chance of O'Donnell getting the Progressive's to participate in that. He says Prim will simply wait until the country collapses under the chaos of this financial crisis. Then he will swoop to the rescue, as the country's last-minute saviour.

'I remember you saying O'Donnell could be the one to knock heads and save the country.' I reminded Tonto.

'Yes, but things are worse now,' Tonto said. 'O'Donnell's made a bad mistake. He should just have told the queen he was not coming back.'

So, there you go: Narváez is out, O'Donnell is in but nobody can stop the revolution from happening. It is only a question of when. And who will get there first — the Democrats, the Progressives or maybe even the Carlistas, if the Church finally decides to get their guns out.

Saturday, 13 January 1866

The sense of expectation here is still manifest. General Prim and two regiments appeared in Villarejo de Salvanes — close enough to Madrid to cause panic. They surely thought the moment was now. But that was two weeks ago. O'Donnell's hand was forced. He had to send the Loyalist Army to meet Prim. But Prim and the nearly 700 men under his command just vanished.

They have been searching for Prim's phantoms. All they can find, following the trail from Villarejo, are cold empty beds, shrugging of shoulders and scratching of stubborn empty heads.

No one knows exactly where Prim's men are, but everyone believes they must be heading north to France. I would believe that too, except Cayetano showed up at my barracks this morning. Once again, a 'situation' needed my presence at home. We were barely out of the barracks when he spoke.

'Why are you looking so pensive, Alonso?'

'I've things on my mind,' I said.

'Such as?'

'What would you all do if I was not here? Suppose I got

myself posted who knows where, like Daniel?'

'Didn't you join the Civil Guard so you could have a permanent in-province posting?' Cayetano reminded me.

I didn't say what I was thinking and wondering lately: why is
it me that must solve all the problems here? I could be pro-
moted if I applied for postings outside of Andalucía. I could
be like Daniel. Be elusive, appear and disappear without
notice or explanation. Just tell the family they cannot know
where I am because their lives would be in danger.

'Do you suppose Daniel could leave his post at a moment's
notice to go to Vélez to sort out some domestic situation?' I
asked.

'You can ask him that yourself. He's there now,' Cayetano
said.

I never got to ask Daniel that question because the situation
awaiting me was far from a routine domestic problem.

I don't know where the other 674 went (Daniel wouldn't say),
but I do know where ten of the Calatrava Hussars are right
now. I've just finished leading them to the harbour at Vélez.
Who would possibly suspect a member of the Civil Guard?
There are fishing boats taking them to Portugal and from
there out to the Gran Canaries.

This was all mother's idea. Daniel had appeared and hidden
six of them on our property. Teresa had taken in two of them.
Cayetano disguised two as priests and smuggled them into his
lodgings at St Juan. Daniel had been ready to stay out in the
foothills with the Hussars but mother would have none of it.
'Do you want to be ambushed in your sleep and leave us all
with a bad conscience?' she argued with him.

Sunday, 21 January 1866

It seems they all made it safely to Portugal. General Prim's already delivered another proclamation out there, about how he will lose neither hope nor courage. He doesn't say much beyond that.

Tonto says Prim is being deliberately vague about whether he would have tried to constitute a Spanish Republic or not. All of this smoke is so he can confuse the Liberals. Meanwhile, the Portuguese Government has invited Prim to 'go elsewhere.' And, since the French said he is not welcome in France, he's gone to London. Our C.O. said he supposed that Prim and his troops would have been welcomed if they had come to Málaga. Little did he know!

LUNCH AT CASA LABRA

RESTAURANT CASA LABRA, CALLE TETUÁN, MADRID.

21 APRIL 1886

IT IS FASHIONABLE these days for some Madrilenians to buy their watches in Switzerland, but not Benito. This is not a matter of patriotism for him, more a hangover of grief and sentimentality. His pocket-watch is a Losada, a watch so often spoken of in endearing terms by his father. It is a thing of dreams: eighteen-carat gold and a fleur-de-lys patterned case. His father, Sebastian Pérez Macías never owned one, nor lived long enough to know that Benito had acquired one and had *In memoriam S. P. M.* inscribed on the inside of the back cover.

Benito consults it ten times inside two minutes. He has more than enough time to walk to his rendezvous. Nevertheless, he hails a carriage.

'Restaurant Casa Labra,' he says and climbs inside.

They speed down Paseo de Recolletos and in a few minutes are at Plaza Cibeles. Benito keeps the carriage window open. He is glad of the incoming air for its calming effect. He leans forward and taps the driver on the shoulder. 'Would you mind slowing down?' he asks. 'We can take the time to appreciate the scenery.'

'Your time. Your money,' the coachman answers and slows the horses.

Benito looks out along the Paseo del Prado at the green-painted iron chairs. Each placed under a shade-giving tree and each occupant idly making conversation with those around them. The shops are already closed when they reach Calle Alcalá but there are still plenty of people on the street. Benito surmises that they are probably all chattering about the assassination of the bishop. No doubt some of them will claim to have attended Mass or taken Communion in one of the several churches where the killer worked.

The carriage deposits Benito in Calle Tetuán at the door of Casa Labra. He enters and waits inside. He reads the menus, studies other diners, drums his fingers on a table. His guests are fashionably unpunctual. He starts to wonder whether they will be unfashionably perfidious and not show up. He reconsiders whether Casa Labra's *sub rosa* reputation — as a safe place for Socialist Party meetings — is more widely known than he imagined. He had only been thinking of the food the ambiance and especially the privacy when he invited them here. Now he wonders if Alonso will show up with a bunch of colleagues from the Civil Guard and 'inspect' the locale — or some other of their euphemisms — and proceed to wreck it.

Finally, a carriage arrives. Benito watches from the window as Alonso steps down and waits for Tránsito. Hopefully Alonso is, like Benito's army lieutenant brother Ignacio, a military man who had idea nor concern of the Casa Labra's story. Alonso holds open the restaurant door for Tránsito. Benito goes to greet them both.

'Excuse us. We had to shake off those odious reporters,' Tránsito says.

'I had to remind some it's not in their interest to harass an officer of the Civil Guard,' Alonso adds.

Benito kisses Tránsito's hand and shakes the hand of Alonso. They look around Casa Labra with its bare, stone walls, its functional zinc counter and its marble-topped tables placed around an L-shaped dining space.

'Pepe, these are the friends we spoke of,' Benito says to the head waiter.

The trio follow Pepe, towards the bricked back room.

'You know this place well, Señor Galdós?' Alonso asks.

'I've been coming here for almost ten years.'

'You'll know the menu then,' Tránsito says. 'Probably as well as Pablo Iglesias from the Socialist Worker's Party does,' she adds with an undertone of teasing in her voice.

'I'm going to take a house speciality,' Benito says. 'Cod with tomato.'

'And wine?' Alonso asks. 'A secret red you'd recommend?'

'House Rioja. Be difficult to improve upon those choices,' Benito says.

'Not so difficult if your friends are from Andalucía,' Pepe says. 'Maybe some *ajo blanco malagueña*, *ortiguillas* and a bottle of *tintalla rota* would be of interest?'

Tránsito and especially Alonso are precisely interested in Pepe's preferences. The privacy of the back room lends an ambiance of discreet relaxation. Soon their conversation flows even more freely than it did at Calle Mayor.

'What the Mother Superior said about Padre Cayetano being unlikely to last in his assignment has been on my mind a great deal since our last discussion. Were you suggesting they had already had it in mind to chase him from the Church?' Benito wastes no time in getting back to his agenda.

'Now I think about it, yes,' Tránsito replies. 'She never hid that. She more or less told him right to his face.'

'I didn't know that!' Alonso says.

'His first day, too! I went to deliver Madre Mariana's afternoon drink: warm milk and a spoonful of acacia honey. When I arrived, she was asking Gabino Sánchez to show Cayetano around the Royal Room.'

'The Royal Room? I can't imagine my brother showing

any enthusiasm for a tour around that,' Alonso splutters.

'He didn't. That was probably his first gaffe. She's proud of that room. It's part of everyone's initiation into El Convento de la Encarnación.'

Benito knows the room they are referring to but despite his inquiries has never been in there. That room is closed to the public. 'I heard most of the paintings are religious scenes substituting members of the last Royal Family,' says Benito.

'The narcissism of the art patron, masquerading as taste,' Alonso says.

Doña Durdal smiles mischievously, 'My favourites were the royal nieces represented as Saint Margaret and a nun.'

Benito feels a seed of complicity emerging between them. He signals Pepe to pour more wine and then raises his glass.

'To justice,' he says.

'And Cayetano,' Tránsito adds.

Alonso raises his glass. 'To my brother's health!' Then he leans across to whisper in Benito's ear, 'I've been thinking about your request. I'll assign my visiting rights this Sunday.'

Benito places his glass on the table, offers a handshake to Alonso. 'Thank you.'

'The following Sunday, I'll assign them to my cousin,' Alonso says and nods at Tránsito.

This declaration has a visibly positive effect on Tránsito's humour. She smiles at both of the others. An irrational hope-fulness has climbed out of the wine bottles. At that moment it feels as though the three of them are in this together.

'Who knows what little piece of information could turn out to be crucial for him,' Benito says. 'I'll not waste the visit.'

Benito's remark galvanises Tránsito. She sits back, straightens her shoulders, looks at the whitewashed brick walls in her line of vision, as though searching for little pieces of informa-tion. 'Her first words to him were — "Take a good look at the

Royal Room, today, Padre Cayetano." — And then she whispers to Gabino Sánchez — "Because he'll not have too many other occasions to appreciate it." — She didn't know Cayetano can lip-read.' Tránsito giggles.

'Which reminds me, it's best to speak a little more loudly than usual and don't look away when you're talking to him,' Alonso says.

'Or worry if he seems to be shouting at you,' Tránsito adds.

'I'll be sure to remember,' Benito reassures them.

'Especially, I wouldn't say too much about your work,' Alonso says. 'He was away for fifteen years and so he missed the fuss of your *Doña Perfecta* novel, but he'd be unlikely to be cooperative.'

'It's not really anti-Catholic, you know,' Benito says and tries to sound relaxed.

'I much preferred your previous material. I've got both series of the *National Episodes*. Very patriotic! You should do more of those.' Alonso scrapes vigorously with his spoon freeing the last morsel of *natillas de avellanas* from his plate.

'I might just do that,' Benito says and considers the money would be useful today.

'And if you need some military insights, I could help you there,' Alonso says.

'Alonso had ambitions of becoming a writer,' Tránsito says.

'Really?'

'Nothing serious,' Alonso says. 'Jottings, a few poems, things like that. Apart from me, no one's actually ever read anything I've written.'

'That's not true,' Tránsito says. 'Cayetano's read the journals.'

'Well, no one else apart from me and my brother,' Alonso corrects himself. He inhales deeply and tips back in his seat before bringing the front seat-legs down with a thud.

'I wasn't allowed to read them,' Tránsito says. 'They were all dusty and damp. And packed regimentally in a crusty old valise along with the pistol and other ancient artefacts and heirlooms.' She finishes her second glass of wine and instantly pours herself a third.

'I'm in admiration of you, Alonso. Bravo for maintaining your journal,' Benito says.

'I'd forgotten who I was until I re-read some of them,' Alonso says. 'And Cayetano did seem to take a pleasure in reading them.'

'He even started to write on them,' Tránsito says.

'You mentioned a pistol?' Benito say, and masks his surprise by reaching over to pour more wine for himself and Alonso.

'An old heirloom; it was in the valise with the rest of the mostly forgotten legacies,' Alonso says. 'I hadn't checked what was in there. Just brought it up like he'd asked.'

'He asked for a pistol?' Benito asks, his voice an octave higher.

'Of course not,' Alonso says. 'He asked for the valise because it held so many discarded objects of the past. My journals, Daniel's lavender oil distiller, those types of things. I had forgotten all about Daniel's pistol.'

'These journals of yours, could I read them?' Benito asks.

'What for?' Alonso replies.

'Maybe it could help.'

'He wasn't searching for anything in them,' Alonso says. 'It was just something to kill the time.'

'If you'd prefer I didn't read them,' Benito says. He restrains his enthusiasm at the possibility of gaining an unexpected insight into the background of the priest's earlier life.

'He always looked forward to your visits,' Tránsito says.

'He could hardly wait to talk about he'd read in your journals, about when you were boys.' Her eyebrows arch and she stares intensely at Alonso.

'Me too,' Alonso says, 'we were getting along much better up here than we had all those years ago in Vélez.'

Benito begins to think about his own family, especially his brothers. He cannot recall the last time he spoke with any of them. Even his favourite brother, Ignacio. In fact, if it was not for Concha acting as conduit he would have no news at all.

'I imagine that chance to reminisce meant a lot,' Benito says. 'Indeed, it's the epitome of normality to be nostalgic. That's something to remind the public of.'

'How can that help?' Tránsito asks.

'Juries are made up of "normal people" drawn from the public,' Benito says and taps the side of his nose.

As the trio leave Casa Labra, Benito reassures Alonso he would not judge his writing skills by the journal he wrote growing up in Vélez.

'Let me think about it,' Alonso says.

'Don't be so reluctant! There nothing incriminating in there, is there?' Tránsito jokes.

As Benito watches the duo walk away into the late afternoon he sees Tránsito slip her arm through Alonso's and Alonso make a little skip in his step before they disappear around a bend. Benito removes his handkerchief and blows his nose. He turns left towards Puerta del Sol from where he will wander up the Alcalá, and that is when he decides Maximiliano Rubín will be the youngest of the Rubín brothers and will keep a journal.

GENEROSITY OF RECTOR VIZCAÍNO
2 Plaza Colón, Madrid
22 April 1886

SHE STANDS UNCHAPERONED on Benito's doorstep. Her smile is a natural complement to the bright clothes she wears today — an ochre-coloured Cordobés hat trimmed with ribbon just a shade lighter, a dress somewhere between orange and ochre, and matching yellow shoes and bag. She is a sunbeam illuminating his stairwell.

'It's good to see you again, Tránsito.'

'You sound surprised.'

'I am, a little,' Benito says. He shrugs and opens the door fully. 'Come in.'

To his disappointment she lingers on the landing. She takes a step back and looks over his shoulder into the apartment. She purses her lips and seems to be silently assessing whatever she sees behind him — perhaps the floral wallpaper pattern and coordinated beige hallway carpet.

'This is an agreeable part of town.'

'We like it here,' he replies quietly.

She turns to peer down the staircase and look out through the full-length, rectangular window that dominates the stairwell. She bends her knees as if to get a better look. He does the same and they both look out over the plaza, above the treetops towards the recently erected, white-marble statue of Christopher Columbus. In one hand, the navigator holds a furled flag topped with a cross, his free arm points across the plaza to the Medinaceli Palace. She seems unaware her eyes are wide, startled looking. Her face has the look of an orphan outside a plush restaurant.

'We?' she says.

The effect the *barrio* has on her and her question unsettles him. For a moment he wants to disown the wealth which he does not possess, admit he is a lodger and his sister-in-law owns this apartment. But he notices a smile tweak the corner of Tránsito's mouth and a playfulness in her eyes too. 'Myself, and the three women I live with,' he says.

'Makes my arrangement seem banal,' she says, then rummages in her bag. 'Quite a menagerie you have.'

'If the first woman is your sister, the second is your brother's widow,' Benito says, 'and the third is the housekeeper, perhaps it's less of a menagerie than it appears.'

'If you say so.'

Tránsito finds what she has been foraging for in the depths of her handbag and removes a rectangular-shaped package. It is wrapped in dullish, bracken-coloured paper and tied with what could be shoelaces.

Benito knows what this package is. Yet it seems too small to hold ten years' worth of anyone's memories. 'I've been looking forward to seeing these,' he says. 'Please do come in.'

'I wouldn't want to keep you from your business.'

'This is my business, now.'

But she remains outside, seems reluctant to cross the threshold.

'Actually, there's something I'd like to show you,' he says. 'A matter I'd like your opinion on. I've been reading his letters.'

'Which letters would those be?' She answers as though barely interested, but her eyes betray her curiosity.

'Those he left at the offices of *El Correo* and other newspapers on the eve of the shooting. I believe you may know something of them.'

She steps over the threshold all traces of hesitation trickle away. Benito closes the door and begins to unlace and unwrap the package. Even before he has it fully open he can smell burnt papers, an odour of singed reminiscences.

'There's been a little incident,' she says whilst looking at her feet.

'What happened?'

Tránsito shrugs her shoulders then reaches into her handbag and takes out an envelope. 'Before I forget, your visitation letter's in here.'

'Can I offer you a coffee?'

'I'd prefer a tea, if that's all right.'

They settle in the salon. Catalina enters with a tray. As the young housekeeper turns to leave the room the two women manage a sideways glance at each other.

'What happened to the journals?' Benito asks again.

'She's very pretty,' Tránsito says.

'Her fiancé would certainly agree with you,' Benito says. He turns over the journals in his hands. Some pages feel damp to the touch. Other pages are a sad mix of limp and crisp. It is difficult to say what is here, what is gone.

'An accident,' Tránsito says.

'How?'

'We were being silly, burning other things: ambrotypes, letters, papers — those sorts of things. Alonso thought it would be better if they didn't get into the wrong hands.'

'So, he threw his journals on the fire?'

'It was my mistake. I didn't realise they were amongst other papers.'

'Pity,' Benito says.

'Many of the entries are still there,' Tránsito says. 'Alonso asks you to tell us if you find anything helpful.' She shakes her head as though she already knows there is nothing here of any use. 'She's engaged?'

'To my friend's son.'

Tránsito sips her tea, smiles over the top of her cup. Benito excuses himself and leaves to fetch the letters. When he returns, Tránsito appears cool. Her smile has evaporated.

'Alonso says you must burn the journals when you've finished with them.'

'Why would I burn them?'

'He feels it would probably be in Cayetano's interest.'

Benito throws up his arms in a gesture of non-comprehension. 'All right, if that's what he wants.'

Tránsito points to the letters: 'How did you come by those?'

'Cayetano delivered them to my friend's office. We believe he also delivered copies to other newspapers. Most likely they'll be published tomorrow unless the newspapers threw them out.'

Tránsito Durdal raises her hand to her mouth, 'Couldn't we do something to stop that?'

'You'd have to talk with your lawyer about that. Usually that's not possible, unless the court demands it. He must have wanted them published. Otherwise why deliver them to the newspapers?'

'He hasn't been thinking straight.'

'Do you know what's in them?' Benito asks.

'These past four months he's been constantly writing letters,' she says, 'then he'd rip them up and rewrite them. I never saw a person write so many letters.'

'But do you do know what's in them?' he repeats.

'Some of them, but he never showed any to me. I snooped when he was not around. In the beginning he was too proud to tell me he had been dismissed.'

Her recounting seems sincere. Even a casual reader of Padre Cayetano's letters could see his heavy burden of pride. It was omnipresent in those twenty-four letters.

'That's what I wanted to ask. I find it quite curious he never actually mentions why he was dismissed,' Benito says.

Her long slender hands push their way up her face and into her hair. Her fingers meet somewhere at the nape of her neck. She gathers up her hair and then softly drops it.

There is something in her gesture, look and tone. This could be how Fortunata — Maximiliano Rubín's adored nemesis — might respond. Benito wants to capture this. He is enchanted. He might immortalise them both: Cayetano and Tránsito, for Maximiliano and Fortunata.

'He doesn't have to mention anything,' she says. 'It's obvious even if it isn't true.'

'What isn't true?'

'Nicolás Vizcaíno's delusions.'

Benito recognises Vizcaíno as an addressee of several of Cayetano's petition letters. 'You know Rector Vizcaíno?'

'I wish I'd never laid eyes on him.'

'How do you know him?'

'From El Convento.'

'Vizcaíno served there, too?'

'No. He just came late at night when he thought no one would know. But he had to stop those late-night visits after Cayetano replaced Gabino Sánchez.'

'He came to visit Gabino Sánchez?'

'Certainly not!'

'Then who?'

'The chaplain! Always late at night, after dark, two hushed voices.'

'Why the secrecy?'

'None of us knew for certain what was going on. You never saw them. You only heard them dragging heavy boxes across the courtyard towards the chaplaincy.'

'So, how do you know either of those clandestine whisperers was Rector Vizcaíno?'

She sat back in her chair, tilted her head upwards, and closed her eyes.

'Well, later, after he dismissed Cayetano, he came to Calle Mayor searching for him. I recognised him straight away.'

'But you said you never saw him, he only visited in the dark.'

'I'm as curious as the next nun. I sneaked outside to spy. That's how I discovered it was small, cumbersome crates they were handling. We never saw those boxes in daylight. Once, I got close enough to hear the two of them whispering. I recognized the chaplain's voice but the other man had a distinctive accent.'

'In what way do you mean, distinctive?'

'Like yours is distinctive — you're obviously not from Madrid. At first, I thought he might have been Portuguese. But I recognised the accent: Galician. Then I heard the chaplain call him rector.'

'Do you know what they were doing shifting boxes around at night?'

'Hiding munitions,' she says without hesitation.

'So sure?'

'What do you think they were hiding? Holy water?'

Benito would not be surprised if the rector had been hiding munitions somewhere in the grounds of the local convent church. Who would be surprised if that was true? After the last Carlista attempt to provoke a revolution ten years ago, everyone has been waiting for the next one. There are still stashes of guns being found in monasteries and churches.

Benito chuckles to think that perhaps there are some now, still hidden, in El Convento.

'After Cayetano left, I suppose Rector Vizcaíno was free to restart his nocturnal visits to El Convento?'

'How would I know?' she says. 'I left there just a few months after Madre Mariana had arranged for Cayetano to be transferred to another parish.'

'Why did Rector Vizcaíno show up at Calle Mayor looking for Cayetano?'

'He came to lend him fifty duros.'

'Vizcaíno came to lend money to Cayetano, after having dismissed him?'

'Cayetano hadn't been dismissed at that moment,' she says. 'He had been asking for extra work. He and Vizcaíno had been having disagreements about that. Then those earthquakes hit Andalucía. Vizcaíno had heard there was a lot of damage in Vélez.'

'He has a caring side?' Benito says and grins.

'I doubt that. More a case of the guilt bothering him,' Tránsito says. Her face darkens. She seems to shrink in her seat.

Benito considers the situation: a loan of fifty duros; that is two hundred and fifty pesetas. Close to what Cayetano could earn in a month. 'Still, it seems generous of the rector,' he says.

'If a person is willing to show "gratitude" you wouldn't imagine how generous the rector said he could be,' Tránsito says spitting the word gratitude. The irony in her voice is both heavy and dark. She crosses her arms and rubs them with her hands, as though fighting back shivers.

'Do you mean what I think you do?' Benito asks.

'You know exactly what I mean. If I'd been willing to show a little more *gratitude*, then that interest-free loan would have become a gift.'

'I see,' Benito says and sighs heavily.

'It was my fault for being so stupid. I should never have invited him in to wait.'

'Why would you do that?'

'I thought he'd come to make things up with Cayetano. It didn't take him long to show he had other things on his mind.'

Benito senses her discomfort, but it is clear too she wants to talk, she needs to get this off her chest. 'You mustn't blame yourself,' he says.

'But I made the whole thing worse. I even said I was Cayetano's sister.'

'Why?'

'Otherwise he would have assumed the same thing you all do!'

'This is perhaps the wrong moment, and I apologise if I'm being too blunt, but what is your relationship with Cayetano?'

'I'm his landlady. Or I was.' Then, pain showing on her face she adds, 'and sometimes his ears too.'

'But you do see how it might compromise him to be living with a woman?'

'He's not the only priest in Madrid. What about you, Señor Galdós? Apparently, you live with three women and you don't seem to consider that compromising.'

It crosses Benito's mind to say that even if there are other priests in Madrid living with women, those women probably look like their own mothers — and are not young, beautiful, cousins once-removed.

'Why was he living with you, anyway?' Benito asks.

'He was broke. Because he was always sending his money to Vélez. After his friend Ferrándiz disappeared the landlord over in Calle de Reloj wanted to charge a market-rent.'

Benito is working out the chronology in his head.

'It was my idea that he come to live in Calle Mayor,' she says. 'We were careful not to tell anyone. They all thought he was still in Calle de Reloj.'

'Then when Vizcaíno heard about the earthquake he went searching for Cayetano in Calle de Reloj?' Benito asks.

'Correct, and that's where he found the landlord's wife, drunk as ever.'

'And she points him in your direction?'

'Worse! She actually says — "If you're looking for the deaf priest. He's living with his girlfriend. Try the 3rd floor at 61 Calle Mayor. And say hello from me". — Drunken dog!' Tránsito says and blushes.

A reminder for Benito: one should always take steps, be discreet, never leave traces. Certainly never, ever, give the drunkard wife of your ex-landlord your new address. In a way, the naïve Padre Cayetano is the architect of his own misfortune. Benito continues to work through the chronology, causes and consequences.

'I suppose Cayetano was angry with Rector Vizcaíno for his behaviour towards you?'

'I never told him about that.'

'Oh?' Benito is unable to hide his surprise.

'He'd probably have challenged Vizcaíno to a duel.' Tránsito sounds serious.

With every word she utters, the priest becomes more and more a Cervantian throwback, and in Benito's imagination more and more a perfect exemplar for an inner life of Maximiliano Rubín.

'Anyway, things didn't get far. I soon calmed Rector Vizcaíno down.'

'So, he was excited?' Benito asks and wonders why he chose that word.

'Of course,' she says, as though there could be no doubting the fact. 'But I asked him about his faith. I think that's when he remembered where he'd seen me before. He left saying if I changed my mind I knew where to look.'

'If you never told Padre Cayetano about this episode just why was there such a degree of animosity between them?' Benito asks. 'Why did the rector agitate to have Cayetano defrocked?'

Tránsito closes her eyes again and appears semi-exasperated, as though this should all be obvious to Benito. 'The first thing Rector Vizcaíno did, after leaving the fifty duros loan, was to go and see Madre Mariana at El Convento. And she did what she had been waiting to do.'

'Which was what?'

'Get her revenge on me for having left. She confirmed to Vizcaíno who I was. And that helped him get rid of Cayetano.'

'How can you be so sure of that?' Benito asks.

'I had a visit from one of the nuns.'

'I see.'

'Without my stupidity they could never have dismissed him,' Tránsito says, her sorrow welling in her eyes.

BOOK THREE

The heart of a mother is a deep abyss at the bottom of which you will always find forgiveness.

Honoré de Balzac
(*La Femme de Trente Ans, Comédie Humaine*)

PART I

MEDDLING IN THE SOUL
Masonic Lodge, 10 Calle Alcalá, Madrid
23 April 1886

APPREHENSION RUNS THROUGH Benito's hollow legs. He is on his way to an encounter. His spidery limbs, skittery and insubstantial, leave little impression on the soft terrain. He tentatively crosses the thin strip of flower bedding that bisects the opposite sides of the wide and bright Calle Alcalá. He dodges horses and coaches as he negotiates the double-crossing. With his body intact, and without provoking any coachman's ire, he arrives on the opposite side of the Alcalá; and thinks: *one day some clever civil servant will create a scheme for safely crossing this wide street.*

He carries on down the street to get to the meeting place. His state of anxiety is not evoked purely through a concern to preserve his body parts, for he has crossed Calle Alcalá a million times. Nor is it around the courtesies of punctuality, for he will arrive early at the meeting place. It is around the uncertainty of his relationship with Luis Simarro.

Their exchange could be critical if he is to have any hope of saving Cayetano. He told José that meeting Luis was a priority. Then he told Concha he was nearly sure Luis would have forgotten all about him. Afterwards he kissed her hand for having taken the initiative to ignore him and just arrange the appointment anyway. Now he is less grateful.

She has sent him out with all of the misplaced encouragement a mismatched pugilist might receive: 'assert yourself, don't hide in the corner, remember what's at stake for you and for your new friend,' were her words. But the closer he gets to the Lodge, the more need he has to recall Concha's accompanying rousing parley, as a motivation to continue.

'What's at stake here?' Concha asked him.

'Whether free will or determinism becomes the dominant view in Spain?'

She rolled her eyes in their sockets. 'No, that's not it. Lives! Reputations! These are the stakes. Goodness, Benito, if you prattle on about free will and determinism, he'll swat you away with a swarm of fleas in your ear. And don't mention your bloody thesis novel.'

She even suggested accompanying him. She probably thought he would never get so far as the Lodge. But she would have been mistaken because here he is now, outside the Nest, wondering exactly how she managed to get the meeting, and regretting that she did.

If he had been in the same spot, this time yesterday, he would have seen how Concha did it. Her plan perfected, her arms swinging, and her lips closed, she had waited in Calle Alcalá until she saw Luis leave the Eagle's Nest and then she *accidentally* bumped into him.

Concha perfectly understood which inclinations of Luis' she should appeal to. If he wanted to have the political influence essential for his big, modern ideas, how convenient was it then that his former friend had just been asked, by Sagasta himself, to sit in the Congress of Deputies?

'Our dear Congress of Deputies, open as always to *cunerismo*,' Simarro had replied.

'Would you have turned it down?' Concha asked.

'Probably not.'

'You think it might it be useful for you to have a friend in there, or not?' she asked.

'Wouldn't hurt,' Simarro agreed.

Outside the Nest, Benito grasps the door handle conceived for a giant. He pushes the enormous, yet oddly anonymous, door. It lumbers open, and he steps into a silent, impeccably well-ordered alleyway. With the solidity of its own might and lumbering weight, the door swings back and snuffs out the noisy clamour and insistence of the street. Bedlam has been banished! He carries on up the alleyway, drifts to his right and enters a granite building through an unlocked entrance. He is immediately confronted by a porter who stands behind a wooden counter in the vestibule.

Benito takes a moment to look the other man in the face.

Several years have passed. Who can say if this is the same porter from the old premises, before the enforced closure? This one has an equally enormous, similar, square-shaped head, but he seems too young. Benito watches him move out from behind his station. His eyes are drawn to the porter's large fists that surreptitiously clench as though crushing a walnut. He decides this is not the same fellow. This porter is charmless and distinctly less welcoming. Benito points to the black door with its shiny brass plate: *Eagle's Nest Lounge.*

'I've an appointment with Doctor Simarro.'

'Wait here.'

Boxer-like knuckles rap out a code on the door. Tappity-tap, tap, tap, tap. The porter waits a few seconds before repeating the rap pattern, then he steps inside.

Forgetting where he is, Benito steps forward too.

'Stay here.' The porter gestures, his thick index finger pointing to a spot a metre from the lounge door.

The door closes. Benito jauntily takes a step forward. The tip of his nose is almost touching the brass nameplate but he can overhear nothing. He takes a half-step back and admires the embossed inscription: *Vnionem Tollerantiam Prosperitatem Ordo Ab Chao devs Mevmqve Ivs* — Fraternity, Tolerance and Prosperity, Order out of Chaos, God, and my Rights: the brotherhood's values.

This nameplate seems to Benito to be bolder, less tentative and more assured than those he remembers. Brass-cleaning vapours irritate his nostrils and eyes. Thus, he dutifully steps back to his assigned spot.

He wondered whether Luis also had become a lapsed member. However, it was Luis' idea to meet here. He looks again at the note Concha passed to him — *I'd be delighted to meet again with Brother Benito*, Luis had written.

As if by itself, the door opens slowly. The porter is out of view, discretely holding it open from behind. Luis stands on the threshold beckoning Benito in to the Nest and already extending both hands.

Although he has rehearsed it, Benito first fumbles then recovers the handshake. Luis laughs. They release hands. The porter slips out from behind the door, closing it as he leaves, and Luis shows Benito into an otherwise empty Nest.

'Benito! How long's it been?'

'Let me think,' Benito says. 'That would be just before you quit Santa Isabel's.'

Luis chuckles and says, 'You think it was me that quit Leganés?' He leads Benito across the lounge to some armchairs positioned on either side of an unlit fire. Luis choses the one closest to some doors that open into a walled garden.

Benito takes the matching armchair facing Luis and absorbs the news. 'Didn't you leave Santa Isabel's to take up advanced alienist studies in Paris?'

'Depends how you look at it.'

'But you've been in Paris all this time,' Benito says. 'I'm

certain of that.'

'Only because of the backwardness there was here in Spain. To tell the truth, it was Santa Isabel's who barred *me* from carrying out my research.'

'I didn't know that.'

'Those simpletons!' Despite the intervening years, Luis' annoyance seems fresh. 'Would you like to know what those Neanderthals accused me of?'

'If you'd like to tell.'

Luis remains seated in his armchair but leans forward and picks up a poker. He begins prodding energetically at the unlit logs piled up in the hearth.

'They said I was meddling.' He stabs the logs, twice in quick succession.

'Meddling?'

'Every time I anatomised a brain, they said I had "meddled in the hallowed site of the soul." Claimed I'd committed a terrible sin and would go to hell.'

A smirk crosses Benito's face.

Luis' face darkens. The poker is stuck in a half-rotten log. He pulls it free and several large logs tumble out of the hearth. The logs cannot escape, because with speed and precision, Luis jumps out of his seat and applies the sole of his boot, pushing them back into place.

'And so, you did go to hell,' Benito says.

'What?'

'Some Spaniards think there's little difference between Paris and purgatory,' Benito answers.

Luis laughs so hard his shoulders shake. 'I don't remember you being this funny before.'

'You always bring out the best in me. Anyway, what does it matter what a pack of priests said about your methods?'

'Here it matters a lot what they say,' Luis answers. 'You

know that better than many.'

'But in Paris, it is science that prevails. Right?'

Luis puts the poker down and smiles.

'You're quite right,' he says, 'at least the scientific method is respected there.'

'But religion is too. There's some mutual accommodation, I understand?'

'If you ask me, we should have followed the French example a little more rigorously,' Luis says quietly.

'In what way?'

Luis looks around the room, as though searching for an eavesdropper and lowers his voice further. 'I'm not just talking about putting the Church in its place but the monarchy too.'

'We tried that,' Benito reminds Luis, 'but our consciences got in the way.'

'North of the Bidosa they don't have qualms about their consciences,' Luis says, 'nor any difficulty in reconciling themselves to their past.'

'Seems like paradise not purgatory,' Benito says. 'You must have felt quite at home.'

'Let's compare revolutions. If you're going to go to the bother of having one then do it like the French. Have no mercy, off with the heads. Don't wait for a hundred more years to pass and then go at it half-hearted like us Spaniards.'

'I'll give you that,' Benito says. 'They did get to it a century before us.'

'And when you do finally do it don't torture yourselves over it either.'

As always was the way, Luis is warm on the topic of forms of government. They are chatting as though they have not been separated for almost six years, as though nothing negative ever happened between them. This is going better than

Benito had hoped for. He wishes he had come to see Luis sooner. Good, too, that they are so quickly on to the subject of politics, one of the diminishing confluences in their rivers of thinking.

'They seem ahead of us in this area as in so many others,' Benito says.

'That's because their institutions serve the people. Not the other way around, like here.'

'But things are changing here, too,' Benito says.

'Their Church understands it place. As for a monarchy, well you can't lead a restoration movement if you're a corpse, can you?' Luis ripples at his own wit but suddenly his smile leaves his face.

It might be the mention of a corpse — caressed or not — that causes this quietness to fall between the two men. Their bonhomie has burst. In the way of their mutual goodwill there remains an unburied, unspoken of, cadaver named Mercedes. Perhaps Benito has been a little hasty in supposing this will go well.

PUENTES' MISSION
Bishop's Palace, Calle Torrijos, Córdoba
25 September 1868

BISHOP JUAN ALFONSO can be seen peering out through the tall, heavily curtained, ground floor windows. Padre Gabino Sánchez is running across the gardens. He rarely runs anywhere. As he enters the bishop's palace, doors slam, and his feet slap in carpet-less corridors, and soon he is standing in front of Bishop Juan Alfonso, who holds a glass of port in each fist.

'It's true then?'

'What is?' Bishop Juan Alfonso answers.

'Narciso's here?' a hard-breathing Gabino Sánchez asks.

'Take a seat, Padre. I think even if it is early, you'll appreciate this little tonic.'

'Not right now,' Gabino Sánchez says, and he places the port on the table next to him.

'Then perhaps you'd prefer a glass of water?' Bishop Juan Alfonso asks and pours some from a jug into a glass.

Gabino Sánchez accepts the water and drinks it straight away.

'He's on a special mission for us,' Bishop Juan Alfonso says.

'For who?'

'Bishop Monzón Puente agreed to send him up.'

'Lord protect him. On a mission for *two* Bishops! What mission?'

'The less you know, Padre, the less you'll be in danger.'

'I'd like to see him.'

'He's not here, right now. Left before dawn.'

'So, when can I see him?'

'Don't worry, he'll be back by lunch-time.' Bishop Juan Alfonso sounds sure of himself.

'You know they're bound to come around here on some ruse,' Gabino Sánchez says.

'Who are?'

'Either of them, it doesn't matter who gets here first,' Gabino Sánchez says. 'Or what pretext they use. Whether it's the rebels or the Isabellinos they'll come snooping for weapons.'

'Well, thanks to Narciso, there'll be nothing to find.' A laugh leaks across Bishop Juan Alfonso face.

'I should have guessed,' Gabino Sánchez says. 'You have him out there now, burying bombs and bullets.'

'We can hardly move them ourselves, can we?' Bishop Juan Alfonso says. 'They're watching us.'

'Not us, you! They're watching you.'

'You think they're fooled by you?'

Gabino Sánchez does not answer. But the truth is he does think they are all fooled by him. Why not? This is why they came to Andalucía in the first place. And why he organised a position for Narciso, as Secretary to Bishop Monzón Puente, down in Granada. And why he was careful to wait a few months before he too moved into the region. He has not been here in Córdoba for so long. He was sure they would be safe here. And they have been safe here, until now.

'Why him?' Gabino Sánchez asks.

'Do you know anyone better?'

'If something happens to him you'll have me to answer to.'

'That's exactly what Bishop Monzón Puente said too. You should relax a little.'

'Relax? Any cleric they find in the vicinity of an arsenal is a dead cleric,' Gabino Sánchez says.

'Don't worry. He knows the risks.'

'Where'd you send him?'

'Somewhere they'd never look, if you must know.'

'Like where?'

'Like the crypt at Nuestra Señora de los Angeles at Alcolea,' Bishop Juan Alfonso answers.

'That's in the middle of nowhere!'

'Exactly.'

'Even Narciso will never find it,' Gabino Sánchez says.

'He knows where it is. He's been there on his last two visits to Córdoba.'

'So now what do we do?'

'We wait,' Bishop Juan Alfonso says. 'As well trained as you have him, he'll be back by lunch time.'

'You bastard!' Gabino Sánchez whispers and then drinks the port in one sweep.

'How perspicacious of you,' Juan Alfonso says. 'Indeed, our Church has many bastards within it, including me. We've been a haven for centuries.' He gives a little nod of the head to salute Gabino Sánchez' speedy despatch of the port. 'Perhaps you'll take a refill?'

Gabino Sánchez is proud to have passed on all that he himself had been taught by the Jesuits who preceded him: veterans who trained alongside his own uncle and who honed their skills during the War of Independence. They were indefatigable. The French occupiers could testify to the ferocity of their fight, their readiness to die for the cause.

Those Jesuits were trained to be invisible too. They knew the terrain and understood, instinctively, how to move around it undetected. The regular Spanish soldiers of the day called them the 'Creeping Jesuits'. A name which continues. The French infantry could hardly spot them until they appeared in front of them with bayonets fixed, crucifixes flying.

But things were simpler. There was a single easily identifiable enemy: the French occupier and he had skin as pink as the flower of the Judas tree, he wore another colour of uniform and barely understood any of the languages spoken in Spain. It was not at all like today, with Spaniard fighting Spaniard.

Gabino Sánchez wonders whether the moment has finally arrived. Will it be the rebels or Isabellinos who will catch them? And who might they make disappear first — him or Narciso? He hopes they execute him before Narciso. He could never suffer the pain of seeing this near son of his go before he goes himself. Or perhaps he is being too pessimistic. Why would *they* even be suspected of anything?

'All right, I'll take that refill.'

'I thought you might.'

Gabino Sánchez sips his second drink of the morning and reflects on Bishop Juan Alfonso's confidence. Yes, he has passed everything of the arts of concealment to his beloved Narciso. He has always believed Narciso is the best he has ever trained, even from the early days at Sigüenza. Bishop Monzón Puente agrees. He said, that Narciso is a chameleon and has become even more effective down here in Andalucía. Narciso goes where he wants, when he wants, and is whomever he wants to be.

'Even his own brother would not recognize him,' Bishop Juan Alfonso says as if reading Gabino Sánchez' thoughts.

Should he need to defend himself or get in touch, Narciso has become an expert on weapons use, as well as how to intercept, reinstate and operate telegraph communications.

He can gather information and disseminate disinformation. He is as capable as any of the other sides' Information Officers. Gabino Sánchez knows they have done a good job by Narciso and so maybe Bishop Juan Alfonso's confidence is not misplaced. But sometimes survival needs more than desire and competence.

'The Lord will keep an eye on your protégé,' Bishop Juan Alfonso says.

'For all our sakes, I hope you're right.'

'Narciso's only problem is he does not fear death. He is like those veterans who believed God was on their side. Those ardent men of faith who might even have welcomed death.'

'That's not true!' Gabino Sánchez says. 'Narciso is not fanatical. And hiding Juan Alfonso's stash is hardly a worthy cause to die for.' He pauses and puts down his glass of port. He reaches low with his right hand to touch the crucifix lying on his midriff. His fingers follow it up until he feels the cord attached to his neck, and with his thumb and index finger, he slowly turns the beads threaded there. He closes his eyes and thinks of Narciso: *Where is he?*

By eleven o'clock, his work finished, Narciso — still dressed in civilian clothes — is in the woods skirting Rio Guadalquivir. He is only two kilometres away from Nuestra Señora when he comes across an army unit. They are perhaps two hundred metres away from him and are methodical in their searching.

He dismounts, holds his horse close and backs into the path. He studies the soldiers. Interested to see which direction they will take. A sensation of foreboding invades. He is certain they must have heard about the arsenal; sure they are now rummaging for rifles. He stands still on the path. He

cannot prevent his horse from whinnying. No point in trying
to go back the way he came. No point either in trying to
outrun them.

He sees them spot him. He smiles at them. There are
maybe a dozen of them, all of them armed. One, a dark, thin
reed of a man, moves forward, coming in his direction. Unable to tell whether they are army turned republican or still
loyal to the queen, he takes the initiative.

'You'll find no boar around these parts,' he tells the slender
soldier.

'It's not boar we're looking for.'

'What are you looking for, then?'

The commanding officer intervenes. He is tall, strong-
looking, a bearded man in his thirties. He speaks as though he
is from here in Andalucía. 'We're looking for soldiers. Perhaps you've seen them?'

'We're searching for royalist scum!' the reedy man interrupts. 'Begging your pardon, sir,' he adds and looks on the
verge of risking saying more, except a look from his bearded
officer cuts him in his stride.

'I've seen nothing,' Narciso says and walks past the reedy
soldier. This close, the man looks even thinner. It seems an
effort for him to carry his rifle. Narciso continues walking his
horse towards the others. He joins them, then passes around
some cigarettes. They are grateful and seem uninterested in
who he is.

Soon he has them talking. He hears the story from the
Andalucían in charge. They were sent up just a few days
before the Cádiz pronouncement, and are billeted in the
barracks at Córdoba. It turns out that within their battalion
there was a group of soldiers still loyal to the queen. Early
this morning those men followed their consciences and
slipped away. Now this Andalucían officer and the rest are on

their tracks.

'Loyalists you say. Likely they'll follow the river north-wards,' Narciso says. 'If they take a left at Andujar then track the North Star it will lead them all the way to Madrid.'

The soldiers register the possibility. Narciso puts his arm into his saddlebag. He removes some ham and wine he had been planning to share with Gabino Sánchez over at the seminary in San Pelagio. He shares it with the soldiers. He knows all the rebel songs — as well as he knows the Isabelli-nos songs — and he joins them in their rebel repertoire. He laughs at all their jokes and even tells some himself. 'Why is Queen Isabel angry with Francisco this week?'

'I don't know,' they chorus.

'She found him in bed with her boyfriend!' He guffaws as much as they do.

They like his variation on the old homosexual prince joke. They start telling their own versions. From there they move on to politics, and then religion. Soon they are telling the gags about the priests: the only profession where everyone else can call a man 'father' except for his own children — who must only call him 'uncle'.

Later, when they have smoked and drunk a little more, it is the commanding officer who suggests that it is time for them to move on. They move away towards the river. He watches them go and promises them: yes, he will take care and if he sees any sign of those deserters he'll ride like the wind right back to his new friends and let them know.

He sits up in the saddle, moves out of the cover of the woods and starts a gallop. He continues to head away from Nuestra Señora. He is only gone a few minutes when he starts to fret about the arsenal and is convinced that the soldiers will stumble upon the church. If that happens, they will likely want to cross over and search it. He is not concentrating on where he is going.

With all the noise he is making, it is not long before he finds himself riding into the midst of the so-called 'loyalist deserters' from Córdoba. There are more of them than he understood. They do not need to introduce themselves; they are still wearing their uniforms. They seem angry.

'You must be the patriots I heard about,' he says as they bring his horse to a standstill and gather in a circle around him.

'Patriots?'

'Well, the others I met had a different name for you, but let's say that not every Spaniard would share their point of view,' he tells them and immediately regrets it.

'So, you've seen 'em?' a huge man with a blood-red face, and Madrid accent, says. He seems to be their leader.

'Those rebels. They mean to kill you,' Narciso tells them.

'Not if we do a little killing first,' Red Face says.

'If you hurry, perhaps you can catch them.' Narciso's keenness to get free of the loyalists might betray him.

'Which way do you suppose we might go?'

'I could draw you a map,' he suggests. 'You can get behind them and give them a little surprise.'

'Why would you do that, exactly?'

'Because as Secretary of the A. C. P. M.,' Narciso says, 'it's my responsibility.'

'The Secretary of what?'

'The Andalucían Commission for the Preservation of the Monarchy,' he tells them. 'Most people just call me the Secretary.'

They seem to have swallowed the illusion. But they are not satisfied with just a map. They make him accompany them. A rifle at his back, his hands tied. He watches as the loyalists ambush their former comrades near the bridge at Alcolea. In the shoot-out, the loyalists kill three and scatter the rest. He sees the scattered republican soldiers riding as fast as they can back across the bridge. The loyalists withdraw back into the woods and take Narciso with them. All the while he wonders what they might do with him. Soon, he hears them discussing it.

'Flip a coin and just get on with it,' Red Face says.

Narciso waits and thinks about all the times he's pulled that same trick. Once, when some of the Church lands in Sigüenza were seized, he got up in the middle of the night and went all over town pasting banners on every prominent wall asking the townsfolk to take action. He signed them as *SCALO* — the *Secretary of the Commission into abuses by Local Officials*. At first everyone believed his posters were authentic, that there really was a Commission into abuses. It got everyone talking, and although it was eventually realized there was no such commission, the fuss was enough to ensure the local parish had no more trouble from the particular official who'd seized the church lands. And a proper SCALO was established in place of his invention.

The next time Narciso tried the tactic was in Granada. He slipped a note under the door of the Chief of Police and denounced the time and place of a secret meeting of republicans. He signed that note the 'Secretary of the Commission for the Protection of the Constitution.' They all laughed at that one. Especially when the absolutionist-loving police showed up and arrested masked republican members of their own extended families.

'Anyone got a coin?' Red Face asks.

Narciso thinks about his mentor, Gabino Sánchez, who by now is likely to have heard from Bishop Juan Alfonso about the mission, and who has probably posted himself or some seminarians outside the walls of the seminary, likely scanning the horizon, and pacing.

'Tails.' Narciso hears one of them say.

He hopes for a single shot to the heart, not in the face or head like they usually do. He wants to be recognisable for his family. He closes his eyes, imagines that someone from the seminary, maybe Gabino Sánchez himself, will eventually come out this way, discover his body and take it back. As Red Face approaches with another soldier — both with pistols in their hands — these are the thoughts that fill his head, and the pictures that flood his inner vision.

'Get off the horse,' Red Face tells Narciso.

Narciso slips off. The second soldier takes the reins, leads the horse away.

'Turn around and start walking,' Red Face orders.

Narciso takes one, two, three, four, ten paces, before he hears what he is expecting.

'Stop! On your knees. Start praying.'

He does as he is told. He prays hard. The bullet does not come. He waits for it. Closes his eyes, repeats his prayer under his breath. Listens. Voices whisper. Then there is a hush. Two clicks, then, nothing. Birds sing, and crickets clack.

After ten minutes Narciso is dizzy with fear. He does not turn around, he is sprawled into the ground as flat as he can, pushing into his own urine. He never fully understands why the loyalists spare him.

NO ENEMIES

Thursday, 3 May 1866

They have me accompanying them to the bank now. It was my uncle Tonto's idea. Personally, he has no money in there to withdraw but my father had a little of his own, and a mission for me.

'Tap your pistol pocket,' Uncle Tonto said when we stood in line.

'Tap you own,' I answered.

Father knew there would be no need for the pistol. He knows and trusts the bank manager. Nevertheless, they still had to argue to have him accept banknotes instead of coins.

'You can keep your paper,' he insisted. 'With the coins at least there's some value in the metal.'

He says he had been thinking for weeks about withdrawing the little amount of savings he had. It was the Duke's factor that tipped him off. When he came to collect this quarter's rent, he gave a little whisper to Father. The factor hears everything at the Duke's place. It seems the Duke was worried about his investments, especially in the joint-stock banks. The Duke withdrew everything.

'Always follow the gentry,' the factor told Father.

Father immediately wrote to Daniel and informed him. Daniel took ages to write back. But when his letter was received there was no doubt in his mind — withdraw every bean, and when the banks go bust this time, at least our generation of Galeotes don't have to do the same Daniel told him and sent a power of attorney.

So, father had me standing in the background and looking authoritative. My curiosity got the better of me. 'How much money did you say Daniel has?' I whispered.

'A tidy sum, in both accounts.'

'Both accounts?'

'He keeps an account for Cayetano.'

I learnt that not only does Daniel bank right here in Málaga, but he transfers some money to our father for essentials and squirrels money away for Cayetano.

It seems Daniel has heard of a doctor in France who knows how to cure the kind of deafness Cayetano has. I had no idea. You think you know a person.

Saturday, 23 June 1866

Have you ever heard of the San Gil barracks in Madrid? You soon will, because yesterday two artillery regiments launched an uprising there. They're already saying that Prim was behind it. No one knows for sure yet.

Now must be the time.

Sunday, 24 June 1866

Some more news about yesterday: the pro-government army lost 80 men and had 400 wounded. Unsurprisingly, some of their officers were killed by their own soldiers. A crazy, half-French soldier called Blas Pierrard Alcedar led the insurgents. He managed to get away, but the insurgents had about 200 men wounded and another 700 taken prisoner. There will be blood to flow when they take their revenge. Prim's been seen in France. Who knows where Daniel is?

Sunday, 8 July 1866

Yesterday Leopoldo O'Donnell announced there will be no more cases of court martial. It's over, but too late for the seventy-six artillerymen who were executed this past two weeks.

Tuesday, 10 July 1866

The tides rush in and rush out again. Some more news from your insane motherland: the queen has dismissed O'Donnell today. Without a hint of irony, she said his regime was 'too brutal' especially over the court martials. Of course, that is all true, albeit this was not her tune two weeks ago when she gave O'Donnell her agreement to organise them. I suppose now his hands are bloody she does not need him anymore.

P.S. Now that she has dismissed O'Donnell, she's appointed Narváez, again.

Tuesday, 5 November 1867

O'Donnell is dead. And we're all nervous. She no longer wanted him in Spain when he was alive, but now Queen Isabel has requested O'Donnell's body be sent back from Biarritz.

She says that O'Donnell is a hero and he deserves a state funeral. Mother says it's more likely the queen just wants to be sure that O'Donnell is really dead. It was only him and Narváez that could protect her. Now she only has Narváez.

Meanwhile, Serrano is making hay. He says that all O'Donnell talked about during his illness this past twelve weeks was how he was looking forward to finally joining his older brother. The O'Donnell brothers might have been on separate sides, but it was still, after all, a single coin: one side a constitutional monarchy, the other side an absolutionist monarchy.

Mother always maintained both the O'Donnell brothers picked the wrong side. 'Still rotten Bourbons whichever one you pick,' she said.

Now Leopoldo O'Donnell is dead, it is Serrano who is Chief of the Liberal Union. But Serrano needs to be careful, because if he keeps on talking the way he has been, he is likely to find himself being banished to Biarritz like O'Donnell was.

Thursday, 23 April 1868

Ramón Narváez is dead. Finally, when he was dying, it seems the Andalucían humour in him resurfaced. They asked him if he was ready to forgive all of his enemies.

'I have no enemies,' he said. 'I had them all shot.'

Only the queen will miss Narváez. Who will protect her now?

THE WRONG DIRECTION

THE MOOD IN the Nest has changed. Benito wonders now if it was a mistake to follow Concha's advice. Yes, he and Luis had so much in common: the Ateneo, the Lodge, Kraussism and Positivism, some common friends too. And let's not forget they both were asked to leave their respective universities — albeit for different reasons, but still — another 'club' they share. And that eight years age difference between them never seemed a problem, they had got along easily. Except, Concha has forgotten one thing; Mercedes wrote to Benito.

Plenty others have written to Benito. He has said yes to dozens of requests to join his *tertulias*. Benito has always been generous with his time, whether with aspiring writers, or curious critics — male or female. It makes no difference to him. But it is undeniable the females who write to him always outnumber the males by quite a margin. Hardly his fault, though, is it? Mercedes was no different to the rest. She was awestruck. She was impressed. She asked for 'one-on-one' tuition. She was not the first to ask for that either.

Despite a certain haughty plainness, Benito was flattered by the persistence of this noticeably young lady: younger even than her boyfriend, Luis Simarro. However, apart from the threat of fracturing an embryonic friendship with Luis, Benito also considered her to have limited talent as an aspiring writer. He discouraged her. He suggested the school of realism was not aligned to her talent as writer. Whereas the school of romantic writing was still thriving, elsewhere. He would give her an introduction. The romantic writers met monthly and had some very interesting creative exercises. But she was insistent, adamant even, that her interests lay elsewhere.

It was José who blabbed — with alert ears nearby — he wondered aloud why Benito could not see what anyone else could see: that Mercedes was just *possibly* more interested in carnal rather than creative games. 'I'd have more fun caressing a corpse,' Benito had replied, and regretted the anti-poetry of his words immediately.

That gossip galloped to Luis. Then Mercedes stopped coming to the *tertulias*. A fact which suited everyone. But Benito's embryonic friendship with Luis moved to its current phase of polite enmity; a fact which really suits no one.

'Perhaps we prefer our revolutions to be calmer affairs,' Benito says. 'Less rolling heads and royal corpses.'

'Seriously, Benito? It was us Latins and our friends the Greeks who invented melodrama. We love the tumult as much as the French,' Luis answers.

'Not all of us. Some are more cut out for it than others,' Benito says. He remembers the younger Luis — unperturbed, cocky and melodramatic on the floor of the Ateneo — this upstart, already an accomplished orator, all swinging arms and emphatic gestures.

This was how Benito had first noticed Luis. He would have liked to have been that way too: unrestrained and fearless with an audience. He has tried, but it never comes naturally. 'We do share the French passion for republican values: liberty, equality, fraternity,' Benito says. 'This could even be Spain's national motto.'

'Talking of fraternity,' Luis says, 'I know you've not been back to the Lodge in years.'

'Do you know how things have been here?' Benito asks. 'I'll tell you. Not very safe. There are moments to be centre stage, like now, perhaps. And moments to slip into the wings.' Benito looks around the lounge, avoiding eye contact. He has been wondering when Luis would arrive at that particular question. He has already thought about how he might answer it. He might tell Luis the truth, that his dalliance with Freemasonry was more a realist writer's experiment than a life choice.

'What you say is true,' Luis says. 'The Brotherhood has had some difficulties here.'

'Less easy to rub shoulders with the Church in Spain than in France,' Benito says. And he remembers another oath he made along with Luis. In his mind, an oath just as important as the Masonic one because it was sworn in the company of Paco Giner de los Rios — their mutual sponsor in both fraternities. 'You know, Luis, it's not that I don't feel the same principles as before.'

'Meaning?'

'Progressive ideas, the advance of truth, those will always remain at the core of my values, and yours too, unless you've changed since you've been away.'

'But letting your membership lapse,' Luis says, 'tut, tut, tut. Very disappointing.'

'At least we're both still members of the Kraussist Society,' Benito says.

Luis crosses his legs and furrows his brow.

'Giner de los Rios would be happy to see us here,' Benito says. 'Us chatting away like the old times.'

At this mention of Giner de los Rios, Luis uncrosses his legs and lets out a long sigh, perhaps pining for those days.

Benito looks over Luis' shoulder towards a large painting of St John the Evangelist hanging on the wall above. He tilts his head as though studying it.

'How is he?' Luis finally asks.

Luis' question pulls Benito away from staring at the painting of St John.

'How is who?' Benito asks.

'Giner de Los Rios.'

'You know he was reinstated in his university chair?'

'Proof again, we're moving in the right direction,' Luis says.

'He's keeping his options open. Kept his own school going. Just in case he gets dismissed again.'

'I really must go and see him, now I'm home.'

'He's bound to want to know everything you've been doing in Paris.'

'He'll never believe the turn things have taken there,' Luis says.

'What turn?'

'It's quite unbelievable. You think Charcot would know better. After all, he's so proud of them having had a university chair in histology since sixty-two,' Luis says.

Benito shakes his head and waits to hear what tragic turn of affairs the French have taken. But Luis is not forthcoming, instead he appears to be sniffing the air.

'Are you suggesting that France in no longer the place where a person can meddle in the hallowed site of the soul without reproach?' Benito asks.

Luis roars with laughter and slaps his own thighs.

'You're too amusing!' Luis says. 'You really have changed, Benito.'

'I was being serious.'

This comment starts Luis off again in raucous laughter and

thigh slapping. 'In the eleven years they have had their histology laboratory in Salpêtrière, in all of that time of anatomising lunatics' brains, they never found a single trace of the human soul.' Luis laughs harder at his own remark. This time he reaches over and slaps Benito's thighs.

Benito laughs along. He imagines Luis up there in his Paris laboratory sharing this same joke with his fellow scientists. He supposes this is not the moment to let Luis know that lately he has found himself wondering about this idea of the soul. Not contemplating whether such a thing actually exists, more reflecting on why, if it were to exist, any particular institution should claim jurisdiction over it. 'What have you been doing since you returned?'

'Getting organised. Setting up my practice. Arranging for my laboratory to be transported here. Then there's this opportunity that's come up,' Luis says, 'but, I believe you know all about that, don't you?'

Benito feels his cheeks burn. 'You're referring to the case of the priest, Galeote?'

'I've been appointed state expert,' Luis says.

'Well, there's no one better qualified.'

'Do you smell that?' Luis asks and sits back in his chair sniffing vigorously.

'Smell what.'

'Open snuffbox,' Luis says and points to a small silver box, the size of pocket bible, sitting on the mantlepiece. 'Cuban and Turkish mix. I'm sure of it.'

'I'm still a cigar man, myself.' Benito says.

'The assassin priest; this is a great opportunity. The perfect occasion for us to mobilise ourselves.'

'Mobilise? Us?'

'Come on, Benito. You can't have missed the big debate taking place right under your nose,' Luis says, and his arms are swinging, emphasising his words, as always was the case.

'Does free will exist or not?' Benito says. 'Yes, I'm aware. I've tried to contribute in my own way.'

'The sides are lining up.' Luis answers. 'On one side are the old bearded fools in cassocks. Those who insist that Spain remains ossified.'

'And on the other side?'

Luis is back on his feet, striding back and forth, poker in his hand, like a baton. 'Us! All those willing to meddle. Determined to carry Spain, on our shoulders, into the future.'

Benito is pleased to be beardless today, and he has not worn a cassock since Mama Dolores forced him to serve as an altar boy in Las Palmas.

'So, what do you say?' Luis asks.

Benito considers saying he has been following this debate extremely closely. Constant headlines, such as *Parliament Split on Whether Lunacy is an Illness*, being so common now. 'I say these are important times for the country.'

'And that's why I needed to be here,' Luis says.

He considers asking if Luis has read *Lo Prohibido*. Has he seen the criticism it received? It was, after all, a subliminal manifesto for *their* degenerate view of the world. Everyone hated it — hah — what does he think of that? But that would mean getting into his plans for the coda.

'Interesting that Paris is not the place to be any more,' Benito says.

'They're headed backwards into speculative fairy stories. It's not proper science.'

'I recall you saying we were on the coat-tails of the French,' Benito says.

'Not any more,' Luis says. 'In five years, Spain will be the new reference for alienist studies. Fitting too, in my opinion, given we were the first country to introduce lunatic asylums.'

'What happened up there?' Benito asks.

'It's all mysticism and voodoo,' Luis says. 'Even my old bosses have performed a *volte-face*.'

'I suppose it's time we had our turn,' Benito says, and warms to the task of flattery. 'And I think I know who'll be at the centre of it.'

'Think again!' Luis says. 'If you believe Charcot, it certainly won't be me. He said I was not open to the possibilities of studying the unconscious mind,'

'Studying the unconscious,' Benito says. 'Very interesting, how's that done?'

'The right question! It's hocus-pocus. They've all been taken in by this young Freud fellow,' Luis says.

'A German?' Benito asks.

'An Austrian,' Luis answers. 'And he's taking them entirely in the wrong direction.'

RUNNING NAKED

Friday, 18 September 1868

Now must be the time for our Glorious Revolution!

This morning General Juan Prim stepped off a boat and strolled ashore in Cádiz. It was afternoon before the news reached our barracks in Málaga. General Prim swept ashore in the full light of day. No waiting for cover of darkness this time. There was even a welcome party right there on the quay waiting for him.

The biggest news is that he was welcomed into Cádiz by Vice-Admiral Juan Bautista Topete.

Who would have imagined that? Even the navy has come out against the queen. And this time it was Topete who made the proclamation. He demanded universal suffrage, freedom of the press, abolition of the death penalty, abolition of conscription and the formation of a constituent assembly, and if all this was not enough, he even ordered a 21-gun salute for Prim.

Topete says that the first job for the new Constituent Assembly will be the establishment of a new constitution. Does that seem like the Spanish navy to you? It feels like we're in France, not Spain. People are saying that Topete spent so much time with O'Donnell that O'Donnell must have hypnotised him, or maybe O'Donnell's ghost is in touch with him.

General Serrano has returned from exile too. He has arrived

in Cádiz on the heels of General Prim. You have to credit it: this time everything seems so well organised. The navy and the army are coordinated. Even our lot has followed suit, at least here in Andalucía we have. Our unit was probably the first of the Civil Guard units in Andalucía to declare for the revolutionary forces.

Now, we'll be keeping the peace by gaoling government and royalist sympathisers!

I understand why we've been having extra manoeuvres these past few months: doubling of the guard on armoury duties, new security procedures checking rifles and munitions. In or out. Some officers must have known all along, our C.O., for sure. I don't believe I've seen him look this happy.

Every telegraph outpost in Andalucía has been commandeered by those sympathetic to the Revolutionary Army or has had its wires cut. All the same, we hear that the news of Prim's arrival in Cádiz has already reached Madrid.

You can hardly imagine the frenzy here in Málaga. A mixture of festival, with a twist of fear, and apprehension about what is to come next.

Mother's always said she would run naked down Vélez high street if the navy ever came out against the queen. I have just come back from Vélez and she is euphoric with the news. Father seems apprehensive.

I didn't have the time to visit Cayetano. Mother will have to go St Juan's in Vélez to tell him the news. He is so uninterested though; he'll likely just shake his head and mutter something incomprehensible in Latin or code which only Daniel might understand.

Talking of Daniel, no one knows where his regiment is. We suppose if General Prim has come out of exile and arrived in Andalucía then Daniel cannot be too far away either.

Monday, 21 September 1868

Well, it happened. Mother ran naked through Vélez. She was not alone — Father accompanied her. They did it in the early hours of this morning. They believe they were unseen by human eyes. We can only hope they are right about that.

Meanwhile, General Serrano is neither naked nor unseen. His troops are well-dressed and armed to the teeth. Along with other army units based in Cádiz, who also declared immediately in favour of the revolutionary movement, they have formed a column and are headed north to Sevilla, then Córdoba, then all the way up to Madrid.

We hear that Topete has placed the entire navy at the disposal of the revolutionary Junta, and General Prim is already sailing up the coast with the fleet raising an army *en route*. Perhaps Daniel is sailing north with General Prim. Or is part of the army marching north from Cádiz. Father says that he hopes Mother will not see the navy's active support as another excuse for more runs around Vélez.

We hear there is some resistance. There is a rumour that General Pavia is leading a column down from Madrid to meet General Serrano. Let's hope that this time Pavia gets what he deserves, and Prime Minister Gonzalez Bravo too finds out it is the country's destiny to become a Republic.

Wednesday, 23 September 1868

I have had to go home again. Mother sent for me, this time because of Gabriel. All the revolutionary excitement and weather storms are too much for him. I found him hiding under his bed. He says that both Daniel and Cayetano visited him last night while he was sleeping.

Mother told me she went to see Cayetano and he had not left St Juan's, and still no one knows where Daniel is. I managed to calm Gabriel but the sight of our father, who has been spending most of today oiling his rifle and patrolling the road outside our home, has made him nervous.

Father is sixty-seven years old and acts as though he has been waiting for this day all his life. His rifle is pathetic, probably as old as he is, and it looks as if it weighs just as much as he does. We hope he does not have to fire it because if it actually goes off the recoil would probably kill him.

HAUPTBESCHÄFTIGUNG
MASONIC LODGE, 10 CALLE ALCALÁ, MADRID
23 APRIL 1886

LUIS IS SEATED, his face rueful, his poker safely replaced in its rightful resting place. It seems a young Austrian has usurped Luis' enchantment of Charcot and Ranvier. The young fellow was already translating Charcot's lectures and running to Berlin and Vienna to spread the news that the great man was ready to tackle the *unconscious*, when Luis got the urge to come home.

'So that's their hauptbeschäftigung right now?' Benito asks the man who ought to know.

'Yes, that's their pre-occupation,' Luis answers. 'You'd never believe the half-baked ideas this young fellow, Freud, has. But he's managed to convince the lot of them. They've gone all mystical.'

'Perhaps he's onto something? Not everything is always observable, or measurable.'

'What happened to you whilst I was gone? You'd never have uttered such nonsense in the past.'

'Does the idea of an unconscious mind necessarily mean turning towards mysticism?' Benito asks.

'In my book it does.'

Luis has been specific to say in his book. That probably means he will entertain there are other 'books'. Even if there cannot be a restoration of a friendship here. Perhaps this need not become all out enmity.

'Well, at least you're back.' Benito says. 'That must mean the country is open to progress.'

'Open, but needs convincing,' Luis says. 'Plenty of educated people here still believe if they discretely make a donation to the nearest bishop they are taking out some form of anti-lunacy protection.'

'You mean should the need arise then said bishop will arrange an admission to an asylum: for their kin?'

'Precisely.'

'And there are others who even say they can predict it,' Benito says.

'I wondered when you'd get around to degeneration theory,' Luis says. His eyes blaze. 'Certainly, we can predict it, but that's not the point.'

They have inevitably arrived at their zenith of friction; when their beliefs, being so diametrically in opposition, must guide them to a zone of departure. Benito knows it and he supposes Luis knows it too. 'What is the point, then?'

'What we do with this capacity to predict,' Luis answers. 'Build asylums, prisons, or something in between?'

Luis is talking of what he calls the 'greatest social problem for alienists today.' It begins with a chain of questions: starting with the most benevolent — What to do with the insane already amongst us? How to protect us and them? How to identify and treat them? — Ending with the more malevolent questions. Such as how to prevent the arrival of the insane not yet amongst us? And this is where the ex-friends reach their ideological fork in the woods.

Benito understands that Cayetano is only a necessary rung in a ladder of possibilities for Luis. But if Cayetano's case can help Luis gain more influence would that necessarily be bad? Even if his ideas on heredity are so wrong? He stares at Luis, sees that the fire in his eyes has dimmed. 'How did you find my dear sister, since you last saw her?'

'Chatty,' Luis says and grins knowingly.

Benito coughs, moves position on his seat, takes another sweeping look of St John.

'Model asylums would be just be the start,' Luis says.

'Well, the existing facilities are hardly "models" of anything one would wish to replicate.'

'That's because those running the current facilities have no scientific ideas on treatment.'

'How could you change things?' Benito asks.

'We'd start with professional training,' Luis says. He is on his feet again, poker less but arms punctuating.

'And you think you "meddlers" can make those changes?' Benito smiles.

'I tell you, we're on the cusp of something. The science is there. A little push for the funding could make the difference.'

Benito reflects on Luis's assertion that the science of heredity is solid. Another version of himself might have the temerity to say: *Well, actually the science is disputable!* Might even ask if Luis dare look inside his own family precedents. If he did would he find stigmata there? But that particular version of Benito is not present in the Nest: 'Can we expect to see the Luis of old?'

'I doubt that.'

'You were on a mission then too,' Benito reminds him.

'I'm not so naïve now.'

'Escuder says you have become our most respected alienist. People will listen to you.'

'I'm flattered.'

'For instance, on what you have to say about this priest Cayetano Galeote.'

'What's your interest in him? Is he another of your liberal crusades?'

'Amongst other things, I'm hoping to help the family.'

'You mean you're writing a response to a poorly penned character in your last novel?' Luis says, mischief in his eyes.

'So, you've heard about that?'

'You can thank Escuder.'

If Benito is alarmed at Escuder it is not because of his indiscretion, but because he seems to be leaning more and more in the direction of the degeneracy disciples. However, at least Escuder is charming at the *tertulias*. Benito will forgive him. For another thing he has an enormous library packed with books on alienist research that Benito may access whenever he wishes.

'You found me out, Luis,' Benito says, and he smiles. 'I'm also gathering material for another character who will display the same trope of hereditary madness.'

'Trope? Is that how you view it?'

'I mean this will be another character who *seems* to be a degenerate, to use your term.'

'Like the priest is?'

'I don't know. You tell me,' Benito says.

'He hears voices. He has the right family antecedents,' Luis says. 'He has an epileptic brother who goes to town with his shoes on the wrong feet. And an uncle, on his mother's side, who is hanging out like a balcony, whom they even call uncle "Tonto". You can imagine the rest of them.'

'Really?' Benito says. 'I've been meeting with his brother who's a Captain in the Civil Guard. I'm hearing stories of excellent scholars, gifted artists in the family.'

'I didn't say the entire family are degenerate.'

'Which ones then? The priest with his old-fashioned principles, who is uncommonly generous, and rather artless? But are those all signs of degeneracy?'

Annoyance clouds Luis' face. His lips become thinner. He

locks his hands together and pushes them away. 'I'm not saying the priest is just thinking aloud.' Luis rotates his hands and loudly cracks his fingers. 'He claims to actually hear voices in his head, which are not his own.'

'I hear voices all the time, don't you?' Benito asks.

'Take my word,' Luis insists. 'And it's no surprise when you look at his family tree.'

'Come on, I've heard what the alienists are saying. It's simply not credible: Baudelaire, Socrates and Darwin. All of them degenerates? Who next?'

'Those are not our claims. We don't all follow the genius equals degenerate school.'

'I'm pleased to hear that. Especially since, as far as I know, none of their brains have ever been anatomised.'

'But the priest's extended family is prone to cases of *dementia praecox*,' Luis says.

'According to whom?'

'Escuder.'

'It's not even a week and you're telling me Escuder's already been to Vélez and studied the family?' Benito's exasperation is unbridled.

'He's still there. He knows what to look for.'

'Escuder looks for what he knows and that's not at all the same thing.'

'Why does it matter so much to you? Your character is fictional. He can be whatever you want him to be. Act whatever way you want him to act. But the priest is real, and he's a killer.'

Now both men are on their feet. Both standing behind their chairs, both pressing their hands down on the backrests.

Luis face looks calmer than Benito's feels.

'You wouldn't deny he's a madman?' Luis says. 'He just assassinated the bishop. Which sane man would do a thing like that?'

'But who's to say this is all *inevitable*?' Benito asks. 'All of it entirely predictable because of who his grandparents and great-grandparents were?'

'Does that matter to you if we conclude he's a degenerate or not?' Luis asks.

'It might.' Benito says. 'But it likely matters more to him.'

'In which case you'd have a cause to crusade for.' Luis' tone holds a mixture of irony and resignation.

'If I'm crusading perhaps it's not simply opportunism.'

'This case can help us get the funds to further our research, help us find ways to treat madness,' Luis says.

'But you'd just using him.'

Luis' eyebrows raise. 'And what about you? What practical help could your crusade do for him?'

'Maybe keep his neck out of the garrotte.'

'More likely place it firmly in it,' Luis says with a grunt.

'Have you considered there might be something else beyond organs and tissues?'

'You've turned religious?'

'I'm not talking about a holy spirit or a soul,' Benito says. 'But imagine something else does exist. Something that can't be seen by dissecting the brain.'

'Such as?'

'An inner world, just as important as the external one.'

'You already know what I think about that,' Luis says. 'Let's suppose this unconscious world exists. What can I do about that? How will I ever recognise who has a diseased unconscious? What treatment could I conceive of and test that might cure them?' Luis enumerates these problems on his fingers.

The force and logic of Luis' argument overwhelms Benito. He shrugs his shoulders and returns to his seat.

Luis follows suit. 'You're a writer, Benito. You're supposed to imagine all sorts of fantasies, but not me.'

'Is it so fantastic to imagine there's something beyond determinism?' Benito asks.

'I'll leave that to you and people like you,' Luis says and his tone is undiluted irony. 'You should think about going to Paris. Maybe I can ask Charcot to introduce this fellow Freud to you?'

'You feel we'd get along?'

'He seems to be on to something that may interest you.'

'No, thanks. I'm planning a visit nearer home.'

'Plaza Moncloa, I'm sure. Then you'll have to admit you are in the presence of a madman,' Luis says.

'We'll see,' Benito answers.

'You might as well look for truffles in the sea as hope to find a trace of free will in cell eleven,' Luis says, and he seems bursting to laugh.

'Until you've anatomised his brain, we'll never know. Will we?'

'I don't discount it. He's as clear a case of degeneracy as I can judge. That fact might save his neck, not your crusade to undermine heredity,' Luis says.

THE SHRIMP THAT FALLS ASLEEP
25 Calle Don Pedro, Madrid.
24 April 1886

BENITO LOWERS HIMSELF from the carriage. He has no wish to alert the exotic pet dogs of the *barrio's* wealthy natives, so he reaches into the carriage for the flowers before quietly closing the door. The only noises he hears in this lonely *barrio* are the sounds of his own heartbeat, and the coach-driver rubbing the hindquarters of Estrella — a half-breed from Jerez de la Frontera.

He whispers, 'If I'm not here in fifteen minutes come back for me around midnight.' He walks to the corner of Calle Don Pedro and Calle de Baijén. Nothing has changed since the last time he strolled around here, as though he was the spectre of Mesonero Romanos — the *barrio* boasts the same grand pretensions, and the same lonely, grey tranquillity prevails in the same cold brick buildings.

The note in his pocket from José Ferreras is typically cryptic: *She's a widow on the search, bound to fall for your charms. Address, 25 Calle Don Pedro, third floor. Ask her about her grandfather, the inquisitor, tell her about yours if you like, and remember all she tells you.* This is José Ferreras' price for passing him her address. He has to sniff for gossip about his host's grandfather even if that has nothing to do with why he has gone there.

José has not said what he would do with the information, but Benito assumes it would be included in another special editorial on Spain's inability to separate Church and State.

As he approaches number twenty-five, a cloud of self-doubt descends. He peers up at the illuminated windows on either side of the street and wonders whether visiting Madre Mariana's sister will make any difference to Cayetano's prospects. The optimism he felt when the idea first presented itself suddenly ebbs away from him. But he thinks again of the Mother Superior's contemptuous refusal to meet him and his irritation with how she treated him, and this delivers the motivation to carry on.

He sent Paco out to purchase and deliver flowers and a note asking to meet. Paco was surprised when Señora Felicé turned the card over immediately and wrote in a looping, expressive script: *Dear Señor Galdós, I would be delighted to meet you. Indeed, I would be disappointed if you did not join me for dinner tonight. Come at nine-thirty.*

The entrance to Señora Felicé's apartment block has monumental double-doors, wide enough to drive a carriage straight through. Benito stands in front of them and in the dim light is trying to locate the bell-chain when one of the doors opens. A tiny, tousled-haired lady emerges, her smallness exaggerated by the immensity of the door.

'I have an appointment with Señora Felicé.'

'I know,' she answers, then grins and winks. 'Third floor on the left. Go quietly, please.'

He tiptoes up the three-flights of stairs. His route is lit by soporific lamplight that falls on the plush carpet which is elegantly flanked on the margins by highly polished wood. He checks the Losada: it is nine-twenty in the evening. He is early. He proceeds slowly and pauses a moment at each landing on the way up. He notes the names on the doors. This is the kind of detail that will impress Ferreras: Ground floor, Señor Francisco Otero González; First floor, Señora Higinia Balaguer; Second floor, Señorita Juana Petra García and

Señor Demetrio José García. He listens at each door, but it is as quiet as a mortuary. The only sounds are the tiny lady's grunts as she slides the well-oiled, heavy bolts of the front door back into position. Soon, that distant noise is gone too.

At nine-thirty precisely, Benito steps onto the third-floor landing. The door to the apartment is colossal. It is lacquered in black and decorated by a polished brass nameplate: *Señora Felicé La de Bringas*. He could be visiting the Bank of Spain instead of a wealthy widow. He tugs on the oversized door-pull and somewhere in the distance a bell chimes more brightly than he expects.

A lady of perfect elegance opens the door. The sight of her poised form and scent of her perfumed presence reaches his eyes and nose at the same moment. In the subdued light, Benito confirms Paco's description for himself. Good looking is not an overstatement. He hands her the bouquet of pink carnations. Their clove-like scent permeates the air and fuses with her perfume to create a combination impossible to ignore.

She leans forward to sample the fragrance and Benito feels a warm current cross his cheeks. 'Thank you, Señor Galdós. Two bouquets from you in a single day, I'm honoured.'

'The privilege is mine, Señora Felicé,' Benito says, and he kisses her hand. 'Thank you, for agreeing to meet me.'

They enter a long hallway. She takes his cape and leads him to a salon. Judging by the piano, the small harp and variety of brass instruments, Benito presumes it also serves as a music room. She points to a comfortable-looking armchair: 'Take a seat, Señor Galdós.'

Whilst she fusses over the flowers, Benito sits.

'Excuse my manners.' She walks to a drinks trolley placed in front of an open window, says; 'I've given my housekeeper the evening off. Please feel free to open the verdeo, whilst I put these in a vase.'

Benito opens and pours. They will be alone. They can talk freely. He is more hopeful than before. Tonight, he may learn something of use in his crusade for Cayetano. As he pours, he tries to recall whom it is this lady reminds him of. There is a vague something about her. It is as though he is looking through ice-frosted windowpanes. On the other side is an outline of someone familiar. It is not Felicé La de Bringas' physical appearance, per se, but her poise and mannerisms.

She re-emerges and stands in the doorway. Benito acknowledges her smile. He notices again her close-fitted, elegant, blue dress. According to Ferreras, she is in her early sixties. Benito has difficulty believing that now. Her feline grace seems timeless. Her high cheekbones are set in skin which is as taut and smooth as a forty year old, and her teeth are marble-white.

It occurs to Benito that Ferreras has made an error. This lady would never be short of admirers. She is surely more hunted than huntress. The phrase *she'd never be short of admirers* comes to mind and it unlocks a labyrinth of associations. Mama Dolores often used that expression when referring to Sisita's mother, Adriana Tate.

That's it!

This is whom Señora Felicé reminds Benito of. She has the lively spirit and elegance of Adriana Tate — undoubtedly Sisita would have had that too had she lived. Mama Dolores had plenty of less pretty phrases for Adriana Tate, 'scheming' and 'loose' amongst them.

He recalls Mama Dolores' rage when she learnt that Carmen, his eldest sister, would marry Adriana's son, José Hermenegildo. She blamed herself. How could she have been so blind to Carmen's trysts with José Hermenegildo?

But worse was to come, when his eldest brother, Domingo,

compounded the treason by marrying Adriana Tate's daughter, Magdalena. Mama Dolores' apoplexy almost did for her. But she was determined the rest of her litter would do better. Torn between her adoration for her brother, José-María, and her dislike of this rich and pretty widow that had 'ensnared' him, she restrained herself from chasing the hussy off the island.

However, with Carmen and Domingo now married into the Tate family, she could only grimace when Adriana Tate laughed and said at the second wedding: 'We're family now, Dolores, and family has to stick together.'

They all saw how much pleasure Adriana took in watching Mama Dolores' fury coursing in her veins. It became so palpable that Mama Dolores' face and neck contorted as she tried to hold the rage inside her. And they all supposed that one day Mama Dolores would exact revenge.

Benito's reminiscences are interrupted by the mellifluous voice of Señora Felicé: 'Flowers taken care of and supper ready in twenty minutes,' she says. 'Perhaps you can tell me what was so urgent.'

'As I mentioned, your sister does not accept visitors. Or at least she wouldn't accept a visit from me,' Benito says.

Señora Felicé smiles the kind of smile a doting mother might after her child has said something amusing. She puts her hand to her chest in mock deflation.

'Oh, and here I was, thinking you wanted to meet me.'

Paco has told Benito that Señora Felicé is good humoured. Now he witnesses for himself the good-natured openness in her smile. 'In fact, I've been looking forward all day to meeting you,' Benito says.

'It's her loss, Señor Galdós. I'm always happy to meet someone new. Yesterday's stranger is today's friend. That's a maxim of mine.'

'I like that maxim,' Benito says. 'It suits you.'

'So serious already? Anyway, it's pleasant to spend time in good company,' she says. 'Especially when it's such an erudite specimen.' She tips her glass to meets his.

Benito knows she is utterly in charge of the situation and confident of her own appeal. There is a vivacity in her manner such that even if she calls him a 'specimen' it is evident she is not being condescending. A gentle breeze of Madrilenian dusk wafts in through the open window, bringing with it the earthy wet scent of the River Manzanares. 'I'm engaged in some research and needed to talk to your sister, but she refused to meet.'

Señora Felicé serves gazpacho, and says, 'Are you surprised, Señor Galdós? You've made quite an enemy of the Church these past years.'

'I've heard those things they say about me. It's exaggerated. I come from a good Catholic family myself, you know. My grandfather was Secretary to the Office of the Inquisition, in Gran Canaria.' José would be happy if he could see how Benito has slipped this into their conversation. Benito, though, is feeling cheap.

'Mine too,' she says. 'Not in Gran Canaria, of course.'

Benito continues, 'Mine was on the maternal side. He passed all his fervour to my mother.'

Señora Felicé hesitates for a moment and appears to be weighing up the significance of what Benito has revealed. It is as though she has something important to say but cannot disclose what is.

'And so?' she says.

'You'd think that would be enough for your sister — me, a good Catholic.'

A cold draft darts in through the open window and causes

a nearby lamp to flicker. Looming black shadows whirl around the wall, and the temperature seems to drop a degree. There is a silence. She leaves her seat and shuts the window. The draft is extinguished and she turns up a lamp. She smiles at Benito. The shadows on the wall dissolve.

'Excuse me,' she says and disappears.

She returns in a moment with another trolley.

'Wouldn't you agree some of your writing has been a touch controversial?' she says.

'You're thinking of *Doña Perfecta*.'

'I read somewhere you based her on your mother?'

Benito has always suspected Adriana Tate of having let this idea slip in society, as a form of revenge on Mama Dolores. He says nothing of that. He has another more neutral and well-practiced retort. 'That character is a composite of individuals. My aim is only to render realism.'

'I've no interest either way. As my sister would tell you the Catholic Church will be here long after you and I are dust.'

'And as I was saying, your sister won't tell me anything,' Benito says.

'What was it you wanted to discuss with her?'

'I was hoping we might talk about Padre Cayetano Galeote.'

'The priest who killed our dear bishop last Sunday?' Felicé sounds perplexed.

'Perhaps she spoke about him to you,' Benito replies.

'The newspapers say he was from San Ginés, then el Cristo de la Salud.'

'His first position here was at El Convento de la Encarnación,' Benito says.

'Oh, I see,' she says. She rises from the table in silence, begins circling, and then searching the drinks trolley. She takes a decanter which she places on the dining table.

'I bought this today after your man came by. It's a tintalla from Las Islas Canarias.'

Benito understands it has not been a mistake to visit. He refills their glasses and places them on the table in front of them. They relax, eat and talk.

'I never met a murderer before,' she says. 'Not that I know of. I only met him once, in passing. I don't think I can tell you much.'

It has not occurred to Benito she might have actually met Cayetano. His hopes rise that this visit will turn out more informative than he had considered.

'Anything might be helpful to form a picture,' Benito answers. 'How did he strike you?'

She cups her chin in her right hand. 'He seemed a likeable rogue. Partially deaf too, although one doesn't notice that at first. Are you sure we really are talking of the same man?'

'Yes, I'm quite sure. How did you meet?'

'It would have been five years ago, when he and Amparo had that big unpleasantness.'

'Amparo?' Benito asks.

'My sister! Amparo's her real name.'

'Of course, she would have taken a new name there. What unpleasantness?'

'I didn't actually witness their row, but I was there the day it happened,' Felicé says.

'When was it?'

'Let me see,' she says, and taps her fingers on the table top. 'Father died on the evening of 10 November. That next morning was a Thursday. I sent Amparo a note and went to see her that same afternoon.'

'I'm sorry to hear about your father,' Benito says.

'He died of consumption, or tuberculosis as some are calling it nowadays. He'd been sick for months. It was a relief in the end.'

'Although it's not always a relief for us who remain,' Benito says.

'Quite right. Amparo had come to see him once, at the beginning of his illness. She sat in the very same seat you're sitting in now.'

Benito fidgets in his seat.

'A nun showed me to her office. I didn't even imagine she had her own office. I would have expected something different, small and charmless. It wasn't at all like that.'

'What was it like?'

'It was bright,' she says. 'There was daylight streaming in from a tall window overlooking an orchard and a garden.'

'Sounds idyllic.'

'But it was business-like too. There was a small writing-desk and two chairs. The walls were deep-green, like grass in April. That was her favourite colour, the colour of her own eyes. I didn't expect that.'

'And this row she had with Padre Cayetano. What could you tell me of that?'

'It was laughable,' she says. 'Apparently, he took a woman in to the Kings Hall or Royal Room or whatever they call it. He told this woman she could take whatever she could manage to carry away. She chose a painting of Queen Margaret of Austria.'

'Just like that?' Benito says and clicks his fingers.

'She smuggled it out in a blanket the priest had taken from the chaplain's house. Amparo was furious. She had to buy it back in the end.'

'Why didn't she just take it back?' Benito asks.

'It was complicated. The woman was the sister of a nun who had recently passed away.'

The tale has the same Quixotic hallmarks of everything

Benito has been hearing and reading of concerning Padre Cayetano Galeote. 'But how come he got involved?'

'He was on his way to say Mass and found the woman sitting outside the church crying. She told him the whole story. Her father had died, and since there were no sons, everything was inherited by her older sister. There was not that much to inherit, but what there was became the property of El Convento. Amparo was in control of it.'

'So, he decided to help? Discuss it with your sister?'

'The woman had already tried that. Told Amparo her husband had cholera and her children were hungry. She asked if she could have some of the money that her father had left.'

'I presume your sister was unwilling.'

'Amparo sent her away.'

'And so, the gallant Padre Cayetano helped her steal a painting?'

'They only found out about it in the afternoon. A nun came and interrupted us. She said the chaplain urgently wanted to see Amparo. When she came back, she was not quite so calm as before.'

Benito knows he should direct their conversation to the subject of Señora Felicé's grandfather but this tale of a row between Madre Mariana and Cayetano is too intriguing to interrupt. Ferreras will have to understand that.

'The chaplain told Amparo the missing painting was a Gonzalez. It could fetch one hundred times the sum that the dead nun had left to the convent. The chaplain said he had seen Padre Cayetano take the woman in there earlier in the day.'

'I'm surprised she did not just send for the police,' Benito says. 'That way she might have got her painting back and dealt with Padre Cayetano at the same time.'

'The chaplain said there was no need to have the police

poking their noses into Church business. Much easier just to send a nun with a proposition for the woman to bring the painting back.'

'So, thanks to Padre Cayetano, the woman got the money that was left by her father, after all?'

'About half of it, I think. Amparo said that the dead nun was entitled to at least one half and so she decided the convent was keeping that.'

Benito reaches across and refills Señora Felicé's glass. 'I wonder why Amparo simply didn't give the money in the first place.'

'I asked her that. She just muttered, *Camarón que se duerme, se lo lleva la corriente* — the shrimp that falls asleep gets carried away by the current — it's an old expression of our grandfather.'

'I see,' Benito says. He makes a mental note of this for José.

'On the way out, we passed that priest.'

'Padre Cayetano Galeote,' Benito says.

'He was talking with a nun. She was asking him why he had to make things worse. He was explaining the woman was desperate.'

'Did he say anything to your sister?'

'No, but she repeated to him that old expression of our grandfather. And he seemed to understand her perfectly well.'

PART 2

GLORIOUSLY YE FELL

Saturday, 26 September 1868

Today we buried Daniel and a part of mother too. Her smile so often present even in adversity, has gone. To see her deranged beyond consolation renders us distressed beyond description.

Father pronounced Don Quixote's epithet over Daniel's coffin:

> Here lies the valiant cavalier,
> Who never had a sense of fear:
> So high his matchless courage rose,
> He reckoned death among his vanquished foes.
> Wrongs to redress, his sword he drew,
> And many a caitiff giant slew;
> His days of life though madness stained,
> In death his sober senses he regained.

And he pretends to be stronger than the rest of us, but we all saw him looking like he wanted to fall into the grave and be next to Daniel.

According to Captain José García, Daniel was killed by deserters from his own battalion. They slipped out of the barracks in Córdoba and went on the run. They doubled back and ambushed Daniel's unit.

This we could not tell Mother. Nor the name of some secret official: a Secretary of the Andalucían Commission of the Preservation of the Monarchy, who knew the lay of the land and drew them a map of how to find Daniel's Unit.

Mother's usual source of solace, Cayetano, can offer nothing. His own state of grief seems equal to hers. He says there is nothing for him here now. He already spoke to the Bishop of Málaga and asked to be assigned to Fernando Pô.

The bishop will not refuse him.

Only the crazy clergy go there and more than half of them never come back: they die of disease. It is no wonder that the British were happy to let their lease expire on Fernando Pô.

Don José García has passed Daniel's Euskaro to me and his bitten crucifix to Cayetano. The Euskaro hangs from my gunbelt, the cross hangs around Cayetano's wrist like it used to hang around Daniel's.

TEMPTATION OF EL CONVENTO
LA CÁRCEL MODELO, PLAZA DE LA MONCLOA, MADRID.
25 APRIL 1886

THE METALLIC SCRAPING of ankle-irons, as he crosses the cell, speaks of Padre Cayetano Galeote's indignity. He sits down at the foot of the thin narrow bed. His back is against the cell-wall. He adjusts his position on the thin mattress.

'I'm so tired. Just so tired. I cannot get any sleep in here,' he says.

At the other end of the same narrow bed, Benito Pérez Galdós watches the daylight streaming in from the cell window, and despite the window being opened he feels the air thicken and warm as the cell seems to shrink. Thanks to Mama Dolores, Benito has learnt a lifetime ago how to avert this oncoming sensation of choking. He hears her voice; harsh and shrill: 'stop gasping like a guppy. All that's required is a little discipline.' He inhales noisily through the nose. Exhales loudly through the mouth. Air flows in and out of his diaphragm. The inner voice hectors: 'slowly, deeply,' as if Mama Dolores were present to command her child.

Attack over, Benito rises and moves towards the cell window. Drops of perspiration appear on his forehead. With a sweep of the back of his hand he wipes the droplets away, then turns to face his sleep deprived companion.

'Asthma?' Cayetano asks.

'It's enclosed spaces,' Benito says. 'I had a nightmare about

307

being in here.'

'Or maybe you have that new phobia.'

Benito returns to the reason he has come here, 'I was saying that Doña Durdal's testimony could be the most important.'

'Forget that!' Cayetano answers. 'I'm not asking her to testify about anything.'

Ultimately it will not be a question of what Cayetano thinks he can agree to. However, since they are getting along so well, Benito omits any correction. He turns a page in his notebook. 'You don't mind if I continue taking notes?'

'Why should I care?' Cayetano answers.

'What were your feelings about your first assignment here in Madrid?'

'What have my sentiments about El Convento got to do with anything?'

'It can let me to see things more completely from your point of view. Doña Durdal agrees this could help others understand why things ended up the way they did.'

Cayetano ignores the point but Benito knows he has been heard.

'Claustrophobia!' Cayetano says and snaps a finger against a thumb.

Benito almost laughs aloud. Despite Simarro's warnings, Cayetano is not only fully lucid but attributing the latest medical conditions. 'How did you get along with Madre Mariana?'

'Señor Galdós, you've convinced Tránsito and Alonso you can help me,' Cayetano says. 'You can start by not mentioning that name again.'

Taken aback by the abruptness of Cayetano's response, Benito nods his assent.

'Before that woman laid eyes on me it was obvious that she

detested me,' Cayetano says. 'I should not have gone there.'

'If only our foresight was as perfect as our hindsight,' Benito says. 'Imagine the suffering we'd avoid.'

'There were signs I might have paid attention to.'

The story-sniffer in Benito prefers Cayetano to talk about Madre Mariana's politics, not just listen to his superstitions. For instance, whether she helped stashed munitions. 'Portents, you say. Such as?' Benito asks.

'The cold for a start! Pavements crunching with frost when I got here. That's surely an ill auspice,' Cayetano says. 'Imagine the M. Z. A. Express pulling in to Atocha and me still dressed for Andalucía.'

'It's often frosty here. From Christmas right until end of January,' Benito says.

'This was the end of February1880,' Cayetano says.

Benito is not surprised that the priest has such a clear memory of the weather on a day his life changed. He is reminded of how often his own important moments can be recalled with the weather attached to them like a limpet attached to a boat. For instance: hot and humid when he first arrived here, one late summer, twenty-five years ago. A lip-cracking dry, cold day when he received the news about Sisita dying in childbirth. A bitter brume with unremitting wetness when he arrived back in Las Palmas in 1871 to bury his father. He remembers too how Mama Dolores talked endlessly of the funereal fog and rain but had no words that day to mark the life of the man in the dirt.

Benito is sure, regardless of whether the priest is sane or insane he is cursed to always remember the weather of last Sunday when he killed the bishop.

All of which reminds Benito to add another note: Maximiliano Rubín must surely remember the climatic conditions when he first meets his own nemesis.

'I had to buy a coat.'

'Well, Madrid is not Puerto Rico,' Benito replies.

'Nor even Vélez come to that.'

'But at least it's close enough, for you to go back to Vélez every September.'

'You know about that?'

'I know some things.'

'Since I got back from the colonies, I've made certain to be in Vélez on 25 September every year.'

'The anniversary of your brother's death,' Benito says. 'I suppose sometimes you wish you'd stayed there.'

'Of course not! The Lord was calling me here, guiding me to Madrid to perform His work.' Cayetano says. His voice is raised. In fact, he sounds a little hysterical. It seems his lucidity has limits. His face tenses and his body sways.

However, Benito is not worried. Cayetano wears manacles, and the guard is a shout away. The prisoner seems harmless. Benito waits and hums an aria.

'You mentioned bad presentiments,' Benito says when the swaying stops.

This question brings Cayetano back from wherever his mind had gone. His eyes are clear again, and his body less rigid. He may not be fully lucid but he is, at least, mentally present. He gestures for Benito to pass him the cup of water that sits on the small round table.

'All these questions, are you aware that you seem more a lawyer than a journalist?'

Benito smiles awkwardly. It was Alonso's idea that he not reveal his true profession to Cayetano. Best not to introduce tension where none is necessary: journalist is close enough, they had agreed. On the other hand, he can imagine himself in the role of a lawyer just like his uncle José-María. Here he is, defending a representative of the Church. An almost perfect scenario for his mother. Except for the fact that the defendant has killed the Bishop of Madrid Alcalá.

'It's just that you mentioned auspices,' Benito says. 'I wondered what you meant.'

'I was thinking about El Convento,' Cayetano says.

Benito knows it well. He has tried to visit it every day this week. But, Madre Mariana will not change her mind. One day he waited hours outside and watched an eerie play of light and shadows on the façade. He sketched it. Cross-hatching its grey granite, taking the time to capture the Anunciación scene. Yet, if she had agreed to meet with him he would never have met her charming sister.

'When I got here,' Cayetano says, 'there was a note for me at my lodgings. I had to go straight to El Convento. It was locked. I stood outside and waited. That façade is frigid. Later I understand where it came from, full of rancour absorbed from her.'

A frigid façade might seem foreboding. Not an entirely irrational thought. Benito wonders whether this is a good moment to mention his failed attempts to meet with Madre Mariana. Perhaps if Cayetano knew he had been called an 'abomination' by her it could make a difference.

'I had a bad feeling whilst waiting there. I thought several times about returning to Atocha. I was on the point of doing it, when Padre Gabino Sánchez appeared.'

'Of course,' Benito says. 'Another one who refuses to meet with me.'

'You shouldn't insist,' Cayetano says calmly.

'But I'm certain he knows more than he says.'

'What he knows won't change anything.' Cayetano turns to face Benito, shakes his head and smiles in some gesture of amused pity. 'Leave the old man in peace. Anyway, you'd never get anything out of him that he doesn't wish to reveal.

But he'll get plenty out of you?'

Benito steps forward towards the cell-window. 'What does that mean?'

'We're all transparent to Padre Gabino Sánchez,' Cayetano says. 'He can see the worm inside you. He reads faces and eyes and knows what you're thinking.'

'You make him sound mystical.'

'I was on the verge of going home. I didn't say anything to him. But then he turns and softly says, "No point in us standing outside here admiring the view. Supposing we go inside and admire that one instead?" In we go, and everything changes.'

'You were seduced into staying?'

'It was like he'd known me for years.'

'I've heard the interior of El Convento is seductive.'

'I wouldn't use that word. It's beautiful, yes but in a spiritual way. There's nothing excessive: carved oak pews; handsome floor in a diagonal pattern of simple black and white stone floor tiles; and somehow the light bounces everywhere, cascades amongst frescoes and statues.'

'I like the poetry in your description. Rather a pity we can't all get to see it.'

'My sister was ecstatic just to hear me talk about the place,' Cayetano says.

'How about the tabernacle? I hear it's unique.'

'Yes, I could take you there now,' Cayetano says and closes his eyes, but opens his arms to help them take a journey in their imaginations. 'Travel down the nave aisle, stop on the chancel step, and from there you have an excellent view of the altar-cross, right in the middle you can see the arched opening of the tabernacle.'

Benito closes his own eyes. He allows Cayetano's words to transport him on this short voyage. 'I'm there I can see it.'

'Cross the chancel. Pass the altar-rails. Now you're stand-ing right next to the tabernacle.' Cayetano says. He seems enraptured by his own recollection and Benito's enthusiasm for the voyage they are sharing.

'I feel as though I can put my hands out and touch it,' Benito says.

'Give me your hands,' Cayetano says. 'Keep your eyes closed.'

Benito does it. He stretches his arms. He feels Cayetano take his hands and place them both on something round, smooth, metallic and cold to the touch.

'Imagine, this is the dome; blue lapis lazuli with bronze angels perched on it,' he says. 'And underneath are miniature marble-columns and jasper capitols.'

'I see them here.' Benito taps his own temple with a fore-finger. 'Now I can imagine the splendours that conspired to melt that crunching Madrilenian frost.'

'Let's not get too carried away,' Cayetano says. 'All of that helped of course but it was Sanchez' charm and the presence of my favourite martyr but especially a steady stipend that made the frost seem unimportant.'

'No regrets, then?'

'I'd be compelled to make the same choice again.'

'Despite everything?' Benito says from his position under the cell window where he has returned to sit on the floor and twists and rolls the ends of his moustache.

Cayetano's gaze fastens on to some imagined spot in the cell wall. His head tilts slowly further back as though the spot moves up the wall and across the ceiling. His stare is now fixed on some ceiling vision. '*Volenti non fit inuiria. Volenti non fit inuiria. Volenti non fit inuiria,*' he says. His eyes are at one moment glassy, the next quietly beseeching. It is as though a tripwire in his mind has been set off. With every repetition of *volenti non fit inuiria* he rocks gently on the bed.

The transformation has been instantaneous, and dramatic. However, Benito does not feel alarmed. He walks calmly past Cayetano and through the open cell door to where the guard sits.

'What's he doing now?' the guard asks.

'I'm not sure. He's repeating the same phrase over and over.'

'Yes, he does that,' the guard says.

'He's saying there's no wrong done to a willing person.'

'Looks like an act to me,' the guard says.

Benito wonders: is it an act or a fact? He cannot quite say either way.

'You want to leave now?'

Benito looks back inside the cell. Cayetano is still rocking, albeit more slowly and repeating his phrase. If Simarro were present he would be delighted to find a rocking automaton in the corner of the cell. Yet Benito has a feeling that Cayetano sneaks a look in his direction and knows he is still here. Perhaps he is being tested, or manipulated?

'No, I'll stay a while longer,' Benito says. 'The Governor said I could stay as long as I feel is necessary.'

SCRUPLES
LA CÁRCEL MODELO, PLAZA DE LA MONCLOA, MADRID
25 APRIL 1886

CAYETANO HAS GONE to sleep. He has closed his non-comprehending, pleading, baby-like eyes, that just minutes before rolled around in his ramshackle face.

The scene precipitates a wellspring of regret within Benito. He is contrite for imagining Simarro was wrong and disappointed for deluding himself that Cayetano has as much agency as Maximiliano Rubín will have. A rocking automaton is not a good development.

By virtue of reading his letters, hearing his story, and seeing his presence in the pages of Alonso's journal, Benito already has sufficient information when combined with his story-weaving experience to stop now. He could tell the guard he has changed his mind and simply walk back the way he came. He could go home and concentrate on Maximiliano Rubín, he has everything he needs. But he is duty bound now. Whatever happens here, he has to go on.

He sees Cayetano stir. 'Your lawyer has several lines of defence,' he says loudly.

Cayetano sit up in the bed and his head lolls as though it is too heavy for his neck.

Benito tries again, 'He says he's found an expert who'll testify that the Bishop's medical treatment was a contributing factor.'

Cayetano is massaging his own wrists and neck. Then

begins uttering something in a language Benito does not comprehend. It could be a prayer, or a curse.

It is the hands around the throat that reminds Benito of his nightmare of last night. In it he had pictured himself in a cell such as this. In his line of sight was a man condemned and already installed in the garrotte. He did not recognise that man's face, but it held a terrified gaze. He was unable to pull himself away until he heard a scream at the moment the executioner started turning the screw. It was then that the man began to ramble. In his nightmare he knew a word, a codeword, that could stop the executioner from tightening the metal collar and prevent the bevel-edged-bolt from screwing all the way through the man's neck. But he could remember the word.

He asked the executioner to stop while he searched for it, but he wouldn't — 'What's the word?' the executioner asked. 'Give me time,' Benito said, 'I'll remember it.' But in the nightmare the word would not come to him. He did not know it. He could only stand and watch the condemned man's tongue loll, and his eyes bulge as the bolt passed through neck arteries, muscles and bones. He placed his hands over his ears to block the screaming.

When it was over, he saw Simarro in a corner, laughing. Simarro had a surgeon's saw and a sackcloth and a basket for the head. And Simarro said, 'I know the word — it's degenerate.'

The sound of Cayetano's laboured breathing calls Benito back to the moment. He decides to try harder to restart their conversation. He removes his handkerchief, soaks it with water from the jug and wipes Cayetano's forehead.

'Did you hear me? He'll say the bishop might have survived with better medical help,' Benito says.

Cayetano rubs his eyes. He is once again full of life. His

face is animated. 'Who'll say that?'

'Doctor Cárceles, the medical expert.'

From somewhere deep inside him, Cayetano makes a lowing sound, and lightly beats his chest. 'No. That's not possible!'

'Shared culpability,' Benito says, and he returns to his side of the bed.

Cayetano stops his light chest-beating, and whispers, 'The Lord does not acquit the wicked.'

'Poor medical care is a frequent line of defence,' Benito says. 'Especially if the victim does not die instantly.'

Cayetano started to moan like an animal in pain. The guard opened the door to look at the scene. Benito waved a hand to say everything is fine.

'There's self-defence, there's provocation, there's diminished responsibility,' Benito said. 'On account of temporary insanity, and there's this one of shared culpability, which in this case means poor medical care.'

Cayetano stops moaning and with his right hand, he forms a pistol, leans over, and, using his index finger as a barrel, sticks it firmly into Benito's stomach, 'He was this close.'

Benito says nothing of the discomfort he is feeling in what used to be a more ample belly.

Cayetano removes his imaginary pistol. 'He let him have three bullets,' he says and smiles less sinisterly this time.

'You mean *you* let him have three bullets.' Benito gives a nervous reciprocating smile.

'I mean *he*. Anyway, there are other things to consider here,' Cayetano says. 'The best medical attention in the world would not have been enough.'

'Perhaps not, but it is a line of defence.'

'It was God's will. Bishop Narciso had his chance. *He* had written to him.'

Benito is saddened to realise that if Cayetano continues like this then Señor Villar-Rivas' insanity line of defence might be the one to prioritise after all. Providing of course Villar-Rivas does not suggest it is inherited, that would be too much.

'It was a matter of honour, a question of family dignity. The bishop should have apologised. The Church should have said they were sorry. But the Lord kept Bishop Narciso silent, and He sent me there so I'd learn the truth.'

'You just said *me* instead of *him*,' Benito says.

Cayetano grinned. 'I'm still practicing.'

'Before, when you were talking about yourself as though you were someone else. You were doing that on purpose!' Benito says.

'*Quos Deus vult perdere prius dementat*,' Cayetano says and he winks at Benito.

'My Latin does not go extend that far.'

'Whom God wishes to destroy he first makes mad.'

Benito winks back.

Without warning, Cayetano rises. His chains rattle and for a moment it seems as though he might lurch forward. His blood-shot eyes look around the cell as though searching for some elusive object and then, just as suddenly, a calmness takes over him. He sits down again and carries on as though nothing had occurred. 'I do feel very tired,' he says.

'Where was it that the Lord sent you?' Benito asks, playing Cayetano's game. 'What truth did you discover?'

'You realise that my parents could not set foot in the street because of the shame they felt?'

'They told you that?'

'Alonso let it out.'

'But in time that would all have gone away. Surely your parents realised your family honour was restored when the

Church agreed to take you back?'

'You can't understand this. My family lives by another code. Simply letting me go back to work could never restore our family name in a place like Vélez. Only a written apology could wash the stain.'

He is wrong because Benito understands plenty. And he has been filling his notebook with context: material he may use when he needs to call on fresh inspiration in creating a deeper Maximiliano Rubín — values, tensions, expectations and family enigmas that might become part of Maximiliano Rubín's inner world.

'On the eve, he went to the palace to plead with Gabino Sánchez,' Cayetano says. 'If anyone could get them to apologise it could only have been him.'

Benito notes Cayetano has reverted back to his use of *he* as though once more he was talking of someone else. 'So, *you* thought you'd just walk in there and ask them to apologise?'

'There's an access through a side-alley. Padre Gabino Sánchez always left the gates unlocked.'

'I don't suppose you could just have made an appointment?'

Cayetano swivels his head, shakes it to say no.

'He could see the two of them in the room talking and laughing about their old days and was about to interrupt when Bishop Narciso mentioned Córdoba in sixty-eight.'

'Córdoba? Wasn't your brother killed near there?'

Cayetano does not answer. Instead, he becomes rigid. Then squeezes his eyes closed, like a man child who does not want to relook at what is in front of him. Finally, he clenches a fist and chokes back on an unpalatable reality. It does not look like an act anymore.

Benito does not tell Cayetano he has read fragments of Alonso's journals, or that they no longer exist. Nor does he ask Cayetano to explain anything more because now he understands everything — Cayetano's revenge was the worst exercise of free will a person can choose.

'If he'd had the Euskaro with him, he'd have shot them both right there,' Cayetano says. His voice is dull but devoid of malice. 'He saw Padre Gabino slapping Bishop Narciso on the back for his quick thinking in invoking another "Secretary" character, and he just slipped out the same way he'd gone in.'

'Have you spoken to anyone about this?' Benito asks.

'Yes, to the Lord,' Cayetano says. 'And the Lord told me this was why he called me here. So, you see now?' Seemingly exhausted, Cayetano rests his head against the cell wall and closes his eyes.

Benito thinks, *Maximiliano Rubín will suffer even greater disappointment but will choose a different path*.

'Perhaps you could have shown yourself,' Benito says. 'They may have given you the apology you were searching.'

Cayetano instantly responds in a convulsive tremble. He reels away from his resting position against the wall. 'Everything changed. What apology could ever suffice?'

'Is that what Daniel would have wanted?'

'Daniel would have understood,' Cayetano says. 'That's why I survived all those postings and never once been ill.'

'You just said I,' Benito says.

'Did I? *Quos deus vult perdere prius dementat*,' Cayetano says and winks again at Benito.

'They say he works in mysterious ways,' Benito answers.

'Let me sleep, please,' Cayetano pleads. 'Just for a short while.'

This time, Benito does not try to rouse Cayetano. Instead he pours himself a full cup of water. Sits at the small desk and writes. He thinks about Villar-Rivas' lines of defence: Self-defence? — clearly not. Shared culpability? — clutching at thin air. Insanity? — nobody would be fooled. This leaves only provocation. Could the Bishop's unwitting involvement in a killing so far off in the past: when the world was less clear and even brothers fought on opposite sides, be considered provocation?

No matter how much Cayetano loved his brother, is revenge a moral or legal defence? Restraint, not vengeance is how civilised citizens exercise free will. But perhaps extenuating circumstances at least lessen the likelihood of a death penalty? Maybe an appropriate duration prison sentence could even appeal to Cayetano's over acute sense of dignity?

Benito takes up his handkerchief again and pours water on it from the jug. 'You have to tell your lawyer about the provocation,' Benito says, oblivious to whether anyone hears him.

Cayetano sleeps on. His vacuous expression has retreated like a tide. When he wakes, he looks around him as though surprised to find himself still in his prison cell, his visitor still present and wiping his forehead with a wet handkerchief.

'I'm sorry, but I've hardly slept since they brought me here.'

'This mad act of yours,' Benito asks, 'is this Villar-Rivas' idea?'

'Of course not.'

'Simarro's then?'

'Absolutely not,' Cayetano says, as firmly as before. 'He might have enjoyed it had he seen it. But I assure you I can do better.'

Cayetano's mouth seems to seize up. He looks at Benito and shrugs his shoulders. His body begins to twitch, firstly a barely noticeable, mild sideways tremor, then a more perceptible movement. Next he rocks backwards and forwards. The bed moves, and squeaks discordantly. Finally, he holds his breath and begins jerking.

'Fascinating performance,' Benito says.

'Is it? Sometimes I do feel as though I am going mad. It's being in here. I need this whole thing to be over.'

'You really must tell your lawyer about the provocation,' Benito says in earnest.

Cayetano crosses to the table, pours some water from the wooden jug into both cups and holds one out. He returns to sit again on the edge of the bed and stares at Benito.

'There's no proof of anything,' Cayetano says.

'Alonso's journals?' Benito says, omitting the fact their existence is tenuous.

'Who's to say they are not entirely fictitious? Perhaps he invented them and brought them to Madrid along with the pistol, knowing what I'd do,' Cayetano says.

'How can you say that? Your brother is doing everything to help you.'

'I know that. But do you see my point? The bishop cannot speak from beyond and say what he did.'

'What if Padre Gabino were to speak out?'

'There is too much to lose.'

'What does he have to lose? He's an old man thinking of the after-life.'

'He has a great deal to lose. For a start, I know he loved Narciso as much as I loved Daniel. And does the country really need to relive that moment?'

Benito understands now, more clearly, why Padre Gabino Sánchez has refused to see him. It is because, even though he is the only credible person alive who can verify Cayetano's story, he would rather let Cayetano die than sully the bishop's name.

'Perhaps the court would show compassion if they understood your revenge.'

'What's compassionate about being incarcerated for life in a lunatic asylum?' Cayetano asks.

'You'd fit in fine, considering how you had me fooled.'

'And anyway, my family would be considered as degenerates, and I can't allow that.'

'So, you'd rather die a slow, painful death?' Benito says.

'I'd rather die a quick and painless death, if someone would only help me.'

'Why be so defeatist? If Padre Gabino will open his door and speak out, surely that will help?' Benito says. 'And there's the manner in which Rector Vizcaíno and Madre Mariana colluded to have you defrocked, that must be taken into account, surely?'

'Doctor Simarro thought I had delusions of persecution when I dared hint at that,' Cayetano says.

'He *has* to consider you as a classic case of degenerate insanity,' Benito says.

'Doctor Simarro said there's no possible defence, unless one is not in charge of their faculties,' Cayetano says. 'He says only he can help me.'

'By taking you on a voyage of self-discovery, or of self-debasement? I've read your letters, seen your chagrin over integrity and nobility. What will you do?'

'There's nobility only in doing the right thing.'

'If Gabino Sánchez will talk, perhaps we can get a reduced prison sentence,' Benito says and his enthusiasm drowns his realism: 'You'd be out of prison in just a few years.'

'You don't understand, I'm already out,' Cayetano says.

'I mean this prison, this physical place.'

'There's no point,' Cayetano answers.

Benito shrugs. Claps his hands together. 'So, do you feel that your relationship with, you know: the Mother Superior, had any connection with what happened?'

'I already told you, I had no relationship with her.'

'Doña Durdal says that the Mother Superior was contemptuous,' Benito's tone is insistent as though he is not prepared to allow Cayetano to sink into *there's-no-point-ism*. 'Did her contempt make you feel differently about the Church?'

'First Simarro comes here with his notebook and half hidden quack theories. Now, you show up with your notebook and your questions. Would you like to look inside too?' Cayetano opens his mouth wide.

Benito begins to laugh.

Cayetano starts to laugh too. 'I don't know why I'm laughing,' he says. 'What's so funny?'

'I've told myself to try to look inside, and now you say that.'

'I still don't understand,' Cayetano says.

'Never mind,' Benito answers.

'Anyway, I consider it all rather providential the way things worked out, concerning the Mother Superior and Padre Sánchez too,' Cayetano says.

'But she moved you out of El Convento.'

'If she hadn't encouraged me to leave there I wouldn't have come under Rector Vizcaíno's supervision. If I hadn't come under his supervision, I'd not have been dismissed. If I'd not been dismissed, I'd never have discovered the real reason for being called to Madrid.'

'Providential. I see,' Benito whispers.

'I'm glad that finally you do.'

'But I shall keep trying with Gabino Sánchez. He's your only hope.'

'That wily old fox will find out what it takes to compromise you too.'

'Impossible! I don't know how to compromise,' Benito says.

'Really? Six years ago, I thought the same. I planned on catching the next train back home. Until he asked if I'd like to see life return from death.'

Benito understands instantly what Cayetano must be talking of. 'You mean the relic of San Panteleon?'

'He'd made up some doggerel. Made it clear who'd be the new caretaker-of-relics in El Convento once he was retired.'

'Doggerel?'

Cayetano sings Padre Gabino Sánchez' doggerel: 'Only two people hold the key; one is the Sacristan, the other is me.' He sings it as though it were a melodious chant handed down from ancient monks. His voice has taken on another timbre. It is incongruous in the cell.

Hairs rise on Benito's arms.

'Quit that singing,' the prison guard shouts from outside the cell door.

'Hard to refuse an offer like that, I suppose,' Benito says. 'Given, San Panteleon's your favourite martyr.'

'Padre Gabino Sánchez always knows where to look,' Cayetano says. 'The martyr who could not be killed until *he* decided it was time for reconciliation with his maker. He knew, instantly, that was my creed.'

THROUGH HER EYES

Monday, 26 October 1868

I am writing this on the terrace of the Central Café in Málaga. I have decided that after ten years of keeping a journal that this will be my last entry. I suppose it should be profound and worthy of a final act but all I shall talk of is a boat that is leaving its harbour.

If you look at life through the eyes of Remedios, every cloud has a silver lining. She sees things differently. And she says things differently too. Words that could sound sacrilegious coming from anyone else drip like honey from her lips and even her contemptible observations come over as simple evidences. Cayetano's carriage had barely pulled away from Central Plaza and the heat of his departing embrace was still warm on us, but this did not deter her.

'Cheer up, Alonso. Now Cayetano's gone you're number-one heir,' she said.

'Who'd be interested in inheriting a tenancy agreement and whatever chattels our family has?' was all I could say to her.

Her answer was to slap me on the back and say, 'You'll probably look back and consider yourself quite fortunate right now.' Since she has gone to live in Málaga as housekeeper and student to Ruiz Blanco she seems even more irreverent than before.

I suppose Cayetano would have gone sooner if he could, perhaps immediately after Daniel's burial. But it has taken weeks for the Rector of St Juan to arrange his assignment to Fernando Pô. Then the new bishop — Don Esteban José Pérez Fernández — would not allow Cayetano to leave without stocking up on quinine. The last priest who had gone there: a young depressed fellow from Toledo, did not take any, and was dead within six months.

'But I'm sure Cayetano will be fine,' the Rector of St Juan told us.

From a purely legal point of view of course, Remedios is right. Last month I had three older brothers: two ahead of me in the succession stakes. Now we have buried one and another is on his way to Málaga harbour where he will take a steam packet to Fernando Pô — probably never to be seen again.

On the terrace, the waiter recognised Remedios. He asked her if she would like her usual and then asked where Don José was. As if she should know the whereabouts of José Ruiz!

'He's gone to see his fiancée,' she said, 'but if you have a message for him, I'd be pleased to pass it on. Perhaps you've sold one of his paintings?'

The waiter seemed conspiratorially happy to tell her they had not sold any of José Ruiz' paintings but they had sold another two of hers and so they had room on the wall to take replacements, if she liked.

'You're doing well then, selling your art?' I asked her.

'At current prices, not well enough to live on,' she told me.

And now there is another problem; José Ruiz' fiancée, María Picasso López, has asked him to find a replacement housekeeper. Ideally find someone very ugly and very old. Someone who is not Remedios. In a month Remedios will have to find somewhere else to live. In the meantime, she has started to pose naked for José Ruiz.

WHAT THE CONFESSOR KNOWS
BISHOP'S PALACE, CALLE SAN JUSTO, MADRID
5 OCTOBER 1886

HIS BOOT HEELS echo up the narrow Calle San Justo. Heavy, wooden, double doors loom across what used to be a welcoming inner entrance to the Bishop's Palace. Thwarted again, he continues on his way along the Calle. He knows of another entrance, tucked away beyond the sight and acquaintance of the casual visitor.

Knowledge of the terrain is the perquisite only of inquisitive natives and someone like him; a non-native whose curiosity has never been idle. For twenty years he has burrowed in all of the city's *barrios*. No passer-by, nor tourist can hope to discover what he knows. For instance, he knows that further along Calle San Justo he can slip through the gates of the narrow alleyway of Callejón Panecillo separating the Bishop's Palace from the Basilica San Miguel. From there he will be able to directly access the living quarters of the last and most elusive name on his list.

But when he reaches the alleyway the gates are chained shut. A heavy, black padlock secures the chain. Despite being barely six months old, the chain and padlock already have the dusty sheen of service in Madrid. He grasps the gate, two-handed, and pulls with force. The chain chatters and clanks but shows not the slightest sign of stress.

He gazes through the gates and sights the doorway of Padre Gabino Sánchez' residence. Shafts of darkness peep through the doorway's periphery, like an inverted antumbra. There is no sound, not a whisper from up there. Behind him, muted music can be heard. He curses quietly and steps away in its direction.

Singing now accompanies the music meandering from the Basilica San Miguel. He enters, sits in the last pew in the north aisle. In the chancel a choir practices, and nearby a small, appreciative group listens. He becomes one of them. Relaxes. Claps when they do and smiles in synch. Yet he is not entirely with them.

His mind drifts and he reflects on why it is he still persists. *Why, why, why?* After all, his coda, *Fortunata y Jacinta*, is complete. And Maximiliano Rubín, for so long his *idée-fixe*, is a pharmacist, not even a priest, and twenty years younger than Cayetano to boot. *Who could even make the link between Cayetano and Maximiliano?*

The thought has barely become manifest in Benito's mind when Simarro's face floats into his consciousness. The alienist would make the link easily. For one thing, the stigmata give the game away. But Simarro will probably not even read *Fortunata y Jacinta*, nor care that in Maximiliano's world, free will wins. *To hell with it! If they prefer pessimism, let them be Simarro's sycophants*, he thinks.

If he was doing this for the future of *Fortunata y Jacinta* he would give up right now, because whatever happens, its future will not depend on whether he ever meets Gabino Sánchez. Tonight, on the eve of the judgement and sentencing, the only future that matters is the life he has sworn to try to save.

A loud percussion startles Benito, slowly transporting him back to the present. A choral melody follows. He recognises it: Boccherini. How appropriate; another immigrant who suffered many setbacks. He allows his thoughts to travel with the music. Boccherini's personal story — his perseverance, his self-belief and his determination — inspires Benito. Against immense odds, Boccherini never gave up, so why should he? He is stirred for one last attempt. In the middle of the melody he stands up from the pew and runs out of the Basilica.

He scurries along Calle San Justo back towards the main entrance of the Bishop's Palace. The inner entrance doors remain defiant and closed. However, this time he pulls on the bell-chain with violence. No response! He pulls again, and again, and again. With each yank of the chain he waits less time before yanking again.

Tonight, no one will rest in there, he thinks. Finally, he hears the sound of impatient feet slapping towards the door. He stops pulling on the chain. The clanging doorbells fall silent. The footfalls stop, but no one answers. He is wavering when the speakeasy flap is unbolted. A young priest peers out.

'What's all this noise?'

'I need to see Padre Gabino Sánchez.'

'He's tired.'

'I'm tired too.'

'Then go home and sleep.'

Benito lowers his voice. 'I've important news for him.'

The young priest readies to close the flap.

'I'm writing a panegyric of the bishop,' he says.

'Come back tomorrow,' the young priest says.

'It's for publication tomorrow. Who knows what mistakes I'll write about fatherless children in Salamanca, if I can't speak with the old man?'

'Who'd you say you were?'

He leans in. 'Benito Pérez Galdós.'

'Well, well, the Liberal Crusader himself. Wait here,' the young priest says, and shuts the flap.

A few minutes pass, then a few minutes more. Benito is readying to pull the chain again. They must know he will not give up. More time passes. Finally, he pulls. Once again, he hears footsteps from inside. He is slightly euphoric when the face of the young priest reappears at the speakeasy.

'All right! All right! He'll see you.'

The young priest opens the doors and allows Benito to pass through before re-bolting them. He carries a lamp and leads the way down a long corridor. It is barely dusk and even though there are tall windows which stretch almost to the ceiling, the place seems ethereally dimly lit.

Threadbare carpets lie next to exquisite woven floor coverings and there are fittings for gas lamps. Even here, like the church Mama Dolores frequents, they burn candles and cling to the past, whilst the gas-powered light of the future awaits connection on their walls.

He hears chanting in the distance as he follows the priest. Occasionally they cross the paths of other priests, mostly slow-moving, half-bent, geriatrics heading in different directions. They nod and stare at Benito, then move in silence into rooms or other corridors.

When Benito and his companion arrive at the other end of the palace, Benito understands they have reached a corridor leading to Gabino Sánchez' living quarters adjacent to Callejón Panecillo.

If they were to carry straight on and push open the door, he might again hear the choir sing Boccherini. The young priest turns to the left, pushes open a set of double doors and leads Benito into a reception room. He points to a sofa, then turns away, taking his lamp and most of the light with him.

Benito sits on the cusp of the couch and looks around. There are lit candles dotted here and there. They offer scant clarity. Nevertheless, he starts to distinguish colours and textures. The couch is burgundy and made of leather. Shapes start to take less sinister forms. A door directly opposite him is wide open. Through it he sees a wall of floor-to-ceiling bookshelves. Every shelf is filled. Naturally, Benito is compelled to go there.

The books are arranged by subject. On the shelf below his knee are books on Philosophy, Rhetoric and Theology. Level with his face are books on Mathematics, Medicine and Poetry. There is a patina of aged paper. It all reeks of wisdom and ancient secrets. Elsewhere he sees modern books; their papers, glues and inks evoke other smells — vanilla, almond and goat.

Many of the volumes are written in foreign languages. The older ones appear to be written in Latin or Greek, a few in Arabic. Some of the modern books are also imports; he sees titles in English, Italian and French.

In any library, Benito is drawn to the section marked *Medicine*. He spies a book authored by a name he knows: Jean Baptiste Félix Descuret: *Les Merveilles du Corps Humain: Précis Méthodique d'Anatomie, de Physiologie et d'Hygiène dans leurs Rapports avec la Morale et la Religion: ouvrage destiné aux ecclésiastiques, aux élèves de philosophie*. This particular book, with its incredibly long title, is not a book he owns. But simply seeing it there and learning that Gabino Sánchez has probably read the same author makes this place seem familiar. In his head he translates from the French: *The Marvels of the Human Body: a Methodical Summary of its Anatomy, of its Physiology, Functions and Relationship with Spirit and Religion: work designed for clergy and students of philosophy*.

In his own collection he has Pedro Felipe Monlau's translation of another of Descuret's tomes: *The Medicine of Passions, or the Passions Considered in Relationship to Illness, Laws and Religion*. It was this very book that sowed the seeds for the parody of Guzmán, and so also spawned his inevitable counterpoint — Maximiliano Rubín.

He thinks, perhaps when Gabino Sánchez shows up he will talk about this later book of Descuret and how it echoes his own ideas; which is that experiences — particularly those of childhood and adolescence — have the power to form and even derange. A power that, in Benito's view of the world, has as much relevance as any supposed degenerative ganglion that Luis Simarro will point to.

Above the section on medicine there are books on history, and above those, on the top shelf, a section labelled *Fictional Works by Spanish Authors*. There are novels by writers he knows: Pedro Antonio de Alarcón, Leopoldo Alas Clarín. He groans when he sees Emilia's name is amongst them. But his insides plummet when he sees that adjacent to Emilia several of his own novels stand spine to spine with hers. And seeing a well-thumbed *Doña Perfecta* amongst them unsettles him.

'For the twisted love of a mother,' Benito says under his breath, and as he says it becomes aware of a presence entering the room.

Gabino Sánchez coughs discreetly from the doorway, then moves across the room with the air of someone who could glide his way around in total darkness, never needing to feel around for his bearings. The fluidity of the septuagenarian's movements seems at odds with his stiffly starched, dark vestments.

Benito returns to the reception room. They shake hands.

'I hope you don't mind. I can't control my curiosity when there's the opportunity to probe a person's library.'

'Not at all,' Gabino Sánchez says, all the time keeping his eyes fixed on Benito. 'I'm pleased to meet you.'

'Likewise.'

Gabino Sánchez crosses the room and pulls open the curtains overlooking Callejón Panecillo. A lighter shade of grey pours in.

'I'm curious to know about your relationship with Padre Cayetano,' Gabino Sánchez says, and he gestures to Benito to sit, whilst he settles himself on a matching sofa.

Benito sits down opposite Gabino Sánchez, clears his throat and smooths his trousers.

'I suppose you want to use him to ridicule the Church in some way,' Gabino Sánchez says.

'Why would I want to do that?' Benito responds.

'It wouldn't be the first time, Señor Galdós, would it?' Gabino Sánchez says. 'I've wanted to ask you for a long time why you so despise our Church? What have we ever done to you?'

'Six months I've been coming here ringing on your bell,' Benito says. 'I could have answered that a long time ago.'

Gabino Sánchez' eyes sparkle, an enigmatic smile discernible in them. 'I hear you don't like it when we interfere in politics. You may not know it but there are many of us in the Church who don't like it too much either.'

Benito has not expected this equanimity. He is unsure of how to respond.

'But sometimes one must have the courage to intervene,' Gabino Sánchez says. 'Otherwise the country might collapse into a moral abyss.'

'I suppose that's a way to justify what you do,' Benito says.

The corners of Gabino Sánchez' lips turn down, 'What is it that you see, an abuse of authority, some undue influence?'

Benito shrugs his shoulders and shakes his head, unable to hide his disagreement.

'What we see is something quite different; an essential duty. Sometimes one must cross boundaries.'

'Or leave it to those whose role that is!'

'An interesting perspective! Let's consider your own position, shall we?'

Benito knows what is coming, but he feels ready.

'You're a writer. You occupy a position of influence in the country. You are someone with a point of view, if you'll pardon my pun. Now, if that's not enough, I understand you've entered politics too.'

Benito clears his throat, pushes up his jacket sleeves.

'Yes, we also have friends following the machinations of the Congress of Deputies. Likely we knew even before you did that Prime Minister Sagasta was coming for you.'

'I've never hidden my political leanings,' Benito says and sucks his teeth.

'Neither have we. We're not judging you. We know how many times you've turned Sagasta down in the past,' Gabino Sánchez says.

Benito sighs, and shrugs his shoulders, as though to say, *Well, thank you for that.*

'But how often have you yourself been deeply critical of *cunerismo?*' Gabino Sánchez says. 'And now here you are, quite content to benefit from your own cronies.'

Benito's face reddens. He feels happy the room is dimly lit.

'No doubt, you have your reasons for this *volte-face,*' Gabino Sánchez says. 'As I'm sure you must have reasons for disliking the Catholic Church as much as you do. And by the way, I hope to get to the bottom of that too before we're through.' He smiles and despite his reproaches still manages to sound a likeable old schoolmaster.

Benito breathes in deeply. He will do whatever it takes to help Cayetano. He will talk about whatever this mystical, sly fox wants to talk about.

'Since you're here, I suggest you pour us both a large glass of port, Señor Galdós.'

Benito has already spotted the sideboard supporting the weight of several bottles tucked behind Gabino Sánchez' couch. He is glad of the diversion. He pours two glasses and hopes he can discretely move on from talking about cronyism.

'To the memory of a great bishop and wonderful person,' Gabino Sánchez says and drinks the contents in a single gulp.

'Here's to that,' Benito says and repeats Gabino Sánchez' gesture before refilling both glasses.

'I suppose we must count you amongst our lost sheep, Señor Galdós?'

'A correct supposition.'

'Since when?'

'Since I've been old enough to decide for myself.'

'I see. So, you're one of the flock forced to attend Sunday Masses?'

Benito grimaces.

'You'd rather not say? Let's see if I can guess. Usually it's the Mother. Every Sunday, I suppose?'

Benito takes another sip of port. He knows this will help him talk about certain matters that have lain latent, wounds barely liminal. It is an odd sensation, but he feels at ease in the presence of this old man, as though he is finally ready to talk. 'For us, it was daily prayers and presence at Mass three times a week. *She* went twice a day.'

Gabino Sánchez takes a sip of his port, swirls it around his mouth, and then gently whistles.

'Twice a day! What was she trying to get away from?'

'What do you mean?'

'Everyone is welcome in our Church. But in my experience when people come so frequently it's often because their own home is not such an appealing place to be.'

Benito's tongue makes a dash around his dentistry. He does not respond to Gabino Sánchez' remark, as he is not sure if this is insight or insult.

'And what did your father make of all this?'

'My Father?' Benito asks.

'His wife spending more time in the local church than the average church cleaner. Or some priests come to that.' Gabino Sánchez chuckles at his own humour.

Benito twirls his moustache-ends. 'I never asked. My father was patient. Not the type to make a fuss. Men like him had been through so many things.'

'He was older, then, than her? How much? A lot?'

'What has this to do with anything?' Benito asks, wondering when they will get around to the real reason he has come.

'Perhaps nothing, perhaps everything,' Gabino Sánchez says. 'I assume he was military and probably fought against the French in the Peninsula War. Likely never took the time to explain to her the things he'd been through. Lots of their generation had that difficulty.' Gabino Sánchez' deductions strike with uncanny accuracy.

'Sixteen years, older. A lieutenant in the battalion of Extremadura,' Benito mutters, barely concealing a certain amount of pride as he speaks.

'Any young wife will resent being shut out of a part of a taciturn trooper's life. In those unhappy circumstances, the Church has ears as wide open as its arms.'

Benito sinks in the coach, wonders: *Mama Dolores? A young, unhappy wife?* She was already wizened when she had him. He cannot recall if he ever saw her smile except in the local church: attending a Mass, a Communion, or someone's Confirmation.

This time, it is Gabino Sánchez who fills their glasses. As he fills Benito's glass, Benito has the impression Gabino Sánchez is benignly weighing him up.

'Didn't you ever enjoy spending time at church?' Gabino Sánchez asks.

How to answer this? Benito's earliest memories of going to

church correspond with feelings of dread. As a young boy he would hear his mother pour ice-cold water into a bathtub and then it would be his turn. Scrubbed and marched off to church. But later, after Sisita arrived in Las Palmas, there were other memories too, happy ones.

'There's something. Your eyes give it away,' Gabino Sánchez says.

The old priest is too perceptive. His manner makes Benito open like a mussel in a pot of warm water. 'Well, there were times I'd meet a friend there. But we could have been anywhere else, and we'd have been just as happy.'

Benito cannot quite see how Padre Gabino Sánchez has got this information out of him. He has not revealed Sisita's name but those happy moments with her and her vivacity somehow communicate themselves through him. Then, inevitably, the disappointment, the anger and the profundity of loss follow and remake his face into another mask. He has said nothing of these sentiments or their source, but the old fox is already on the scent of a scandal.

'You know, Señor Galdós, one mustn't imagine that because a person goes to church twice a day that the Church is responsible for their acts. I understand you're an advocate of free will. We're responsible for our own acts. Don't you agree?'

How could Benito disagree with the old man's logic? He finds himself disarmed, even charmed by Gabino Sánchez. They talk on, uninhibited. The longer they talk the more loquacious they become, and the more frequently they tip themselves another glass of port. Finally, Benito is ready to take his chances. 'I really came here to talk about Cayetano.'

'I know you did.' Gabino Sánchez sips his port and pushes himself back into the couch.

'I could write a panegyric of the bishop, if you wanted me

to,' Benito says.

'I'll write one myself. I doubt if anyone could have loved their own son any more than I loved Narciso.' Gabino Sánchez swallows hard and steadies his voice.

'I'm sorry for your loss. It must seem so senseless.'

'There's always a sense, always a greater plan. A man in my position is bound to believe that.' The light in Gabino Sánchez' eyes fades, and the lilt in his voice falters.

Benito wonders, is this the moment to tell him he knows about the "Secretary" and what happened near the bridge at Alcolea? The port is potent but somehow it still feels too soon to play that card. 'I talked with Tránsito Durdal. She says Cayetano is innocent.'

'Innocent of what?'

'Of immoral conduct.'

The old man shakes his head slowly and sadly, as though there is a grief that laps around his heart. 'Does she not consider the shooting of Narciso to be an immoral act?'

'She means there was nothing immoral in Cayetano's lodging with her.'

'Well, some parishioners would find it hard to distinguish between lodging with and living with,' Gabino Sánchez says. 'Anyway, whether they were or whether they weren't changes nothing.'

'It might change a lot. If the Church agreed he was innocent of that charge. Perhaps the court would take that into consideration?'

'He's not on trial for having lodged or lived with Tránsito Durdal,' Gabino Sánchez says.

Benito places his glass on the floor, port spilling over the lip as he does so. 'But he was provoked,' he says. His voice a little louder than before.

'You think so? I suggest you forget whatever ideas Padre

Cayetano's filled your head with. Anyway, the court will have no truck with them.'

'The judge won't even let him speak,' Benito says.

'Because no one wants unverifiable allegations, especially in this moment of fragile fraternity.'

'But you could speak for him,' Benito says.

'He has a lawyer to do that.'

'But you know the truth.'

'The truth is whatever his "provocation" was, he murdered Narciso.'

'But if no one speaks up for him he'll be sentenced to death.'

'Or they might just say he's mad,' Gabino Sánchez says.

'He'd rather die than bring that shame on his family.'

'Would they prefer he was judged sane and put to death, or considered insane and allowed to live?'

'How about judged sane, provoked and given a short prison sentence?'

'Impossible! You keep claiming provocation,' Gabino Sánchez responds. 'But after having slain a man loved by so many, don't you think that if he were to escape with his own life that would be adequate compensation for a possible misunderstanding concerning his living arrangements?'

'You think he will escape with his life if no one speaks the truth?'

'I remind you, the bishop himself forgave Cayetano.'

'They know that but they're itching to have his neck.'

'Well, it will all be in God's hands.'

'God is not going to be in the courtroom.'

'But Villar-Rivas is,' Gabino Sánchez says. 'I understand he'll plead diminished responsibility due to insanity.'

'But he's not insane,' Benito says. 'He was provoked.'

'There you go once more. Let's indulge ourselves for a

moment. Let's say a couple of living individuals know the truth.'

Benito feels a small victory has been won in getting Gabino Sánchez to arrive here. Perhaps he can lure the guileful personal confessor one more step? 'Let's say, there's Cayetano. There's you, of course. And now there's me.'

'You surely know I must abstain from talking on the matter,' Gabino Sánchez says. 'Reputations of loved ones prevent it.'

'Cayetano could speak of it.'

'I doubt he will,' Gabino Sánchez says. 'At such a fragile moment in our history, he, better than any of us, understands what's at stake.'

'But his life lies in the balance. And if you will not speak for him...'

'Revenge solicits revenge. I know this is not what Cayetano wants,' Gabino Sánchez says. 'Go and ask him if you don't believe me.'

Benito has spent months watching and listening to the court proceedings, he knows even if Cayetano was ready to allege anything the court would not give him leave to speak, nor listen to what he has to say.

'That leaves only you, Señor Galdós,' the old confessor says. 'What will you do for the sake of peace?'

'That depends on you, Padre.'

'A little compromise on your side, and the Church will plead for leniency,' Gabino Sánchez replies. 'You see? This situation does not depend on me at all.'

LUSTRE OF MAGNIFICENCE
BISHOP'S PALACE, CALLE SAN JUSTO, MADRID
5 OCTOBER 1886

HE WAS STARTLED when they opened their doors. He was stupefied when Padre Gabino Sánchez opened his memories. Because Sánchez surely knew he had come here searching for a way to save Cayetano.

For six months he has studied Padre Gabino Sánchez from across the courtroom. As each court session passed, the old man seemed more and more haunted by his inability to prevent the killing.

It would have taken nothing so dramatic as throwing his body in the path of those bullets. There was always another, far simpler, action. But he never chose it. Now, having failed to prevent the shooting of his beloved Bishop Narciso, it seems his obsession is to ensure that the world retains the same idealised memory that he does.

Even now, on the verge of judgement, on the lip of Cayetano's death sentence, the old confessor will not confess. He will not blab of the bishop's role in the killing of Cayetano's brother, far less admit the Church's own negligence.

'You've asked what *I* will do,' Benito says, 'but you know the testimony has already all been heard.'

'If you don't like the sentence you can ask Villar-Rivas to appeal,' Gabino Sánchez says. 'See if you can get them to call on your unverifiable testimony.'

'You'd be called back to testify,' Benito answers, 'and you cannot lie.'

'It would not be a lie to say I was not present. Nor can I can confirm anything you allege.'

'Wasn't there something that could have prevented all of this?' Benito asks.

'It was God's will,' Gabino Sánchez replies.

'Are you saying God wanted Narciso dead?'

The old priest sits his glass on the floor. He looks momentarily ill at ease.

'All those letters Cayetano sent,' Benito says. 'To the prime minister, to the queen, and even to the pope. All pleading to be heard.'

'What would you have had us do?' Gabino Sánchez says.

'I don't know, but the judge said Cayetano's intentions were clear in those letters. Why wasn't the bishop warned?'

Gabino Sánchez shrugs his shoulders at Benito's port-fuelled impertinence.

'Why would we have done that? Narciso had never even met Cayetano.'

'But surely he read Cayetano's letters?'

'We never passed any of those to Narciso.'

'Why?' Benito asks, his tone straining.

'We didn't wish him to become anxious.'

'So, you did think there were grounds for anxiety?'

'Perhaps some in that last letter. I discussed that one with Vizcaíno. But he felt it was not the best moment to go troubling the bishop. And anyway, he had his own way of ensuring the bishop's safety.'

Benito has been wondering when they would get around to Rector Vizcaíno.

'I've been hearing quite a lot of Rector Vizcaíno,' Benito says.

'Narciso was fond of him,' Gabino Sánchez says.

'And you?' Benito has in forefront of his mind those confidential matters that Tránsito Durdal revealed concerning Vizcaíno's generosity. He hides his frustration at not being able to make allusions. He will not betray her confidences.

'He means well,' Gabino Sánchez says. 'But no, I wasn't taken in by the young rector.'

'What do you mean?'

The old priest taps the side of his nose and adds a sly wink. 'Nicolás is quite engaged in the Carlista cause.'

'Like you and Narciso are?'

'Were!' Gabino Sánchez says. 'But Nicolás is engaged much more than we ever were. Even at his age.'

'Hasn't that all been settled?' Benito says.

'Well, we believed so. We had certainly not come to Madrid to start all of that again.'

Benito has not expected Gabino Sánchez to be so open about his past. Yet, the old man seems rather at ease talking of it. 'So, how did you come to learn about Rector Vizcaíno?'

'One old toreador always knows when he is in the presence of another, no matter the disguise.'

'You caught him?'

'Certainly not! But there was something in the way he stuck out his jaw. How he constantly walked with his shoulders back and his nose in the air, as though performing a drill. Nicolás Vizcaíno was always in a hurry. He always had some place more important to be.'

'But you permitted him to stay on as Rector? Let him dismiss Cayetano and those other priests?' Benito's voice is judgemental.

Gabino Sánchez laughs. 'Given our own past, we were hardly in a position to be too critical.'

Then, as though reading Benito's mind he places a finger

to his lips and shakes his head.

'Let's not become too distracted. Curious as you may be to know more about that chapter in our history.'

'The rector could stay but others had to go?'

'Narciso's priority was to clean up the bishopric. His message was clear right from the beginning — "Our mission is to purify this diocese. Wherever we find apostasy we must destroy it. Burn it to the ground by the power of our fire". No one heard the message better than Nicolás.'

Benito itches to be direct with the old priest, tell him what Tránsito Durdal has revealed to him concerning Vizcaíno, but he gave his word to her.

Gabino Sánchez brings his hands together in a quick clap and holds them close to his chest as though praying: 'Of those four priests relieved of their posts, Vizcaíno had dossiers on three of them.'

'Quite zealous, it seems,' Benito says.

Gabino Sánchez points his clasped hands at Benito. For a moment there is a steeliness that flashes in the old man's eyes, it dissipates in the wake of a forced but still charming old priestly smile.

'I'd choose to say, vigorous, rather than zealous.'

Benito understands that somehow a criticism of Vizcaíno's zeal will be considered in Gabino Sánchez' mind as a criticism of Narciso. This would be of no help to Cayetano. He decides to steer the conversation elsewhere. 'What do you imagine the judge will make of Villar-Rivas' suggestions concerning the quality of medical intervention?'

'You're referring to Juan?' Gabino Sánchez opens the palms of his hands and holds them out as if to say, there's nothing here.

'According to Villar-Rivas, Doctor Creus' actions in the gatehouse were a contributory factor,' Benito says.

'He did everything he could,' Gabino Sánchez says. 'It's not often Villar-Rivas will get a witness to cry the way Juan Creus did. He and Narciso were very close. Even as boys at the seminary.'

'They never mentioned that Doctor Creus had been a priest.'

'He was never ordained. He and Narciso only trained together for two years in Sigüenza.'

'I suppose not everyone has what it takes to be a priest,' Benito says.

'He certainly made a better doctor,' Gabino Sánchez says. 'Although his medical training turned him a touch more pompous.'

'He didn't seem over conceited when Villar-Rivas was questioning him,' Benito says.

'Villar-Rivas didn't see Juan on the eve of Palm Sunday,' Gabino Sánchez says. 'We had a little get together. Several rounds of hombre and glasses of brandy. Juan soon got going, as usual, denigrating the young surgeons of Madrid.'

'What has he against the young generation?'

'For a start, they're insufficiently grateful for the path-forging work of his generation,' Gabino Sánchez says. He leans back into the couch, sighs loudly and tilts his head as far as the couch neck-rest permits. 'When Juan left, I reminded Narciso, politely of course, that since Juan had not actually practiced surgery for some years he may be a little out of touch.'

When giving evidence, Doctor Juan Creus Manso did not appear quite so opinionated. The tragedy of being on the scene and yet unable to save his cousin seemed to have oblit-erated any previous sense of superiority. The man even cried, and his tears were evidently heartfelt. Despite the fact the doctor's testimony was not helpful for Cayetano, Benito still felt empathy for the doctor.

'We must forgive our family their eccentricities,' Gabino Sánchez says.

'Is that so?'

'I believe it is. When there's sincere repentance for one's absence of perfection, there's surely room for true forgiveness.'

Benito is pierced by Gabino Sánchez' sagacity. It may be time for forgiveness, and compromise. 'Will you come to the court tomorrow,' Benito asks. 'And ask for leniency?'

'Let's consider what needs to be done for everyone's sake,' Gabino Sánchez says. 'Let everyone follow their own conscience. I'm sure that is what Cayetano would wish.'

As he leaves the lair, Benito believes he has decrypted Padre Gabino Sánchez' remarks. Tonight, he shall write to his mother, before it is too late.

TO BORROW A PHRASE
2 Plaza Colón, Madrid
6 October 1886

FROM WHERE HE sits in his study, the door ajar, he hears his sister's voice. She is clear and authoritative. 'Benito's not seeing anyone today,' she says.

'He's expecting me,' José Ferreras answers.

It is true. Benito is expecting him. Because yesterday at the close of the court proceedings they had agreed to travel in together for today's rendering of the judgement. However, after finally meeting with Gabino Sánchez last night, Benito no longer knows if he has the stomach for it. He rises and quietly closes the door to his study. He can hear them chattering as they make their way towards his sanctuary, excitement evident in their voices.

'And the others are downstairs too, waiting in the carriage,' José tells Concha.

The knock on his sanctuary door arrives. 'Come in.' he says. They push open the door, and Benito steps forward to greet them with a sigh.

'This might change that look on your face,' José Ferreras says, waving a torn-out newspaper page.

Benito takes and unfolds the page. It is not another article from one of the many newspaper or journals reporting on Luis Simarro's persuasive testimony on the 'Degenerate in the Dock.' This is a page from *Madrid El Cómico*. It can mean only one thing.

Too wrapped up in his apprehension for Cayetano, Benito has not been bothering to seek out the literary sections of the mainstream Madrid newspapers or specialist press. He already guesses this must contain the first critique of Maximiliano's appearance. He wonders if the critics will focus on why Maximiliano Rubín has been wheeled on to the stage in part two.

It is no surprise to him that *El Cómico* is the first to publish a review. He is curious to discover if it has been signed and whether Clarín himself has written this critique or asked someone outside to do the job. It is not always certain.

'Who wrote it?' he asks.

'Read it and you'll see,' José says.

Apprehension in his eyes, Benito flattens the page on his writing table and begins to read. José and Concha remain in the room; twin sentinels taken root. They watch Benito scan for the reviewer's *nom de plume*. After a moment, Concha begins to fidget, shifting from foot to foot. 'Are you going to share it?' she asks.

'All right, all right, I'll read it,' he says: '*Señor Galdós' portrayal of the troubled but saint-like redemptor Maximiliano Rubín shows unusual insights. To borrow a phrase from Mr Wilde, that well-known critic of Pall Mall, this character has all the hallmarks of imaginative reality so prevalent in the great works, such as La Comédie Humaine.*' his voice is pitched high as he cites the comparison with his favourite Balzac masterpiece. He pauses to gather breath, glances over the top of the page and sees José and Concha smiling at each other.

'Well, go on then,' Concha says.

'If you insist,' he says and reads the rest of the review: '*This is a visceral leap in characterisation, distinctly richer than Guzmán of Lo Prohibido. Señor Galdós is back! He has shown himself to be pre-eminent amongst his contemporaries. He is a writer capable not only of taking on the mantle of Balzacian tradition but of enriching it. I look forward to seeing how he develops this story and this character in particular.* Satisfied?' Benito says, and puts the review in his back pocket.

Concha puts her arms on her hips. 'Well, she has a nerve.'

'What else could she say?' José says. 'The character is a masterpiece. Soon they'll all be writing the same thing.'

'Perhaps she's less of a bitch than I thought,' Concha says.

'Come on Benito,' José says, 'let's go and see what the presence of the country's "pre-eminent" realist writer might do to help rescue Maximiliano's alter-ego.'

Benito sighs. 'Last night I met with Padre Gabino Sánchez. The situation is more complicated than we thought.'

'He finally agreed to meet with you?' José says.

'Yes.'

'How is it more complicated?' Concha wants to know.

'Reading Alonso's journals and then talking with Cayetano I discovered something that could be considered serious provocation for Cayetano's revenge. Last night Gabino Sánchez confirmed it.'

José whistles and Concha puts a hand to her mouth.

'This is excellent You must tell Villar-Rivas straight away,' José says.

'It's not possible because Gabino Sánchez will never admit to it,' Benito says.

'Why would he deny it?' José asks.

'Because it's just the kind of situation some extremists need,' Benito says. 'It risks tipping us back into the cycle of civil wars that we're trying to leave behind.'

'Is that what he says?' José asks.

'And Cayetano would agree with that,' Benito says. 'We can say nothing of this to anyone. All we can say is that the Church will plead for leniency.'

'This is still great news,' José says. 'And anyway, with this judge any proposed provocation will only prove premeditation.'

Benito puts on his jacket and hangs his head.

'Don't look so miserable,' José says. 'You tried. Anyone would think it was you on trial.'

'But I fear the worst,' Benito whispers.

'Hasn't he said himself no matter what happens he's had his vengeance?' Concha says.

Benito does not answer. He and José leave the room, say their goodbyes to her. As Benito moves down the stairs, his hand glides over the dark, polished, wooden banister. It feels cold. His knees tremble as they pass the doors to the other apartments in the building. He wills someone to open their door and detain him there for a while with some domestic crisis or neighbourly favour to ask. But no one appears.

José opens the street door. His carriage is stationed in front of the apartment building. The carriage windows and curtains are open. Benito sees and salutes Tránsito and Alonso. Alonso opens the door and extends a hand. Benito pulls himself into the carriage. Alonso looks bright and vital in his green uniform and tricorn hat.

Tránsito is dressed entirely in black. 'Cayetano will be so pleased to see you there,' she says. She offers Benito her ungloved hand. Against the black of her clothes her unmade face is as pale as egg-white.

Amongst the four of them, only José seems to have enthusiasm for the journey. 'They'll not wait for us, you know,' José tells the coachman.

The others gasp in unison at José's keenness. They settle down into their places in the carriage. They stare vacuously here, there, and anywhere, as long as they do not have to look into the eyes of each other. Through the open carriage window, the sounds of life proceeding normally can be heard in

Plaza Colón.

Somewhere on the far side of the carriage, a band are practicing something tuneless, whilst on the near side there are cries from the pedlars: 'Half-price fish. Today only!' The fish-sellers come every day except Sunday and say exactly the same thing. Buckets containing their live specimens are on display, freshly appropriated from the Manzanares by children and by washer-women wives. The aroma of fish is fresh and grassy — not yet as pungent as it will be by late afternoon.

Those in the carriage are also fish out of the water. None can find the right expression. Several times one of them coughs as though about to mouth something. Then, possibly knowing the syllables on their tongue do not hold the correct tone or weight, they let the moment go. Perhaps they are worried that their words might appear too prosaic.

Benito feels in his pockets for the familiar shape of his notebook. He takes it out and looks through his notes from last night's meeting with Gabino Sánchez. He considers this will be his last day spent sitting in the courtroom, taking notes, sketching and listening to them all.

'Do you think Villar-Rivas might ask Cayetano to pretend to be mad?' Tránsito asks.

'Legally he cannot make that suggestion,' Alonso answers.

'And anyway, Cayetano will never agree to that,' Benito adds.

Benito appreciates that Villar-Rivas is not beyond this tactic. However, it is clear to him that Judge Salva — perched in his large chair on its plinth, looking down at Villar-Rivas and the others — will be quite ready for that trick. And who knows what Judge Salva really thinks about the varied manifestations of Padre Cayetano that he has seen — the noble dignified priest; the upright simple man; and those other incarnations which have arrived more recently as the bolt begins to thread? Can anyone find the real Cayetano amongst these apparitions?

Then there is the jury. What will they give most credence to? Especially since so much has changed during this past six months. Nothing holds the same solidity. Ideas and words which seemed so well understood in April have spun away, and any shared meaning has become hard to pin down in October.

'He's not mad, just angry,' Tránsito says, as the carriage hits a pothole.

'Sorry, to be the one to have to point this out,' José says, 'but if we all shot someone every time we got angry, then our over-population problem could be resolved rather quickly.'

The stinging truth of José's observation causes Benito's eyeballs to pop like a Filipino Tarsier. Tránsito slaps both hands to her chest. Alonso's face stiffens.

'I didn't say Cayetano's anger justified his actions. I'm just saying he's not the mad degenerate the state expert is painting him as,' Tránsito says through her teeth.

Benito realises in the storm and rage of the court proceedings the word that has most lost its solidity is that one: degenerate. Some veneer of meaning has rubbed away under duress. Judge Salva has permitted Luis and the other state experts to stretch the meaning of that term.

And the judge himself has led the wearing down of Cayetano. He would not let Cayetano speak freely, no matter how often or how reasonably he asked. If he quietly asked to speak, they refused to listen. So Cayetano had to scream to be heard. When he screamed, the judge and prosecution lawyer implied he was bad and mad. And when he talked about *dignity* and *honour*, they cut him down with words such as *revenge*, *unprovoked* and *premeditation*, which all seem so much more concrete and violent the way they said them.

'Anyway, I have to tell you,' Benito says, 'I have a deal with Gabino Sánchez. He's sworn the Church will plead for leniency in the sentencing.'

'Well, anyway this is excellent news,' Tránsito says.

Their carriage picks up speed and they are jostled. They lurch into each other. José Ferreras closes a window and instantly the hubbub from outside no longer reaches their ears. They speed to hear the verdict and there is only the sound of their breathing, and the carriage wheels rattling, and its green and red livery squeaking.

Outside the sun shines brightly. Inside Benito thinks of his compromise. Cayetano was right about that. Gabino Sánchez knew precisely what to offer, to buy his silence. He finds himself praying that it is worth it.

THE SENTENCE

THE COURTROOM DOORS are already being opened to
the public as Alonso leads Benito, José and Tránsito through
to their reserved bench. Almost immediately, Cayetano is
brought in, escorted by two guards. He shambles across the
room and occupies his usual spot, but his demeanour is devoid
of dignity, sapped of its usual nobility. Benito cannot take his
eyes off him. There is no more stubborn pride carved in that
face. He stands there, his hands manacled, a wretch who
loiters and twitches.

In a few moments the courtroom is packed and uncomfort-
ably warm. Despite the size of the crowd there is an unnatural
stillness. As though all are reluctant to move or breathe aloud
for fear of missing a word. Judge Salva enters to start proceedings. He asks the prosecution lawyer to sum up the prosecution case. The prosecution summation passes in a blur.
Benito, in any case, is not listening to it, because he is fixated
on watching Cayetano whose expression suggests he is perplexed to find himself here.

Judge Salva gives leave to Villar-Rivas to make his final
pleading. From where he sits, Benito can look into the eyes of
the defence lawyer. He sees a determination in them as Villar-
Rivas raises the volume. The lawyer laments Cayetano's
"unjustified defrocking." He reminds the jury that the prosecution has already conceded that point, and he stares at his

confrère as though daring him to contradict. The jury foreman looks at his watch. Villar-Rivas presents his next thread:
"poor medical care." Again, he raises the tone. The defence
expert witness remains convinced that the medieval medical
care applied was a "contributing factor" to the eventual death
of the bishop, which — he reminds the jury and ladies and
gentlemen present — took place the next day, whilst his client
was already locked up. Someone in the jury is scribbling on a
pad of paper. Benito cannot tell if this a good or bad sign.

Villar-Rivas is not finished. He raises an arm. 'Ladies and
gentlemen of the jury, I'm holding here in my hands.' He
waves some papers in the air, 'An appeal for leniency.' The
same jury member scribbles again and some of the public
nudge the person next to them and say, "It's an appeal to spare
the neck." Villar-Rivas carries on, 'Signed by the new Bishop
of Madrid Alcalá, Sancha Hervás and hand delivered to me
this very morning.'

Benito is awed at the defence lawyer's performance. He
supposes the entire public, and maybe the professionals
present too, are equally impressed. They stare at Villar-Rivas'
hand still held aloft, as though he is *Themis* holding the scales
of justice. Their eyes follow as he spins around, brings his arm
down and points to Cayetano; 'But here, ladies and
gentlemen, is our best defence. You have seen with your own
eyes and heard with your own ears: *this* defendant cannot be
responsible for his acts, for he was at that moment quite out
of his mind.' Villar-Rivas approaches Cayetano and whispers
something in his ear.

Luis Simarro laughs aloud at Villar-Rivas' histrionics but
Judge Salva brings down his gavel with a bang: 'The state's
expert alienist will desist from laughter.'

Villar-Rivas passes the new bishop's appeal for leniency to
Judge Salva, who reads it and passes it to the court recorder.

Padre Gabino Sánchez has kept his word; as Benito knew he would.

'The court will take due consideration of Bishop Sancha Hervás' remarks,' Judge Salva says.

'Has the accused anything to say in his own defence?' Judge Salva asks.

Seconds pass before Cayetano begins to deliver an incoherent rambling, part Spanish, part Latin and part some guttural code unknown to any of them. No one in the courtroom can decrypt a single sentence. Cayetano's incoherent rambling is accompanied by shaking of his arms and an increase in volume. Finally, he jerks his head in wild circles and stares into the air like a tethered dog pursuing the trajectory of a housefly.

Benito looks at Cayetano and knows in that instant Gabino Sánchez was right about Cayetano too: he will not risk the peace of the country for an allegation he can never prove.

Judge Salva begins to read a prepared preamble. He starts out quietly but augments his volume as he proceeds in the statement. His voice soon booms across the courtroom. He speaks about Padre Cayetano Galeote's arguments with Rector Vizcaíno. His letters to all and sundry making clear his 'premeditation' to exact revenge for what he considered an offence against the 'dignity' of his family name. A name which he himself dragged into the dirt, whilst committing a deed witnessed by two thousand of the faithful. Then Judge Salva tells the jury foreman the jury should leave the courtroom to consider a verdict. He looks around the courtroom and he lets his gaze linger in Benito's direction before returning to his notes.

This could be the last moment to rise up and speak out in Cayetano's defence, but Benito cannot rise. He has given his word to Gabino Sánchez, and anyway who amongst them could believe the truth? It is clear, only the Church's plea for leniency and Cayetano's own play-acting can save Cayetano. Benito looks over to Cayetano, who still wears his priestly vestments, but no longer has the form of the noble cleric, whom Benito came to know in the prison cell. He has fully transformed and in his place stands an ignoble madman who continues to murmur an unintelligible rant.

It is not long before the jury return. The foreman passes their verdict to Judge Salva. The judge makes a play of reading it. He keeps everyone waiting. They hear clocks tick; someone sobbing; some people blowing their noses. Finally, Judge Salva clears his throat. 'We have heard the defence argue that this killing was carried out whilst the accused was "not himself" and the state expert talks of "degenerate origins" and would have you believe the accused is insane on account of them.'

The courtroom erupts, in boos. Alonso nudges Benito and Benito sees two Civil Guards fix their bayonets. Judge Salva smashes his gavel down on his desk. 'Order!' The courtroom quietens. Judge Salva picks up his notes. 'However, the prosecution has shown us clear evidence of the accused fully in charge of his actions; of the accused planning; of the accused utterly responsible for his deeds.' He pauses to allow his words to settle in every corner of the courtroom.

From the rear, a gruff voice shouts out: 'The garrotte's too good for 'im.'

The crowd collectively exhales. There follows another thud of Salva's gavel and then another hush before the judge repossesses the courtroom.

'Cayetano Galeote Cotilla, you are found guilty of murder and sentenced to pay the sum of ten thousand pesetas in financial compensation to the successors of Bishop Narciso Martínez-Vallejo y Izquierdo.' Salva pauses to read his notes.

Benito searches Cayetano's face, sees that Cayetano is smiling.

Salva continues, his tone is unwavering. 'Additionally, you are sentenced to be taken from here to a place where you will be put to death by application of the State's sole approved instrument for civil executions.'

The hush descends into their gut. Only the quiet sobbing of Tránsito Durdal is heard.

'I hear the whole family are mad,' the same gruff voice from the back of the court, pierces the hush.

Hearing this slur on his family, Cayetano roars, raises his manacled hands and begins to beat them against his chest. He pulls at his hair and the noise and the violence of his actions causes the crowd to cower until the guards pull Cayetano's arms back down by his sides.

'Silence!' Judge Salva's voice booms again and by the time his gavel hits the desk, order is restored in his court.

Alonso comforts Tránsito Durdal, whilst José Ferreras slips away for *El Correo's* late edition, and the guards begin to clear the courtroom.

Benito remains seated. He closes his eyes. His compromise with Padre Gabino Sánchez is a failure. Cayetano's performance was masterful. Simarro must have been delighted to have witnessed it. And yet, Judge Salva has seen through it too.

Benito's throat is dry. His cheeks are damp. He sheds tears for the madman who providentially came into his life when the need was greatest. Benito consoles himself with the knowledge that elsewhere he has been able to tell a truth — about a certain person who seems bad but is not.

THE END

ACKNOWLEDGEMENTS

In the course of researching and creating this work of fiction, I have been privileged to engage with an enormous amount of material of various types: including biographies, academic journals and newspapers; as well as to watch old films and listen to audio recordings too numerous to mention individually here. However, I would especially like to acknowledge my debt to the following excellent academic sources: (a) *Analyses Galdosianos*, the esteemed journal of the Asociación Internacional de Galdosistas; (b) The *Bulletin Hispanique;* and (c) The biography: *Pérez Galdós Spanish Liberal Crusader*, by H. C. Berkowitz, Madison, 1948.

I also wish to thank those beta readers of various versions of the novel. Their encouragement has been crucial in keeping me motivated all the way through this project. Thank you: Ailie Collins, Tim Olsen, Lori Vitali, Elaine Brown, Graziella Chilosi and also I want to tip my hat to my wonderful cohort and teaching staff from University of Glasgow, Creative Writing M.Litt. (Class of 2016/2017) for the stimulating creative environment and inspiration.

I am enormously grateful to the Cabildo de Gran Canaria for their permission to use the 1894 portrait of Benito Pérez Galdós painted by the exceptional Joaquín Sorolla y Bastida and to graphic artist Audrey Beauhaire of *Anythink*, Paris for her patience and indulgence whilst designing and producing the cover for this novel.

Special thanks to Elena Battista (Foreign Rights Agent) and to Zoe James (Editor) for their support, enthusiasm and savvy.

NOTES

Benito Pérez Galdós (1843 - 1920)

The year 2020 is the centenary of the death of Benito Pérez Galdós — the most famous Spanish writer whom many English-speaking readers may not know by name or reputation. Regarded by contemporaries and twentieth-century literary critics as probably *the* most important writer in Spanish letters after Cervantes, Galdós was one of the world's most accomplished practitioners of realist writing, and a prodigious writer of historical fiction. Think Balzac, Tolstoy, or Henry James and add in a productivity factor of multiples, as well as an insatiable curiosity for figuring out what makes a person tick.

Considered a masterpiece[1], *Fortunata y Jacinta* became his best-selling and one of his most critically acclaimed novels. I am delighted to say it is one of several of Galdós works available in English. I thoroughly recommend it. Within it, the depiction of *Maximiliano Rubín* is particularly celebrated for demonstrating Galdós' extraordinary depth of medical knowledge and foresight.[2]

Benito Pérez Galdós was not simply a writer but also a lover of literature: English, French, Russian; contemporary or classic. Although there are many Cervantian influences in his work, one also finds Shakespearian. A fan of Dickens, he translates Dickens' debut novel: the *Posthumous Papers of the Pickwick Club*, into Spanish. He was also an inaugural winner of the UK's Royal Society of Literature's *Benson Prize* — a prize subsequently awarded to other literary greats such as Philip Larkin, J. R. R. Tolkien and E. M. Forster.

---

[1] H C Berkowitz, Pérez Galdós Spanish Liberal Crusader, (Madison, pp 219, 1948)

[2] M. Stannard, Maximiliano Rubín and the Context of Galdós's Medical Knowledge (Anales Galdosianos, vol 48, 2013)

Five of his novels were adapted for film (directed by directors such as Luis Buñuel, and JL Garci) and won many awards, including The Cannes International Film Prize, and being Oscar-nominated for best foreign film, as well as being serialised in several Spanish-speaking countries around the world.

I hope that through: *The Providential Origins of Maximiliano Rubín*, Galdós may come more to the attention of English language readers in his centenary year.

Luis Simarro (1851 - 1921)
Luis married Mercedes in 1886 and Benito was not invited to the wedding.

Simarro's diagnosis of Galeote as a degenerate madman, though not accepted during the trial, was subsequently validated by the court and supported by the Royal Academy of Medicine. In another victory, Simarro was back in court several months later, pitted against his ex-mentor, J. M. Charcot who had been hired by a wealthy family in Spain to declare a family member insane. Simarro found this particular subject to be sane. After a controversial court case, Simarro's position was upheld in that case also.

The anticipated reforms in the provision of facilities for the insane, and redistribution of authority (away from religious charities towards qualified medical professionals) did not materialise for another twenty years.

Simarro is acknowledged as having introduced his friend, Santiago Ramón Cajal, to the methods of the Italian histologist, Camillo Golgi. Cajal spent a decade perfecting the methods Simarro had shown him. Subsequently Cajal and Golgi were co-awarded the *Nobel Prize for Science*.

Cayetano Galeote Cotilla (1839 - 1922)

Cayetano's death sentence was transmuted to a life sentence in an asylum for the insane. He was transferred from the model prison in Plaza Moncloa to Santa Isabel asylum in Leganés just a dozen kilometres south of Madrid, where he lived to celebrate his eighty-second birthday before dying in his bed on 3 April 1922. It is a matter of serendipity that the last scene of *Fortunata y Jacinta* has the fictitious character Maximiliano Rubín check himself into the same asylum of his own free will.

Joaquín Sorolla y Bastida (1863 - 1923)

Sorolla's influences included Velazquez and Goya. He has been described as Spain's most celebrated artist covering the period between Goya and Picasso. He was a very close friend of Luis Simarro and in 1897 painted Luis at work in his laboratory. Examples of Sorolla's work can be seen in rare itinerant expositions, such as was the case at U.K.'s National Gallery in London between March and July 2019 and Ireland's National Gallery in Dublin between August and November 2019 where *Sorolla: Spanish Master of Light* was presented in collaboration with the Museo Sorolla. Or on permanent display at the Museo Sorolla, located at Calle General Martínez Campos, Madrid. The original Galdós portrait is on permanent display in the Casa-Museo Pérez Galdós, 6 calle Cano, Las Palmas de Gran Canaria.